Make time for friends. Make time for Debbie Macomber.

Dear Friends,

Welcome back to Cedar Cove! There's been lots going on in town since your last visit. Olivia, Jack, Grace, Maryellen, Jon and everyone else are eager to fill you in. You're probably curious about who started the fire that destroyed The Lighthouse restaurant – and are you in for a surprise. So many of you wrote to tell me who you thought was responsible – and only one person guessed right.

In addition to the solution of that mystery, you'll get an update on all the characters. I'm also going to introduce you to someone new, a chess player I loved the instant he turned up on the page. Bobby Polgar is one of my most unusual male characters. But wait – there's more! (I love it when I get to say that.) If you're interested in further updates on the characters, log on to my webpage and click on the Cedar Cove button. The characters themselves have written letters and as a bonus have included favourite recipes. (That's because the author loves to cook and to eat – so the characters do, too!)

If you're not online, you can contact me at my office, PO Box 1458, Port Orchard, Washington 98366, USA. I really enjoy hearing from my readers; I read and value every one of your letters.

Now relax and step out of your own world for a few hours and into the world of Cedar Cove. We're so glad you stopped by. I hope you have a good time and that you'll want to come again.

Debbie Macomber

Debbie Macomber

6 Rainier Drive

MIRA

Published in Great Britain 2010
MIRA Books, Eton House, 18-24 Paradise Road,
Richmond, Surrey, TW9 1SR

© Debbie Macomber 2006

ISBN 978 0 7783 0368 8

59-0510

Printed in Great Britain
by Clays Ltd, St Ives plc

To Martha Powers
My walking partner, fellow career dieter and best of all
My friend

Some of the Residents of
Cedar Cove, Washington

Olivia Lockhart Griffin: Family Court judge in Cedar Cove. Mother of Justine and James. Married to Jack Griffin. Lives at 16 Lighthouse Road.

Jack Griffin: Editor of the *Cedar Cove Chronicle*. Recovering alcoholic. Married to Olivia. Recently suffered a heart attack.

Charlotte Jefferson Rhodes: Mother of Olivia and of Will Jefferson. Now married to widower Ben Rhodes.

Justine (Lockhart) Gunderson: Daughter of Olivia. Married to Seth Gunderson. Mother of Leif. The Gundersons live at 6 Rainier Drive.

Seth Gunderson: Justine's husband. Co-owner, with Justine, of The Lighthouse restaurant, which was recently destroyed by fire.

James Lockhart: Olivia's son and Justine's younger brother. In the Navy. Lives in San Diego with his wife, Selina, and daughter, Isabella.

Stanley Lockhart: Olivia's ex-husband and father of James and Justine. Now lives in Seattle.

Will Jefferson: Olivia's brother, Charlotte's son. Married and lives in Atlanta.

Grace Sherman: Olivia's best friend. Librarian. Widow of Dan Sherman. Mother of Maryellen Bowman and Kelly Jordan. Now married to Cliff Harding. Lived at 204 Rosewood Lane.

Cliff Harding: Retired engineer, now a horse breeder living in Olalla, near Cedar Cove.

Cal Washburn: Horse trainer, employed by Cliff Harding.

Maryellen Bowman: Oldest daughter of Grace and Dan Sherman. Mother of Katie. Married to Jon Bowman. Pregnant with their second child.

Jon Bowman: Photographer, married to Maryellen. Father of Katie.

Joseph and Ellen Bowman: Estranged father and stepmother of Jon.

Zachary Cox: Accountant, married to Rosie. Father of Allison and Eddie Cox. The family lives at 311 Pelican Court.

Anson Butler: Boyfriend of Allison Cox. Suspect in The Lighthouse fire.

Cecilia Randall: Navy wife, living in Cedar Cove. Accountant, working for Zach Cox. Married to Ian Randall. Mother of Aaron.

Rachel Pendergast: Works at the Get Nailed salon. Friends with widower Bruce Peyton and his daughter, Jolene. Romantically involved with sailor Nate Olsen.

Bob and Peggy Beldon: Retired. Own a Bed & Breakfast at 44 Cranberry Point.

Roy McAfee: Private investigator, retired from Seattle police force. Two adult children, Mack and Linnette. Married to Corrie, who works as his office manager. The McAfees live at 50 Harbor Street.

Linnette McAfee: Daughter of Roy and Corrie. Moves to Cedar Cove to work as a physician assistant in the new medical clinic.

Gloria Ashton: Police officer on Bremerton force. Linnette's friend and neighbour – recently discovered to be her sister, adopted at birth.

Troy Davis: Cedar Cove sheriff.

Pastor Flemming: Local Methodist minister.

Teri Miller: Hair stylist at Get Nailed. Friend of Rachel Pendergast.

One

Justine Gunderson woke suddenly from a deep sleep, with the vague sense that something was wrong. A moment later, she remembered, and an intense sadness pressed down upon her. Lying on her back, she stared up at the dark ceiling as the realization hit her yet again. The Lighthouse, the restaurant she and Seth had poured their lives into, was gone. *Gone*. It had burned to the ground a week ago, in a blazing fire that lit up the night sky for miles around Cedar Cove. A fire started by an unidentified arsonist.

Without bothering to look, Justine knew her husband wasn't in bed with her. Only a week had passed since the fire, but it felt like a month, a year, a lifetime. She didn't think Seth had slept more than three or four hours at a stretch since that shocking phone call.

Folding back the sheet, she climbed slowly out of bed. It was barely four, according to the digital readout on the clock radio. Moonlight filtered through a gap in the curtains, creating patterns on the bedroom walls. Justine slipped her arms into the sleeves of her robe and went in search of her husband.

As she'd suspected, she found him in the living room, pacing. He moved ceaselessly, his angry strides taking him from the fireplace to the window and back. When he saw her, he continued to walk, looking away as though he couldn't face her. She could tell he didn't want her near him. She barely recognized this man her husband had become since news of the fire.

"Can't you sleep?" she asked, whispering for fear of waking their four-year-old son. Leif was a light sleeper and although he was too young to understand what had happened, the child intuitively knew his parents were upset.

"I want to find out who did this and why." Fists clenched, Seth turned on her as if she should be able to tell him.

Tucking her long, straight hair behind her ears, Justine sank into the rocker in which she'd once nursed their son. "I do, too," she told him. She'd never seen Seth this restless. Her strikingly blond husband was of Swedish extraction, a big man, nearly six-six, with broad shoulders to match. He'd been a commercial fisherman until soon after their marriage. That was when they'd decided to open the restaurant. The Lighthouse had been Seth's dream, and with financial assistance from his parents, he'd invested everything—his skill, his emotions, their finances—in this venture. Justine had been at his side every step of the way.

In the beginning, while Leif was an infant, she'd kept the books and handled the payroll. When their son grew old enough for preschool, she'd assumed a more active role, working as hostess and filling in where needed.

"Who would do this?" he demanded again.

The answer eluded her just as it did him. Why anyone would want to hurt them was beyond her comprehension. They had no enemies that she knew of and no serious rivals. It was hard to believe they'd been the target of a random firebug, but maybe that was the case. So far, there'd been little real progress in tracking down the arsonist.

"Seth," she whispered gently, stretching her hand toward him. "You can't go on like this."

He didn't respond, and Justine realized he hadn't heard her. She longed to ease his mind, to reassure him. Her fear was that the fire had destroyed more than the restaurant. It had stolen Seth's peace of mind, his purpose and, in some ways, his innocence. He'd lost faith in the goodness of others and confidence in his own abilities.

Justine's innocence had been devastated one bright summer afternoon in 1986, when her twin brother, Jordan, had drowned. Justine had held his lifeless body in her arms until the paramedics arrived. She'd been in shock, unable to grasp that her brother, her twin, was gone. He'd broken his neck after a careless dive off a floating dock.

Her entire world had forever changed that day. Her parents divorced shortly afterward and her father had quickly remarried. To all outward appearances, Justine had adjusted to the upheaval in her life. She'd graduated from high school, finished college and found employment at First National Bank, then risen to branch manager. Although she'd had no intention of ever marrying, she'd been dating Warren Saget, a local builder who was the same age as her mother. Then she'd met Seth Gunderson at their ten-year high-school reunion.

Seth had been her brother's best friend. She'd always felt that if Seth had been with Jordan that day, her brother might still be alive, and her own life would've been different—although she wasn't sure exactly how. It was ridiculous to entertain such thoughts; she recognized that on a conscious level. And yet…it was what she believed.

All through high school she'd barely spoken to Seth. He was the football hero, the class jock. She was the class brain. And never the twain had met until that night nearly six years ago, when she'd run into him at the reunion planning meeting. Seth had casually mentioned that he'd had a crush on her during their high-school days. The look in his eyes told her he'd found her beautiful then and even more so now.

They hadn't experienced an easy courtship. Warren Saget hadn't wanted to lose her and made a concerted effort to pressure her into marrying him. He'd instinctively understood that Seth was a major threat. Warren bought Justine the largest diamond she'd ever seen, promising a life of luxury and social prominence if she agreed to be his wife.

All Seth had to offer Justine was a twenty-year-old live-aboard sailboat—and his love. By that time, she was so head-over-heels crazy about him that she could scarcely breathe. Still, she struggled, unwilling to listen to her own heart. Then, one day, she couldn't resist him anymore....

"I'm calling the fire marshal this morning," Seth muttered, breaking into her thoughts. "I want *answers*."

"Seth," she tried again. "Honey, why—"

"Don't *honey* me," he snapped.

Justine flinched at the rage in his voice.

"It's been a full week. They should have some information by now, only they're not telling us. There's something they don't want me to know and I'm going to find out what. If I have to bring Roy McAfee in, I will!" He looked directly at her then, probably for the first time since she'd entered the room.

"Seth, I like and trust Roy," she said, referring to the town's only private investigator, "but the fire department's already investigating. So is the insurance company. Let them do their jobs," Justine said in a soft voice. "Let the sheriff do his."

Splaying his fingers though his hair, he released a slow breath. "I'm sorry, I don't mean to take my frustration out on you."

"I know." Justine got up and walked into his arms, pressing her body against his, urging him to relax. "Come back to bed and try to sleep," she said.

He shook his head. "I can't. Every time I close my eyes, all I can see is The Lighthouse going up in smoke."

Seth had arrived a few minutes after the fire trucks and stood by helplessly as the restaurant, engulfed in flames, had quickly become a lost cause.

"I can't believe it was Anson Butler," Justine said, thinking out loud. She'd liked the boy and had trusted him—which, according to her friends and neighbors, had been a mistake.

"You don't *want* to believe it's him," her husband returned, the anger back in the clipped harshness of his words.

That was true. Seth had hired Anson several months earlier. The teenager was paying off court expenses because of a fire he'd set in the city park. He'd had no explanation for why he'd burned down the toolshed. All Justine really knew were the few details Seth had divulged at the time he'd taken the boy on.

To his credit, Anson had turned himself in to the authorities and accepted full responsibility for his actions. That had impressed her husband, and on the recommendation of their accountant and friend, Zachary Cox, who'd become something of a mentor to the boy, Seth had agreed to give Anson a job.

At first the teenager had made an effort to prove his worth. He'd shown up early for his shifts and put in extra hours, eager to please his employer. Then within a few weeks, everything had fallen apart. Tony, another dishwasher, had taken a dislike to Anson and the two had exchanged words. From what she understood, they'd also gotten into a shoving match once or twice. As a result of their animosity, the tension in the kitchen had increased. Seth had talked it over with Justine and she'd suggested they separate the two boys. Seth decided to make Anson a prep cook. Tony didn't like the idea of Anson getting a promotion, while he'd been on staff longer and remained a dishwasher.

Then money had gone missing from the office and, although others had access to the money box, both Tony and Anson had been seen entering the room. When questioned, Anson claimed he'd been looking for Seth because a supplier had a problem. Tony insisted he needed to talk to Seth about his schedule. Both boys were suspects, so Seth felt he had no choice but to lay them both off. The money was never recovered. Seth blamed himself because he'd left the safe open, lockbox inside, while he was briefly out of the office.

A week later, The Lighthouse had burned to the ground.

"We don't have any proof it was Anson," Justine reminded her husband.

"We'll get proof. Whether he's the culprit or somebody else is. We'll find whoever did this." Seth's hard mouth was set with determination and his body tensed.

"Try to sleep," she urged again. Despite his reluctance, she led him back to their bedroom.

Together they slipped under the sheets and she moved her body close to his. Seth lay on his back, eyes open, as she slid her leg over his and draped her arm across his powerful chest. He held her tight, as if she were the only solid thing left in a world that had started to crumble. Kissing his neck, Justine purred in his ear, hoping that if they made love, the restlessness in him would ease and he'd be able to relax. But Seth shook his head, rejecting her subtle offer. She swallowed down the hurt and tried not to take it personally. All of this would be over soon, she told herself; soon everything would be back to normal. Justine *had* to believe it. Without that hope, despair would encroach, which was something she had to avoid at any cost. She fought to maintain a positive outlook, for her husband's sake and for the sake of her marriage.

When Justine woke again, it was morning and

Leif was climbing onto her bed, wanting breakfast. Penny, their cocker spaniel-poodle mix, followed him, eyeing the bed.

"Where's Daddy?" she asked, sitting upright, rubbing her hand tiredly over her face.

Her son dragged his teddy bear onto the bed, blue eyes soulful. "In his office."

That wasn't a good sign.

"It's time we got you ready for school," Justine said briskly, glancing at the clock. Quarter to eight already. Leif's preschool class was held every morning, and even though their own schedules had fallen apart, Justine and Seth had done their best to keep Leif's timetable consistent.

"Daddy's mad again," the four-year-old whispered.

Justine sighed. This was almost a daily occurrence, and she worried about the effect of so much tension on their son, who couldn't possibly understand *why* Daddy was mad or Mommy sometimes cried.

"Did he growl at you?" Justine asked, then roared like a grizzly bear, shaping her hands into make-believe claws. With Penny barking cheerfully, she crawled across the mattress after her son, distracting him from worries about his father.

Leif shrieked and scrambled off the bed, racing for his bedroom. Justine followed and laughingly cornered the boy. Leif's eyes flashed with delight as she set out his clothes. He insisted on getting dressed on his own these days, so she let him.

After saying a perfunctory goodbye to her husband, Justine delivered Leif to preschool. When she pulled back into the driveway, Seth came out the door to greet her. The April sky was overcast, and rain was imminent. The weather was a perfect reflection of their mood, Justine thought. A sunny day would've seemed incongruous when they both felt so fearful and angry.

"I talked to the fire marshal," her husband announced as she got out of her car.

"Did he have any news?"

Seth's frown darkened. "Nothing he was willing to tell me. The insurance adjuster's taking his own sweet time, too."

"Seth, these things require patience." She needed answers as much as he did, but she certainly didn't want the fire marshal to rush the investigation.

"Don't you start on me," he flared. "We're losing ground every day. How are we supposed to live without the restaurant?"

"The insurance—"

"I know about the insurance money," he said, cutting her off. "But we won't get anything for at least a month. And it isn't going to keep our employees from seeking other jobs. It isn't going to pay back my parents' investment. They put their trust in me."

Seth's parents had invested a significant amount

of the start-up money; Seth and Justine paid them monthly and she knew Mr. and Mrs. Gunderson relied on that income.

Justine didn't have any solutions for him. She recognized that he was distressed about more than the financial implications of the fire, but she had no quick or ready answers. "What would you like me to do?" she asked. "Tell me and I'll do it."

He glared at her in a way she'd never seen before. "What I'd like," he muttered, "is for you to stop acting as if this is a temporary inconvenience. The Lighthouse is *gone*. We've lost everything, and you're acting like it's no big deal." Justine recoiled at the unfairness of his words. He made it sound as if she was some kind of Pollyanna who wasn't fully aware of their situation. "Don't you realize the last five years are in ashes?" he railed. "Five years of working sixteen-hour days and for what?"

"But we *haven't* lost everything," she countered, hoping to inject some reason into his tirade. She didn't mean to be argumentative; she simply wanted him to see that although this was a dreadful time, they still had each other. They had their child and their house. Together they'd find the strength to start over—if only Seth could let go of this anger.

"You're doing it again." He shook his head in barely controlled frustration.

"You want me to be as angry as you are," she said.

"Yes!" he shouted. "You *should* be angry. You should want answers just like I do. You should—"

"More than anything," she cried, her own control snapping, "I want my husband back. I'm as sick as you are about everything that's happened. We've lost our business, and to me that's horrible, it's tragic, but it isn't the end of my world."

Her husband stared at her, incredulous. "How can you *say* that?"

"Maybe you're trying to lose your wife and son, too," she yelled, and before she could change her mind, she slipped back inside the car, slamming the door. Seth didn't try to stop her and that was fine with Justine. She needed to get away from him, too.

Without waiting for his reaction, she backed out of the driveway.

With no real destination, Justine drove into town, a few blocks from where Leif attended preschool classes. Her son would be in school for another two hours, and she had nothing urgent to do, no one to see, so she walked down to the marina.

Struggling to find meaning in the disaster that was battering her marriage, she sat down on a wooden bench in Waterfront Park and gazed out at the cove. The sky was even darker now, and the water crashed against the rocks near the shore. She needed to think. Everything would be all right when she got home, she told herself. Seth would be sorry for what he'd said, and she—

"Justine, is that you?"

She glanced up to see Warren Saget coming toward her. She offered him a weak smile. She didn't welcome his company—didn't want to see anyone right now, but especially Warren, who'd let it be known that he still had feelings for her. When she'd declined his proposal, he hadn't taken it with good grace, and she tended to avoid him.

Without waiting for an invitation, he sat down beside her. "I was sorry to read about the fire."

The *Cedar Cove Chronicle* had published a front-page spread about the arson, and everyone in town had been talking about it all week.

"It was…a shock," she mumbled, suddenly cold.

"You're going to rebuild, of course?"

She nodded. She couldn't imagine Seth not wanting to rebuild. Within a few months, all of this would be behind them, she told herself again. Everything would be all right. There was simply no other option.

A chill raced up and down her arms as she remembered that this was exactly what she'd believed the day they'd buried Jordan. It was over, she'd thought then. All the relatives would go home and school would start and everything would go on the same as before. Only it hadn't. How naive she'd been, a thirteen-year-old girl who'd trusted her parents to maintain the steady course of her life. They hadn't; they couldn't. Their own suffering had made them unable to cope with hers, destroying their marriage and tearing their family apart. Far from being over, the grief had barely begun.

"Warren," she said, panic rising inside her all at once. She reached for his hand, gripping it hard. She was hyperventilating; she couldn't get her breath. She heard herself gasping for air. The world began to spin.

"What's wrong?" he asked, and his voice seemed to come from a long way off. "Are you ill?"

"I…don't know," she said on a choked whisper, the panic settling in. Suddenly she felt an overwhelming need to find her mother.

"What should I do?" he asked, placing his arm protectively around her shoulders. "Should I take you to the clinic? Call for an Aid Car?"

She shook her head, feeling small and lost and childlike. "I…I want my mother."

Warren didn't hesitate. He leaped to his feet. "I'll get her."

"No." She tried not to sob. She was an adult. She should be more capable of dealing with the events in her own life. Looking at Warren, she forced herself to take deep, even breaths. She forced her heart to stop racing.

"I think you're having a panic attack," Warren said, brushing damp hair from her temple. "My poor Justine. Where's Seth?"

"H-home." She couldn't, wouldn't tell him anything more.

"Should I phone him?"

"No! I—I'm fine now," she said shakily.

Warren slipped his arm around her and held her head against his shoulder. "Don't worry about a thing," he whispered soothingly. "I'll take care of you."

Two

Clutching her textbooks, Allison Cox rushed from her first-period American History to her French class. She slid into her desk and ignored the whispers that ceased abruptly as soon as she entered the room.

No one needed to tell her the topic of conversation. She knew. Everyone was whispering about Anson. Her friends assumed he was the one who'd burned down The Lighthouse. He wasn't! She refused to believe he was in any way responsible for the fire. Anson wouldn't do anything so underhanded to the Gundersons. Not only had they been good to him, he wasn't that kind of person. He wasn't cruel or vindictive. Allison didn't care what anyone thought or said—she wouldn't lose faith in Anson or the love they shared.

Turning, she glared over her shoulder at Kaci and Emily. According to her so-called friends, she was walking hand in hand with denial. Fine, they could think whatever they wanted; it had nothing to do with her. They could condemn Anson, but she wouldn't.

The class bell rang, and she slowly turned around, ignoring the flow of gossip. Yes, Anson had disappeared right after the fire. Yes, he'd burned down the shed in the park. But she just couldn't accept that he'd had anything to do with what had happened at The Lighthouse.

She'd convinced herself that Anson would return to Cedar Cove soon. With all her heart, she believed he'd be back by graduation. She clung to that hope, focused on the date—June fourth—and refused to doubt him.

The afternoon dragged by. Every day had since she'd seen him the night of the fire. After her last class she couldn't get away fast enough. She hurried off the school grounds to her part-time job at her dad's accounting firm. As she walked to the building owned by her father and his partners, she reviewed the facts as she remembered them. She did this often; she went over and over every detail she could recall. Logically, she understood why someone who didn't know Anson might conclude that he was an arsonist. Okay, so he'd made that one mistake last fall, with the park shed. But he'd owned up to it, taken his punishment and moved on.

It'd been a week since she'd seen him—the longest week of her life. She remembered how he'd come to her that night. She'd been asleep and he'd tapped against her bedroom window, waking her. It wasn't the first time he'd appeared in the middle of the night, only now he wouldn't come inside. He'd explained that the only reason he was there was to tell her goodbye.

She'd argued with him, but he'd been adamant, insisting he had to leave. So many questions remained unanswered, including the issue of the missing money. Anson swore he knew nothing about that and she believed him. Mr. Gunderson was wrong to blame Anson for a crime he didn't commit.

Worse, according to the terms of his plea agreement, the agreement Anson had made with the court after the first arson, he'd pledged to stay in school and make restitution.

But Anson hadn't been in school the week before the fire, and Allison had been worried sick, wondering where he was and what he was doing. No one seemed to have any idea, and no one seemed to care, either. Not even his mother.

Anson had said he was leaving and wouldn't tell her where he was going or when he'd be back. He'd kissed her goodbye and although she'd pleaded with him to stay, to talk things out, he'd disappeared into the night.

The next morning, on one of the worst days of her

life, Allison's mother, Rosie, woke her and said Sheriff Troy Davis needed to ask her a few questions. That was when she'd learned about The Lighthouse. As best she could, Allison answered the sheriff's questions—except she didn't tell him everything.

She couldn't.

Not even her parents knew the full truth.

She dared not tell her dad for fear he'd lose his trust in Anson—and in her.

Allison was grateful for this job at her father's office. Even though it was only part-time, it distracted her from her troubles for at least a few hours a day.

Her father had tried to help Anson. Allison appreciated the way he'd stepped in and stood at Anson's side after that fire in the park. Her father had been the only one, too. Anson's own mother had turned her back on him; Cherry Butler had as much as said that her son deserved whatever he got. Nor did she seem terribly concerned that Anson had now disappeared. According to Cherry, he'd come back when he was ready, and until then, she wasn't wasting any time worrying about him. Allison was horrified by his mother's attitude.

If Allison had run away, she knew her parents would never stop looking for her. And they wouldn't ever give up on her, like Anson's mother had on him.

But then, that was what Anson had said the night he left—that Allison was lucky. She had parents who loved her and cared about her. Anson claimed no one gave a damn about him. He was wrong. Allison cared. Her parents, too, were concerned about him, although of course their primary goal was to protect Allison.

Some kids were born lucky, Anson had told her, and she was one of them. He wasn't. He insisted that he had to make his own luck.

As she opened the front door of Smith, Cox and Jefferson, Allison noticed that the reception area was full of clients who'd waited until the last minute to file their taxes. With only four days to go until April fifteenth, she sensed the uneasiness in the room. It was like this every year.

Mary Lou, the receptionist, returned Allison's smile. "There's someone to see you in the kitchen," she said.

For a fleeting moment Allison thought it might be Anson. It couldn't be, though. The minute he showed up, the sheriff's office would become involved. Her father would be duty-bound to call them. Because Sheriff Davis suspected Anson would try to contact her at some point, her parents had discussed the possibility and the action they'd have to take. The matter was out of her hands and her father's, too. Allison had no choice but to accept that.

"Who is it?" she asked.

Another smile appeared on the receptionist's face. "You'll just have to check it out for yourself."

Allison was puzzled, since it wasn't like Mary Lou to be so mysterious.

The kitchen, located behind the office, wasn't a real kitchen—more of a lunchroom, with a microwave and a small refrigerator, plus a table and four chairs. Most days, Allison stuck her schoolbooks and purse in a cupboard there. As she walked into the room, she saw a baby carrier—complete with baby—resting on the table.

"Cecilia!" she cried, delighted beyond words. Her father's assistant had been a good friend to Allison, a better friend than either of her parents would ever know.

Three years earlier, Zach and Rosie Cox had divorced. It had been a terrible time for their family, especially Allison. She'd rebelled, hanging out with the wrong crowd. Her grades had slipped drastically and she'd stopped caring about much of anything.

When her father offered her a part-time job, she wasn't fooled. She'd been well aware that the only reason he was willing to hire her was to keep an eye on her after school. She'd taken the job, but she'd gone into it with a bad attitude.

Then she discovered she wouldn't be working for her dad. He'd assigned her to assist Cecilia Randall, and the young navy wife had helped Allison understand her own behavior—what she was doing and why. Cecilia's parents had divorced when she was ten and she understood the pain Allison was feeling.

Cecilia had guided her out of the self-destructive rut into which she'd stumbled.

As soon as Cecilia saw Allison now, she opened her arms wide for a hug. "I decided Aaron could do with a day out in the sunshine," her friend said, wrapping her arms around Allison and pulling her close. The baby was only three weeks old, so Cecilia hadn't been out of the office long. It felt like an eternity, though, because so much had happened.

Clasping Allison's shoulders, Cecilia leaned back and studied her. "You look…"

"Dreadful," Allison muttered. With everyone else, including her parents, she could pretend, but not with Cecilia. She wasn't sleeping nights, and she'd grown so weary of carrying this burden of worry and fear.

"Anson," Cecilia whispered.

Allison nodded.

The baby began to cry, demanding attention. He was loosely covered with the blanket Allison had knit. At first glance she thought Aaron resembled Cecilia's husband, Ian, but as she studied the baby, Allison saw plenty of his mother in him, too.

"Oh, Cecilia, he's adorable," she whispered, giving Aaron her finger to hold. The infant immediately clutched it with one tiny hand, and she was surprised by the strength of his grip.

"He's already spoiled," Cecilia said, smiling fondly down on her son. "It's bad enough that I'm at his beck and call, but you should see Ian. You'd think the sun rose and set on this baby."

Because Cecilia and Ian's first baby had died shortly after her birth, Allison knew how precious this child was to her friend. Aaron started to fuss again, more loudly this time. Cecilia lifted him out of the carrier and sat down at the table. "I think I'd better nurse him for a few minutes," she said, draping the blanket over her shoulder while she unfastened her blouse and expertly arranged her son.

"Sit," she ordered Allison, gesturing with her head at the chair beside her.

Allison willingly complied. "I've wanted to talk to you so badly," she said. Thankfully, no one had come in search of her. Busy though the staff was, they seemed to know that Allison needed this time with Cecilia, just the two of them.

"You can call me whenever you need to," Cecilia assured her. "I worried about you when I didn't hear anything."

"I couldn't—"

"I know," Cecilia said as she nursed her infant son. Her gaze was focused on Aaron. With her free hand, she stroked the wisps of hair at his temple.

"Do you remember that when we first met, I was going out with Ryan Wilson?"

"The kid with the paper-clip earring?" Cecilia asked, grinning down at her son as if to suggest she dreaded the day he'd become a teenager. "I believe your father might've have mentioned him."

Allison felt embarrassed now to recall how foolish she'd been. Ryan was trouble, and getting involved with him had been a blatant attempt to pay her parents back for their selfishness—what she saw now as their temporary insanity. Soon after that, her parents had reconciled, and before the summer was out they'd remarried.

"Anson isn't anything like Ryan." She shook her head. "People might think he is, but Anson's a much better person. He's smart and loyal and kind. Ryan isn't any of those things. He isn't even in school anymore. I have no idea where he is." But she had no idea where Anson was, either….

"I know that," Cecilia said calmly, "and the reason I do is your father. He would never have gone out of his way to help if he thought Anson would hurt you."

"He *has* hurt me," Allison protested, clenching her fists. "I don't understand why he ran away." She wondered if Anson considered what a terrible position he'd put her in. She realized that he didn't have the luxury of thinking about anyone but himself. He had to escape, had to run. However, he'd left Allison to face his detractors, alone, and she was afraid.

"Sometimes people don't know how to deal with pain," Cecilia said, her gaze still on her baby. "The only way they can react is by running."

"That only makes things worse," Allison said.

"You're wise to recognize that," Cecilia told her. "But unfortunately, Anson hasn't figured it out. My guess is he's hurt and confused, and taking off was kind of a knee-jerk reaction to pain."

"Where would he go?" As far as she knew, Anson didn't have any family. His mother was a sorry excuse for a parent, and he'd never known his father. Not once had Anson mentioned grandparents or uncles or aunts. She'd racked her brain, trying to work out where he could possibly find a hiding place. She hoped he was safe and had enough to eat.

"Mom and Dad said the minute he contacts me I need to call Sheriff Davis."

"And they're right."

Allison agreed, although she didn't like it. "Anson is what the sheriff called a person of interest." She was interested, too, darn it. She had questions of her own.

As soon as Aaron was finished, Cecilia buttoned her blouse and placed the baby over her shoulder, rubbing his back. "Everything's going to work out, Allison. If Anson is innocent—"

"He is," she said vehemently.

Cecilia raised her head abruptly, staring at Allison. Her dark eyes seemed to burn straight through her. "There's something you're not telling me, isn't there?"

Allison swallowed convulsively.

"I can see from the look in your eyes." Cecilia paused, waiting. "Allison? Have you heard from him?"

"No."

"Allison?" she asked again, her voice calm. "You'd better tell me."

"I…I'm not sure…."

"Why are you afraid?"

Lowering her head, Allison bit her lip. "No one else knows," she murmured. Last week, when the sheriff had come to speak to her, she'd answered all his questions—to the letter. But he hadn't asked about this particular thing, and Allison hadn't volunteered the information.

"You can trust me," Cecilia added. "You know I want only the best for you."

Allison nodded. "You won't tell anyone?" She tried to keep the pleading out of her voice.

"If you ask me not to say anything, I won't."

"Not to *anyone*," she insisted.

"I promise."

"Okay." Allison took a deep breath. "If I tell you…you might think—you might believe Anson set the fire."

"You're not withholding evidence, are you?" Cecilia asked urgently. "Because that would change everything."

"No! I couldn't do that."

Cecilia sighed with relief. "Good, because that would make you an accessory."

Sheriff Davis and her parents had already explained this. "I answered all his questions truthfully," she said.

Cecilia frowned. "This was a sin of omission, then?"

Allison slowly released her breath. "That night…when Anson knocked on my bedroom window."

She glanced up and Cecilia nodded, encouraging her to continue.

"We talked, and…and then he came into my room." Her mother had been really upset when Allison admitted that; she could only imagine what Rosie would say if she knew the rest.

"Yes?"

Allison hesitated again. "He…he was in my room for a few minutes and then he left and when he did—" She nearly choked on her words.

Cecilia leaned closer.

Allison could hardly make herself say it. "I…I could smell smoke." Her throat was painfully dry. "Not at first, I didn't, because all I could concentrate on was not letting him leave. I noticed a smell but I didn't think about it. Later I did, and when I realized what it was, I cried myself to sleep."

"Anson smelled of smoke?" Cecilia whispered the question.

"Like that other time," Allison said shakily. "As if…as if he'd been standing close to a bonfire."

Cecilia's shoulders sagged and she closed her eyes. It was just as Allison had feared. Now even Cecilia believed Anson had burned down The Lighthouse.

Three

Arching her back, Maryellen Bowman shifted positions on the sofa, her temporary bed. The family living room had become her prison as the pregnancy moved into its final trimester. Jon was gone for the afternoon with Katie, their three-year-old daughter, so the house was quiet, peaceful. Maryellen knew she should try to rest. The problem was, she couldn't.

Worries assailed her from all sides. She worried about her unborn baby and this difficult pregnancy. She worried about the pressures her husband was under as he struggled to support their family now that The Lighthouse, where he'd once worked as chef, was gone. She worried about his photographic career, her marriage and all the mistakes she'd made. The worst one had come from the best intentions. Maryellen had tried so hard to heal the rift between Jon and his parents, and it had nearly destroyed her relationship with her husband.

She found it impossible to rest, and yet that was what the doctor had ordered—bed rest for the remainder of this pregnancy. She was forbidden to climb stairs or exert herself in any way.

Yet how could she lie around when so much needed to be done? Leaning against the sofa, she closed her eyes and fought back depression. It'd never been like this when she carried Katie. That pregnancy had been normal in every respect.

Then she'd miscarried their second child. The emotional costs of this third pregnancy had yet to be calculated. Still, they both desperately wanted their child. All Maryellen could do was follow her doctor's instructions, try *not* to worry and pray that the baby would be born healthy and whole.

Because she was bedridden, everyone had pitched in. Her mother, especially, helped as much as she could, coming by twice a week with dinner and looking after Katie as often as her own busy life would allow. This gave both Jon and Maryellen a much-needed break. She hated to intrude on her mother, since Grace and Cliff were newly married and just now setting up house together. Grace had her own adjustments to make without taking on Maryellen's problems.

The phone rang and Maryellen grabbed it, eager for any distraction.

"Hello," she said, hoping her voice disguised the self-pity she'd fallen into.

"It's Ellen Bowman. Is everything all right?"

Her mother-in-law's sympathy nearly overwhelmed her, bringing her close to tears. Maryellen felt dreadful, about as low as she'd been in her entire life, other than during her brief first marriage. "I'm okay," she managed to tell her.

"And Jon?" Ellen asked hesitantly.

"He's…" Maryellen was willing to stretch the truth about her own state of mind and health, but she couldn't lie about her husband's. "Not well, Ellen. He's not doing well at all."

Her mother-in-law grew quiet. "Joseph and I thought that might be the case. I know Jon's angry. He's made it abundantly clear that he doesn't want anything to do with either of us. His attitude's killing his father. But I know you've tried to talk to him, and we both appreciate your efforts more than we can say."

Maryellen had paid a high price for interfering between Jon and his parents and she dared not do it again. She and Jon had actually separated for a time, just before the miscarriage, because of her attempts to effect a reconciliation. Afterward, they'd sidestepped the whole issue. But earlier in the month, soon after she'd begun her regimen of bed rest, Jon had conceded that they didn't have any choice other than to ask his family for help.

Yet he hadn't made the phone call, hadn't contacted them in any way, at least not that Maryellen knew about. Instead, they struggled from day to day until she feared their lives were about to implode. Neither Jon nor Maryellen could continue living with this constant, unrelenting stress.

"Jon was going to phone you," Maryellen said. "He told me."

"He was?" Hope elevated Ellen's voice.

"He hasn't, because, well, because he's afraid, I think, and proud. Too proud."

Ellen laughed softly. "He's like his father in that regard."

Maryellen smiled and tried to relax. This nervous tension was bad for the baby, bad for her, bad all around. At her last appointment, Dr. DeGroot had emphasized the importance of staying calm. When he'd said she should try to keep her life stress-free, she'd nearly laughed out loud.

"Joseph and I ordered the *Cedar Cove Chronicle* mailed to us here in Oregon," Ellen said, "and we read about the fire at The Lighthouse. We know Jon went back to work there."

"Yes, it's terrible news." Without his job as chef, Jon was left with only his photography earnings to support the family. His work was displayed in a Seattle gallery and sold well, but the money he made wasn't nearly enough to cover their living expenses, particularly now that Maryellen no longer had medical insurance.

"Jon's not working anywhere else, then?"

"His photographs are selling nicely," Maryellen felt obliged to tell her. "He's so talented." It was through his art that Maryellen had first come to know Jon Bowman. He'd brought his photographs for display at the Harbor Street Gallery, where she was employed as manager. They were among the most popular in the gallery.

Unlike some of the other artists, Jon preferred to keep a low profile. It wasn't until after Katie was born that she'd learned this man she loved had spent time in prison. In order to save their younger son, his parents had lied and Jon had been sentenced for a crime he'd never committed.

"Joseph and I want to help," Ellen insisted. "What can we do?"

"I'm not sure…" She didn't feel comfortable stating the obvious—that she needed someone here, in the house, looking after Katie, preparing meals, cleaning.

"There's something wrong," Ellen said sharply. "What is it?"

"I'm—I'm having problems with the pregnancy," she admitted. "I'm on complete bed rest." The baby gave her a hard kick as if to remind her.

"What about Katie? You can't possibly be taking care of her if you're confined to bed."

"I'm not. I can't. She's with her father," Maryellen said. Jon was doing his best to sell his work and take care of their child, run the household, and everything else.

"But how can he do that?" Ellen asked, clearly concerned.

"He can't." Maryellen was unwilling to explain further.

"We're coming," Ellen announced. "You both need us."

Maryellen sighed, feeling a surge of relief and simultaneous anxiety about Jon's reaction. "I can't ask you to do that."

"You didn't," Ellen said. "Our son will just have to swallow his silly pride. His family's at stake here. As far as I'm concerned, this is God's way of bringing us all back together. Jon can't very well ignore us now. He's our son, and Katie and this new baby are our grandchildren." Ellen sounded like a force to be reckoned with.

"Let me talk to him first," Maryellen urged.

"You do that if you want, but it doesn't make the least bit of difference what he says. Joseph and I are coming to Cedar Cove, and that's that. Leave everything to me, Maryellen," she insisted in a determined voice. "I'll be in touch."

They ended the conversation and afterward Maryellen did feel better. She didn't know what she'd say to Jon. Maybe she wouldn't broach the subject, after all. Maybe she *would* leave everything to Ellen and Joseph. She was so weary of fighting him on this. He'd relented once and agreed to ask his family for help and then done nothing. She couldn't face that battle again.

Just as she was beginning to think it was time for

Jon and Katie to return home, she heard a car pull into the yard. Trying to look rested and relaxed, she attempted a smile, waiting for her husband and daughter to walk into the house.

Instead the doorbell rang.

Visitors? In the middle of the day?

Before Maryellen could move, the door opened and Rachel Pendergast and Teri Miller entered, letting in warm spring air and sunshine and laughter. They worked at Get Nailed, the salon where Maryellen had her hair and nails done. Or used to...

"Rachel? Teri?" Maryellen couldn't have been more surprised—and delighted. "What are you doing here?"

"We are on a mission of mercy," Rachel declared. She set a white take-out bag on the coffee table in front of Maryellen, then reached for her hand. Shaking her head, Rachel gave a disparaging sigh. "Just look at those nails," she muttered.

"And I was thinking you could do with a haircut," Teri said cheerfully. "And since we were coming, we decided to bring lunch for all of us."

Maryellen felt like laughing and crying at the same time. "How did you know I've been longing for some TLC?" she whispered, endeavoring not to weep.

"A little birdie told us," Rachel said, grinning. She walked into the kitchen and collected three plates.

"This place is beautiful," Teri said. Hands on her

ample hips, she glanced around. "Rachel said Jon did most of the work himself. Mighty talented husband you've got there, my friend."

Maryellen had to agree. She liked both women immensely; Rachel had done her nails for years, while Teri had only recently started cutting Maryellen's hair. Teri had a flair for the outrageous and was genuinely entertaining. More than that, she was a kindhearted and compassionate person—as her visit today proved.

Over the years, Maryellen had gotten to know them both pretty well, and at one time had tried to set Teri up with Jon. Now she was astonished that she'd ever thought of such a thing. Teri and Jon were completely unsuited, but Maryellen hadn't even considered that. She'd been fighting her own attraction to him and had managed to convince herself that if he turned his attention elsewhere, he'd forget about her and vice versa. However, Jon was interested only in her.

"We brought you teriyaki chicken with rice and veggies," Rachel said as she pulled containers from the white sack.

Maryellen's appetite had been almost nonexistent for weeks. Jon had to coax her to eat at every meal. But all at once she was ravenous.

"That sounds fabulous."

"Good." Rachel handed her a filled plate and a pair of chopsticks.

Maryellen sat cross-legged on the sofa while her two friends arranged ottomans on the other side of the coffee table. The three of them dug into their lunch as Teri explained that it was from a new take-out place on the outskirts of Cedar Cove. They all proclaimed the food to be delicious and worth getting again. Teri had been considerate enough to leave a menu with Maryellen. "For when you guys just want to order in."

"I think I should cut your hair short," Teri said next. "Really short. You've got better things to do than fuss with your hair."

Maryellen smiled. It was all she could do to get it combed every day. "Jon won't like that."

"Hey, he isn't the one who has to wash it and brush it," Teri said. "He'll get used to it."

Maryellen could imagine how he'd react. The last time she'd had more than a trim was soon after Katie's birth. Until then, Maryellen had worn her dark hair long and straight, reaching the middle of her back, much as it did now. Jon had never actually *said* he didn't like her new style, but she could sense that he'd been disappointed. He often told her how much he loved her long, glossy hair, how beautiful he found it.

"Okay, what do you mean by *short?*" Maryellen asked.

Teri's dark eyes twinkled. "Wait and see."

"I hope you realize I can't afford this," she felt obliged to remind her friends.

"That's not your concern," Rachel was quick to tell her. "It's all been taken care of."

"And," Teri added, "included in the fee was a more-than-generous tip."

"Who did this?" Maryellen asked, although she could guess.

"Your fairy godfather," Rachel told her. "That's all I'm going to say."

"Cliff." Just as Maryellen had thought. Her new stepfather, Cliff Harding, had arranged this.

"Like I said," Rachel scolded, drawing two fingers across her mouth, "my lips are zipped."

The next two hours were such a pleasure. Teri washed her hair in the sink, and while she cut, dried and styled it, Rachel worked on her nails. God bless Cliff for this—and so much else. Ever since her mother and Cliff had met, she'd been impressed by what a loving, thoughtful man he was.

"Tell me the latest gossip," Maryellen said as the two women continued their beauty treatment.

"Well," Teri said, sighing deeply, "the *biggest* news is that Nate Olsen's back in town."

Nate was the young warrant officer Rachel had been seeing. Her friend had an ambiguous relationship with a widower named Bruce Peyton, which had gone on for three—or was it four?—years. Then this navy man had entered her life. Maryellen wondered which one Rachel would eventually choose.

"Would you stop!" Rachel cried. "Nate and I are dating casually, that's all."

Maryellen doubted the "casual" part but didn't comment.

"What about Bruce?" she asked, knowing how close Rachel was to Bruce's daughter, Jolene.

"We're just friends." She brushed off the questions, sounding a bit impatient, but Maryellen suspected Rachel's feelings for Bruce went deeper than she realized.

"You know what I don't understand?" Teri said, expertly wielding her scissors. "Rachel has *two* men on the line and I haven't hooked a single one."

"You should've put in your bid at the bachelor auction," Rachel teased, referring to the charity event at which she'd "bought" Nate.

"Those men were far too expensive for my pocketbook," Teri muttered, still clipping. Long pieces of hair fell to the floor.

She bent to gather up Maryellen's hair. "Want to donate this to make a wig for a cancer patient?" she asked.

"Sure!" Maryellen felt good about giving to someone in need—especially since she'd received so much herself. "That's a wonderful idea."

A few minutes later, Teri switched on the television to check the weekend weather. "Hey," she said, stepping back from the screen as the local news broadcast concluded. "There's a big chess champion-ship coming to Seattle."

"Do you like chess?" Maryellen asked.

Teri shrugged. "I don't know much about it. It's a lot like checkers, isn't it?"

Rachel and Maryellen exchanged looks.

"Well, not really," Rachel answered. "It's a little more complicated."

Soon after the two women finished, packed up their supplies and left, Jon and Katie got home. He seemed exhausted and Katie did, too. When Jon saw Maryellen, he did a double take.

"Do you like it?" she asked tentatively, putting her hand to her head. Then she went on to explain how this change in her appearance had come about—mentioning her satisfaction at donating her hair for a cancer wig.

Jon nodded. "That's great," he said. "And I love your new look. I've always liked your hair long but this is…nice. Nice," he repeated. "It suits you and I can see that it's much more practical."

Maryellen was pleased at his response, which seemed exactly right to her. Katie crawled into her lap then and laid her head against Maryellen's shoulder. Within minutes, the little girl was fast asleep. Mary-ellen settled Katie on the sofa beside her.

She didn't ask Jon how his day had gone. His weary expression told her everything she needed to know. He'd spent the day doing errands—getting groceries, film, visiting the library.

"Sit with me awhile," she urged, sitting upright.

"I've got stuff I have to do."

She patted the empty space next to her. "Jon," she whispered. "Please."

He hesitated, and she knew he felt torn between the need to work while Katie napped and his desire to be with his wife. Her smile must have won him over because he sank down at her side and slipped one arm around her shoulders.

"I love you so much," she said.

Jon kissed her forehead. "I love you, too."

"In a few months, this will all be over."

"It feels like it's gone on forever," he murmured.

"Getting through these last few weeks of the pregnancy… That'll be the most difficult. Things will get worse before they get better."

He released a deep, pent-up sigh. "We'll be fine."

"I think so, too." She turned her head in order to meet his gaze. "Your stepmother phoned this afternoon," she said, not bothering with a preamble.

Jon stiffened but said nothing. Then he asked. "Did *she* call or did you?"

"She phoned," Maryellen assured him, refusing to take offense at the question. "They read about the fire at The Lighthouse because they get the *Chronicle*. She called to see if everything was all right with us."

He didn't respond for a long moment. "So they know I'm not working?" he finally asked. "At a job, I mean?"

"They know," she said. "I told her about the problems with the pregnancy, too."

He wasn't happy about that, she could tell, but he didn't say anything.

"I didn't ask her to do it, I want you to understand that."

"Do what?"

"Come here and help. Ellen insisted. She said these are her grandchildren and we need help."

Still Jon refused to comment.

"Say something," she said, fearing his reaction. On top of everything else, she couldn't bear his anger. It would break her.

"They can't stay here."

She nodded.

"I don't want them around the house when I'm here." The arm that cradled her lay heavily on her shoulders.

"I'll make sure they understand that."

He sighed. "I don't like this, but I'll do it for you and Katie and for the baby."

"Thank you," she whispered.

"It doesn't change anything, Maryellen."

"I know." She pressed her head against him. A minute later, she felt him relax again.

"Love does that to a man, doesn't it?"

"Hmm?" she murmured.

"Makes you do things you don't want to for the people you love. Things you never thought you'd do."

Maryellen knew what he was saying. Jon had vowed that he would not allow his family back in his life after what they'd done to him. Yet here he was, setting aside his deepest convictions because Ellen and Joseph were willing to help in this impossible situation. He'd agreed to let them into the fringes of his life for Maryellen's sake and Katie's. There might be no forgiveness in his heart, but he'd set aside his anger to serve his wife's needs.

"Love makes us put other people first," she said. "Isn't that what you mean?" *Isn't that what love is?*

Four

Justine could barely stand to look at the burned-out husk that had once been The Lighthouse. Most of the structure had collapsed and the charred remains were a blight against the vivid blue backdrop of the cove. Yellow crime-scene tape stretched across the parking lot. Even now, two weeks after the fire, the acrid smell of burned wood and smoke hung oppressively in the air.

Seth stood at her side and Robert Beckman, the insurance claims adjuster, was with them. He made notes on a clipboard as they surveyed the site together. Leif, thank goodness, was in preschool. As much as she could, Justine wanted to protect her son from all this.

Her panic attack the week before had shaken her. She hadn't told Seth about meeting Warren. There seemed no reason to do so. Knowing she'd been anywhere close to the other man would only upset him, although her husband had nothing to worry about. Her love for Seth and their family was rock-solid. Warren had been kind to her, and for that she was grateful. He'd asked her to join him for lunch; she'd declined and hadn't talked to him since.

"How much longer will the investigation take?" Seth asked, keeping pace with the adjuster.

Justine wrapped her hand around his arm in silent entreaty. Seth was still bitter and impatient, yearning to move forward after the fire and resentful of every delay. Already he was talking about rebuilding, eager to get their business and their lives back on track. More than eager, he'd become obsessive. Every drawback, every question, frustrated him. He couldn't sleep and the stress had begun to affect his emotional health.

"I know it seems to be taking a long time," Robert said in a soothing voice. "But—"

"It's already been over two weeks," Seth snapped. "What else is there to investigate?"

"You'll have to forgive my husband, Mr. Beckman," Justine said quietly. "As you can imagine, this fire has been very difficult for us."

"I completely understand," the older man assured her. "As I was saying, I know it seems like a long time, but I do promise you that we're working as quickly and efficiently as we can."

"I didn't mean to snap." Seth gave a helpless shrug. "It's just that every day we're not open for business we lose customers and staff." Word had come that morning that their head waiter had taken a job in Tacoma. Dion wouldn't be easily replaced. It was inevitable that the rest of their staff would find other employment, as well. No one could go without a paycheck for long.

"The company recognizes that, but we can't do anything until the fire marshal gives us an opportunity to survey the damage thoroughly. And because this is a criminal investigation, it's simply going to require more time."

Justine knew that Seth had made numerous phone calls to the fire marshal in an effort to get the investigation moving.

"I've contacted an architect," Seth explained, and Justine barely managed to conceal her shock. She'd had no idea. "We've been discussing design plans," he went on, "and I'd like to set up a construction schedule. I can't do that until the fire marshal releases the property."

"Well…you may have to wait a while."

"When can we rebuild?" Seth demanded.

Robert Beckman slowly shook his head. "Since the fire appears to have been arson, the company would like to bring in a 'Cause and Origin' investigator." He paused. "This is in addition to what your local people are doing."

"What will he do?" Justine wanted to know. "Your investigator, I mean."

"His—or her—primary purpose is to confirm the preliminary finding of arson. Our investigators do that by looking at flame patterns to see where the fire started."

"How could anyone tell anything from a heap of ashes?" Impatience rang in Seth's voice.

"It's astonishing the information they can derive from the site. They're able to distinguish exactly where the fire originated. They can determine the accelerant. Sometimes there are other clues they can find by sifting through the debris. There are certainly cases in which their investigations have led to the apprehension and conviction of arsonists. I remember one instance in which—"

"That's all well and good, but what should I tell the architect?" Seth broke in. He ran his fingers forcefully through his hair.

Justine was horrified that Seth had already spoken to an architect and wondered when he'd done this. He'd been gone a couple of afternoons but hadn't mentioned where he was or with whom. Nor had Justine questioned him. The truth was, it had been a relief to have him out of the house. Seth found it impossible to remain in any one place. When he was home, he stalked from room to room, unable to work at anything or even read for more than a few minutes. Unable to relax.

"Your policy covers loss of income for a year," Robert Beckman continued, flipping a page on his clipboard. "If construction time goes over that, we can request an extension."

"So the sooner we get started, the better, don't you agree?" Seth asked. "For the company *and* for us."

Robert gave another of his soothing replies, and unwilling to listen to any more, Justine walked across the parking lot to stand at the farthest edge, which overlooked the cove. The wind carried a briny scent on this overcast day, shrouding the pungent smell of smoke.

The view of the cove always calmed her. She absorbed that peace now, needing it to settle her pounding heart. Seth had taken matters into his own hands; without so much as talking to her, he'd held discussions with an architect. When they'd first conceived the idea of The Lighthouse, Justine had been involved in every aspect of the planning. Now Seth had excluded her.

The fire and its aftermath were so much worse than she would ever have believed. Her husband had turned into a stranger, a man Justine neither knew nor liked. The temptation to escape, to pack a suitcase and disappear, grew stronger every day. Warren had offered her the use of a summer cottage on Hood Canal. It sounded so peaceful there. Leif would love to walk along the beach, exploring, wading in the water. She could picture him now, digging for clams with his small shovel, his laughter spilling out into the wind. Not once since Leif was born had they taken a family vacation. The Lighthouse had filled every waking minute. Only in the absence of the restaurant and its demands was she beginning to see how completely it had taken over their lives.

"Justine." Seth placed his hand on her shoulder as he came up behind her. "Everything's going to be all right, sweetheart," he said, his voice conciliatory.

"I know." The fire, the destruction of the restaurant, was no longer her main concern. What worried her was the effect it'd had on her husband.

"I realize I've been a little cranky lately."

She smiled and pressed her hand on top of his. To say he'd been "a little cranky" was an understatement of major proportions.

"Everything will be all right," he said again, "once we find out who did this to us."

"Will it?" she asked, but apparently Seth didn't hear her because he didn't respond.

Justine tilted her head to one side so her cheek could rest against his hand. "You're already talking about rebuilding," she murmured.

"Of course. I want to get started as soon as possible. Don't you?"

She shrugged. "I don't know anymore."

"What do you mean, you don't know?" He laughed and seemed to assume she was joking. "We're in the restaurant business. This is how we make our living. Unless we rebuild, we won't have an income."

"Yes, but…"

Her husband went still for a moment. "I can't go back to fishing, Justine."

Being a professional fisherman was a hard, dangerous life, and they'd agreed that Seth would give it up for good. His father had encouraged him in that decision.

"I wouldn't want you to fish," she said, turning so she could slip her arms around his middle. "I'm just not sure I want to be a restaurant owner anymore."

Seth gripped her shoulders, his fingers digging into her flesh. "You *don't* mean that. You don't know what you're saying."

"I…I do," she countered. "At least I think I do. We went into this business with absolutely no knowledge of what we were letting ourselves in for. We were totally naive about what owning a restaurant takes out of you."

According to statistics, eight out of ten new businesses fail, and restaurants headed the list. The only reason theirs had been successful was the sheer force of their combined efforts—and a degree of luck.

"We made a few mistakes," Seth said, then added with a wry grin, "okay, we made a *lot* of mistakes in the beginning, but we learned quickly and we've come a long way."

"We hardly spend any time together, as a family." This was the one thing that distressed Justine the most.

Seth didn't agree or disagree with her.

"You were at the restaurant all hours of the day and night, and so was I." She supposed that now wasn't a particularly opportune moment to broach her concerns, not while Seth was still so upset.

"I *had* to be there. You know that."

"I'm not blaming you for any of this," Justine told him, gazing into his intensely blue eyes. He was frowning at her and in him she read confusion and pain.

"Are you suggesting I haven't been a good husband?" he asked.

"No! That isn't what I meant at all. I love you and you love me. I could never doubt that." Then, reluctantly, she said, "I'm afraid, Seth."

"Afraid? Afraid of what?"

"I'm not sure. I had a panic attack last week. I didn't know what it was at first. I felt like I wasn't getting enough air and that I was going to pass out."

Concern darkened his eyes. "When? Why didn't you mention this earlier?"

"How could I? You've been so angry, so restless. I didn't want to add to your worries."

He slid his arms around her, drawing her close. "I'm sorry, my love. So sorry."

"I am, too. About everything."

He lifted his head. "What do you have to apologize for?"

"Because I don't think I can go back to the way things were before, with you gone so many hours. With me at the restaurant virtually every day. I don't want our son spending every night with babysitters. I don't want to go back to the constant worries over money and meeting payroll. It was always something, wasn't it?" Once she started listing her concerns, she couldn't seem to stop. "This was never our plan, remember? I was going to do the books and fill in occasionally, but occasionally became every day. Leif is being raised by strangers and you have less and less time for us."

Seth frowned at her. "You never said any of this before."

"That's because I hardly ever saw you, and when I did, we were usually talking about the restaurant. We wanted to have a second child and kept putting it off."

"But—"

"We've had practically no time to be a family. It doesn't make sense to have a second baby." She stared at him. "I know what you're thinking."

"I doubt that."

"You're thinking that you aren't about to let all this hard work go to waste. That you didn't slave away for the last five years to end up with nothing more than a pile of rubble."

He looked startled, as though her observation had surprised him.

"We both need to decide what's really important," she said, nearly choking on her words. "Is working thirteen- and fourteen-hour days worth what it's doing to us, to our son and to our marriage?"

"Yes," he stated without question. "You're exaggerating, Justine. It isn't all bad."

"I agree, but for me, the bad outweighs the good. I'm no longer sure the sacrifice is worth it. I love you so much," she whispered, bringing her hands to his face, blinking back tears. "I want my husband back—the man I married. The man who proved to me I could love and be loved. I want to find what we once shared and I'm so afraid it might be too late."

Seth crushed her to him then and held her tight. She felt him shudder, and he didn't speak for a moment.

"I had no idea you felt this way," he finally said.

"I didn't know it myself until the fire," she admitted.

"What *do* you want?"

"That's a mystery to me, too," she said with a shaky laugh. "I guess I want us both to think long and hard before we decide whether or not to rebuild The Lighthouse."

She could tell from his sudden tension that he'd prefer not to reconsider but to go ahead with his plans to rebuild. Justine swallowed, wondering if anything she'd said had gotten through to him.

"I'm not making any promises," Seth told her.

"But we can talk?" she asked.

"All right," her husband agreed. "We can talk."

Five

With the *Cedar Cove Chronicle* folded to the classifieds, Cecilia read through the listing for rental houses one more time. Other navy couples had warned them that it was next to impossible to rent in a middle-class neighborhood without including the wife's income. Cecilia and Ian didn't want to do that. They'd never be able to save for a house if most of their monthly pay went into rent. They wanted a home of their own, especially now that they had Aaron.

"The house is at 204 Rosewood Lane," Cecilia said as Ian drove. She turned to check on Aaron, who was sleeping peacefully in his carrier in the backseat.

"Don't get your hopes up," Ian warned.

"It's too late—they already are." Cecilia so badly

wanted this to work out. Her parents had divorced when she was young and from that time forward, Cecilia and her mother had lived in apartments. She'd always dreamed of one day having a home with a yard and a garden and a real neighborhood. Ian had grown up in a house, and living in one again didn't mean nearly as much to him as it did her. He was willing to wait until they could afford their own.

She'd phoned about several possible places, and the one on Rosewood Lane was represented by an agent. Judy Flint, who worked for Cedar Cove Real Estate, was meeting them at the house.

He drove onto Rosewood Lane and Cecilia immediately liked the area. The street was lined with elm trees already in leaf and there were tulips and daffodils in front of almost every house. This was the kind of neighborhood where children rode their bicycles in the street, and the sidewalk was used for jump rope and other kid games. She saw a white picket fence and held her breath, hoping that 204 was the house number there.

It was.

"Oh, Ian, *look!*" she cried, breathless with excitement. "It's perfect." In fact, it was even better than she'd dreamed. It was a white, two-story house with a large dormer over the front porch. Although this was clearly an older home, that didn't bother Cecilia and if anything, made its appeal stronger. She especially liked the wide porch and brick columns.

"It's all right, I guess," Ian said as he parked the car by the curb.

Cecilia playfully slapped his arm. "You like it, too."

"Yeah." He shrugged. "Looks like a good family home."

He'd hardly put the vehicle in park when she unfastened the seat belt and climbed out. Judy Flint, the agent, was waiting at the front door, and the owners were due to show up later, if warranted. It seemed a bit unusual, but they'd requested a meeting with any potential renters.

Ian extracted the baby carrier from the back seat and carried a napping Aaron onto the porch with him.

"Aren't you adorable?" The agent smiled at the baby. "I see you're right on time," she told Ian and Cecilia in a friendly voice, still smiling at Aaron.

Cecilia had been ready an hour early and the wait had seemed interminable.

"I think my wife wants to rent it sight unseen, but I'd like a tour," Ian said, teasing Cecilia.

"Step inside," Judy invited as she held open the screen door.

Gazing all around, Cecilia walked into the house. Even without furniture, the living room had a sense of warmth that came from the brick fireplace, polished oak floors and off-white walls. It was easy to imagine what this place would look like filled with their things.

She was still examining the living room when Ian called from the kitchen.

"It's a little small in here."

"I'll be there in a minute," Cecilia called back. She was studying the fireplace with its built-in bookcases on each side. This was the perfect location for a rocking chair, where she could nurse Aaron, read, daydream....

Ian returned to the living room. "Remember this is the first house we've seen. We've only started to look. There are plenty of other rentals on our list."

"I'll remember," she promised, but Cecilia had made up her mind. This was it. All she had to do now was convince her husband. If they delayed, someone else would quickly snatch it up.

Ian disappeared, and a few minutes later she heard him say, "I'm going to check out the garage." Apparently he'd already been through the ground floor and she had yet to move beyond the living room.

Taking in every detail, Cecilia made her way into the kitchen. Ian was right; the area was smaller than she would've liked but it was adequate. She noticed that the back door had a doggie entrance. Perhaps they could get a dog sometime, she thought dreamily. A compact laundry room off the kitchen led to a hallway. She followed that and came to the larger of the two bedrooms. The master bedroom was painted a soft shade of yellow that looked fresh and new. The closet was small but again adequate.

"There are two other bedrooms upstairs," Judy, the agent, told her. "Four bedrooms in all."

"Four bedrooms," Cecilia repeated. It felt like a mansion.

"The basement is unfinished."

"It has a basement, too?"

"The owner didn't use it for anything other than storage."

Ian bounced back into the house and the instant he did, Cecilia could tell he was happy. "The garage is great! Want to come see?"

"Sure." Cecilia exchanged a smile with Judy Flint. Men and their garages. She trailed him outside and into the detached garage. Judy went with them and highlighted a number of features. There was plenty of room for Ian to work on his car, while leaving space for storage.

"I do want to remind you that this is the first house we've seen," Cecilia teased, throwing his own words back at him. "So don't get too excited."

"This is the best home I have available in your price range," Judy inserted.

Ian's eyes held Cecilia's. "What do you think?" he asked.

"I think we'd be foolish to let this opportunity pass us by."

Ian reached for her hand and gave it a gentle squeeze.

"Would you like me to contact the owners?" Judy Flint asked.

Ian responded with an enthusiastic nod.

The agent walked outside, and Cecilia watched as she opened her cell phone.

"It's everything I'd hoped for," Cecilia whispered. "Everything."

"Four bedrooms is a lot for just the three of us."

"There'll be other babies," Cecilia said. "We could fill those bedrooms in no time."

Ian's eyebrows shot up and Cecilia giggled.

She was so happy she could barely contain herself and she could see Ian was just as pleased.

She thought he might have kissed her right then, except that the agent returned. "The owners are in town and they'll be here in about ten minutes."

As Cecilia and Ian finished exploring the rest of the house, including the two upstairs bedrooms, she noticed that another car had parked out front. An older gentleman, wearing a large cowboy hat and boots, and a middle-aged woman started up the walkway toward the house.

Judy Flint opened the front door for them and introduced Grace and Cliff Harding. Cecilia smiled shyly at the other couple. When Aaron began to fuss, she lifted him from the carrier and held him against her shoulder.

"I know it's unusual for the owners to ask for a meeting with potential renters," Grace said.

"We don't mind," Cecilia assured her. She recognized Grace from the library. Before she had her own computer, Cecilia had made several trips to use the ones in the library whenever Ian was at sea, so she remembered Grace, who'd been helpful and friendly. "We like your home very much and we'll take the very best care of it."

The older gentleman put his arm around his wife. "Grace and her family lived here for over thirty years and she wants to be sure it's in good hands."

"It will be," Cecilia promised her. She understood why Grace would want to interview anyone who might be renting her house. It must be hard to let strangers move into a place that you'd lived in for much of your life. And yet Cecilia understood why she was willing to walk away from her home of thirty years. Cliff Harding cherished her. She saw it in the way he touched his wife, the way he looked at her.

"You're in the navy?" Cliff Harding asked Ian.

Ian nodded. "Yes, sir."

"So you could be transferred," Grace said, glancing at her husband. She seemed a little unsure.

"We could." Cecilia's heart would break if they had to leave Cedar Cove but she'd go wherever Ian was assigned.

"Ms. Harding is asking for a one-year lease," Judy explained.

Ian paused. "That could be a problem," he said. "There've been a few rumors about the *George Washington* being transferred to San Diego. That might not mean anything, but then again, it could." He'd mentioned this to Ceclia earlier, and she could only hope the rumors came to nothing.

"Would you consider a lease-to-own option?" she asked. She should've talked this over with Ian first and wished she had, but if that *was* an option, she wanted to know.

Again Grace looked at her husband. "I…don't know. I'd like some time to think that over."

"Sure… Ian and I aren't even sure we could afford to own a house this big."

"We'll discuss all of that later." Ian gestured around him. "As my wife said, we'd take care of your home the same way you have," he told Grace. "But if you need a one-year lease, we won't be able to sign it."

Cecilia held her breath while she waited for Grace's response.

"Should we look elsewhere?" Ian pressed.

After the briefest of hesitations, Cliff Harding shrugged and seemed to leave the matter up to Grace.

Cecilia wasn't sure what else to say, so she asked, "Is there space to plant a garden?"

"Oh, yes, I've always had a garden—roses and bulb flowers and perennials. Pretty well everything should be coming up, but there's certainly room for more. And the yard gets plenty of afternoon sun."

"I've always wanted a garden," Cecilia confessed. She patted Aaron's back gently and soon the baby was sleeping contentedly on her shoulder.

Together the four of them walked around the house, while Judy waited inside. Ian and Mr. Harding were deep in conversation, and Cecilia had some questions for Grace, as well.

"I do hope you'll agree to rent to us even without a lease," Cecilia said when they'd finished.

Grace smiled at her husband and nodded. "My hope was that this home would go to a family just like you. This neighborhood's a good place for a family and you'll fit right in."

For a moment, Cecilia thought she might cry. "Thank you both so much."

"Hey," Mr. Harding said, raising his hands. "This is strictly Grace's decision."

Judy Flint rejoined them then. "I'll get the paperwork going right away," she announced. "Are you prepared to write me a check this afternoon?"

"Sure am." Ian removed his checkbook from his hip pocket.

"When could we move in?" Cecilia asked, and had trouble keeping the excitement out of her voice.

The Realtor turned to Grace, who smiled. "As far as I'm concerned, once the paperwork's signed, you have my blessing."

"Thank you," Cecilia said over and over. "Oh, thank you." She couldn't stop smiling.

Six

Linnette McAfee had been looking forward to this afternoon with Cal all week. Because of her work as a physician assistant at the Cedar Cove Medical Center, her days off rotated. Fortunately, Cal's job with Cliff Harding allowed him to adjust his work schedule to hers. If not for such an understanding employer, Cal and Linnette might never have found a chance to be together.

Linnette's mother, Corrie, had purchased a date for her with Cal at the Dog and Bachelor Auction, a charity event for the local animal shelter. For more money than Linnette could believe, her mother had set her up with Cal Washburn and at the same time purchased an Australian shepherd for her brother, Mack. Both gifts had worked out exceptionally well. Lucky had become her brother's constant companion, and Linnette—well, she'd fallen in love with Cal. That wasn't how she'd felt about him in the beginning, however.

All she'd known about Cal Washburn was that he was a horse trainer and that he talked with a mild stutter. Besides, she'd had her sights set on Dr. Chad Timmons. Chad, however, wasn't interested, despite Linnette's continued attempts to attract him.

Her mother had pestered her to go out with Cal, and Linnette had finally capitulated. To her surprise, she'd enjoyed herself. When he'd asked her out again and kissed her, Linnette was even more surprised. She hadn't expected to enjoy his company, much less his kisses.

And so their courtship had begun. *Courtship* was an old-fashioned word and that suited Linnette, because she considered herself an old-fashioned woman. Cal seemed to appreciate that about her. Their relationship moved slowly—which, she had to admit, she was starting to find a *tiny* bit frustrating— but she recognized that this was the kind of people they were. Cal's stutter made him rather shy, even with her.

Cal was waiting for her when Linnette pulled onto Cliff Harding's horse ranch in Olalla, about twenty minutes south of Cedar Cove. His welcoming smile made her smile, too. Linnette was thrilled by their feelings for each other, but she was also a little intimidated because of the physical attraction between them. In her early twenties she'd been so intent on her medical studies, she'd never really had a serious relationship. Cal was the first.

"Hi," she said, as she climbed out of her car. He was tall and lean, with deep blue eyes. Their color was so intense she was convinced she'd never seen any bluer.

"H-hi. Hello." He didn't need to say any more for her to know he was glad to see her. He didn't need to speak for her to know how he felt. Almost before she was ready, he slid his arms around her waist and, after checking to be sure no one was watching, he pulled her close and kissed her with a hunger that sent her mind whirling into space.

When their kiss ended, she leaned her forehead against his chest and dragged in a deep breath. "You missed me, didn't you?"

"I—I d-did."

"Cal," she said. Because his kisses had such a powerful impact on her, she had to clear her throat. "Cal," she said again. "I got your message and packed us a picnic lunch. What did you have in mind?"

"Y-you'll s-s-see." He took her by the hand and led her into the barn, where he had two horses saddled and ready to ride.

Linnette hesitated. "Ah… Have I mentioned that I've never been on a horse?"

"Yes. D-d-don't worry."

"I am worried," she protested. "Okay, I *have* ridden before. I remember it now. When I was five years old, my dad let me ride a pony at the Puyallup Fair. I was terrified and he had to walk around the circle with me."

Cal chuckled. "You'll be ok-kay. Sheba—" he pointed toward the brown horse "—is an older m-mare. V-very gentle."

"Promise?" The horses Cal had chosen were a whole lot bigger than that pony had been. Although she might be projecting her own fears, the mare seemed to give her the once-over and then snorted as if to say Linnette would regret it the minute she climbed onto her back.

"Promise," Cal assured her.

She figured Cal had a romantic interlude planned, and her nervousness was about to ruin everything. In an effort to buy time, she returned slowly to her car and retrieved two sack lunches from the passenger seat.

Cal walked with her and kept his hand on the base of her neck. "D-don't-t-t be afraid."

"Afraid? I'm not afraid," she lied. She thought she did a good job of it.

Cal seemed to believe her—or else he was equally good at pretending.

"So Sheba's mine?" she asked as he took the sack lunches out of her hands and stored them in saddle-bags on the larger of the two horses.

"Yup." He gestured with his head toward the mare. "L-like I said, Sh-Sh-Sheba's gentle."

"Gentle is good," Linnette murmured as she

walked around and stood in front of Sheba, allowing the mare to get a good look at her. Sheba nodded her head a couple of times, apparently acknowledging Linnette's presence. Maybe in Sheba's view, Cal had vouched for her, Linnette thought whimsically. Tentatively, Linnette raised her hand and petted the mare's dark muzzle.

With Cal's help she mounted. As soon as Linnette was in the saddle, Cal adjusted the stirrups and handed her the reins. She felt very high off the ground—and correspondingly vulnerable. A fall off this horse could cause her serious injury. And yet she didn't dare let Cal know how frightened she actually was.

After asking if she was comfortable, to which she nodded in response, Cal mounted the other horse, a chestnut gelding. He led the way out of the huge barn. Without needing any direction from Linnette, Sheba obediently followed Webster, Cal's horse.

Although it was barely noon, the sun was out and the day promised to be glorious. Cal had given her some basic instructions, but riding was awkward at first. Linnette bounced and her teeth chattered until she learned to relax. Cal kept their gait slow and easy. When she felt confident enough to raise her head, she stared avidly at him, so handsome in the saddle, so natural. She remembered what she'd heard Cliff say once—he was a born horseman.

"Gloria?" Cal asked in that shorthand way of his.

He was asking about her sister, the one she'd only recently met. Her parents had fallen in love when they were both in college. Her mother was still a teenager when Gloria had been conceived—and then the romance had fallen apart. Disgraced and afraid, Corrie had moved back home with her family. Several months later, she'd had a baby girl and given her up for adoption. After the birth she'd returned to college. Without knowing about their child, Roy had sought out Corrie and they'd reunited. Only after they were engaged did Corrie tell him she'd had his baby. They'd agreed never to speak of the matter again, and they hadn't, until Gloria tracked them down.

Needless to say, it was a shock to discover she had a sister. Linnette had been astounded, overwhelmed, bewildered. At the same time, she was excited. She'd always wanted a sister and, unbeknownst to her, the woman who lived in the same apartment complex and had already become her friend was also her sister. The bond between them had grown steadily stronger.

"Gloria's fabulous," Linnette told Cal. "We went out to dinner on Monday after work. The whole family's getting together for Easter, and Gloria will be joining us." This would be a real test for their family, Linnette realized. She knew her parents loved Gloria and welcomed her into the family.

It wasn't the same, though, and Linnette recognized that, as did Gloria. Her adoptive parents had died in a plane crash and she had virtually no family left. She'd gone in search of her birth family for that very reason. Linnette's parents, Corrie and Roy, were trying to make up for lost time, trying to fill in the gaps, exchanging information with Gloria about her history and theirs.

Cal was watching her intently as she spoke.

"It isn't that we don't want her or don't love her," Linnette went on to explain. "You know we do. What we don't have is a shared past. She had another mother and father who raised, loved and nurtured her, and they're her true family, her true parents." Everyone, however—including Gloria—was determined to make an effort. This Easter would be their first holiday as a family.

The horses trotted in single file now as they entered the woods. Linnette followed Cal on a narrow path, which made conversation difficult. The scent of fir and ocean mist pervaded the morning air.

It was just as well that they couldn't continue their conversation, Linnette decided. She had something important to discuss with Cal and had to figure out how best to approach it. She'd been doing a lot of thinking about his stuttering and wanted to tell him about the research she'd done on speech therapy. Yet she also wanted to make sure he understood that she loved him for the man he was.

After ten minutes or so, they emerged from the forest and onto a shore. Wavelets lapped against a pebble beach; the tide was in and sparkled in the sunlight.

"Oh, my goodness," Linnette cried, astonished at how secluded this beach was. Mount Rainier, capped with snow, rose off in the distance. Puget Sound spread out before her like an emerald blanket, with Vashon Island so close it seemed she could easily swim over.

"Y-you like it?" Cal asked, his blue eyes clear and alive.

"I like it very much."

Cal slid off his horse and then helped her down. He left both horses to roam while he set a blanket down on the beach and brought out their lunches. Leaning against a large driftwood log, they sat side by side to eat.

It was perhaps their most romantic date. When they finished their lunch, they stayed where they were, absorbing the beauty of the view. Cal slipped his arm around her and every now and then they'd kiss. His kisses were soft, sweet, his mouth lingering on hers.

Linnette thought about what she wanted to say and almost lost her nerve. She was reluctant to mention anything that might destroy the tranquility of the moment.

"Can I ask you something?" she said after several minutes. "Something I've never asked before."

"O-k-kay."

"Have you had the stutter all your life?"

As she'd feared, Cal tensed.

"Cal," she said, scrambling around. She knelt in front of him and cradled his face in her hands. "I have a reason for asking. Please don't take offense."

His eyes delved into hers, as if to gauge how much he could trust her. She didn't flinch, didn't back down and held his look with her own, letting her love shine through her eyes.

"Always," he said. "All m-my l-life."

She rewarded him with a series of slow kisses. "Did you know that when we're kissing and touching, you don't stutter?"

He frowned briefly. "I don't?"

"Nope. When you're talking to the animals, you don't, either." She'd observed this earlier and been struck by it.

Again he seemed unsure he should believe her.

"Have you ever been to a speech therapist?" she asked.

Resistance narrowed his gaze and he glanced away. "N-n-no."

She turned his face back to her so he couldn't avoid meeting her eyes. "That's what I thought." She took a deep breath. "There's an excellent therapist here in Kitsap County." She'd investigated therapists in the region and checked out their credentials.

"Y-y-you w-w-w-want me to g-go?"

"That's entirely up to you," she told him, ignoring the fact that his stutter had instantly become more pronounced, which seemed to happen as a reaction to stress. The gravel on the beach was cutting into her knees; still, she stayed where she was. "I'm just letting you know there's help if *you* want it." She placed the emphasis on him. This was up to Cal, and whatever he decided was fine with her.

When he didn't respond right away, Linnette sat down beside him once again. Cal draped his arm around her shoulder and brought her against his side. She felt peaceful and calm in his embrace.

"W-would y-you go with m-me?"

"For the first visit, anyway—if that's what you want."

Leaning over, Cal kissed the top of her head. "Y-you g-got on Sheba."

He was telling her that although she was apprehensive about riding, Linnette had climbed into the saddle—and that he was willing to take a risk, too. He would see a therapist about his speech impediment, despite his intense need to protect his own privacy.

"I owe my mother a big debt of thanks," Linnette whispered more to herself than to Cal.

"Oh?"

"She paid a lot of money at that auction so I could meet you, and now that I have, I think she got the bargain of the century." She grinned. "What I really mean is that *I* did."

Seven

As Rachel Pendergast was putting a load of clean clothes in her dryer, the phone rang. She reached it just before the fifth ring, which was when her answering machine always came on.

She'd been waiting to hear from Nate all day and dove breathlessly for the receiver. "Hello."

"Rachel?"

It was a young girl's voice, instantly recognizable as that of nine-year-old Jolene Peyton. They'd been good friends for the last four years. Soon after widower Bruce Peyton had brought his young daughter into the salon for a haircut, Jolene had decided she wanted Rachel to be her new mother. At the time, it had created an embarrassing situation.

Bruce still grieved for his wife, who'd died in a car accident on her way to pick up Jolene from kindergarten. He'd been adamant about having no interest in any kind of romance—with anyone, Rachel included. She accepted him at his word and over the next few years, as Jolene and Rachel continued to meet, Bruce and Rachel had become friends. They occasionally went out to dinner, mostly to discuss Jolene, since Bruce often sought her advice. Because she'd lost her own mother when she was relatively young, Rachel identified with the child.

In other words, there was nothing romantic between her and Bruce. Rachel was seeing Nate Olsen, although the time they actually spent together was limited, since the navy's demands came first.

"I need someone to take me shopping," Jolene said in a small, uncertain voice. "Dad said I could buy an Easter dress."

"I'd be happy to go with you," Rachel assured the youngster.

"My dad wants to talk to you, all right?" The little girl's voice was more cheerful now.

"Rachel," Bruce said. "Would it be a bother?"

"Not at all." The truth was, she could do with something new herself. "I'd love it."

"When can you go?"

Since Easter was the following weekend, Rachel figured it would need to be soon. "How about this afternoon?" she suggested. She had a rare Saturday free, which she'd arranged on the off-chance that Nate would be available. But it was already midafternoon and she hadn't heard from him, so she assumed he wouldn't be calling.

"This afternoon is perfect," Bruce said.

Rachel heard Jolene shout with glee in the background.

"I'll bring her by in an hour if that works for you," Bruce said.

"That would be great."

They discussed a price range for the new outfit and after a few words of farewell, ended the call. Rachel always enjoyed her "girl-time" with Jolene. When she'd started fourth grade, Jolene had asked her to attend the school's open house, and with Bruce's blessing, Rachel had gone. Afterward Jolene had written her a lovely thank-you note, which Rachel treasured. She had a stack of artwork that Jolene had colored or drawn or constructed for her. These were things a little girl would normally give her mother, and Rachel felt honored to play that role— part-time surrogate mom—in Jolene's life.

As Rachel finished brushing her hair, her phone rang again. Even before she answered, she had the sinking feeling it would be Nate.

It was.

"Are you free?" he asked.

"I will be later," she told him. Nate was working on some major project aboard the aircraft carrier. Because of it, they hadn't been together in more than a week.

"I thought you took the day off," he complained.

"I did." She didn't mention how many favors she'd had to call in to arrange a free Saturday. "When I didn't hear from you, I figured you were still hung up on this project."

Nate groaned. "Can you cancel whatever you've got planned?"

Rachel refused to do that to Jolene. "No. It's Jolene. I'm taking her shopping for an Easter dress."

The line went silent. "All right," he said reluctantly, his disappointment obvious. "I would've phoned sooner if I'd had the chance."

"I know." Rachel was disappointed, too. "What about later?"

"What time?"

"I'm not sure." She wouldn't know that until she got to the shopping mall. "Say six?"

"That's too late," he muttered. "I have a commitment this evening—a stag I have to go to. Dinner and, uh, entertainment. The whole deal."

"Well…we'll get together soon," she assured him. It was the best she could offer.

"Soon," Nate agreed with a sigh.

They spoke until the doorbell rang. Assuming it was Bruce and Jolene, Rachel ended the conversation with Nate and opened the door to discover Teri Miller waiting there. "Turn on your television," Teri insisted, storming into the small rental house.

"My television?" Rachel said. "What for?"

"Remember when we were over at Maryellen's last week?" Teri moved toward the television and reached for the remote. Not giving Rachel a chance to respond, she turned on the set and flipped though channels until she found the one she wanted.

Rachel stared at the screen, unable to figure out the program, which seemed to be some sort of... sporting event? She quickly surmised that it had nothing to do with sports. A group of mostly men were gathered around game boards, and everyone seemed intent and deadly serious.

"They're playing chess," Rachel said. She couldn't imagine why this was important to her friend.

"It's one of the biggest chess tournaments in the world, and they're in Seattle."

"Seattle," Rachel repeated. "Right. I remember. We heard the announcement at Maryellen's."

"Bobby Polgar is playing," Teri said excitedly, standing transfixed in front of the television. She pointed at a man bent over the board just as the camera closed in on the slouching figure.

"Who?" The name was vaguely familiar but Rachel didn't care about chess. She knew the basics of the game, or had at one time, but that was it.

"Bobby Polgar is the top-ranked player in the United States," Teri explained. Again Rachel wondered why this mattered to her friend. "He's in a match with some guy whose name I can't pronounce. From Ukraine."

"And this interests you?" Rachel asked.

"Yes. At least, Bobby does. I think he's kind of cute." She shrugged dramatically. "I know why Bobby's losing this match."

"You do?" She sent Teri a puzzled frown. "I don't get this, so give me a hand here," Rachel said. "As I recall, you know next to nothing about chess." She remembered that Teri thought chess was a lot like checkers, which of course, it wasn't.

"I have no idea how to play," Teri said. She glanced at her watch and immediately became agitated. "But that's beside the point. Listen, I've got a ferry to catch. I'm going to Seattle to help Bobby."

Rachel stared at her. Life-of-the-party Teri was going to "help" a chess grand master? Someone she'd only seen on television? Someone who was expert at a game she didn't know the first thing about? "Teri, are you all right?"

Her eyes widened. "Of *course* I'm all right. This is a mission of mercy. By the way, can I borrow twenty bucks?"

"I'll get my purse." They often helped each other out when one was short of cash. Rachel retrieved her wallet and took out the money. This was so unlike Teri. She knew her friend to be impetuous, but this was extreme.

"I realize you just have a few minutes, but start at the beginning. Just talk fast."

Teri drew in a deep breath and spoke in a rush. "I was cutting that snooty college professor's hair this morning. That Dr. Uptight."

"Dr. Upright," Rachel corrected.

"Whatever. The point is, the entire time I was cutting her hair she was on her cell phone getting updates on the chess championship. She couldn't believe Bobby Polgar was behind. I was curious, so after I finished her haircut, I turned on the TV at the salon and I saw him playing his first match, the one he lost." Teri said all this apparently without taking a breath.

"And?" Rachel urged.

"And he needs a haircut."

"Bobby Polgar needs a haircut?" What did that have to do with anything?

"Yes, he does," Teri said. "He kept brushing his hair out of his eyes. His hair is distracting him. He's long overdue for a cut and I decided to do something about it. I'm going to the tournament and I'm going to offer to cut his hair."

Rachel could list at least a dozen obstacles her friend was likely to encounter before she got to Bobby Polgar, if she ever did. However, Teri wasn't easily dissuaded once she'd made up her mind.

"I'm doing this for my country," she announced with melodramatic flair.

"Good for you." Grinning, Rachel patted her on the shoulder. "Let me know what happens, okay?"

"I will," Teri promised, practically running out the door to her car.

No sooner had Teri left than Bruce and Jolene arrived. Rachel was still waving Teri off when the nine-year-old dashed up the sidewalk toward her, hugging Rachel around the waist. Bruce followed at a much slower pace. "What time should I pick her up?" he asked.

"I'll drop her off at home," Rachel told him. He didn't live far out of her way and it wasn't as if she had other plans.

"I've got a better idea," Bruce said. "Why don't I meet you somewhere and the three of us can have dinner together?"

"Can we, Rachel?" Jolene asked, pigtails bouncing as she leaped up and down. "Can we? Can we?"

"That sounds like fun."

Three hours later, Rachel and Jolene pulled into the parking lot at the Pancake Palace, where they'd agreed to meet for dinner. The food was cheap and plentiful, and this was Jolene's favorite place in Cedar Cove to dine. She liked to dip her French fries in her cream-topped hot chocolate, a culinary activity that made Rachel wince.

Bruce was waiting for them in a booth near the front. The moment they walked in the door, he gestured to them. Jolene ran to his side as if it'd been weeks since she'd last seen her father. Rachel joined them a few seconds later.

"How'd it go?" Bruce asked, sliding over so his daughter could slip in beside him.

Rachel hid a smile when Jolene chose to sit beside her, instead.

"Daddy, we had *so* much fun. Shopping is great! We bought me a pink dress *on sale*, so we had money left over for tights *and* a purse."

"Men don't generally appreciate fifty-percent-off sales unless it involves hardware," Rachel told the little girl. She reached for the menu and scanned it, deciding on a ham-and-cheese omelet.

The waitress came for their order and disappeared with quiet efficiency. Jolene chattered for a while, then selected a crayon from the juice glass filled with them and started to color the paper place mat, which had a connect-the-dots outline of a bunny.

Rachel and Bruce picked up the conversation. They always seemed to have plenty to talk about, although she saw Bruce infrequently. Over the years they'd become comfortable with each other. They'd shared a kiss now and then, but they had no romantic illusions. In any case, Bruce still loved his wife, and Rachel was seeing Nate. In fact, Bruce was someone she'd confided in when she'd first learned Nate's father was a U.S. congressman.

"I didn't think you ever had a free Saturday night," Bruce said in an offhand way. "Don't you and Nate usually go out?"

"I wish. The navy comes first, and he's working on

some hush-hush project that's kept him tied up for a few weeks now." She didn't point out that although they did manage to talk every day, it was almost always late at night when they were both exhausted.

She and Bruce lingered over coffee, while Jolene had a second hot chocolate. It was after eight by the time Rachel returned home. She'd enjoyed dinner as much as she had the shopping—which had netted her two new sweaters. Afterward, they'd all gone down to the Cedar Cove waterfront for a walk and an ice-cream cone. She'd described her odd meeting with Teri, and Bruce had laughed.

"If anyone can get past security to see Bobby Polgar, it'll be Teri," Bruce said.

"You think so?"

"I know so." Bruce nodded confidently. "She isn't one to let a little thing like security guards or TV cameras stop her."

Rachel suspected he was right. If anyone could talk her way into meeting the top-ranked American chess champion, it'd be Teri.

She'd just unlocked her front door when the phone rang. Running to answer it, she threw down her shopping bags. As she'd hoped, it was Nate.

He told her he was calling from the stag, and she could hear shouts and laughter in the background. He didn't seem to be enjoying himself.

"Where were you?" he demanded, sounding tired and argumentative.

"I told you I took Jolene shopping."

"Until after eight? You said you'd be back by six."

"Yes, but…" But he hadn't suggested anything after that, since he'd had his own plans. "We finished up around six and then met Bruce for dinner at the Pancake Palace."

Nate went quiet for a long moment. "You didn't say anything about you and Brucie having dinner," he muttered sarcastically.

"Well, no," she agreed, "that didn't come up until later. Don't tell me you're jealous."

"Yes," he stated matter-of-factly, "I am. I haven't seen you all week."

"I know, and I've missed you like crazy. This dinner thing didn't mean anything, Nate. You know that. It was Bruce's way of thanking me for taking Jolene shopping."

"Okay," he said in a grudging voice.

"Dinner meant nothing, I promise you."

"Okay," he said again. "Look, I've got tomorrow afternoon free. Do you think you could squeeze me into your busy social calendar?"

"I'll see what I can do."

"Good."

They arranged to meet at the waterfront, and after a protracted good-night, Rachel replaced the receiver. She took a long shower, then got into an old flannel nightgown and sat in front of the television, hoping the ten o'clock news would have a story on the chess tournament. She half expected to see an item about a disruption, with Teri being hauled away by armed guards.

As the news began, her mind wandered back to the dinner with Bruce. She felt that their relationship had subtly changed in the last few months. She wasn't sure how it'd happened or what it meant. She hadn't lied or misled Nate; dinner tonight *wasn't* a romantic tryst. Far from it. Yet something seemed different. Rachel could only wonder why that was.

When the news anchor spoke about the chess championship, she mentioned only a few of the details—the most prominent being that after his stunning first-match defeat, Bobby Polgar had taken the second match and then the third, winning the championship.

Eight

After pacing the hallway outside the sheriff's office, Seth Gunderson sat restlessly on a nearby bench. Apparently Troy Davis had some news about the fire. Even after nearly a month, Seth had trouble adjusting to the reality of his and Justine's loss. It felt as if he were in the middle of Leif's toy kaleidoscope, the pieces of his life tossed about willy-nilly, forming random patterns that made no sense to him.

Despite his best efforts, Seth discovered himself lashing out at those around him. He felt guilty about the way he'd behaved and was thankful for Justine's patience, although they'd had a spat just that morning.

Her comment a couple of weeks earlier that she might not want to rebuild had come as a shock. In his opinion, she wasn't thinking clearly. He refused to let some unknown arsonist make his decisions for him. And the more his wife tried to convince him to consider options other than rebuilding, the more he shut her out. One thing was certain: Seth couldn't sit around the house like this much longer. He was going stir-crazy, with nothing to do but fret and fume. Since Justine's announcement, he hadn't even found any pleasure in considering new designs for the restaurant.

The office door opened, and Troy stepped into the hallway. "Sorry to keep you waiting," the sheriff said, extending his hand.

Seth stood and the two exchanged handshakes. Troy gestured toward his office, then went back inside and sat at his desk. Seth took the chair across from him.

"I was on the phone with the fire marshal when you arrived," Troy explained.

Anxious to hear the latest update, Seth leaned forward. "So what's the news?"

Troy tipped his chair back and locked his fingers behind his head. "There's one detail that might be significant, but I'll get to that later. The inspector hired by the insurance company confirmed what we already knew—that the fire was purposely set. An accelerant was used, probably gasoline. It started near the kitchen, then spread to your office and quickly engulfed the main dining room."

"Suspects?"

"As you know, I've interviewed the employees," Troy told him, dropping his arms and picking up a folder on his desk. "Plus former employees," he added.

Seth frowned. "Tony Philpott?"

Davis nodded slowly. "He'd recently been laid off, correct?"

Seth pressed his hands against the side of his chair. "I was forced to lay off both Tony and Anson Butler because of the money missing from my office. Both had access and opportunity. Between you and me, I think Tony was the one who took it, but I can't be sure. We never found it, and I don't have any proof. It was an unfortunate situation, and I probably didn't handle it as well as I should have."

Seth wished now that he'd dealt with the whole mess some other way. In retrospect he could understand Anson's anger. Yet he *did* have a bad track record and despite the boy's attempt to prove himself, Seth wasn't entirely satisfied that he could trust him.

"Philpott was out of town at the time of the arson," Troy said. "His alibi checks out."

Seth released a sigh. He didn't want to think Anson had anything to do with the fire, and yet what else was he to believe? The boy was already responsible for one arson in town, and The Lighthouse had gone up in flames right after he was laid off. All the pieces seemed to fall together, and for once the pattern made a horrible kind of sense.

"Have you ever seen this?" Troy surprised him by asking. "It's what I was referring to earlier." He held out a photograph of a large pewter cross, then passed it to Seth.

Seth studied the photo and shook his head. He couldn't remember seeing it before, but that wasn't saying much. He never paid much attention to jewelry.

"Where did you find it?" The cross looked partially melted, so it must have been either in the fire or close to it.

"The fire inspectors came across it in the rubble, near the office. It might mean nothing, but then again…" He shrugged. "At this point we just don't know. I'll keep you updated on anything we learn."

Seth stood up. "Thank you, Sheriff. I appreciate everything you've done."

On his way out of the office, Seth checked his watch. Ten. The entire day stretched before him, about as empty as a discarded beer bottle. This past month was the first time since he'd bought the old Captain's Galley restaurant and remodeled it that he'd had nothing to do.

Before this, there weren't enough hours in a day. His schedule was full; he'd constantly had meetings and plans and new ideas. His lack of purpose was killing him. Of course, he could go back home, but his relationship with Justine was strained. He loved his wife, but he didn't understand her anymore. Right now, he needed breathing room, a place where he could collect his thoughts, try to figure out what came next.

Seth had always done his best thinking on the water and it seemed natural to go down to the marina. He kept his sailboat moored there but couldn't remember the last time he'd taken her out. The air was crisp and clean, and he breathed deeply as he strolled over to the waterfront. Sailboats and motorboats of various sizes were secured in their slips, bobbing gently, peacefully, in the dark-green waters.

"Seth."

At the sound of his name, he turned to see his father walking toward him. Seth smiled. He'd always been close to his family. He and his father had once been partners in a fishing enterprise, which took them to Alaska for a number of months each year. The money was good, but the work was dangerous, and when Justine came into his life, Seth knew it was time to make a career change. His father's help had been instrumental in starting the restaurant.

"You spoke with the sheriff?" Leif Gunderson asked when he joined him.

Seth nodded. He hadn't mentioned this to his father, which meant Leif had been talking to Justine. "There's nothing new to report about how the fire was set—we already know that—or by whom. The inspector found a pewter cross in the ashes. That's the biggest news. But I have no idea who it belongs to and we can't be sure it's even connected to the arsonist."

Leif frowned, as if pondering this latest bit of information. They sat on a park bench outside the marina. "How are things at home?" his father asked.

Seth figured his wife had given him an earful. Then again, it wasn't like Justine to share their personal problems with others. "What makes you ask?" Seth murmured. He reached down and picked up a pebble and threw it into the water.

His father picked one up, too, and tossed it toward the cove. "I didn't mean to pry. It's just that you looked like you wanted to talk."

All at once Seth realized he did need to confide in someone. Someone who knew him well, yet could maintain a perspective on the whole situation and everyone involved. Someone whose advice he trusted. Who else but his father? Sighing deeply, Seth braced his elbows on his knees. "Justine and I had an argument this morning. It wasn't over anything important. We're both on edge these days with the fire and all."

His father didn't respond for a moment. "That doesn't sound good."

"The problem is, I don't know what to do with myself these days. I wanted to start rebuilding as soon as possible. Then, a couple of weeks ago, Justine dropped this bombshell about not being sure rebuilding was such a good idea. She seems to believe we should just forget about the restaurant." Seth lowered his voice.

He sucked in his breath and waited for his father's reaction. He assumed Leif would react the same way he had—with shock and disbelief. The fact that he didn't immediately say anything surprised him. "So, what do you think?" Seth pressed.

His father leaned back, closing his eyes. "Did she give you a reason?"

Seth had been too shocked to take in much of what Justine had said. At the time, he'd figured it was simply her way of dealing with the aftermath of the fire. "My wife is talking nonsense," he said. "We *need* the restaurant. It's how we make our living. Okay, she's right—I do put in a lot of hours and the work is demanding. The profit margin isn't exactly what we'd hoped, but we were doing pretty well."

He looked at his father, but Leif still didn't give any indication of what he was thinking.

"It's total nonsense," Seth insisted a second time. "Of course we should rebuild!"

"What do you plan to do while you're waiting for everything to come together?" his father asked instead.

If Seth had the answer to that, he wouldn't be hanging around the marina. "I don't know." This gave the matter of rebuilding top priority in his mind. Filling his days with the reconstruction project would ease his depression. Seth had been raised with a strong work ethic; he'd worked summers and after school from the time he was thirteen. He didn't know what to do with himself when he wasn't working. Outside of his role as a husband and father, his identity, his sense of who he was, came from what he did. Without work, he had no purpose.

Leif quirked a brow in his direction. "Do you love Justine?"

That question came as another shock. "More than my life." Seth had loved her when they were in high school and he'd carried a torch for her years afterward, too. She'd gone off to college and he'd half expected her to marry some rich boy there. But she'd returned to Cedar Cove, starting work at the bank. He'd never believed she would love him, didn't even think it was a possibility.

"You might listen to her, then," his father advised.

"I *do* listen, but she's talking foolishness."

"You might be listening, but you're not hearing her."

At that, Seth turned to stare at his father. "You're saying I should let all those years of work go down the drain?"

"No. I'm saying you need to *listen* to your wife."

"What am I supposed to do?" Seth flared. Everyone seemed to have an opinion but no one had offered him a solution.

His father didn't answer. A moment later, he casually continued the conversation. "I was talking to Larry Boone the other day," Leif said as he tossed another pebble in the water. "You remember Larry, don't you?"

Seth nodded. His father had purchased a fishing boat from the other man. Seth had owned a half interest in the boat and when they sold it, they'd invested that money in the restaurant.

"Larry's looking for a salesman and asked if I'd be interested in coming out of retirement. The way he figured it, I'd been around fishing and boats all my life. He's selling pleasure crafts, too, and offered me a commission that sounded almost too good to be true."

Seth thought his father was probably glad of an excuse to go back to work. Adjusting to retirement hadn't been as easy as he'd assumed it would be. "Are you going to do it?" he asked.

"I considered it," his father said, grinning. "But then I talked to your mother, and she was dead set against it." Leif rubbed the side of his face. "She's been waiting all these years for us to travel. She's got her heart set on buying one of those RVs and driving across the country. She isn't about to let me take up a second career at this stage."

Seth chuckled, understanding his father's advice. "So that's the reason you're telling me I need to listen to my wife. You're listening to yours."

His father chuckled, too. "You know your mother. When she wants something, she makes sure I hear about it."

Seth did know and love his mother, and he had to agree she generally found ways of getting what she wanted. He loved the give and take of his parents' marriage, and their ability to compromise.

"I don't much like the idea of driving one of those battleships," Leif admitted, "but I'll do it, and by the time we get back, my guess is I'll be able to park that thing as slick as any boat I ever steered."

Seth didn't doubt it for an instant.

"I phoned Larry this morning," he went on, "and told him I had to refuse."

"Was he disappointed?"

"He was," Leif said, "so I gave him your number and suggested he call you."

"Me?" Seth asked. "You think I can sell boats?"

"Why not? You know as much about fishing as I do, and what you don't know about pleasure crafts you can learn. The money's good, and it'll help you fill in the time until you decide about the restaurant."

Seth needed to talk to Justine. This idea suddenly seemed right to him, but he wanted a few days to mull it over.

He sat with his father a while longer, chatting companionably about friends and neighbors, then headed home. Justine was vacuuming when Seth walked in and didn't hear him. He stopped to admire her as she worked. Her long hair flowed unrestrained down her back and her lithe body moved gracefully as she pushed the vacuum cleaner. Justine's concentration on any task was always complete; it was one of the many traits he loved.

He regretted their argument and was sorry for the things he'd said.

When she turned and saw him standing just inside the door, she jumped, startled. "Seth!" She switched off the vacuum cleaner. "When did you get home?"

"Just now." He walked toward her. "Where's Leif?"

"Preschool. I need to pick him up in half an hour." Her gaze didn't meet his as she swept the hair away from her face. "Did the sheriff have any news?"

He shook his head. "He showed me a picture of a pewter cross. You might take a look and see if you recognize it, although there's no guarantee it's connected to the arsonist." He paused. "If the sheriff doesn't get any leads from that, I feel we should contact Roy McAfee."

Justine didn't respond to any of those statements. "I'm sorry about this morning," she murmured instead.

"I am, too." He walked toward her, and she stepped into his embrace. "We need to talk," he said, holding her close.

"Okay."

"How about if I take you and Leif out for lunch," he said. "I ran into Dad, and he had a suggestion I want to discuss with you." He went on holding her. For the first time, he saw clearly that his anger was putting their marriage at risk. He loved Justine and his son. Dammit! He wasn't going to lose them, too.

Nine

Olivia Lockhart-Griffin wondered if job shadowing was such a good idea. The high-school guidance office had contacted her a couple of weeks earlier to make the arrangements, and in a moment of weakness she'd agreed. The high-school girl sitting in front of her looked terribly young, but her eyes glowed with sincerity and keen interest. Olivia had believed in the justice system as a girl of that age, and she did now. The difference was that years of experience had shown her its weaknesses as well as its strengths.

"So you'd like to be an attorney?" Olivia glanced down at the girl's name on the sheet of paper. "Allison?" she added. Allison Cox. Cox. That name sounded vaguely familiar.

"Yes, Judge, I would," Allison said, her back straight.

"Any particular reason?" Olivia asked.

The girl nervously flipped a strand of dark hair over her ear. "I'm hoping to learn how to use the law to help someone who doesn't have a lot of options."

Olivia nodded. It sounded as if the girl had a personal agenda; however, there wasn't time to delve into that now. She needed to get to court. "I'll be spending the morning in court, listening to a variety of cases. You can sit in the jury box near the court reporter. We'll take a short break midmorning, and then stop for lunch around noon. I have a luncheon engagement with my mother. You're welcome to join us if you'd like, and then we'll return to court about one-thirty." She smiled at the girl, who nodded. "Depending on the cases, I generally stop for the day at four. I stay a bit longer to read case files for the next day, but you'll be free to go then."

Allison made a notation on a yellow pad. "Thank you for giving me this opportunity."

"You're welcome. Is there anything you'd like to ask me before we head into the courtroom?"

The girl offered her a tentative smile. "I…I asked the guidance counselor if I could be assigned to you specifically. You might not remember this, but about three years ago my parents were in your court. They were getting a divorce."

That was why the name seemed familiar. Olivia did recall the couple and their situation.

"Mom and Dad had decided on joint custody of

my brother and me. You said you didn't like Eddie and me moving between houses every few days, so you gave us the house and had Mom and Dad move in and out."

Olivia smiled. "I remember. But professional ethics prevents me from discussing any case if there's a possibility the parties might come before me again."

Allison nodded. "They remarried, you know."

Olivia didn't, and was pleased to hear it. "That's wonderful." Checking her watch, she stood and reached for her black robe. Pulling it on, she left her chambers. Allison followed and she introduced the girl to the court reporter, who escorted her to a seat near the bench.

The court cases on that morning's schedule probably opened Allison's eyes wider than anything she'd read or seen on television. The child custody cases always tore at Olivia's heart. The state's position was to leave the child with the primary residential parent, in most cases the mother, if at all possible, as long as the child's welfare wasn't in jeopardy. More times than she cared to admit, Olivia wanted to shake these young parents and ask them to take a hard look at what they were doing to themselves and their children. Too often, their minds were addled by drugs or alcohol. Sadly, she doubted anything she said would sink in. Of course she dealt with other cases, too, but these were the ones that stood out most prominently.

Olivia noticed Allison taking copious notes and could only imagine what the high-school senior must be thinking, looking at the ravaged lives of those who stood before her.

Shortly after court went into session, Charlotte Jefferson Rhodes slipped onto a bench at the back of the courtroom. Within about a minute, she'd taken out her knitting. Olivia smiled. Charlotte was an inveterate knitter. More than that, she was exceptional in every way, and Olivia's admiration for her continued to grow.

Case in point, her mother and friends were responsible for the new medical clinic in town. It'd taken a senior citizens' demonstration and an arrest to get the council to respond. Word of Charlotte's arrest had spread faster than chicken pox through their small community. Not long afterward, the council had made some major concessions that allowed the establishment of a medical facility in town.

The irony of it was that this same medical center had saved Jack's life. Olivia's husband had suffered a heart attack the year before, and the EMTs had told her that if they'd had to drive him all the way to Bremerton, Jack wouldn't have survived.

At the time of the demonstration, Olivia had been embarrassed by her mother. Now she'd be forever grateful that there was a medical clinic in Cedar Cove, and it was mostly due to Charlotte, her second husband, Ben, and their friends.

Olivia was accustomed to seeing her mother in court, although she didn't come by as often as she used to. Since Ben Rhodes had entered her life, Charlotte had better things to do than sit and listen to Olivia.

At noon, the court broke for lunch. Allison and Charlotte met Olivia in her chambers, and Olivia made the introductions.

"Would you care to join us?" Olivia asked the teenager. She didn't expect the girl to accept, and she was right. They agreed to meet again at one-thirty.

"What a lovely young lady," Charlotte commented after Allison had excused herself.

"She is," Olivia agreed. "Where would you like to have lunch?" Her favorite place had always been The Lighthouse. Olivia missed it even more than she would've thought.

"How about the Wok and Roll," Charlotte said. "Grace tells me Maryellen likes their chicken hot sauce noodles, and I have a hankering to try that."

"Sounds good to me." Olivia was just grateful her mother didn't suggest The Taco Shack, which happened to be Jack's favorite. She'd had about all the tacos and enchiladas she could stand for a while.

"Speaking of Grace, have you seen her lately?" Charlotte asked as they walked through the courthouse and to the parking lot behind.

"She's so busy, we haven't talked all week. She's had to temporarily give up her Wednesday night aerobics class."

"My goodness, you two have been going to that class for years," Charlotte exclaimed. "What's happening? Is Cliff keeping her all to himself?"

"No." Using her remote, Olivia unlocked the car doors and opened the passenger side for her mother. "Nothing like that. She's helping Jon and Maryellen as much as she can. Kelly's pregnant, too, you know." Olivia slid into the driver's seat. "Grace rented out the house on Rosewood Lane and you won't believe who her tenants are. The Randalls! Do you remember them?" At her mother's blank expression, Olivia elaborated. "You were in court the day I denied their divorce. A young navy couple. Apparently they have a baby now and were looking for a house to rent and Grace met them. She remembered the case. Then, while she was talking to Mrs. Randall, my name came up. That's when Grace learned this was the very same couple. It's a small world, isn't it? Grace wanted me to know how well everything worked out."

"That's good news. And how's Maryellen?" Charlotte asked, concerned about Grace's oldest daughter.

"She's doing well, especially now that Jon's parents have arrived. They showed up last week and Grace told me it's made a world of difference."

"Where has Jon's family been all this time?" Charlotte asked. "Well, never mind, they're here now, and I know Maryellen and Jon must be thankful for the help. Some babies have a few problems coming into this world. That's why God created grandparents."

Olivia smiled at her mother as she pulled out of the parking lot and headed down Harbor Street toward the Chinese restaurant.

"And Jack? How's he? I do hope he isn't working himself into another heart attack," Charlotte said next.

At the mention of her husband, Olivia had to smile. "He's as cantankerous as ever. He's also back at work full-time."

Charlotte's eyebrows shot up. "I thought you weren't going to let that happen."

As if Olivia had any real control over Jack. "I couldn't stop him. He has an assistant editor now, and he's home every night as close to five as he can manage. He's lost thirty pounds, but I swear it was like chiseling it off an ounce at a time."

"I think he might've cheated now and then," Charlotte whispered.

That was an understatement if ever there was one. Jack did cheat—but not as often anymore. The heart attack had frightened him off double cheeseburgers for life, thankfully. Still, there was the occasional bowl of ice cream and a few cookies, but overall, Jack's self-control had been impressive.

"What about you and Ben?" Olivia asked as they drove into the parking lot at the Wok and Roll.

"I have news about David, Ben's son," Charlotte

said as she climbed out of the car. "You remember him, don't you?"

Olivia wasn't likely to forget David Rhodes. Ben's youngest son had asked her to fix a reckless driving ticket he'd gotten while visiting Cedar Cove. He hadn't taken kindly to her refusal.

The conversation was halted by their arrival at the restaurant. Once they were seated and sipping tea they resumed talking. Their order for chicken hot sauce noodles was already in the kitchen.

"You mentioned David Rhodes," Olivia said.

"Oh, yes." Charlotte reached for her purse and took out a linen hankie, dabbing at the corner of her mouth. "Sad to say, Ben's son is an embarrassment to him. He felt sick at heart when he learned David had approached you about the traffic ticket. He was mortified by that."

In Olivia's view that was the least of David's sins. She wasn't about to forget or forgive the fact that he'd attempted to swindle her mother out of thousands of dollars. If not for Justine's quick thinking, he would've gotten away with it. After some fast talking on David's part, her mother had written him a check. They'd met for lunch at The Lighthouse, just the two of them, but Justine had been on the alert. Much to David's chagrin, she'd swiped it right out of his hand. That was the same afternoon he'd picked up the reckless driving ticket. He probably should've been charged with driving under the influence, too, Olivia thought.

"David does have his problems," Charlotte said, "but I feel he's genuinely trying."

Olivia would believe that when she saw it.

"Ben got a check from David this week for a thousand dollars toward a loan he received from his father several years ago."

This was promising news. Perhaps David Rhodes *had* learned his lesson. Although Olivia took a rather jaundiced view of that possibility.

"Ben didn't say much, but I could tell he was pleased." Charlotte beamed. "It distresses me to see Ben estranged from his son. I know it bothers him, although he won't talk about it."

"David's a grown man, Mom. He isn't going to change. He is who he is, and that's who he'll remain—unless something drastic happens."

Her mother sipped her tea. Then casually, as if discussing the weather, she said, "Your brother's his own person, too, and he isn't likely to change, either."

A chill went down Olivia's back. So her mother knew. Will lived in the Atlanta area with his wife. They'd never had children, and while outwardly the marriage appeared stable, Olivia knew there were problems. Problems she suspected were due to her brother's infidelity. She'd never discussed with her mother what she'd recently learned about Will. How could she? But it seemed Charlotte was well aware of her son's weaknesses.

Olivia had been disillusioned by Will. Shortly

after Grace discovered that her first husband, Dan, had committed suicide, Will had contacted her. Before long, Grace and Will were involved in an e-mail relationship. Will had misled her friend, lied to Grace and said he was getting divorced. While not completely blameless, Grace had been vulnerable to his undeniable charms and naive about his motives. She'd trusted him—and nearly lost Cliff because of Will's selfish lies.

"Will isn't a good husband," Charlotte murmured. "It pains me to say so. Georgia wrote and said she'd had enough. Will was involved with someone at work. Georgia has decided to file for divorce."

The fact that he'd had an affair didn't come as any shock to Olivia. "I'm sorry to hear that."

"I called Will and spoke to him," Charlotte continued. "Georgia's moved out, but he seems to think she'll change her mind. Apparently she has in the past."

The waitress came with their order and two bowls. Steam rose from the noodles bathed in their seasoned chili sauce, topped with broccoli and slices of chicken. Although it smelled heavenly, Olivia found her appetite was gone.

"Georgia isn't going to change her mind this time," Charlotte said calmly. "I spoke to her, too, and heard the determination in her voice. It's over and frankly, I don't blame her."

Olivia was saddened to learn that her brother had

destroyed his marriage. She remained angry with him for what he'd done to Grace. He'd apparently thought Olivia would never learn of his deception but she had, and she'd let him know how upset she was. He'd brushed off her chastisement, with the implication that she was overstepping her bounds. In Will's opinion, this wasn't any of her business. But it was, and Olivia refused to forget what Will had done to her best friend.

Once they were off the subject of incorrigible sons—David and Will—Charlotte and Olivia made Easter plans. Everyone was coming to Olivia's for dinner, but Charlotte had planned brunch for Easter morning, following church services. She was baking her cinnamon rolls, which were Jack and Ben's favorite.

Charlotte and Olivia chatted about some of Charlotte's knitting friends as they finished lunch. Then Olivia paid for their meal and they returned to the courthouse.

Allison Cox met her outside her chambers, waiting as Olivia flipped through her phone messages, something she hadn't had a chance to do before leaving with her mother. The one on top made her smile. It was from Grace, and it said she'd see her at aerobics class that evening.

Ten

Allison was convinced of two things: Anson would be back before graduation and she'd hear from him by Easter. The more she thought about it, the stronger the idea became. Anson *would* call her by Easter. She knew it. She felt it. She lived on that hope.

Her day in court with Judge Lockhart-Griffin had been revealing, to say the least. People did stupid things and seemed shocked when they were held accountable in a court of law.

Anson wasn't like the people who stood before the judge. He'd been working hard to do the right thing, and then it seemed everything had blown up in his face. No one believed he was innocent. Yes, he was angry and disillusioned with the Gundersons—understandably because they'd laid him off—but that didn't mean he'd started the fire.

She sat on her bed and studied her notes from the day in court. The phone rang in the distance and she left it for Eddie to answer, since he considered it his duty to check all incoming calls. He was okay as brothers went, she supposed, but sometimes he could be a real pest.

"Allison!" he shouted as if she were deaf. "It's for you."

"Who is it?" she demanded.

"Some guy. He didn't give his name."

Only half interested, Allison reached for the receiver in her room. She paused. "Hang up, Eddie." When she heard the click, she said, "Hi," in an indifferent voice.

"Allison."

Her heart stopped. It was Anson.

"Where are you?" she asked, gripping the phone with both hands.

"I can't tell you."

"Are you okay?"

"Sort of."

She wasn't sure what to make of that.

"I needed to hear your voice," he said. "I know what happened at The Lighthouse. Everyone thinks I did it, don't they?"

She couldn't lie to him. "Yes."

He didn't respond for a moment. "I swear to you, Allison, it wasn't me."

"I believe you." It was hard to speak past the lump

in her throat. In her joy at hearing from him, she nearly floated off the bed. "How did you get past Eddie?" That was a crazy question when so many others were far more important.

"I had a friend of mine call. I'm using a throw-away cell phone. No one'll be able to trace it. I don't want to get you into trouble."

"Do you need anything?"

"No…just the sound of your voice. I knew if I heard it I'd be okay."

"I will be, too," she said breathlessly. She longed to tell him how desperately she missed him and how difficult it was to go to school every day and defend him. Anson didn't need to hear any of that. His troubles far outweighed hers.

"Has it been bad for you?" he asked. "Did the sheriff question you?"

"Yes. I…told them about you coming to my window that night."

"That's okay—you had to tell the truth."

"You…you smelled of smoke. I was too upset to realize it right away…. I—I didn't say anything to the sheriff."

He didn't comment or explain. Instead, he asked. "Is there a warrant out for my arrest?"

"No." She lowered her voice on the off-chance Eddie was listening. "But the sheriff says you're a…a person of interest."

He seemed relieved to hear that. "No matter what anyone tells you, Allison, I swear I didn't do it."

"I know." She closed her eyes and held her breath, as if to keep him close. Then she wondered if he had a specific reason for reaching out to her, if he needed her help. "Should I send you some money?"

"No. I'm fine."

Her heart pounded so hard that her pulse echoed in her ears. The money box had been taken from the office the night of the fire. Allison had heard the sheriff mention it to her father.

Anson hadn't been able to save any money because everything he'd earned as a dishwasher and later as a prep cook had gone toward restitution for the fire he'd set in the park. If he left Cedar Cove with money, it hadn't come from his employment. She wanted to ask what he was living on, but she was afraid of the answer, afraid of the truth.

"Come back, Anson," she pleaded softly. "My dad will help you."

"He can't," he returned, "not this time. I appreciate everything he did, but this is bigger. I'm eighteen now, Allison. This isn't going to be handled in juvie. I'd be tried as an adult and I can't risk that."

"Please." She didn't want to beg. "I can't stand not knowing where you are or what's going on."

"It's too late, Allison. I'm sorry—sorrier than I can ever tell you."

"It *isn't* too late. It can't be." Anson didn't seem

to understand that they'd never be together if he didn't clear his name.

"Where I am," he began, then stopped abruptly.

"Yes?" she urged.

"There's no going back for me. I shouldn't have phoned."

"No! I'm so glad you did."

"I have to go now."

The reluctance in his voice made her feel like crying. She wanted to argue with him, plead with him to talk to her for just a few minutes more. Instinctively she knew it wouldn't make any difference.

"Will you call again?" she asked.

"I don't know."

"Please." All her love was in that word.

"I'll try. Believe in me, Allison. You're the only good thing that's ever happened to me."

"I believe in you. With all my heart I believe in you—I believe in us."

The phone disconnected.

For a long time, Allison just sat on her bed, holding the receiver. Tears pooled in her eyes but she held them back, unwilling to let them spill over.

Some time later, she heard the garage door close as her mother came home from work. Rosie Cox was teaching fifth grade this year at one of Cedar Cove's elementary schools.

"Allison," her mother said as she walked past her

bedroom door. She knocked once. "Would you mind peeling five potatoes for dinner?"

"Sure." She tried to sound normal, as though everything in her world was exactly as it should be. Apparently she failed, because her mother opened her bedroom door and glanced in, her face showing signs of worry.

"Everything all right?" she asked gently.

Allison shrugged. "Sure, why not?"

Her mother stepped into the room and sat on the edge of the bed. "I remember when you were three years old and you decided you were perfectly capable of pouring your own bowl of cereal." She smiled as she spoke. "It was early one Saturday morning and you sat in the middle of the kitchen floor, where you emptied the contents of an entire box into a single bowl. I walked in, and you looked up at me with almost the same how-did-this-happen-to-me expression you have now."

Allison had heard that cereal story a dozen times. "I didn't do anything," she insisted, and she hadn't.

Her mother patted her hand. "Does this concern Anson in some way?"

Allison wanted to deny everything, to vent an anger that came from frustration—and fear. Being defensive was how she would've responded a few years ago. But she knew that ploy wouldn't work. Lowering her head, she whispered, "He phoned."

Exactly as Allison had suspected, her mother snapped to attention. "When? Just now?"

Head still bent, Allison nodded.

"We have to tell the sheriff," her mother said. "You know that, don't you?"

"Mom," she cried, "we can't! Anson swore to me he's innocent. He told me he didn't set the fire and I believe him."

Her mother slid one arm around Allison's shoulders. "If that's the case, we don't have to worry. We want Sheriff Davis to solve this so Anson can come home, right?"

Allison wanted that more than anything.

Her mother called the sheriff, who arrived about the same time her father did. Everyone gathered around the kitchen table, and Sheriff Davis questioned Allison again and again. He reviewed every detail of her brief conversation with Anson. Halfway through, the sheriff's cell phone rang. He excused himself to answer it, going into the other room, then returning to the kitchen a few minutes later.

"The phone is untraceable," he announced. "We don't know where he is."

That was what Anson had told her, but she was relieved to hear it, anyway.

"Do you think he'll phone again?" Sheriff Davis asked, pinning her with a look.

"I...I don't know." But Allison prayed that he would.

"You have any idea how he's living?"

"No."

"What about money?"

"He said he didn't need any."

Her parents exchanged a quick glance, knowing that she'd offered to give him what she had. She tried to defuse the tension, saying, "I asked him to come back, but he said he couldn't."

"There might be a very good reason for that, Allison," Sheriff Davis said. "An innocent man doesn't need to hide. If he calls you again, you tell him I said that, all right?"

Allison met his eyes and nodded. "I'll tell him," she promised.

Eleven

The day before Easter was always a busy time at Get Nailed. A lot of their clients attended church and wanted to look their best. She knew it was an important religious feast day, but Teri wasn't much interested in church. It wasn't how she'd been raised. Her mama was a single mother with three kids, struggling to make ends meet. She could barely keep them fed and clothed, let alone teach them about church. Teri, the eldest, had dropped out of high school at sixteen to attend beauty school and had her license the day she turned eighteen.

She was good at her job, but it wasn't the career she really wanted. Teri would've liked to spend her time around books. Be a librarian or even work in a bookstore or something like that. She was constantly reading. Her house had stacks of paperbacks in every room—romances and mysteries and biographies. Any title that caught her eye. Most of her extra cash went to books. With her lack of a social life outside the salon, they were great company.

Being a stylist suited her well enough, and it paid the bills. Fortunately, she was talented and kept up with current styles; she also had a decent clientele. Her first customer of the day was Justine Gunderson, who came in for a trim.

"I heard about what you did," Justine teased her as she sat in Teri's chair. Word had spread throughout the community. People talked, of course, and she'd been questioned again and again about meeting Bobby Polgar.

Teri studied Justine's thick, straight hair, which hung down her back—the kind of hair they had in shampoo advertisements, healthy and shiny. Teri's own had been dyed, cut and permed so often she'd forgotten the original color. Dishwater blond, she guessed. At the moment it was dyed brown with red highlights, and she wore it ultra-short and spiked with gel. She was thinking of dyeing it black next week when there was a lull in the schedule. She'd see if she could get Jane to do it for her.

"I'm impressed," Justine said. "You cut Bobby Polgar's hair."

People still talked about how she'd appeared at the televised chess match and bullied her way in to see the world-famous chess player. For pride's sake, she'd made it seem easy; in truth it'd taken a lot of effort.

Her arrival had caused a scene with those unpleasant security people. When they found her scissors, the guards acted as though she was some dangerous lunatic. She'd made such a fuss that Bobby himself had come out to see what she wanted, which was the only reason she'd even had a chance. He'd listened to her assessment that he needed a haircut and agreed to let her do it.

With several bodyguard types following, she'd been escorted in to Bobby Polgar's suite. When she entered, all kinds of people were milling about, giving him advice and making suggestions about the next chess match with the Russian. The moment Teri stepped into the fray, Bobby had lifted his hand and the room went silent. He'd stared at her, so she stared back. She'd told him to sit down, draped a towel over his shoulders and retrieved her scissors from one of the security people.

"Like I said, your hair is what's distracting you," Teri had told him. "You don't need other people's advice. You know what you're doing better than anyone." In retrospect, it was a bold statement and Teri couldn't quite understand why she even cared about this man and his silly chess match. All she knew was that she had this compelling urge to go to him and cut his hair. Go figure. She was the impulsive type and…well, it'd worked. Didn't matter if she couldn't explain it.

Most everyone wanted to know what Bobby had said to her. This was the confusing part. A few minutes after she showed up, Bobby had asked everyone else to leave, and then it was just the two of them. She wished she had some fantastic story to tell, but she didn't. She'd simply cut his hair and left. The entire time she was in that room, he probably didn't say a dozen words to her. Not until she was back in Cedar Cove did she learn that he'd won the next match and the one after that.

"Have you heard from him since?" Justine asked.

Teri arranged the cape over Justine's shoulders and fastened it. "Me? Nah. I didn't even tell him my name."

"He didn't talk to you?"

"Not really. Nothing I'd consider a conversation, anyway." In fact, Bobby Polgar hadn't even bothered to pay her, which was a damn shame since she'd had to borrow twenty bucks to get to Seattle. But then, to be fair, Teri hadn't asked for payment.

"What's Bobby like?"

Teri held up a comb as she thought about Justine's question. All week people had been asking her that and she was never sure what to tell them. "It's hard to say, seeing he wasn't all that communicative. He's intense and…" She wanted to say "peculiar" but that didn't seem quite right. "Strange," she finished. "He's just strange."

"They say he's one of the greatest chess minds of our time."

"He is *the* greatest chess mind of our time," Teri corrected. That much she'd garnered from Bobby himself, not to mention his handlers.

"So you're a fan?"

"Not of Bobby, and not of chess, either. They don't teach you much about the theory of chess in beauty school, you know?"

"So what interested you in Bobby?" Justine asked as they walked to the shampoo bowl.

"I don't know," Teri said slowly. "I saw him on television one morning and thought he was interesting looking. Then he lost that chess match. I knew what was wrong and that I could help him. I do stuff like that. People need something, and I do what I can. My mother's the same way, God bless her." Her mother also had a tendency to fall for the wrong guys, another trait Teri was afraid she'd inherited. At least Teri didn't see any reason to marry them. She'd been through three or four rocky relationships, none of which had lasted more than six months. They'd all ended with her wanting to kick herself for being so stupid. Teri liked to think of herself as savvy and smart; life, however, had a way of proving her wrong.

Teri lowered Justine's head into the shampoo bowl. Their eyes met, and Teri offered her a quick smile as she turned on the water.

"Thanks, Teri," Justine said, suddenly intent.

"For what?"

"For not asking about the fire. That's all anyone ever talks about. I haven't gone out of the house in weeks, except when it's absolutely necessary, because every time I do, people bombard me with questions."

The truth was, Teri had forgotten about the fire. With her own small world spinning around her brief moment of notoriety, the destruction of The Lighthouse had slipped her mind.

"You okay?" Teri asked. One look at Justine said she wasn't.

Justine didn't seem to hear and closed her eyes. Teri had discovered that there was something about working on women's hair that had a relaxing effect on them and led to confidences and disclosures they might make at no other time. Barriers were lowered, and they discussed their lives and problems with surprising openness. Teri was convinced it had to do with her being admitted to their personal space, as well as her undivided focus and the soothing atmosphere at the salon. She sometimes said she should put out a shingle advertising that she did hair with free counseling on the side. She certainly had enough experience to know what *not* to do when it came to unhealthy relationships.

"Seth and I are having a few problems," Justine confessed, sounding sad and lost. Her voice was so low Teri had to strain to hear. "We'll be all right…. It's just that things are difficult now."

"Which they're bound to be after something this upsetting," Teri reassured her. Again, their eyes met.

"We haven't made love in weeks," Justine whispered. "Not since the fire. Seth is so angry. He doesn't know how to deal with this." She closed her eyes again, and Teri gently squeezed her shoulder.

"Don't you worry," Teri said. "Everything will work out, you wait and see." She didn't mean to serve up platitudes; every word was sincere. Teri had seen it happen over and over. Some trauma would upset a family and it was the marriage that took the brunt of that strain—but if the relationship was strong, husband and wife could survive it together.

"How long have I been cutting your hair?" Teri asked. It wasn't a rhetorical question.

"I don't know," Justine replied. "Six or seven years for sure."

"That's what I thought. I remember when you were dating Warren Saget. I never did understand what you saw in that geezer, but who you decided to date was your business. Then Seth came along and— oh, my goodness—you were dumbstruck. I ran into you down by the waterfront one Saturday, and I saw the way you looked at each other. You two were crazy in love, no mistake about *that*."

Justine's eyes stayed closed as Teri washed her hair, but she smiled. "I remember those days, too. We couldn't keep our hands off each other."

Teri grinned. "You pretended Seth meant nothing

to you. I made the mistake of mentioning his name one time, and you nearly bit my head off."

"I most certainly did not," Justine protested.

"Did, too," Teri retorted, working the shampoo into the long, thick hair. "I'll bet Seth still looks at you the same way he did back then. There's no denying that man loves you and you love him. Just hang in there, okay?"

Justine opened her eyes and blinked up at her. "I hope you're right."

Denise, the part-time receptionist, approached Teri as she finished the shampoo. "There's someone here to see you," she said.

Teri wrapped the towel around Justine's head. "Did you get a name?"

"He wouldn't give me one."

"*He?*" Joan, Jane and the other girls all stopped what they were doing and stared at her.

"Go check it out," Rachel suggested from where she sat doing the mayor's wife's nails.

Teri led Justine to her station and dried her hands. "I'll be right back," she promised.

A tall, extremely thin man hovered just inside the salon. He glanced nervously around, as though afraid one of the stylists would tackle him, tie him up and dye his hair pink.

"I'm Teri Miller," she said, hand on her hip. She wasn't buying anything and she didn't have time for chitchat, either.

"Bobby Polgar would like to speak with you," he announced, clearly expecting her to drop everything immediately. "He's in the car outside."

"Oh." Her first reaction was astonishment.

"Miss Miller," the thin man added, "Mr. Polgar doesn't like to be kept waiting."

"Is that right?" Teri muttered, frowning at him. She remembered now that she'd seen this guy at the chess match with Bobby and had assumed he was either a friend or employee. "Well, it so happens I'm busy, and I'm going to be busy all day. Kindly tell Mr. Polgar that if he wants to see me, he should make an appointment like everyone else."

"Teri," Joan cried in utter exasperation. "Don't be an idiot. He probably wants to thank you."

"As he should," Teri reminded her friends. The man owed her, and all she'd gotten for her trouble was an escorted exit from the competition. Not only had Bobby Polgar not paid her, he hadn't seen fit to thank her, either.

"Miss?" the man asked again.

Everyone in the salon seemed to be watching her, waiting for her to decide.

For a second she was tempted to walk out to the car and listen politely while the great Bobby Polgar deigned to grant her an audience. But frankly, she wasn't that hard up. Nor did she want to give this…chessman the idea that she was at his beck and call.

"Please thank Mr. Polgar for coming," Teri said smoothly, "but explain that I have a full schedule today and am unavailable until after six o'clock." With that, she turned to see her friends and customers staring at her.

"I don't think Mr. Polgar will be pleased," the man said.

Teri shook her head. In her opinion, too many people already catered to Bobby Polgar's likes and dislikes. It was about time someone stood up to him.

When she returned to Justine, it seemed the entire salon had gone silent. "What?" Teri demanded.

Activity resumed, and she heaved a sigh of relief.

A few minutes later, Denise was back. "That skinny guy asked me to give you this." She handed her a hundred-dollar bill.

Teri shrugged and stuffed it in her hip pocket. Apparently there was even more money in chess than she'd guessed. A hundred bucks for a haircut was about four times what she normally charged. She'd say one thing for Bobby Polgar—he was a decent tipper.

When Teri finished Justine's cut, Grace Harding arrived for a perm. Grace tried to book all her perms on weekends because she worked full-time at the library.

In fact, Grace's perm was the first of three Teri had scheduled for the day.

By six that evening, her feet hurt and she hadn't

managed to have lunch. She was hungry, tired and feeling irritable about a certain spoiled chess player who was far too accustomed to getting his own way. Still, Teri was gratified that Bobby Polgar had made the effort to find out who she was and where she worked.

Actually, that was a noteworthy feat. She hadn't given anyone her name, although now that she recalled, some of those pushy security people had checked her identification.

Teri was the last person to leave the salon that night. She set a final load of towels in the dryer, turned off the lights and headed out the door, locking it carefully before leaving the mall. Her feet hurt, and she was looking forward to a soak in her tub, a microwave pizza and a good book.

The stretch limo in the rear of the mall lot caught her attention right away. As soon as Teri appeared, the car started moving in her direction.

Teri froze.

Sure enough, the car slowed to a crawl and stopped directly beside her. The door opened. Apparently she was supposed to get in, no questions asked.

She bent over and looked inside.

Just as she'd suspected, there sat Bobby Polgar. This car could easily seat ten thin people or maybe eight women her size. Yet the only person inside was the chess player.

"Why wouldn't you see me?" he asked.

"I told your driver I was booked for the day. I was."

"Do you have time now?" He gestured toward the seat next to him. She studied him critically—he was of average height and build and wore glasses with dark frames. Quite nerdy looking, really. He didn't appear to give much thought to fashion…or anything other than chess.

"Why?" she asked, genuinely curious.

Her question seemed to surprise him. "So we can talk."

"What do we have to talk about?" she demanded.

"Are you always this much trouble?"

"No," she told him truthfully. "But I had a very busy day and I'm tired."

He frowned as though he found her statement puzzling. "You weren't busy last Saturday?"

"I had a lighter schedule. I rescheduled two afternoon appointments in order to get to Seattle." She didn't mention the money she'd borrowed.

"Your diagnosis was correct," he reminded her. He leaned forward and offered her his hand. "I won the match."

Capitulating, Teri reluctantly climbed inside the limo, which was the biggest one she'd ever seen. She ran her hand over the plush upholstery and gazed up. The ceiling had lights that changed color every few seconds, subtle pastel colors that gave the interior a soft, flattering glow.

"Would you like something to drink?" Bobby asked.

"What've you got?"

"What do you want?" was his reply.

"A beer sounds good."

"A beer," he repeated as if he'd never heard the word before.

"Preferably a cold one."

Bobby pushed a button and spoke into an intercom. "A cold beer for the lady, James."

Teri nearly burst out laughing. "Your driver's name is James?"

"That amuses you?" He wore the same puzzled look he had earlier.

She did a poor job of hiding her amusement. "It's just so…clichéd."

"Is it?" he asked, his expression still bewildered.

The car took off.

"Hey, just a minute," Teri said, glancing around, suddenly unsure. "Where are we going?"

Bobby stared at her. "To get you a cold beer. Don't worry. James can be trusted."

"I trust James. You're the one who's got me worried."

Bobby Polgar nearly smiled. "I like you. You're a little on the fat side but—"

"And you're on the rude side," she interrupted. "Now take me back to my car."

"In a minute." He seemed to be in no hurry.

She crossed her arms. Never had she dreamed she'd be riding in a vehicle like this. "I thought you would've left the area by now."

"Aren't you pleased to see me?"

She shrugged. "Not particularly."

He frowned.

Teri supposed that Mr. Bobby Big Shot wasn't used to someone unwilling to pander to his gigantic ego. "You know, you didn't pay me last Saturday. That's fine, although payment at the time *is* customary. I didn't intend on charging you—but it would've been nice if you'd offered."

"You got the money?"

"Yes, thank you. That was a pretty hefty tip."

"You deserved it."

"You didn't bother to thank me, either."

"No," he agreed, "I didn't. I don't think much about anything other than chess."

As if she hadn't figured *that* out.

The car stopped. About three minutes later the door opened and James, the man who'd come into the salon earlier, handed Teri a cold beer.

"Thank you, James," she murmured, stifling a laugh.

The driver began to close the door.

"James," Bobby said simply, "I'd like one, too."

James did a double take, obviously wondering if he'd heard correctly. "*You*, sir?"

"Yes, me."

"Right away, sir."

The door closed. "You like yes-men, don't you?"

Bobby studied her a moment and once more,

came close to smiling. "When you're as rich and celebrated as I am, most everyone is a yes-man."

She flipped back the pull tab and took a long, thirsty swallow. "Not me."

"So I noticed."

The door opened again, and James gave his boss a second can of beer. Bobby took it and examined the top. He reached for the tab, but apparently couldn't get his finger under it.

"Oh, for the love of heaven," Teri muttered. She grabbed it, balancing her own can between her knees. "You're helpless."

Bobby met her gaze and then he did smile. "You're the first person to really see that, Miss Teri Miller. I *am* rather helpless."

Twelve

"Cal's here," Linnette said loudly, peering out the living room window on Easter afternoon. She'd been helping her mother in the kitchen, preparing dinner, and had begun to set the table. Dropping the curtain, Linnette hurried to the front door, but then felt she needed to give her family a reminder. "Mom, Dad, please don't embarrass him," she cautioned.

Her father glanced up from the Seattle newspaper, which he read from front to back every Sunday. "About what?"

"He's been seeing a speech therapist in Silverdale and he's kind of self-conscious. Sometimes he hesitates between words, but don't pay any attention to that, okay?"

"No problem." Her father went back to reading the paper.

"Don't worry, sweetheart," her mother said from the kitchen doorway.

The doorbell chimed and Linnette opened it to Cal, who couldn't have looked handsomer had he tried. He wore a tan leather jacket, polished boots and pressed jeans. His beautiful blue eyes searched hers out, and Linnette reassured him with a grin. Reaching for his hand, she pulled him into the house.

"Hello, Cal," her father said, briefly lowering the paper.

"Welcome, Cal," her mother called from the kitchen.

"It smells good in here," Cal said without stumbling over a single word.

Linnette's heart swelled with pride at his fluent delivery. "That's the ham. Mom coats it with brown sugar and maple syrup and tops it with cloves. I've never tasted any ham better than hers. It's just wonderful, so be sure and compliment her."

"Okay."

"I'll package up some of the leftovers for you. There's always plenty."

"Hey, don't be giving away my ham," her father chastised in a humorous tone.

Cal looked around the room and Linnette knew what he was thinking. She answered the question he'd wordlessly asked. "Mack's on his way," she said. "He phoned. Apparently the bridge traffic is a nightmare."

"Gloria?"

"Will be here by four."

"She's working. Low man on the totem pole," Roy explained. "In this case, low woman."

Her newfound sister was a Bremerton police officer. Before moving to Cedar Cove, Roy had worked for the Seattle Police department. Linnette found it interesting—and very fitting—that Gloria had chosen the same profession.

She'd initially made contact with her birth parents by sending anonymous postcards, flower arrangements and other benign but puzzling messages. Eventually, Roy unearthed the mystery and Gloria was welcomed into the family. However, they were still finding their way with one another, treading carefully, creating a new dynamic. This afternoon would be a test.

"Gloria said we should start without her," Linnette murmured, "but I told her we wouldn't."

"She'll call if she gets held up," Roy said confidently. He'd spent quite a bit of time with Gloria, and at first Linnette had been afraid that sharing her father would be difficult, since she and her dad had a close relationship. But it didn't bother her at all— mainly, Linnette believed, because she had Cal. Since their working hours often conflicted, they weren't able to see each other as often as they would've liked. If it was up to Linnette, that would be every day. But she had to be content with phone calls and seeing each other twice a week, if that.

Lately Cal had been in town more often because of his visits to the speech therapist. He usually stopped in to see her on the way to his appointment or afterward. The progress he'd made in such a short time was truly impressive.

"I was putting the finishing touches on the table," Linnette said. "You want to help me?"

"Linnette." Her father's voice betrayed some impatience. "Cal's our guest. I don't think it's good form to ask him to set the table."

"Yes, Daddy," she muttered, smiling at Cal.

Cal grinned back and sat down on the sofa. Her father handed him a section of newspaper, which Cal accepted.

Linnette returned to the kitchen. "The least Dad could do is talk to him," she told her mother.

Corrie shook her head. "You know your father."

"This is the man I'll probably marry." She truly hoped that was the case. Cal hadn't brought up the subject of marriage yet, but as far as Linnette could tell, they were definitely headed in that direction.

The doorbell rang again, and before anyone could answer, Mack walked into the house bearing a tall lily with three huge blooms. Her brother had trimmed his hair and actually looked decent. Well… halfway decent. This was an effort to appease their father, Linnette guessed. He wore jeans, sandals and a flowered shirt that made her shudder slightly. He needed a woman to help him dress better, but she wasn't volunteering. Lucky followed him in and settled by the fireplace.

"Happy Easter, everyone," he said. "When's the Easter egg hunt?"

"You're too old for chocolate bunnies," Corrie laughed, coming out of the kitchen. She kissed her son on the cheek and made a fuss over the lily, then placed it in the center of the dining room table.

Cal stood, and the two men shook hands. Linnette was immediately concerned. She hadn't mentioned to her brother that Cal was working with a speech therapist and feared Mack might say something that would unintentionally embarrass him.

"What's for dinner?" Mack rubbed his palms together, as if he was ready to start eating that minute. "I'm starved."

"Good. We'll begin as soon as Gloria gets here."

"You mean you didn't make those little cheese rolls?" Mack asked, clearly disappointed.

"Yeah," Roy said, setting aside the newspaper. "What about a few appetizers to tide us over?"

"They're coming," Corrie said. "Roy, could you see what everyone wants to drink?"

"Mom bakes these little cheese-filled biscuits Mack loves," Linnette explained for Cal's sake. "You'll want to taste them, but don't overdo it or you'll ruin your dinner."

"I won't," he promised.

"No matter what holiday it is, Mack wants

Mom to bake cheese biscuits. Easter, Thanksgiving. Christmas…"

"Groundhog Day," her brother added, as their father got to his feet to offer drinks.

"They sound good," Cal agreed.

"I'll have a beer, Dad."

"Me, too, Mr. McAfee," Cal put in.

Mack suddenly turned to him. "Hey, Cal—"

Linnette kicked his ankle.

"Ouch. What was that for?" Mack demanded.

Linnette blushed. "Oh, sorry, did I kick you?"

"Yes, and it hurt." Her brother rubbed his ankle.

"Come help me in the kitchen, would you?" she said pointedly and half dragged her brother out of the living room. As soon as they were out of earshot, she whispered fiercely, "Don't embarrass Cal! He's seeing a speech therapist about his stutter. Having everyone comment only calls attention to it."

"The only person embarrassing Cal," her brother said in a whisper, "is you. Give the guy a break."

"What are you talking about?"

"You're suffocating him," Mack insisted. "And if you keep doing that, you're going to lose him."

Linnette started to tell her brother he was being ridiculous but then the doorbell rang a third time. Gloria had arrived. She still wore her police uniform. "I didn't take time to change," she said, "I hope that's all right."

"Where's Chad?" Linnette asked. She knew that

Chad Timmons, the physician she worked with at the clinic, was interested in Gloria.

"I didn't ask him to join us," Gloria said as she removed her jacket; Roy took it to hang in the hallway closet.

Linnette was disappointed for Chad, who'd been hoping for an invitation.

"Can we eat now?" Mack asked impatiently.

"Did I hold up dinner?" Gloria wanted to know.

"Not at all," Corrie assured her. "I thought you wanted appetizers," she reminded her son.

"Oh, yeah."

"Well, they're on the way."

They all sat in the living room, waiting for Corrie. Linnette was at Cal's side and took his hand, entwining their fingers. Her mother had returned to the kitchen and now carried a plate of Mack's favorite cheese biscuits, along with a veggie tray and dips. Roy passed out drinks—beers for all the men and glasses of white wine for the women.

"You'll love this dip Mom makes, too," Linnette said, dipping a carrot stick in a rich creamy mixture and handing it to Cal.

"I was in Cedar Cove earlier this week," Mack said as he filled a small plate. The cheese biscuits were still hot, and he burned his finger. "Ouch, dammit."

"You didn't come by," Corrie murmured.

"By the time I finished, all I wanted to do was get home and take a hot shower."

"Finished what?" Linnette asked her brother.

Mack straightened and looked around the room. "I applied with the Cedar Cove fire department," he announced.

"What does the application process involve?" Gloria leaned forward, serving herself a small plate of appetizers.

Mack took a gulp of beer. "I had to complete a physical test, and I'm not talking about some doc listening to my heart, either. This was running up flights of stairs and stuff like that."

"How'd you do?" their father asked.

From the gleam in his eyes, Linnette knew her brother had passed. "All right, I guess. I'm taking the written exam next."

"I guess you like this sort of work, since you're a volunteer firefighter," Roy said. "At least you know exactly what you're in for." The two hadn't always gotten along, but Linnette could see they were both making an effort. Roy didn't add that he'd much prefer having his son a firefighter than working for the post office, although that wasn't exactly a secret.

"I do," Mack responded. "I hope they hire me— and the truth is, I wouldn't mind being closer to everyone on this side of the water. If I do get the job, it means I'll be attending firefighting school for ten weeks. There's one near North Bend."

"We'd love having you live closer," Corrie told her

son, her face glowing with happiness. "And ten weeks will pass quickly."

"I might be leaving for a while, too," Cal said.

"Leaving?" Linnette cried. Why hadn't she heard of this before? That he'd chosen to bring it up at a family function distressed her. "Where are you going and why? You won't be gone long, I hope."

"M-mustangs," he said, faltering over a word for the first time that day.

"What about mustangs?" she said, pressing him. When they were alone, she'd ask him more, but already she didn't like the sound of this.

"Wild mustangs—f-feral horses—are being rounded up by the Bureau of Land Management. Then they're sold. Cliff and I—"

"Cliff is sending you away? When?"

Cal ignored her questions. "These wild horses, some of them, are being slaughtered. The BLM m-m-makes them available for adoption, and several rescue organizations—"

"Cliff wants to add mustangs to his herd?" Linnette asked, too upset to allow Cal to finish. "He can send anyone. He doesn't need to send *you*."

"Linnette," Gloria said gently, "let Cal talk."

"I'm going to v-volunteer with the BLM and help round up mustangs and get them to the adoption centers." He seemed to speak without stopping for breath. "I want to see that they're p-protected. A lot of them are sold at auction and, like I said, some end up being slaughtered. I hope to work with one of the rescue groups to prevent that."

"How long will you be away?" she asked.

Cal shrugged. "A month, maybe more."

"A *month?*" That was completely unreasonable. Wouldn't this be a hardship for Cliff? Furthermore, it would be difficult on them as a couple. Surely a man didn't walk away from a relationship this strong without discussing the prospect with the woman in his life. She didn't understand why Cal hadn't mentioned his interest in volunteering before now. Nor did she appreciate the fact that he'd revealed it in front of her family and not told her first.

Perhaps Linnette was overreacting, but Cal was doing so well with his therapy and their relationship was everything to her. She couldn't bear it if he left—even for a short time.

"I think that's a wonderful thing for you to do," Corrie said. *Thanks, Mom,* Linnette thought irritably.

"I do, too," Mack concurred. "I've read about what's happening to those wild horses and it's a crying shame."

It was a crying shame, all right, Linnette mused. But the only one *she* felt sorry for was herself. She didn't want Cal to leave Cedar Cove, but it almost seemed as if he couldn't get away fast enough.

Thirteen

The Monday after Easter, Maryellen woke in good spirits—despite another night on the sofa. She missed sleeping with her husband, missed the intimacy they'd shared. Once this baby was born, she vowed she'd never sleep on a sofa again as long as she lived.

Easter Sunday had been wonderful. When church services were over, Joseph and Ellen had taken Katie to a community Easter egg hunt. Katie had gleefully collected a basketful of colorful plastic eggs. She'd proudly showed her treasures to Maryellen and then later Jon. Her husband had conveniently disappeared when the Bowmans returned with Katie.

Katie had needed a week or so to become accustomed to Jon's parents, but by then her daughter realized she had these two people completely wrapped around her little finger. Joseph and Ellen lavished their granddaughter with attention and love. Katie was thriving, and Maryellen would be forever grateful for their presence.

The Bowmans' arrival had gone a long way toward bringing Maryellen peace during this complicated pregnancy. Her mother and Cliff helped as much as they could, and had decided to delay their wedding reception until after the baby's birth. Grace visited at least three times a week and brought Maryellen library books to keep her entertained.

Charlotte and several ladies from the Senior Center had been out, too. Charlotte had taught Maryellen how to knit and she'd caught on quickly. Under Charlotte's tutelage, she'd started a baby blanket. However, none of these distractions was enough to keep Maryellen's mind off the financial difficulties caused by her unemployment. Jon couldn't work and take care of both Katie and her. Now, at least, he was able to spend the days taking photographs and had sold a few to the *Chronicle* and other area papers, as well as providing prints to the galleries that carried his work. He'd even applied for a few jobs, which had come to nothing.

Joseph and Ellen's presence had made a difference that was as profound as that between night and day. Jon couldn't deny that their generosity had changed everything; still, he avoided all contact with his parents. He left in the morning and called every night before he got home. His call was the signal that his parents should leave.

Maryellen was distressed that he could be so cold-hearted toward his family. Distressed and scared, too. If he could so completely turn off his love for them, then he might be capable of doing the same to her and to their daughter.

She knew very well that the only reason Jon had allowed his family into his life was for her sake and Katie's.

He refused to acknowledge their help or show them any appreciation. Joseph and Ellen had remained respectful of his wishes. The minute he notified Maryellen that he was on his way home, they packed up and left. The fact that dinner was waiting for him on his return was never mentioned or credited to his parents. As much as possible, he ignored their very existence. Maryellen felt dreadful for his father and stepmother.

When she heard Jon tiptoe down the stairs in the early dawn, Maryellen smiled. Their time alone on Easter Sunday had been special and she refused to ruin today with any unpleasantness.

"You awake?" he whispered.

She nodded and held out her arms to him. Jon joined her on the sofa, lying beside her. He placed his hands on her growing abdomen. They giggled and cuddled close.

"After this baby's born, I'm never sleeping without

you again," he said, spreading warm kisses on her throat until he reached her lips for a series of deep, probing kisses. Groaning, he tore his mouth from hers and buried it in the hollow of her neck. After a moment, he whispered, "I miss you sleeping with me."

"I miss you, too." His body was so familiar to her and so beloved. She reveled in the feel of him pressed against her. Had their circumstances been different, they would've made love. It wouldn't be long before all of this was over, Maryellen reminded herself. She had to repeat that thought frequently throughout the day—and night.

"Katie's still asleep," Jon told her.

"She had a busy day yesterday. Oh, Jon, I can't tell you how good Ellen is with her."

Her husband went rigid, just as he always did whenever she mentioned his parents.

Maryellen rubbed his back. "Did you see the giant Easter basket they bought her? It's got a plush bunny and—"

"I don't want them spoiling her rotten."

"Sweetheart, that's what grandparents do." She paused. "They love her so much," she murmured.

Without a word, Jon slipped off the sofa and went into the adjacent kitchen to start a pot of coffee. She watched him grind beans, then add water.

"I knew this would happen," he said to her from

the doorway a moment later, his voice ringing with resentment.

"What?" she asked, sitting upright now. "You're afraid I'll refer to your parents in casual conversation? *That's* what you fear? Do you have any idea how ridiculous that sounds?"

"The minute they got here, you were championing their cause. It's not going to work, Maryellen. I told you that before and I'm telling you again now. Nothing's changed between them and me. Not one damn thing."

She flinched at the harshness of his words. "But Jon—"

"I will not talk about it anymore. I let them come because you wanted it, and for no other reason."

"They've been a tremendous help. How can you deny what your parents have done for us? Jon, they left their home. They're staying at one of those hotels off the highway, and all because they want to be near us during this time. The least we can do is show some appreciation."

"They didn't help *me*," he said with unrestrained anger. "Instead, they lied. They should count their blessings that I didn't get them charged with perjury. Then they would've gone to prison like I did."

Maryellen forced herself to remain calm. "Yes, they did lie, and because of it you went through hell. They paid the price for that, Jon, and they paid dearly."

"No, Maryellen," her husband said, "*I'm* the one who paid. *I* was the one behind bars. Do you know how I got through those years? Do you really want to know? By hating them. I swore I'd never have anything to do with either of them again."

It pained her to hear the bitterness in his voice. Jon was a passionate man, who felt everything deeply. Anyone who studied his photography could see that, could sense his emotion.

A picture as simple as an empty rowboat tied up at a dock was sharply evocative. One reviewer had said that the abandoned rowboat was an object that had its own integrity and yet also symbolized lost dreams. Maryellen loved that review, and she'd clipped it and kept it in a special file. She agreed with every word. Years ago, she'd fallen in love with his art, long before she even knew the man.

So, it was no surprise that Jon's emotions, both positive and negative, had such potency. His hatred for his parents was uncompromising. He loved with this same intensity. Maryellen could never doubt the depth of his feelings for her and their children. He'd sacrificed for her; he'd even been willing to give up this land, and the home he'd built with his own hands, for her and for Katie and the new baby.

The silence between them seemed to throb like a fresh wound. The only sound was that of the coffeemaker gurgling. Jon returned to the kitchen to pour himself a mug and heat water for herbal tea in the microwave.

"Thank you," she said when he brought her the tea.

He sat down across from her. "I don't want to argue, Maryellen."

"Me neither." She offered him a sad smile.

"I love you," he said. "I won't allow my parents to come between us. I can't. They took everything else away from me, and I won't let them steal you and Katie, too."

She sipped her tea and tried to see the situation from his point of view. "I was just thinking how unusual this is. It's the reverse of what normally happens, where the wife doesn't get along with her in-laws."

Nodding, Jon cupped the mug. "I like my in-laws just fine," he said. "It's my own family I don't care for." He checked his watch and stood, ending their conversation. "I need to get ready for an interview."

The comment caught her off guard. Jon hadn't said anything about applying for another job. He took photographs that sold in galleries, and she hoped to begin managing his career later this year, finding ways to give him more exposure and license his work. Maryellen had been reading about it on the Internet, using a laptop computer Cliff had lent her.

"An interview?" she echoed. "You didn't say anything about that."

"It's nothing great," he said as he headed up the stairs.

"But…you always tell me when you're going to a job interview." A couple of opportunities had come his way recently, neither of which had panned out. Jon had talked to her at length before and after each interview. One had been for a construction job with Warren Saget's company. However, Jon had discovered that Warren used shortcuts and inferior materials. He was currently building an apartment complex and rumor had it that there were already major problems on the site. Although he possessed excellent carpentry skills and would gladly have taken on a construction project, Jon and Maryellen had agreed that, for ethical reasons, he shouldn't work for Warren Saget. Seth Gunderson wanted him back at the new—as yet unbuilt—Lighthouse, but Jon couldn't wait that long. He'd applied for some restaurant jobs, too.

"I'm sure I mentioned this," Jon threw over his shoulder as he dashed up the stairs to their bedroom.

No, he hadn't; Maryellen would've remembered it. She had the unpleasant sensation that he was hiding something from her. Only, she couldn't imagine what it would be, or why. When he came down the stairs, dressed and freshly shaved, Maryellen was ready. She'd slowly made her way to the kitchen, where she sat at the table.

"Tell me about this interview," she said as he popped a slice of bread in the toaster. He placed a bowl with instant oatmeal in the microwave and sliced a banana for her breakfast.

He glanced up. "It's nothing special," he countered.

"Is it a cooking job?"

"No," he said curtly.

"Apparently it's something you don't want to tell me about. Something you'd rather not mention." She shook her head. "You've never kept secrets from me before," she said softly, unable to disguise the hurt. "Please don't start now."

He released a pent-up sigh. "All right, if you *must* know. The interview's with a portrait studio in Tacoma."

"But Jon, that's great!" It was probably a waste of his talent, but she wasn't going to say that.

"I'll be photographing schoolchildren and…"

Maryellen swallowed hard and struggled to hide her dismay. This was so far beneath Jon's abilities. It would stifle his creativity, kill his passion for photography. No wonder he'd been reluctant to tell her about this interview.

An involuntary sob escaped and she covered her face with both hands.

"Maryellen, don't." He came to kneel in front of her. "Honey, it's the only thing available. It'll pay the bills, even if it doesn't provide any benefits." He wrapped his arms around her.

"You'll hate it." He was willing to waste his considerable talent at this menial job, and all because of her.

Kissing the top of her head, he said, "I've had

worse jobs. This won't be for long, I promise you. I won't be home much, but—"

"You *want* it that way. You want out of the house because…because you can't stand the thought of your parents being here, and that's my fault, too. Sometimes I think this baby's going to destroy us."

"Don't," he warned gently. "Maryellen, you can't think like that. This baby is a gift."

"I can't let you do this. Jon, please. I just can't bear it."

"Sweetheart, don't." He took her face between his hands and kissed her again and again. "I love you. I'm doing this for us. As soon as the baby's born, everything will be different. I promise."

"Oh, Jon."

"It's all right," he said soothingly. "Everything's going to be all right."

Maryellen so badly wanted to believe him. She smiled absently as he brought her breakfast to the table, although she could barely eat.

Jon left shortly afterward, and Maryellen tried hard to conceal her feelings when Ellen and Joseph came in. Ellen immediately went upstairs to get Katie dressed, while Joseph washed the few soiled dishes and straightened the books that were scattered around the living room.

Midmorning, he took Katie outside for a walk in the sunshine, and Ellen brought Maryellen a cup of tea. "I thought I'd make a chicken pot pie for dinner this evening," she said. "It used to be one of Jon's favorites."

"I'm sure he'll appreciate it," Maryellen said, but she had to wonder if Jon would even notice.

Fourteen

Justine was grateful to hear from her mother and even happier to see her. Late Wednesday afternoon they met for tea at 16 Lighthouse Road, the house where she'd grown up and where Olivia still lived. In a sense, Justine would always think of it as home. Leif had a play date with a friend from his preschool, and it was good to be with Olivia, just the two of them.

"Jack's out doing an interview with Pastor Flemming about the church's work with hurricane relief," her mother explained as she carried the teapot and a plate of oatmeal cookies to the kitchen table.

This was Olivia's way of telling her that the timing of this visit was intentional—a chance for the two of them to be alone. Only a few years ago Justine couldn't have imagined sharing her troubles with her mother. They'd rarely talked or discussed anything of importance. Now it seemed only natural to do so.

"What do you want to talk about?" Justine asked. If her mother had purposely arranged this time to make sure they weren't interrupted, then there had to be a reason.

Olivia glanced up from pouring the tea into china cups. "I guess I wasn't very subtle, was I?"

"It's all right, Mom. I'm your daughter—you don't need to be subtle with me."

"Why don't you tell me how you're doing first?" Olivia set the teapot in the center of the table, then took her seat.

Justine reached for her cup and added a teaspoon of sugar, making lazy circles with her spoon. "I've decided to go back to work part-time for First National Bank." She said this casually, as if it were a small thing. It wasn't. "I'll be out of the house for part of every day." She was silent for a moment, wondering whether to talk about the underlying reason. "Getting away from Seth helps me deal with all the stress," she admitted. She had to either spend time away from her husband for a few hours every day, while Leif was in preschool, or slowly go insane. She was relieved that Seth had talked to Larry Boone about taking the job at the boatyard but as yet nothing had come of it. She didn't know if the hesitation was due to Seth or the other man. Seth was so volatile that Justine hadn't asked for fear of causing problems.

These last few weeks, living with Seth had felt like being trapped. His thoughts and all his efforts seemed to be focussed on finding the arsonist. Despite their brief attempt at resolving the tension between them, Seth was as driven as ever. The fire had consumed far more than the building that had housed their restaurant; it had consumed her husband, too. This angry, unreasonable person wasn't the man she'd married and Justine felt she no longer knew him.

"How does Seth feel about your taking this job?" her mother asked.

The sugar had dissolved but Justine continued her gentle stirring. "I…haven't told him yet, but I don't think he'll care one way or the other." She doubted he'd even realize she was gone.

"Oh, Justine." Her mother read the pain in her response. She leaned across the table and laid one hand over hers.

"The funny part is, I forgot to pick up my birth control prescription at the drugstore the other day and then I thought, why bother? Seth hasn't even come near me since the fire."

"He's upset."

Seth was more than upset, and making love couldn't compete with his need to be angry. Every bit of tenderness in him seemed to be gone. All that remained was his sense of unfairness and rage.

"To say he's upset doesn't even begin to cover it, Mom. Seth is impatient and edgy and determined to find out who started the fire. It's become an obsession. He wants me to be angry, too, and he can't understand why I'm not."

Olivia sipped her tea and sat back. "You're angry about this," she murmured. "Aren't you?"

"Yes, of course I am. But I want to let it go. I'm trying to. I'm choosing to look at this the way I would any other traumatic event. We need to move on."

"And Seth's not ready to do that?"

"No. And my lack of righteous anger complicates the issue," Justine went on, a bit wryly. She'd given up reasoning with Seth. Any sort of acceptance on her part, or desire to advance to something new, only angered him further.

"He spoke to Jack recently," her mother said thoughtfully.

This was news to Justine, but then she knew little of what Seth did these days.

"He approached Jack about putting a picture of that pewter cross in the paper. Apparently that was Roy's idea. He and Seth think someone might recognize it and give the sheriff a lead. At this point, the investigation's stalled."

"Is Jack going to do it?"

Her mother selected a cookie from the plate. "I believe he said he'd talk to the sheriff first and see if that would help or hinder the investigation."

Since Seth rather than the sheriff had spoken to Jack, Justine assumed that Troy Davis was reluctant to release this information. Most likely, Seth had gone behind the sheriff's back in an attempt to keep the investigation alive.

"You need to tell Seth you're going back to work," her mother advised.

"I will." But she wasn't in any hurry. They were barely speaking. For Leif's sake, they each made an effort to be civil in his presence. As far as Justine was concerned, though, they might as well be room-mates. Or strangers.

"Is that why you had lunch with Warren Saget?" her mother asked, staring directly at her.

Shocked, Justine widened her eyes. Warren had taken her to lunch last week, but he'd been careful to ensure they wouldn't be seen. They'd met at a small, out-of-the-way restaurant in Gig Harbor. It'd happened only once and Justine had felt guilty about it ever since. How her mother knew was beyond her, but it explained the invitation for tea in this private setting.

"You heard about that, did you?" she asked, hoping to make light of the incident.

"I did, and I probably wasn't the only one. I didn't know Warren was back in your life."

He wasn't, but saying so would only raise other questions she didn't want to answer. "Warren's a friend of mine," she said tersely.

"Is he, Justine?" her mother asked point-blank.

It seemed that an explanation would be necessary,

after all. "Soon after the fire, Seth and I had an argument. I had to get away so I went down to the waterfront. While I was there, Warren joined me. All of a sudden I had a panic attack. I've never had one before and Warren was extremely kind to me."

"Oh, Justine! How frightening."

She nodded. "I didn't know what was happening, but he calmed me down and talked me through it. Then last week he asked me to lunch and it seemed to mean so much to him, I couldn't say no." She sighed. "I shouldn't have gone. I regret it now."

"Have you thought what Seth would say if he knew?"

Justine had foolishly believed no one would ever find out. Including her husband. So much for that theory. If her mother had heard about the lunch, then there wasn't any reason to believe Seth wouldn't eventually hear about it, too.

"Who told you?" she asked.

"An attorney friend. It wasn't like Sharon came running to tell me, either. She hardly knows you and mentioned that she saw you in Gig Harbor with your father. I knew it couldn't have been Stan and surmised you must've been with Warren."

"It won't happen again, Mom."

"It's none of my business. This is your life, but I'd hate to see you do something stupid that'll hurt you and your marriage."

Her mother was right. She had to talk to her husband, let him know how damaging his actions had been. Confrontation had never been easy for her but they needed to reconnect with each other before it was too late.

Justine went home soon afterward. She wasn't supposed to pick up Leif until dinnertime, and she'd hoped to find Seth.

To her disappointment he wasn't home. Maybe she'd drive over to her grandmother's place. Just as she got ready to turn around and leave, the front door opened and Seth stepped inside. Penny, their small dog, trotted over to greet him.

She and Seth stood several feet apart and stared as though they'd never seen each other before. For the longest time all they did was look. Neither moved. Neither spoke.

A tightness gripped Justine's throat, and all at once tears filled her eyes and clogged her throat. She couldn't continue living the way they were, couldn't go on pretending everything was fine when it so clearly wasn't.

With all her heart she loved Seth, and she couldn't bear the thought of losing him. If she didn't do something, she *would* lose him. They'd lose each other.

Out of need and fear, she took one step toward her husband. He did the same. Before she knew it, Justine was in his arms and Seth was kissing and hugging her as though they'd been reunited after a lengthy absence. He tangled his fingers in her hair as he brought his mouth to hers. Tears spilled down her face and she was sobbing and kissing him back, all the while pulling his shirt free of his waistband. She needed her husband, wanted him.

Justine wasn't sure how they made it to the bedroom. Ravenous as they were for each other, they didn't even completely undress before they fell on the bed, gasping and panting.

By the time they'd made love, Seth was half on the bed, his feet on the floor, while Justine was pinned to the edge of the mattress. They broke into wide grins.

"Oh, Seth," she whispered, "I've missed you so much."

He straightened and they climbed onto the bed, lying on their sides, facing each other. He kissed her chin and traced her cheekbones with one hand.

"I've been the biggest fool who ever lived," Seth told her. "We lost the restaurant. That's tragic, but I still have what's most important in my life. You and Leif."

Tears clouded her eyes and she attempted a smile.

Seth continued to stroke her face. "I went down to see Larry Boone this afternoon."

Justine bit her lip.

"I took the job, Justine. I'm going to be selling boats."

A small cry of happiness escaped as she wrapped

her arms around Seth's neck and hugged him with all her might.

"I'm so glad," she said, sobbing openly. "Everything's going to be fine." That was when she told him about her lunch with Warren. From the way his mouth tightened and his eyes narrowed, she knew Seth wasn't pleased. But once the truth was out, Justine felt as if a backpack loaded with rocks had been removed from her shoulders.

"I won't see him again," she said. She gave him a long, involved kiss.

"You promise?" Seth asked.

"I promise."

Then she told him about the job at the bank, which she'd be starting the following Monday.

His eyes revealed his astonishment. "When did you arrange this?" he asked, still frowning.

"A week ago."

"You *want* to work?"

She did—for a dozen different reasons. She needed the escape into another world. She needed something to do; like him she'd been at loose ends. When they'd had the restaurant, she'd worked nearly every day and now there was a void. The money would come in handy, too. "Just a few hours a day. Do you mind?" If he did, she'd tell the bank she couldn't do it.

"No—it's totally up to you."

Although Justine hated to bring up the subject of

the restaurant, she felt it was necessary. "What about The Lighthouse?"

A pained look came over Seth, as if even talking about it distressed him. "I don't know. I just don't know." His gaze held hers as he used his index finger to outline the shape of her lips. His touch was gentle and his eyes filled with tenderness. "Whatever we decide, it doesn't need to be this very minute. We'll take things one day at a time."

"Okay." Justine sighed and rubbed her bare foot along the outside of his leg. "I was so afraid I was going to lose you."

"Never," he whispered. "I would never have let that happen."

And yet Justine feared it almost had.

Fifteen

Allison Cox checked the address and space number a second time, uncertain whether she had the right trailer house. Anson had never told her which one he and his mother lived in. When she'd asked the manager, the woman had pointed to the back of the park, saying, "Cherry's at the end. Space fifteen. When you see her, tell her the rent payment's past due, would ya?"

"Ah…"

The woman had frowned. "Forget it, kid. I'll deal with her myself."

With more than a little trepidation, Allison walked up the rickety steps of number fifteen. The thought of Anson living in this poor excuse for a home nearly broke her heart. After a brief hesitation, she knocked at the thin door.

"Who is it?" the woman inside shouted.

"Allison Cox." She spoke as loudly as she could without yelling.

The door slowly opened. Dressed in a housecoat, Anson's mother stood on the other side of the screen door, holding a cigarette. Her hair was lank and dirty, and it looked as if she hadn't been out for a while.

"Who are you and what do you want?" she demanded. One arm was tucked around her waist; ash fell to the floor when she flicked her cigarette with the other hand.

"I'm a friend of Anson's," Allison explained. "I…" She lowered her voice in case someone was listening. "He phoned me and I thought you might want to hear how he's doing."

Anson's mother laughed as though the statement amused her. "Sure," she said, unlocking the screen. "Come on in and tell me what you know about the little bastard."

Allison flinched at the word and resisted the urge to retaliate. If Anson was a bastard, then that woman was responsible for it. Biting her tongue, Allison stepped inside. The trailer was in shocking disarray. The kitchen sink was piled with dirty dishes and the countertops covered with junk. The living room obviously hadn't been picked up in months.

There was a stale, musty smell—smoke, spilled booze, judging by the rye bottle lying on its side, and just…dirt. The smell of squalor. "Excuse the place," Cherry said with a dismissive gesture. "It's the maid's day off."

Allison smiled weakly at the woman's attempted joke.

Cherry shoved a stack of trashy grocery store magazines from one of the chairs, indicating Allison should sit there. "Where's he at?" she demanded before even Allison had a chance to sit down.

"He, uh, didn't say."

"Did you tell him the sheriff's looking for him?"

"Well, no… He already seemed to know that."

"He's goin' to prison this time."

"Mrs. Butler, Anson didn't set that fire."

The woman snickered. "First off, I ain't never been a Mrs. anybody, and second you and I both know Anson did it. You don't need to pretend for my sake, sweetie. My son likes fires. He nearly burned the house down when he was six years old playin' with matches. When he was ten, he and a group of his little friends started a brush fire that got me in a whole lot of trouble. Next thing I knew, Child Protective Services are all over my ass like I was the one who lit that match." She paused and inhaled deeply on the cigarette, then smashed it out in a glass ashtray overflowing with ashes and crumpled butts. "Last year he gets himself in *real* trouble by burning down that toolshed in the park. Far as I'm concerned, he's just building bigger fires. It started when he was a kid and it hasn't stopped." When she finished, she walked over to the refrigerator and opened it. "Want a beer?"

Allison slowly exhaled. "No, thanks."

Anson's mother grabbed a bottle, twisted off the cap and took a swig. "Problem is," she said without looking at Allison, "I never was mother material."

Allison didn't say anything, although she definitely agreed.

"You say he called you?"

"Yes."

"What did he want?"

Allison hated the implication. "He didn't *want* anything. He said he needed to hear the sound of my voice. He told me he didn't start the fire."

"And you believe him?"

"I do."

"You tell the sheriff he phoned you?"

"No." Technically she hadn't. It was her mother who'd contacted Sheriff Davis.

"Good," she said and nodded approvingly. "If he calls you again, don't, okay?"

Allison couldn't promise one way or the other, so she didn't say anything.

"He wrote me," Cherry said, shaking another cigarette out of the pack.

Allison sat up. "You have an address?" she asked excitedly.

"I wish. Little bastard owes me money."

"Can I see the letter?" Allison pleaded.

His mother shrugged. "It's around here somewhere." She walked over to the toaster and sorted through a tall stack of flyers and bills until she found what she was looking for. She held the envelope out to Allison.

Allison stood, but before she could take it, Cherry yanked it out of her reach. "You ain't gonna mention this to the cops, are you?"

"No," Allison promised, her heart in her throat.

Cherry gave her the letter.

Sitting down, Allison removed the single sheet from the envelope and read.

Dear Mom,

I asked a friend to mail this for me. Don't try to trace me because I'm not anywhere close to where this letter is postmarked.

Allison stopped reading and examined the envelope, which had a Louisiana postmark. She hated that he was so far away and hoped what he said was true.

I know you're probably mad because I took the money out of the freezer. There was almost five hundred dollars there. I counted it and as soon as I can, I'll pay you back every penny. I know you were saving that money to fix the transmission on the car. I wouldn't have taken it if I'd had any other choice.

If you're done being mad, then there's something else I want to tell you. I didn't start that fire.

This was underlined several times.

I've done a lot of stupid stuff in my life but I didn't do this. Believe me or not…that's up to you.

I don't know if I'll be able to write you again so consider this an IOU for the money—$497.36.

Take care of yourself, and if you're smart you'll get rid of that guy you think looks like Tobey Maguire. He's a piss-poor imitation.

Anson

Allison replaced the letter in the envelope. "Anson borrowed almost five hundred dollars from you?" she asked softly. *That* explained why he didn't need any money. Yet it'd been weeks since she'd seen him. That money couldn't have lasted long.

"He didn't borrow anything. He *stole* it," Cherry said, puffing on a new cigarette. "I'm never gonna see that cash again. It's gone and so is Donald." She took a crumpled tissue from her housecoat pocket and blew her nose. "And he did too look like Tobey Maguire."

She seemed more upset about Donald than her own son, Allison mused.

"Anson was nothing but trouble to me from the day he was born," Cherry said, suddenly angry. "It would've been a whole lot better if he'd been a girl. I knew the minute that nurse told me I'd had a boy this wasn't gonna work. But as soon as I saw him, I knew I was gonna keep him." She shrugged her shoulders and took another puff. "The kid would have done a hell of a lot better if I'd given him to that lady from the state. She said she had a home ready and waitin'. But I wouldn't listen to her. Oh, no. I figured this kid came from me and that he'd love me."

"Anson does love you."

"Yeah, right," she muttered. "That's why he did what every man I ever loved did. He left and took something of mine with him. In his case, it was that five hundred bucks. He might as well have taken my car for all the good it's doing me with a busted transmission." She ground out the half-smoked cigarette. "Not that five hundred bucks would've paid for a new one."

"Despite what he did, Anson's a wonderful person," Allison felt obliged to tell her. "And he's smart, too. He's really good in languages and science. He could've gotten top grades."

His mother blinked as if this came as a surprise, and then shook her head. "The problem is, he's a man. I never could hold on to one. His own daddy dumped me soon as I got pregnant and then disappeared. I found out later he was married, anyway."

"I'm sorry."

"Yeah, well he wasn't my first mistake or my last." She gulped down another swallow of beer. "You go ahead and believe in Anson if you want," she said, giving Allison a shaky smile. "He needs someone who will. I don't believe in myself anymore, so I don't have it in me to believe in him."

"I love Anson," Allison admitted.

Cherry looked away for a moment, and Allison thought she saw the sheen of tears in her eyes. When Cherry looked back, she pointed the bottle at her.

"Time for you to go."

Allison nodded. "All right." On impulse, she opened her purse and took out a small pad. Tearing off a piece of paper, she wrote down her phone number. "If you hear from Anson again, would you call me?"

Cherry didn't answer.

"I'll let you know if he phones me."

When Cherry turned her back, Allison laid the sheet on the table and quietly left the trailer.

Sixteen

When Charlotte left the Garden Club meeting, she stopped by her friend Helen's on Poppy Lane. Ben was playing bridge with some other men, and then later Charlotte would meet him for soup at the Pot Belly Deli, one of her favorite lunch spots. Their homemade soups were not to be missed. However, she'd promised Helen Shelton a quick visit before lunch. Her friend was working on a Fair Isle sweater for her only granddaughter and wanted Charlotte to take a look. At one time or another, Charlotte had tackled just about every type of project in the knitting world, and Fair Isle was no exception. Helen found this sweater a challenge; Charlotte admired the way she'd refused to give up, although she'd had to restart more than once before she figured out the correct tension.

Charlotte and Helen were both widows. They'd begun as casual acquaintances, but their friendship had grown through their involvement in the Senior Center. Now Charlotte considered Helen one of her dearest friends. She knew Helen had been in France during World War II, but only recently had she learned that Helen had been part of the French Resistance. This information came to her by accident, when Charlotte happened to see a faded poster while visiting her friend. She'd asked about it and then, reluctantly, as though every word had to be forced out, Helen explained that as a young college student, she'd been trapped in France after the German invasion.

Determined to support the Allies, she'd joined the French Resistance, helping downed American and English pilots find their way back to England. Although Charlotte had tried to ask further questions, Helen sidestepped them. Instinctively Charlotte had realized that her friend didn't want this information shared. The only person she'd ever told was Ben. The friendship between Helen and Charlotte had deepened from that day forward.

Helen met her at the door of her duplex and immediately ushered her inside and out of the drizzle. No one used umbrellas in the Pacific Northwest—or residents didn't, anyway. An umbrella was a sure sign of a tourist.

Now, as she sat in Helen's living room with a cup of tea, Charlotte examined the body of the sweater, which was knit in the round. This was the method Charlotte had recommended and it seemed to be working well.

"It's all in the tension," Charlotte said, looking closely at Helen's knitting. She nodded. "Nice job." Holding a strand of yarn in each hand was a learned skill, but one grew accustomed to it quickly enough. "Ruth's going to be thrilled when she sees this."

"I certainly hope so," Helen said, shaking her head. "I can't tell you the number of rows I've had to take out."

"You're doing just fine."

Helen set her tea aside. "Ruth's engaged—did I tell you?—and I'm thinking of knitting something for her wedding."

Since Helen was already knitting her granddaughter this difficult sweater, Charlotte was loath to suggest a wedding coat, which was meant to be worn over the wedding dress following the ceremony. She'd come upon a 1970s pattern for one and was quite taken with it. Perhaps she'd find an excuse to knit it up herself.

"Let me look through my patterns to see what I can dig up," Charlotte said.

Helen thanked her with a smile. "I'd appreciate that. Any suggestions are welcome."

Charlotte finished her tea and bade her friend an affectionate farewell, promising another visit soon. She put on her raincoat, collected her large purse and stepped into the May drizzle. With gas prices what they were, Charlotte had decided to walk. Fortunately the Garden Club meeting room, Helen's duplex and the deli were located only a few blocks apart.

By the time she arrived at the Pot Belly Deli, Ben had secured a table and was reading the menu. As soon as her husband saw her enter, he stood, giving her a discreet kiss on the cheek and helped her remove her coat. The fact that Ben exhibited such impeccable manners had endeared him to her from the very start. Such courtesies didn't play much of a role in social relationships anymore, so when they existed, she felt they were often indicative of real respect. In Ben's case that was definitely true. Those protective, caring gestures—opening a door, helping her into a car, walking on the curb side of the street—touched her. She and Ben believed in treating each other with politeness and consideration. Her first marriage, to Clyde, had been marked by those same small displays of love.

"How did the meeting go?" Ben asked after seating her and reclaiming his own chair.

Charlotte was afraid he'd ask. "I was elected president again," she said with a slight grimace. "Everyone's so busy these days, and no one else wanted the position." The Garden Club didn't require a lot of her time, but it was a monthly commitment that took her away from him.

His lack of response unsettled her. "Are you upset with me, dear?"

Ben lowered the menu and his eyes widened at her question. "Why would I be upset? If I were a Garden Club member, I'd want you as president, too. You're the perfect choice. You're organized, practical, responsible—and the most incredible woman I've ever met."

The things this man said. Things that made her heart expand with joy. "Oh, Ben, I do love you."

Smiling, he set the menu aside. "I know, and I consider myself the most fortunate of men because you do."

They both ordered the chicken-and-wild-rice soup, with large chunks of warm-from-the-oven sourdough bread. The restaurant owner had once told Charlotte that the sourdough starter had come from Alaska and was more than a hundred years old. Whether or not the story was true, the bread did have a flavor that couldn't be matched.

"I stopped by the house before I came down to the deli," Ben told her as they got ready to leave. "Justine phoned and asked if we could see her at the bank before one."

Charlotte had heard only a few days ago that her granddaughter had gone back to work for First National part-time. Justine had served as manager until shortly after her wedding to Seth. She sincerely hoped the young couple wasn't having financial problems, although she didn't think so. Olivia had told her that Justine and Seth were getting interim insurance payments. She had the feeling that her granddaughter had returned to the bank more to structure her time than for financial reasons. Justine had never been a girl who liked being idle.

After their bill was paid, Ben helped Charlotte on with her coat and together they left the deli. Although she'd enjoyed their lunch, Charlotte missed The Lighthouse. It had become a popular place in the community and she was so proud of everything Justine and Seth had done. Any meal there was a notable dining experience. She couldn't begin to understand why anyone would burn it down. She had to believe it'd been a random act of violence. Surely no one would wish her granddaughter and Seth any harm.

Perhaps because this was a Monday, the bank didn't seem too busy. Justine sat behind a desk set against the far wall and stood when she saw them.

"Hello, Grandma," she said, smiling. "Ben." She came forward to meet them and kissed Charlotte's cheek, then led them toward her desk. "Sit down, please."

Charlotte couldn't remember her granddaughter calling her into the bank even once. There must be some problem with Justine's finances, after all. Her gaze seemed to avoid Charlotte's, as if she was embarrassed about something.

"What's wrong, dear?" Charlotte asked, holding her purse on her lap and leaning forward in the chair.

"Ben," Justine said, looking directly at him. "You deposited a check for a thousand dollars a while back."

"That was from David, his son," Charlotte explained before Ben had a chance. Although he hadn't said anything, she knew Ben had been pleased with David's gesture in repaying him part of the money he owed. Father and son were estranged, and Charlotte had done her best to bring them together. Ben didn't discourage her efforts, yet she had the distinct feeling that he thought it was a waste of time. Certainly David was a problem child.

"The check was returned—insufficient funds," Justine said, keeping her voice low. "I'm so sorry. As soon as I saw the name, I took the check and handled it myself."

Ben remained stoic. "The truth is, I'm not surprised. Could I have it, please?"

Justine handed it to him and without so much as glancing at it, Ben tore it in two.

"Ben!" Charlotte was shocked at her husband's action. "I'm sure there's a logical explanation for why this happened."

"It's worthless," her husband said without emotion. "I should've known that from the first. David's had constant financial problems from the time he was a youth. He's never been able to repay me a dime he's borrowed. That's why I refuse to lend him money anymore."

"Oh, dear," Charlotte murmured, genuinely saddened by this turn of events.

"His lack of financial sense is the reason he went

to Charlotte for a loan, which infuriated me more than just about anything David's ever done in his life," Ben continued.

"You can't let money stand in the way of love," Charlotte admonished. She made sure her tone was without censure.

"Don't misunderstand me," Ben said, his words weighted with sadness. "I love my sons, both of them. David, however, has never grown up or learned to accept responsibility. It's always someone else's fault, always a temporary condition. Everything will be better later, and instead of facing the truth, he looks for an easy out or a quick fix. His immaturity has cost him deeply, and his excuses have only led him further into debt."

Charlotte placed her hand on her husband's. "You aren't to blame."

"I made a call to David Rhodes," Justine said, interrupting their conversation.

Charlotte turned her attention back to her granddaughter.

Justine seemed decidedly uncomfortable. "David asked if I'd hold the check until the first of the month, which I did."

"And when you resubmitted it, the same thing happened. It was returned because of insufficient funds," Ben finished for her.

Justine confirmed his suspicions with a nod. "I couldn't hold on to it any longer."

"Of course not," Ben assured her with such a facade of calm that even Charlotte was nearly fooled. She, however, knew her husband far too well—and knew that Ben was both embarrassed and unsettled. "Please, if anything like this ever comes up in the future, do not do my son any favors."

"I'm sorry, Ben," Justine said sympathetically.

"No, *I'm* sorry." Ben got to his feet.

"Thank you, Justine, for letting us know," Charlotte said. With a polite nod, Ben took her arm.

"We should phone David," Charlotte suggested as they left the bank. She still felt there must be some kind of explanation. She *had* to believe that or she'd give up on Ben's son the same way he had, which was exactly what she wanted to avoid. To Charlotte, it was important to build good relationships with Ben's children.

When they got home, Ben excused himself and went into the bedroom. The urge to follow him left Charlotte's stomach in knots. She knew how bad he felt and wished she could alleviate his disappointment. At the same time, she recognized that he needed to be alone.

As she walked into the kitchen, the answering machine light was flickering. She pushed the message button and heard David Rhodes, speaking clearly and distinctly. "Dad, give me a call once you're home."

As soon as the message had finished, Ben entered the kitchen.

"Did you hear?" she asked.

Ben nodded.

"Will you phone him?"

Her husband shook his head adamantly. "There's no point. I already know what he wants."

So did Charlotte. Surely David had phoned to apologize. He wouldn't be foolish enough to ask for another loan. This situation must be just as embarrassing for his son as it had been for Ben.

The phone rang and Ben glared at it accusingly.

"Shall I answer it?" Charlotte asked.

"No," Ben snapped. "It's David." Then, as if realizing how harshly he'd spoken, he gathered Charlotte into his arms. "My son can't say anything that I haven't heard a hundred times before. He's sorry—and I believe he is—but it never makes any difference."

"Oh, Ben." Charlotte understood; she really did. It was almost as if Ben was talking about *her* son, Will. David had been careless with money, Will with people's affections. *Women's* affections. Charlotte knew the kind of man he was and yet she chose to look the other way and ignore his faults. A mother did that. She wasn't sure what else to do, even now that his marriage had failed. She didn't feel it was her place to interfere between a man and his wife. Yet Charlotte knew that not only had her son been unfaithful, he'd taken advantage of Grace, a woman almost as close to her as her own daughter. Yes, she acknowledged that Grace had played a role in this, too, but she blamed her son far more than she did Grace.

No one had told her what had gone on between them; no one needed to. She'd figured out that it was Will with whom Grace had been involved over the Internet. Her married son had led that lovely woman down a path of promises he had no intention of keeping, and to her detriment, Grace had followed him. Now Will's own marriage was in shambles and he was blaming Georgia, the woman who'd stood by him all these years. No, Charlotte understood far better than Ben realized what a disappointment one's children could sometimes be.

Seventeen

Since Easter, almost two weeks ago, Linnette had barely spoken to Cal. He'd joined her and her family, sat with them, talked with them and then as casually as could be announced that he was leaving for Wyoming on some wild goose—correction, wild horse—chase.

He didn't seem to have noticed how upset she was. In fact, at the time, Linnette had been too unnerved to do more than make a token protest. Since Easter, though, she'd given a great deal of thought to the situation. It'd taken her this long to work up the courage to confront Cal and let him know her feelings. If he was serious about their relationship, the same way she was, then the least he could do was discuss this with her.

She'd been working long hours at the clinic to

cover for colleagues on vacation. She'd left two messages on his answering machine, and he hadn't answered either one. Of course, he was busy, but so was she. Yes, she knew that several of the mares were pregnant and that he was training a couple of yearlings. But what about *her* work commitments? Anyway, even if she wasn't very familiar with horse ranching she remembered that Cliff raised quarter horses, not mustangs. She didn't understand his and Cal's sudden interest in an entirely different breed of horse. Her only option was to talk to Cal, face to face. She'd explain her position and beg him to give up this crazy notion.

On the long drive out to Olalla, she smiled as she recalled how her sister, Gloria, had teased her, calling it Oo-la-la once she'd seen Cal. Linnette had talked to her about this situation, and Gloria had agreed with her decision, cautioning her to stay calm, stay focused. That had offended Linnette just a little, since she saw herself as calm and clearheaded. But she was grateful for Gloria's go-ahead.

Linnette hadn't given Cal any advance warning. The idea of driving to Wyoming by himself, especially now that he was doing so well with his speech therapy, troubled her. She didn't want to give him an opportunity to come up with rationalizations and trumped-up reasons, either.

The least Cal could've done was present his plan to her, so they could talk it over before he made a decision. He hadn't considered her feelings at all, and that hurt. She'd finally realized why this whole idea of his bothered her as much as it did. Ultimately it came down to the fact that she'd played no part in it.

When she arrived at the ranch, she didn't immediately see Cal. Various horses milled around the fenced pasture to her right. She wasn't sure exactly how many Cliff owned now—several dozen as far as she could tell. On previous visits Linnette had learned the names of a few of them. Cliff's stallion was called Midnight, and the brown-and-white yearling cavorting around the pasture closest to the fence was Funny Face. And there was Sheba, of course, the mare she'd ridden a few weeks ago.

When she'd parked and left her car, Cliff was emerging from the barn. He was a good-looking man, probably older than her parents, with a striking, vital presence. She thought he looked better than he ever had, and being a romantic, Linnette felt sure the difference was due to his marriage.

"Hi, Linnette," Cliff said as he came closer. He led a big dark-brown horse who stomped and snorted, making her nervous. She saw that the animal was already saddled. "Cal didn't say you were coming by."

"He doesn't know." She turned toward the corral and saw Cal standing there, a rope in his hands. The animal apparently recognized his intentions and whirled to avoid him.

Linnette watched, fascinated, as Cal expertly spun the lasso, all the while moving slowly toward the horse. With an ease that seemed entirely natural, he tossed the rope. His aim was true, and the lasso settled around the horse's neck. The stallion suddenly reared up, pawing frantically in the air. Linnette gasped and covered her eyes.

Cliff touched her shoulder in a reassuring gesture, and Linnette made an effort not to step apprehensively aside as the black horse thrust its neck toward her. "It'll be fine. Cal's working with a new stallion I just bought. He wouldn't do anything that might hurt the horse or himself."

When she found the courage to look again, she saw Cal standing in the corral, the stallion now backing away from the restraint. He kicked up dirt and reared again.

An involuntary sound of protest came from her lips as she rushed to the fence. She stared in horror as Cal went down. Cliff stood there, watching, too, and she wondered why he didn't seem more worried about the fact that Cal knelt on the ground, hunched over as if in pain.

"He's fine," Cliff assured her again. And as she looked intently at Cal, she saw him get up, still holding the rope. Her heart was in her throat as he shortened the distance between the stallion and himself, speaking quietly to the massive horse.

Linnette stared in amazement as he neared the

animal and, after a few minutes, ran his hand down the sleek, sweat-drenched neck. She couldn't believe he'd managed to do that—or that the stallion was allowing it.

Linnette didn't understand what had just happened. All she knew was that she had to get to Cal—talk to him. Find out for herself that he was all right. Despite herself, she was impressed that he'd subdued the stallion so quickly.

She climbed the fence and swung her leg over the top rung when Cliff stopped her.

"Stay here," he ordered. "Cal will be back in a few minutes."

Sure enough, as soon as he'd slipped a halter on the stallion and led him into the barn, he joined Linnette and Cliff. He was frowning slightly. "What are you doing here?" he asked. She noticed that he hadn't greeted her or expressed any pleasure at seeing her.

"I came to talk," she said. Her heart was still racing. Cal's world was so different from her own, she reminded herself. So filled with risks and dangers that were commonplace to him, but completely foreign to her.

When he didn't respond, she couldn't help asking, "Are you *okay?*"

"Yes," he said brusquely. Then he seemed to relent a bit. "I'm perfectly fine," he said in a friendlier tone.

"But…you could've been injured! What if that horse had kicked you? Or stomped on you? Or…or…"

"He didn't, did he?"

In the back of her mind she registered that he'd spoken without stammering or hesitation. "Why do you take these kinds of risks?"

He didn't seem to realize how badly she'd been shaken by seeing him in danger. Her knees would barely support her.

"Come on," Cal said, ignoring her question. He slipped an arm around her waist as he drew her away from Cliff. "Let's talk, since that's why you're here."

"I don't want you to go," she blurted out. "I know you feel you're doing something noble and good but is it really *necessary?* And doesn't this seem like a bad time?" She was afraid he hadn't considered all the consequences of leaving. "You're doing so well with your speech therapy…and…and you said yourself that there are mares ready to deliver. Surely Cliff needs you." Desperately she looked in the other man's direction, but Cliff had already mounted the brown horse and galloped off, giving her and Cal privacy. "And what about me?" she added.

"Cliff's encouraging me to go," he said patiently. "My speech therapist thinks it's fine." He shrugged. "I need to do this."

"But—"

"This is *my* life, L-Linnette," he said and for the first time his voice faltered slightly. "I make my own decisions."

"Of course you do." She was astounded—and frightened—by the intensity of his declaration.

"P-perhaps I sh-should've told you earlier. Actually, it's been in the works for some t-time."

"Why *didn't* you tell me?"

He removed his hat and wiped his forearm across his brow. "Because I knew you were going to object, so I k-kept putting it off. You're right—I should've said something sooner, but I'm telling you now. L-like I said, this is important to me, and I'm going with or without your approval."

"All right," she murmured, backing down with a sigh of resignation. Nothing she said was going to make any difference at this point.

"Good. Then we're clear on that." His voice was devoid of expression.

"Perhaps you could explain *why* this is so important to you," she suggested.

Together, but not touching, they walked over to the fence. Leaning against it, Cal braced his boot on the bottom rung. "Mustangs are being trapped by the Bureau of Land Management and because of a t-t-technicality in the law, once they're sold, too many of them are being slaughtered."

He'd mentioned some of this when he'd visited on Easter Sunday. She hadn't paid much attention to the details, though.

"Why?" she asked. "How can they do this?"

"United States law allows mustangs over the age of ten to be sold 'without limitations,'" he explained.

"In other words," she said, "they're being caught

and sold and whoever buys them can do what they want with these horses."

"Th-that's what's happening, yes."

"But it doesn't necessarily mean they're being killed," Linnette argued.

"I wish you were right. Unfortunately that's not the case. These beautiful beasts are being used for dog food here in the States or sold for human consumption in Europe."

That couldn't be true. It just couldn't. Although she knew little about horses, she was reluctant to accept that the government would allow this kind of senseless slaughter.

Several minutes passed in silence before Cal turned to look at her. "Can you understand why this is so important to me?" he asked.

Linnette did understand. What she didn't grasp was why *Cal* had to go. He was only one person and there wasn't much he could do by himself.

She pressed a finger to Cal's lips. Her eyes filled with tears and she couldn't see him clearly. "How long?" she asked, speaking around the knot in her throat. "How long will you be gone?" She wanted him to hold her, reassure her, but he didn't.

"A month, six weeks at the most."

"What do you intend to do with the mustangs?" She wiped away her tears with the sleeve of her sweater.

"There are various agencies that adopt them out.

Like I told your family at Easter, I'll be volunteering with the BLM and working with one of the agencies. Once the horses are captured and checked for health problems, they're available for adoption or auctioned off. I'll buy a few for Cliff and me, and I'll help the wild horse rescue group in whatever way they need." A smile slowly emerged. "I'll do everything I can to prevent even a few of them from being sold for slaughter."

Unwilling to wait for him to make the first move, Linnette threw her arms around his neck and rested her head against his shoulder. "What about us?" she asked. She could hear a distant truck, growing louder as it approached.

Cal stroked her hair with tenderness. Although his touch was gentle, an uneasy feeling refused to leave her. Something had changed between them, and she didn't know what. Or why.

Just then, the truck she'd heard rolled into the yard. Cal dropped his arms and stepped away from her.

"Who's that?" she asked.

"The vet."

Vicki Newman climbed out of the pickup and headed toward them, striding like a movie cowboy. Linnette had never met the other woman, although her name routinely came into conversations. She often stopped by the ranch for one reason or another. These horses seemed to require constant medical attention, Linnette thought, unable to curb her cynicism.

Placing his hand lightly on her shoulder, Cal made the introductions.

Vicki Newman nodded and held her gaze. She wasn't attractive or even very feminine looking, Linnette noted critically. Her light-brown hair was long and severely tied back, which sharpened her features. She wore jeans and a faded shirt.

"Nice to finally meet you," Vicki said.

"You, too," Linnette told her. After an awkward moment, she realized she was in the way. Whatever business they had to conduct, she clearly wasn't needed. "I, ah, guess I'd better get home."

Cal walked her to her car and kissed her cheek. As she drove away, Linnette glanced back and saw Cal and Vicki with their heads together, talking. It intensified the anxiety that roiled in her stomach.

Eighteen

"Come on, Olivia," Jack shouted over his shoulder as he jogged several paces ahead of her on Lighthouse Road. Fortunately traffic was light for a Saturday afternoon.

"Jack," she panted, struggling to keep up. "Slow down." She'd never thought she'd see the day that Jack Griffin could outrun her. But now that he was down thirty pounds and working out regularly, he'd become an exercise convert. His heart attack had been the motivation—and the warning—that he needed.

Trying to catch up, Olivia trotted along, breathing hard by the time she reached his side. "How much farther?" she panted.

"Around the next corner is three full miles."

As soon as they rounded the curve in the road,

Olivia stopped, slumping against the speed limit sign, exhausted. She leaned forward to catch her breath. "I can't keep up with you anymore," she said, gulping air into her lungs.

Jogging in place, Jack looked exceptionally proud of himself. "You might want to lose a few pounds."

"Jack!" She straightened and glared at him, hands on her hips.

"Just kidding," he said, chuckling.

"No, you weren't." The thing was, she probably *could* afford to lose five pounds. Except that at her age, it wasn't as easy as it had once been. Despite all her hard work, those few stubborn pounds refused to budge. It would be easier to melt them off with a blowtorch, as she'd recently told Grace.

Grace and Olivia were back to meeting every Wednesday for their aerobics class. Afterward they went for pie and coffee at the Pancake Palace. However, Olivia had forsaken dessert in the last few weeks. But she might as well have indulged in that coconut cream delight for all the good it'd done her to go without.

"I was thinking we should take a nice, hot shower when we get home," Jack suggested, jogging circles around her. He jiggled his eyebrows suggestively.

"Jack Griffin, you're outrageous."

"Yeah, but you love it."

He was right; she loved everything about this man. After being single for nearly twenty years, she'd had to make a real adjustment to return to married life. Jack had been divorced for almost as long, and he'd had to make his own compromises.

It had taken Jack's heart attack to show her—*remind* her—what really mattered in life and in marriage. She loved her husband. That fact was immutable; everything else was negotiable.

She only hoped that her daughter's marriage was equally strong, equally capable of surviving a crisis.

They started the three-mile walk back to the house, their pace more leisurely than before.

"Oh, oh," Jack said after a moment. "You've got that look. Better tell me what you're thinking about."

Olivia sighed and supposed she should get straight to the point. "Justine mentioned that Warren Saget's been coming by the bank a lot."

"Doesn't surprise me," Jack muttered. He shared her distaste for the other man.

Her daughter's relationship with Warren had always made Olivia uncomfortable, and her disapproval had driven a wedge between them for a long time. Good grief! Warren was Olivia's age, old enough to be Justine's father. In fact, Olivia had worried that her daughter was seeking a father figure in him. Stan had been a good husband and father until their son's death. Afterward, it was as if her ex had abdicated those roles. In retrospect, Olivia believed this was how Stan had dealt with Jordan's loss. Stan had remarried almost immediately after the divorce, and while he'd continued with child support payments, he'd had practically no emotional involvement with either Justine or her brother, James.

"Did she tell you what Saget wants?" Jack asked, frowning.

"Not really. She just said he's making a lot of unnecessary visits to the bank. I don't think she's told Seth about it."

"Maybe she should—to avoid any misunderstandings."

Olivia agreed with him, but it wasn't her decision.

"Warren knows Justine isn't interested in him, right?" Jack asked.

Justine had assured Olivia she'd made that abundantly clear. "She loves her husband and family."

"I wouldn't trust Warren Saget," Jack said, walking faster now. Olivia picked up her pace, too. "Justine would be well advised to stay away from him," he said.

"I agree."

"Do you figure he's trying to get on her good side? Because he wants the contract to rebuild the restaurant?"

"Perhaps," Olivia said, but she doubted it. Warren's company was successful, despite a number of complaints and even lawsuits through the years. Olivia had never understood how he stayed in business and yet he did. Warren had lost some of those lawsuits, and won others, and still he thrived.

What bothered Olivia most was the way he kept turning up in her daughter's life, like the proverbial bad penny. Olivia knew it'd been hard on Warren's ego when Justine left him and married Seth. Five years had passed. Surely he was over her daughter by now.

"Did you hear about Sandy Davis?" Jack asked suddenly.

Olivia shook her head. Sandy was the sheriff's wife; she and Troy Davis had been married nearly thirty years. Sandy had been diagnosed with multiple sclerosis as a young adult. She'd spent the last two years in a nursing home.

"She died yesterday."

"I'm so sorry," Olivia murmured. She'd always admired Troy and the way he loved and cared for his wife. He rarely talked about Sandy or her condition, seldom disclosing his own troubles.

"The funeral's going to be low-key," Jack said. "That's what Troy and his daughter told me when he brought in the obituary. Pastor Flemming is doing the service."

"Poor Troy," she said, wishing she could think of some way to help. "We'll definitely go to the funeral."

"I let your mother know," Jack told her. "Charlotte and the ladies at the Senior Center are organizing the wake. Most of them knew Sandy."

An involuntary smile came to Olivia. "My mother's so funny about these wakes. She claims that's where she finds her best recipes. The whole event becomes a recipe exchange."

Olivia expected Jack to be as amused as she was and glanced over at him to see that he wasn't smiling.

"That's the way she handles losing her friends," her husband said. "If she can concentrate on something other than the fact that she's lost another friend, then she doesn't feel as bereft."

Jack's insight didn't surprise her. He was skilled at recognizing the motivations beneath people's actions. "When did you get so smart?" she teased.

Jack chuckled. "About the time I married you."

"Good answer."

"You still interested in that shower?" Olivia asked in a sultry voice as they neared the house.

"You bet I am." Her question added an extra bounce to his step.

Olivia broke into an unhurried trot. "Wanna race?"

Jack declined. "I think I'd better conserve my strength—for later."

"Excellent idea. Otherwise I might wear you out completely and I wouldn't want to do that."

Jack cast her a teasing, sexy look. "Oh, but I was hoping you'd at least try."

Olivia couldn't keep from giggling like a schoolgirl. One of the great gifts of her marriage was laughter. Jack tended to see the humor in situations, even serious ones, and he could be a very clever mimic. "I don't know what I ever did without you, Jack Griffin."

"I don't, either."

"We don't have anything planned for this evening, do we?" he asked.

"Well…" Olivia hated to break this to him. "Actually, we do."

"We do?" Jack whined.

"Grace and Cliff invited us to dinner to give Cal a nice send-off to Wyoming."

"He needs *us* to send him off?"

Olivia would rather stay home, too, but she'd promised her friend. "I told Grace we'd be there."

Jack gave a deep, resigned sigh. "What's Grace cooking?"

"I didn't ask."

"I'm going to need lots of incentives. Like her rib roast and those mashed potatoes she does."

They reached the house and Olivia jogged up the steps only to find Jack surging ahead of her. "Jack," she cried when he entered the house. He hadn't bothered to wait for her, either. "Where are you going?"

He looked back, raising his eyebrows. "To turn on the shower, of course."

"Of course," Olivia echoed. "I'm right behind you."

Nineteen

Ever since the phone call from Anson, Allison had been waiting, waiting for him to contact her again. It'd been almost three weeks, and she was afraid she wouldn't hear from him a second time. As graduation grew closer, she hoped and prayed that the investigators would uncover *something*, anything, to prove his innocence.

"Dinner," her mother shouted from the kitchen. Allison reluctantly left her bedroom. After her parents had remarried, they'd insisted on eating as a family every night. Sometimes, like this evening, Allison considered it a major pain, but mostly she enjoyed it. Silly though it sounded, eating together had brought them all closer. With everyone's hectic schedule, the habit had fallen by the wayside, and Allison hadn't thought she'd really missed it. But if sitting down with her family at dinnertime helped keep her parents' marriage intact, she'd do it.

Her mother had cooked Eddie's favorite meal tonight, spaghetti and meatballs. That should make her little brother happy, since food, computer games and basketball were his three passions. She remembered how much Anson liked Eddie and had even played basketball with him a few times.

Without being asked, Allison set the salad on the table and brought out two bottles of dressing from the refrigerator door. Her mother thanked her with a smile.

Her father sliced the French bread while Eddie sat at the table waiting. Typical boy attitude. Like it was his right to have everyone wait on him.

After saying grace, they passed everything around and Allison served herself some salad and just enough spaghetti to deter any comments or questions. Her appetite hadn't been good since Anson's disappearance and she'd lost several pounds. Again and again she'd reviewed their brief phone conversation. He'd told her so little, for fear of putting himself at risk. The less she knew, the better. Allison understood that. Still, she couldn't help worrying about him.

"How was school?" her mother asked.

Eddie shrugged, digging into his meal with unrestrained gusto. He was already taller than Allison and still growing. "Bor-ing."

"Allison?" Her mother turned to her.

"Okay, I guess. I got accepted into the University of Washington." The letter had come that afternoon.

Her father set his fork down and stared at her. "You're only thinking to mention that *now?*"

She nodded carelessly. "I knew I'd get in."

"Such confidence," her mother said, looking at Zach with a smile.

"Congratulations, Allison." Her father raised his water glass, and the others joined in the toast.

Really, Allison couldn't see what all the fuss was about. Both of her parents had attended UW and it was expected that she would, too. She'd encouraged Anson to apply for a scholarship there, and if he'd stayed in school, if he'd pursued it, she was positive he would've been accepted.

No one seemed to realize how intelligent Anson was. He picked up languages easily, as she'd mentioned to his mother; he'd also helped Allison get through her chemistry class. Without him she would barely have passed. All that stuff came to him with very little effort.

"What about you, honey?" her mother asked, directing the question to Zach.

"I attended the Rotary meeting this afternoon and sat with Seth Gunderson."

Allison's ears perked up. She kept a file with whatever she could find out about the Gundersons, the restaurant and the fire. Obviously, she didn't possess the resources or the finesse of the authorities, but she collected every bit of information she could.

"How are Seth and his family doing now?" her mother asked.

"All right, it seems. He's selling boats."

"Boats?" Eddie echoed, a smear of tomato sauce on his chin. "That's a switch, isn't it?"

"Not really. He was a fisherman before he went into the restaurant business," Zach explained.

"Oh." Uninterested, Eddie returned to his meal.

"Apparently the arson investigators found a cross in the fire," her father added. "There was a picture of it in last night's paper. Seth hopes someone might recognize it and come forward."

Allison froze. She hadn't read yesterday's paper.

"What an interesting twist." Her mother met Allison's gaze, and Allison didn't dare look away.

"*Has* anyone come forward?" she asked, her heart in her throat. Anson had worn a pewter cross. That didn't mean anything, she was quick to tell herself. "But whoever wore it might not be responsible for the fire," she said. "It could've belonged to anyone, right?"

Both her parents and Eddie stared at her.

"What makes you ask?" her father asked, watching her intently.

Allison lowered her head and swallowed hard. "No reason," she mumbled. Only there was…. As soon as she could do it discreetly, she was going to find that newspaper and take a look.

No one at school had said anything about the article, not anyone, and Allison knew why. They were afraid to; afraid she'd get defensive and angry the way she always did when anyone dared suggest Anson was involved in the fire.

When dinner was over, Allison escaped to the privacy of her bedroom. Her mother, who had an uncanny ability to read her moods, came to see her shortly afterward. She held the local newspaper.

Allison pretended not to notice.

"Don't you want to see the picture?" her mother asked, sitting on the bed beside her.

Allison thought of lying and acting as if it didn't matter at all. Instead, she shrugged. "I suppose," she said in a dispassionate voice.

"Anson wore a big cross, didn't he?" her mother asked gently.

"It's not his," she said before she'd even glanced at the photograph. "And even if it is, that doesn't mean anything."

Her mother was slow in answering. "It might not. But then again, it might."

"He wouldn't do it, Mom," Allison insisted and although her mother didn't argue, Allison wondered who she was working so hard to convince—her family or herself.

Her mother handed Allison the paper, which was

open to the picture. One look, and Allison closed her eyes, so sick at heart that she couldn't bear to read the caption or the article below the photograph.

"Anson wore a cross like this?" her mother asked.

Allison bit her lower lip hard and nodded.

"You need to tell the sheriff you recognize it as his, sweetheart."

A sob threatened to burst from her chest, but Allison managed to hold it back. "I will."

Rosie slid her arm around Allison's shoulders. "I'm sorry," she whispered.

Unable to speak, Allison nodded again. "It's not him," she said. "It's not Anson." He wouldn't lie to her. He'd told her he hadn't started the fire and she believed him.

After a moment, her mother stood and left the room. Allison remained on the edge of her bed. She had to think, to sort everything out. Whenever she least wanted to remember it, the conversation with his mother kept running through her mind.

Playing with matches. According to her, Anson had nearly burned the house down as a youngster. Later he'd started a brush fire with friends and then there was the toolshed at the park. Fires fascinated him; his mother had been quick to tell her that. According to Cherry, he was just setting bigger ones now.

Even his own mother thought Anson was responsible for burning down The Lighthouse. The only person who still believed in him was Allison. And yet every shred of evidence she'd collected pointed directly at him.

For the first time, her faith in Anson wavered. She *wanted* to believe, and prayed that he was innocent. But how could she maintain her faith in the face of everything she'd learned?

The phone rang, and on the slight chance that it might be Anson, Allison leaped on it before Eddie could.

"Hello," she said, hoping she didn't sound as breathless as she felt.

"Allison, it's Kaci. Did you get your acceptance from UW?"

"Yeah, I'm in."

"Me, too. Want to go out and celebrate?"

Allison didn't feel much like celebrating. "Not really."

"What's wrong? You sound really down."

Kaci was Allison's best friend. "Anson," she whispered.

"Come on, Allie, you've got to stop pining for him. He's the one who walked out on you. Remember?"

Allison didn't say anything, *couldn't* say anything.

"I didn't mean that," Kaci said apologetically.

"I know," Allison assured her and then, because it all seemed so hard, she started to cry. "Oh, Kaci, I think he might've done it."

"No way! Hold on, I'm coming over."

Before Allison could protest, the line was disconnected.

Ten minutes later, the doorbell rang. Allison didn't go out to greet her friend. If her parents saw her tears, they'd be asking questions and she couldn't cope with that right now. Kaci let herself into Allison's room and immediately flopped down on the bed. "All right, talk."

Instead of speaking, she handed the newspaper to her friend. By now, Allison had read the short article two or three times. The cross had been found in the hallway outside the restaurant office and near the kitchen. Apparently it had fallen into a crack in the wood floor, protecting it from the worst of the fire.

Kaci read the piece and then set it aside. "Is it Anson's? He wore one identical to it."

"I told you he came to me the night of the fire," Allison said, keeping her voice low.

Kaci leaned closer.

"What I didn't tell you was that Anson smelled of smoke."

As though horrified, Kaci pressed her hand over her mouth. Allison hadn't confided in anyone except Cecilia, whose silence she could trust. "I…I'd never seen Anson like he was that night. I asked him what he did—I was sure he'd done something. He said—" she stopped long enough to regain her composure "—Anson said it was better for me not to know."

Kaci's shoulders sagged. "He did it, didn't he?"

"I...I don't know. I asked him outright and he swore he didn't. He asked me to believe in him. And I do, I do." Her throat started to close up again. "He said I'm the only person in his life who's ever had faith in him."

"If he asked you to help him now, would you?" Kaci asked.

Allison hung her head, unable to answer. What she had with Anson was more precious than any other relationship in her life, outside of her family. She loved him, but she had to stop deceiving herself. She couldn't continue to believe in him just because she wanted to. It was time to accept the fact that Anson might be guilty.

Twenty

"Come here, Grammy's girl," Ellen Bowman called, chasing Katie around the kitchen. Over the weeks, the formalities had been dispensed with. Joseph had become Grampa Joe and Ellen was Grammy.

Letting out a squeal of glee, Katie made her grandmother run after her in a mock game of tag. Jon's stepmother was endlessly patient with the little girl. Maryellen felt grateful—and deeply moved—to see how much Jon's family loved her daughter.

Nevertheless, Jon still kept his distance. Nothing Maryellen said or did seemed to help, so the situation continued unchanged.

"It's time for your nap, young lady," Maryellen reminded Katie. The child had no interest in sleeping if Grammy and Grampa Joe were available—as they always were, at least on weekdays. Katie had grown so close to her grandparents. Joe was just as enthralled with his granddaughter as his wife, and they spent countless hours entertaining the child; it was as if she'd become the focus of their existence.

"I'll take her up," Joe offered.

"No, I will," Ellen said.

Maryellen's father-in-law laughed. "How about if we *both* go upstairs with her."

The three of them disappeared up the flight of stairs and Maryellen figured it would be at least an hour before Katie fell asleep. Katie would insist that her grandparents read to her first and then sing to her and heaven knew what else. Only after that would Katie consent to have her nap.

Maryellen treasured the peace and quiet. Since Joe and Ellen had arrived, the pregnancy had been almost free of problems. Her stress had all but disappeared, thanks to her in-laws. She missed Jon, who still held his job photographing students in Tacoma schools. Never once had he complained, but Maryellen knew he hated it. She hated it for him.

But there *was* good news from the research she'd done online. One of the largest licensing agents in the business had agreed to review Jon's work. This was no small success; if Jon was accepted as a client, it would change everything. His work would be licensed for use on book covers, calendars, ads, all sorts of places. Jon might never know where or when his photographs would appear, which was a bit disappointing; however, the up-front money and the royalties would more than compensate for that. Maryellen was thrilled to know that someday they could be on the road and look up at a billboard and see Jon's work.

She hadn't told him yet because she didn't want to get his hopes up. For now, this was her secret and she held it close to her heart. One thing was sure: if he was accepted and his work became popular, their current money problems would be over.

Maryellen's general health had improved, and the doctor was pleased with how well the pregnancy was progressing. Judging by all the fetal activity she experienced, the baby was feeling just as good.

Caressing her abdomen, Maryellen felt fortunate to have carried this child as long as she had. In three weeks—but more likely two, according to Dr. DeGroot at her last appointment—she'd finally meet this baby of hers. As with Katie, she and Jon had decided they didn't want to know the sex of their child before the birth.

The phone rang and Maryellen answered as quickly as she could. Since he'd been hired by the portrait studio, Jon occasionally phoned to check on her. He didn't often, and she knew that was because he didn't want to risk talking to his parents.

"Hello," she said.

"Hi, Maryellen, it's Rachel. I was just calling to see how you're doing."

"Hi, Rachel." Maryellen responded, delighted to hear from her friend. "I'm feeling…pregnant."

Rachel laughed. "Cliff came in to ask me if you're ready for another beauty treatment."

Her stepfather was both kind and generous and he, like her mother, had been more than accommodating. Grace had joked that they'd hold the wedding reception, two baptisms and baby showers all at one time, during the summer. Her sister, Kelly, was due to deliver her second child a few weeks after Maryellen. The family had a lot to celebrate.

"I'm fine, actually," Maryellen said. "My hair's still looking okay." In fact, she planned to let it grow again. "I'll call Cliff and thank him."

"What about your nails?"

Maryellen examined her hands and sighed expressively. "That, my friend, is a different story."

"I thought so. Let me book you an appointment."

"It's so far for you to come all this way," she protested, although Maryellen would love to see her.

"Don't you worry about it. I'll be there at one o'clock on Wednesday."

"Thanks—and when you get here be prepared to fill me in on all the gossip."

"I will," Rachel promised. Lowering her voice, she added, "You heard about Teri and that chess player, didn't you?"

"You mean about her going over to Seattle and cutting Bobby Polgar's hair?"

"Oh, there's more. Much more."

Maryellen sat up straighter. "Tell me now. I don't want to wait until Wednesday."

Rachel gave a small giggle. "He came to Cedar Cove a little while after the chess match, which he won, in case you didn't know."

Maryellen did. "To Cedar Cove? Bobby Polgar was in Cedar Cove?"

"Not once, but *twice*."

"Twice." This was even better than she'd imagined. "Tell me more."

"Bobby's from somewhere back east. I can't remember where Teri said."

"New York," Maryellen supplied. Not that she was a keen follower of chess players—or chess, for that matter. But she'd read a lengthy article in the *Smithsonian* magazine about Bobby a few years ago, and for some reason remembered a lot of it. He'd been playing chess from the time he could walk. By the age of three, he was beating grown men in local chess clubs. It didn't take him long to gain recognition. She recalled one picture in which this child, this little boy, sat with his small hand extended across the chessboard for a sportsmanlike victory shake.

"Anyway," Rachel continued, "he came to Cedar Cove the first time to pay Teri, something he failed to do when she went to Seattle."

"I hope she took the money." In Maryellen's view, Teri had earned it.

"She did, and they had a beer together, too."

A beer? Somehow she couldn't picture the great Bobby Polgar drinking beer with Teri Miller. "What about the second time?"

"He came back a week later. They must've gone out to dinner but I can't say for sure because Teri's been very quiet ever since."

"Teri? Quiet?"

Rachel lowered her voice even more until Maryellen had to strain to hear. "The truth is, I think she's falling for him."

That was bad news. Bobby Polgar was the last man in the world Maryellen could see with a woman like Teri—irreverent and funny. She had a wicked sense of humor and a heart of gold. But Teri and Bobby Polgar, one of the world's intellectual geniuses? It'd never work.

"Speaking of romance, how's it going with you and Nate?" Maryellen asked.

"Good. I'll tell you all about it on Wednesday," Rachel said.

"I can't wait." For years Maryellen had watched the girls at Get Nailed bemoan the lack of romance in their lives. Then within a year or so, they all seemed to be finding love, and in the most unlikely places, too.

Rachel had been attracted to Nate Olsen after the first date. But then Nate had informed her he was seeing a girl back home; disappointed, Rachel had tried to forget him and gone about her life. All of a sudden Nate was back and she'd fallen head over heels in love.

After her conversation with Rachel, the afternoon sped by. When Ellen brought Katie down, following her nap, she baked brownies, letting her granddaughter "help," while Joe did some work in the garden.

"These are Jon's favorite," Ellen said, cutting the brownies and setting them on a plate on the kitchen counter.

Conscious of the time, the older couple packed up their things and left by five. A half hour after they'd returned to their hotel, Jon came home.

Because the sun was still shining brightly and the garden smelled of lilacs, Maryellen had moved awkwardly outside to sit on the deck. She wanted to be in the fresh, clean air, enjoying the scents of spring. The deck afforded Katie a small play area, too, and Maryellen could keep an eye on her.

"Hey!" Jon said happily when he found the two of them outdoors. "How are my girls?" he asked, sweeping Katie into his arms.

Maryellen smiled as Katie wrapped her own arms around his neck and offered him a sloppy kiss. She chattered away, and Jon pretended to understand every word.

"She has a surprise for you in the kitchen," Maryellen told him.

After hugging Maryellen and gently rubbing her belly, Jon went inside with Katie. "It's brownies," he called out. "My favorite."

Soon he was back, holding the plate aloft. "You mean to tell me my girls baked me brownies?"

Katie was so proud to see her father enjoying what she'd made—with her grandmother's notable assistance—that Maryellen let him assume she'd been in the kitchen herself. Jon broke off a corner and shared it with her. Katie poked it into her mouth and instantly wanted more.

"Greedy little girl, aren't you?"

Maryellen laughed. "And who's got that whole plate?"

Jon chuckled. "Point well-taken." He sat down, relaxing in the wooden deck chair, and looked out over the view. Vashon Island was visible in the distance and so was the distinctive shape of Mount Rainier.

Legs stretched out before him, Jon slipped his arm around her shoulders. Maryellen savored the warmth and comfort of his embrace.

"I know this has been a difficult pregnancy for you," he began. "I'm glad it's almost over."

"It has been hard in some ways, and in others it's been…wonderful."

Jon seemed taken aback by her comment. "Wonderful? How?"

"It's brought us together."

"True," he agreed.

"I don't know if I ever would've had the courage to leave the gallery. Everyone relied on me, and it was so easy to put off giving my notice. Then all of a sudden I didn't have any choice."

"I'd like you to be home with our babies."

"It's where I want to be—and with you, too." Her love for Jon seemed tangible and strong.

Jon reached for a second brownie as Katie sat contentedly at his feet. "Once when I was in junior high, I ate a plate of these on my own."

"I know. Ellen told me about it." She'd mentioned his stepmother without thinking and felt him stiffen.

Jon stared suspiciously at the one in his hand. "She didn't bake these, did she?"

Reluctantly Maryellen nodded.

Jon threw the brownie back on the plate as if it had lost its taste. "I wish you wouldn't do that," he said.

"Do what?"

"Set me up like that. What did you and Ellen do, sit around all afternoon making plans to break down my defenses? The way to a man's heart is through his stomach, right?"

"Jon, stop it," she snapped. He'd ruined a very pleasant interlude. "We did nothing of the sort."

She could tell by his lack of response that he didn't believe her. "I'm going upstairs to change," he muttered, taking the brownies and walking into the kitchen through the open French doors.

It seemed so hopeless, Maryellen thought sadly. He refused to bend on this matter, refused to forgive his parents or accept their remorse.

A few minutes later, Jon was back, wearing jeans and a T-shirt. "I think I'll mow the lawn," he said as though nothing had happened.

Maryellen hoped physical labor would improve his mood. "Good idea," she said curtly.

All at once Katie let out a cry and Jon rushed into the kitchen, Maryellen following at a slower pace. She discovered her daughter pulling the brownies out of the garbage can where Jon had tossed them.

"It's all right, sweetheart," Jon tried to tell her.

"Grammy," Katie cried, kicking and screaming on the floor. "I hate you. I want my Grammy."

Jon looked at Maryellen for help, but she didn't know what to tell him. His thoughtless act had broken their daughter's heart.

Twenty-One

Since she'd been on her feet all morning, Teri welcomed a break before her next client showed up. Sitting in her own cubicle chair, with her back to the mirror, she ate hot, salty French fries and sipped a diet soda. One of the other girls had picked up some takeout for lunch, and Teri had ordered her ultimate comfort food. The drink was a concession to calorie cutting.

Rachel finished with her nail client, then joined Teri in the adjacent cubicle. "You've been quiet all morning," she said. "That's not like you."

Teri shrugged. She'd been feeling depressed for the last few days and didn't want to talk about it. She hadn't been able to stop thinking about Bobby Polgar since he'd rolled into Cedar Cove in that stretch limo with his driver, James. Apparently Bobby had never learned to drive. He'd come to see her again, and after that, he'd been calling her every day.

"Is it Bobby Polgar?" Rachel asked, keeping her voice low so as not to attract attention from the other girls or their clients.

Teri nearly dropped her Diet Coke. "How'd you know?"

Rachel's smile was shrewd. "How many years have we worked together?" She didn't wait for a response. "In all that time, I've never seen you this...subdued."

"He calls me every night." The crazy part was that Bobby phoned at exactly seven, Pacific Daylight Time, regardless of where he was. Not one minute before or one minute after, always precisely at seven. The man got around, too. Just last week he'd been in China and the week before that he'd been somewhere in Europe. Prague, if she recalled correctly. His home was in New York City, although she doubted he was there even twenty percent of the time. He always seemed to be on the road. She hadn't figured out what he did in all those exotic locations once the chess match was over. When he called, he asked her ordinary questions about her day. To be fair, she asked him pretty much the same kind of thing. Mostly she wanted to know where he was calling from. If he was in his hotel at the time, he'd describe whatever he could see from his window. He told her about his chess matches in terms that were light years beyond her understanding. She told him about her customers and how many color jobs, perms or haircuts she'd worked on, the conversations she'd had and what she was reading.

"You like him, don't you?" Rachel asked, peeling a banana and taking a bite.

"No!" Teri declared.

"You don't?"

"I've been waiting all my life to fall in love," Teri muttered, and it was true. Rachel knew about all the losers Teri had been involved with through the years. After she'd graduated from beauty school, she'd been too stupid to know any better. She seemed to learn life's lessons the hard way. Once a guy had emptied her entire bank account, and she'd had no one to blame but herself. She'd actually given him her ATM card and her PIN number! Given it to him because he needed twenty bucks and she had a perm going and couldn't leave. Talk about stupid. Only it wasn't twenty bucks he'd walked away with. Instead he'd taken the maximum amount, which happened to be exactly what she'd had in her savings.

Then there was Ray. She'd made the mistake of letting him move in with her. It was only until he got a few things straightened out financially, he'd claimed, and then they'd be married. What a joke. Within a week he'd "lost" his job, and she found herself supporting him. It took six months and a sheriff's deputy to get him out of her apartment.

Her history with men was abysmal. Her judgment

was bad, just like her mother's. Teri no longer trusted herself when it came to men, and she didn't understand why Bobby Polgar seemed to be so fascinated with her.

"I told him not to phone me again," she said. She'd come to look forward to those ridiculous phone calls from Bobby, but she had absolutely *nothing* in common with him.

"Has he called since?"

"No." For two nights Teri had sat by the phone, waiting. Hoping he'd call despite her demand. Wishing he would.

"Oh, Teri," Rachel said, with a resigned sigh. "You're afraid, aren't you?"

"Damn straight I am!"

"And yet you were the first person who told me I shouldn't let the fact that Nate's father is a congressman keep me from loving Nate."

"It's different with you," Teri argued. "You're much smarter than me. You never let a loser move in with you and suck you dry."

"That doesn't make me smart."

Teri snorted softly. "It does in my book." She didn't mention her mother. Rachel's mother had died when she was young and she'd been raised by an aunt. Teri's mother had married four or five times. Maybe it was six; Teri had lost count. She had a couple of siblings she'd practically raised herself. Her half sister, Christie, was married to a drunk and going through a divorce.

Her half brother, Johnny, was seven years younger and in college, and he was staying there if she had anything to say about it. She helped him with tuition and routinely checked on him to be sure he was studying and his marks were good. That kid was graduating and doing something decent with his life if she had to kill him to make it happen.

"I don't know what Bobby sees in me anyway," she said, and popped another French fry in her mouth. She barely had a high-school education. Okay, a GED, but she was top of her class in beauty school. In the looks department, she was all right, she supposed. Average attractive. Her hair color changed depending on her mood. Currently it was black and short, but she was thinking about bleaching it.

"I know why Bobby likes you," Rachel said. "You're a breath of fresh air to him, and you're different from everyone else he knows." She grinned. "He's probably never met anyone like you."

"I don't even play chess," Teri muttered.

"That makes you all the more attractive to him. Chess is his entire life. It's all he knows. You've opened up a whole new world to him. Plus, you're fun and sassy, and he doesn't intimidate you like he does everyone else."

Again and again Teri had examined her memories of that Saturday in Seattle, when she'd bullied her way in to see Bobby and cut his hair. She'd done crazy stuff before, but this was a new high—or maybe a new low. Even after analyzing the incident to death, Teri still couldn't explain what had driven her to do it. Now she was paying the price and as with every other relationship in her life, the price was too high. She was falling in love with this geek and it wouldn't work. Not in a million years.

"Anytime you want to talk," Rachel said, standing up, "I'm available. Just remember the advice you gave me about Nate."

Sharing her problems wasn't something Teri did often. She was closer to Rachel than practically anyone, but talking about Bobby, even with the person she considered her best friend, was difficult.

"Thanks," she said, dumping the rest of her fries in the garbage. Anyway, there was nothing more to say about Bobby, since she hadn't heard from him in two days. Painful as it was, she'd made her point; he wouldn't call her again.

Nevertheless, Teri was sitting by the phone that evening, just in case Bobby had a change of heart. At exactly seven, her doorbell rang. Irritated, she grabbed her portable phone and carried it to the door.

There, standing directly in front of her, holding a huge arrangement of bright red roses, was the ever-courteous James. The vase probably weighed more than he did. "Good evening, Miss Teri," he intoned.

"What are you doing here?" she asked.

"Would you mind opening the door a little wider so I can bring these in?" James asked breathlessly.

Teri unlatched the screen door but she wasn't letting him inside her home. No way. "I'll take them," she insisted, placing the phone on her small hallway table. She accepted the display from him and instantly regretted it. The vase had to weigh a good fifty pounds. She lugged it over to the coffee table and set it down, sloshing water as she did. "How many roses are there?" she asked, utterly astonished.

"Six dozen."

Teri groaned. They must've cost a fortune. *Six* dozen roses? No man had ever given her more than a single rose.

"I hope you like chocolates," he said next. "I have ten pounds from the top six candy companies around the world. Bobby didn't know if you had a preference, so he wanted all the bases covered."

"*Ten* pounds of chocolate?" No man had *ever* bought her chocolate. Men generally knew not to give an overweight girlfriend candy.

"They're in the car, along with the perfume."

"Perfume?" Hands on her hips, Teri studied Bobby's driver. "What's this about?"

"Well, Miss Teri…" James removed his driver's hat and exhaled. "Bobby asked a colleague what women like, and his friend said flowers, candy, perfume and sentimental cards."

"Where's Bobby?"

"In the car," James told her. "I'm double-parked outside. Bobby's in there signing the cards."

"Cards?"

"The sentimental ones. He bought a dozen."

Sure enough, the stretch limo was parked in a lot reserved for the occupants of the apartment complex. Several of her neighbors had stepped outside to gawk at it. Her neighborhood wasn't accustomed to seeing cars that required uniformed drivers.

Teri marched past her neighbors and opened the passenger door. Without waiting for an invitation, she climbed inside. Yup, there was Bobby Polgar, pen in hand. Boxes of chocolates were stacked beside him, as well as a pile of sealed envelopes and a stack of expensive perfume boxes.

"*Why* are you here?" she asked, sitting across from him. She tried to sound stern, and yet she couldn't deny her thrill of happiness.

"You asked me not to phone you again," he answered, eyes widening behind the dark-rimmed glasses. "I didn't call."

"But—"

"I would've arrived two days ago but I was in the middle of a match."

"Bobby." He made it so difficult to be angry. "Why are you here?" she repeated, at a loss to understand this man.

He didn't speak for a long time, and then he blurted out, "I need a haircut."

"Anyone qualified to cut hair can do that. You

didn't have to fly halfway around the world for me to do it."

"I didn't want anyone else."

"Why the roses and the chocolates—and everything else?" She gestured toward the perfume. According to James, Bobby had solicited advice on the gifts women preferred, and been given these generic suggestions. The real question was why he felt he needed to present her with gifts at all.

He shifted uncomfortably as he glanced around the vehicle. He seemed to look everywhere but at her. "I didn't know what I'd done that you'd ask me not to phone. I liked talking to you. I looked forward to it."

"I did, too," she reluctantly confessed.

"You did?" He wrinkled his brow. "Then why did you make me stop?"

If he hadn't figured it out, she couldn't explain it.

"Experts have calculated that I've committed to memory over a hundred thousand possible chess configurations," he said. "I look at a chessboard and within seconds I can figure out how any move my opponent makes is going to play out. I know chess, but I don't know women. I want to know you. I like you."

"I like you, too. In fact, I like you a lot and that frightens me."

"Why?"

She might as well tell him the truth. "I'm not all that intelligent."

He shrugged, apparently unconcerned. "I don't think that's true. But even if it is, I'm smart enough for both of us. Did you like the roses?"

"They're beautiful."

"May I kiss you now?"

She laughed and then realized he was serious. He watched her, anticipating her kiss. He met her eyes and extended his hand to her.

Crouching, she made her way toward him. Because of all the candy and perfume stacked next to him, she had to sit on his lap. She slid her arms around his neck, then removed his glasses, folded them and slipped them into his pocket. When she'd finished, she gave him an encouraging smile and leaned forward so their lips could meet.

As kisses went, this one was pretty tame. Bobby might know plenty of chess moves, but that was the only kind of move he knew. He sure didn't have a lot of sexual finesse. Well…he might possess enough brains for both of them, but she had enough experience.

Bobby cleared his throat after two follow-up kisses, each lengthier and more intense than the one before.

"That was very nice," Bobby whispered. He seemed to have difficulty speaking.

"Yes, it was. Are you ready for your haircut?"

He cleared his throat a second time and nodded.

Most of her neighbors had gone back inside when Teri emerged from the limousine. Thank goodness for tinted windows! If any of the stragglers recognized Bobby, they didn't say anything. Bobby gave his driver instructions to return in a couple of hours and accompanied Teri into her small apartment.

Had she known she was going to have company, she would've cleaned the place up a bit. Bobby didn't seem to notice that she wasn't giving Martha Stewart any competition. In fact, he didn't seem to notice anything but her.

"What?" she muttered, uncomfortable with the way his eyes followed her every move.

"There's something different about you," he commented.

"I dyed my hair black." She pulled out a kitchen chair and gestured for him to sit. She kept a spare cape in a bottom drawer; she took it out and wrapped it around him, fastening it at the neck.

"Why did you change your hair color?" he asked. "I liked it the way you had it the last time I saw you."

"I was in a black mood," she said and went briefly to her bedroom to retrieve scissors and a comb.

She'd just started trimming his hair when he announced, "I want to marry you."

Teri lowered her arms and exhaled harshly. "Stop it."

"I mean it."

"I'll cut your hair, but I am not marrying you."

"Why not?"

"You don't even know me!"

"Is that important?"

"Yes," she said, shocked he'd ask such a fundamental question. "Love helps, too."

Bobby frowned. "I'm not good with emotions."

No surprise there. "Go figure," she teased.

Bobby smiled slightly. "Will you let me kiss you again?"

She continued to clip the sides of his hair. "Probably."

"Tonight?"

"How much chocolate did you bring?"

"Ten pounds. Is it enough?"

"Plenty," she assured him. Just to show him how much she appreciated good chocolate, she straddled his lap. Scissors still in her hand, she hooked her arms around his neck. With a surge of joy she didn't bother to examine or to question, she gave Bobby Polgar, world chess champion, a kiss that could've won a competition of its own.

Twenty-Two

"There's someone here to see you," Frank Chesterfield, the bank president, told Justine late Friday afternoon. She normally worked mornings, but Frank had asked her to take care of some pending loan applications so she'd agreed to stay. She'd gone into the vault and before she could ask who it was, Frank was gone.

Most likely Warren Saget had stopped by for another chat. He was still doing that despite her lack of encouragement or welcome. He chose to ignore her wishes and persisted in visiting her far too often. It wasn't that Justine disliked Warren. He was her friend and had proved it the day of her panic attack.

She could do without seeing him right now, though. Seth had been depressed for several days, since the official end of the arson investigation. The building, or what was left of it, had been released to them and quickly demolished. Seth had watched it all, watched the trucks hauling away the charred remains of their dream. Justine was concerned about him and resented Warren's frequent appearances, despite his kindness to her.

She was married and she loved her husband and no friendship was worth risking her marriage over. Seth had made his feelings toward the other man plain. He didn't want her seeing Warren, no matter how platonic the relationship. Justine had every intention of abiding by his wishes. She wouldn't want him lunching with an old girlfriend, either.

However, it wasn't Warren waiting at her desk, it was her husband. She felt a stirring of excitement, of delight untainted by anger or sadness. "Seth!"

He stood as she approached. "Hi." His smile told her all was well. "I've come to make a deposit."

Justine blinked. "Okay," she murmured, "I'll take it to the teller's cage."

"Aren't you interested in what I'm about to put in our bank account?" he asked, the gleam in his eyes signalling his pleasure.

"Of course."

"It's my first commission check." Two weeks earlier, Seth had made his first sale; he'd downplayed the event but Justine had been very proud of him. Taking her lead from Seth, she'd acted equally casual.

"Congratulations, Seth," she said now.

"Thank you." He did seem pleased with himself.

Standing, he withdrew his wallet from his hip pocket, ceremoniously removed the check and handed it to her.

Justine took one look at the amount and had to sit down. "*This* is your commission check?" she asked, hardly able to form the words.

"Yup."

"For *one* boat?"

"Yup."

She looked again. "What did you sell, the *Queen Mary?*"

Seth's laughter echoed against the bank walls. "No, my darling wife, it was a fishing vessel, not unlike the one Dad and I used in Alaska."

"This is a lot of money." Although the restaurant had done well, this amount was more profit than they'd made in three months at The Lighthouse.

He smiled in acknowledgement. "Larry says I'm a natural and if so, it's because I know the business. I lived it, worked it and, well, I've made two more sales from referrals."

"Oh, Seth!" she gasped. "I couldn't be happier for you." As far as Justine was concerned, the money was secondary. They could certainly use it, but what really mattered was the contentment she saw in her husband's eyes. She felt a renewed hope that the arsonist hadn't devastated their marriage along with the restaurant.

"I already picked up Leif and he's spending the

night with my parents," Seth told her. Their son had been at a birthday party for the afternoon.

Justine gave her husband a slow smile. "He is?"

"Oh, yes."

"And where will we be?" she asked.

"We're going out to celebrate."

That happy smile was back on Seth's face. "Sounds wonderful to me," she said.

"Jay and Lana are joining us in Silverdale."

Jay and Lana were former classmates and good friends. With the restaurant demanding so much of their time, Seth and Justine had rarely seen any of their friends in the last few years.

"After dinner," Seth went on, interrupting her thoughts, "I have another small surprise for you."

"Better than stealing me away for a celebration dinner with friends?" This was more than they'd done in months and months; when they were operating The Lighthouse, they'd simply never had the time.

"Much better," Seth promised in a low voice.

"I'll finish up here," she said, glancing at the clock. The bank closed later on Fridays; however, she planned to leave at six. "Then I'll go home and change."

"Not necessary," Seth told her.

"But…"

"As a matter of fact, why don't you leave now?" Her boss stepped up to her desk. He winked at Seth, and Justine wondered how much Frank knew about this surprise of her husband's.

"Should I drive out and meet you in Silverdale?" she asked, reaching into the bottom drawer for her purse.

"No need to do that, either," Seth said, taking her arm in his.

"But my car…"

"Is at home."

Justine's jaw sagged. "When did that happen?" She'd driven to work that morning and parked it at the far end of the lot, where employees left their vehicles.

"Jay and I came by earlier," Seth explained. "I picked up your car and then drove back here."

"I would like to change clothes." If they were going out for the evening, she'd prefer to wear something fancier than business attire.

"I figured as much, so I brought another outfit with me." He opened the bank door as he spoke and they walked toward his car, parked near the entrance.

"Very cute, Seth, and where am I supposed to change? A gas station restroom? I don't think so." She leaned against his car. "I suppose I could use the employee bathroom, but…"

"Hmm, that's a good point," he muttered, his eyes bright with love and anticipation. "I guess I'll just have to take you to the hotel earlier than I'd planned."

"What?"

"We have a hotel room for the night, complete with champagne."

"Oh, my goodness." Justine covered her mouth. "Pinch me, because I must be dreaming."

Seth brought his arms around her waist and laughed. "Why don't I kiss you, instead?"

This was an offer she couldn't refuse. "It's a deal."

The evening was everything Justine could have imagined, and more. After a lengthy dinner with excellent wine, the four of them drove to the hotel and had drinks in the elegant lounge while a three-piece ensemble played. Justine needed a couple of mixed drinks to fuel her courage before she agreed to step onto the dance floor. She was glad she did. Any excuse to have Seth's arms around her was worth potential embarrassment.

Jay and Lana had to get home to relieve their babysitter and left at midnight. Shortly after that, Seth was feigning a yawn.

"All right, all right," Justine teased. "I've got the message."

Smiling, Seth reached for her hand. In the elevator, he stood behind her, arms around her waist as he kissed the side of her neck. "I'm ready to collect on all those promises you've been sending my way all evening."

"And what about that surprise you promised me?"

"You'll see when we get to the room."

"Oh, Seth, I love you so much." She turned in his arms and held him close. It felt as if she had her husband back at last—as if the burdens of the months since the fire had fallen away.

"Just wait until you see what I bought you to wear to bed," he whispered with a low groan—obviously picturing her in it.

"Do you really want me to take the time to change?" she whispered.

"True," Seth murmured. "No, don't bother. The minute you put it on, I'll be taking it off."

Justine closed her eyes and smiled. "That's what I thought."

The elevator doors glided open, and Seth swung her into his powerful arms as though she weighed next to nothing. He headed down the long hallway toward their room. It was a small comedy of errors as he tried to hold her while attempting to open the door with the room card. Justine dissolved into giggles and then they were both laughing. He had to put her down before he managed to get the door unlocked.

Seth didn't bother to turn on the lights. He shut the door and pressed her against it, kissing her with hot, urgent hunger.

"Oh, Seth," she breathed, her head spinning. "I was so afraid I'd lost you."

"Never." His hands worked at the tiny buttons on her silk blouse. "I think you'd better get out of this before I accidentally rip something."

She giggled again and took over the task of unbuttoning the blouse.

They made love that night and again in the

morning. Lying there, spent, Justine felt utterly relaxed in her husband's arms, utterly tranquil and at peace.

"Seth," she whispered, thinking aloud. "I need to ask you something."

"Anything." He stroked her bare back, letting his hand roam from her shoulder blades to the curve of her waist.

"After a night out—the first one in over a year— are you sure you want to rebuild the restaurant?"

His hand stilled, and she feared she'd destroyed the moment.

"I don't know anymore, Justine. I just don't know."

Twenty-Three

On Sunday at noon, Nate drove to Rachel's with a picnic lunch. She met him on the sidewalk outside her front door, too eager to wait. Throwing herself into his arms, she sighed as he hugged and kissed her. It was weeks since they'd spent more than a couple of hours together.

His work schedule was hectic, but so was hers. Her days off were Sunday and Monday, although lately she'd been working Mondays, too. As soon as the navy wives had gotten word that she did both hair and nails, her schedule had started filling up. Her bookings were practically overlapping. The money was great, but she needed a break.

"Where would you like to go?" Nate asked, smiling down at her.

"How about Point Defiance Park?" she suggested.

The Tacoma park was always lovely, but especially at this time of year with the rhododendrons and azaleas in bloom.

"Perfect." Nate kissed the top of her head. "I can have you all to myself?"

"Of course." Rachel knew the question referred to the time she spent with Jolene. Nate didn't complain much, but he wasn't pleased—and she realized it was her relationship with Bruce that troubled him, not her friendship with the little girl.

"Good."

The day could not have been more ideal for their outing. The sun shone brightly in a clear blue sky, and a light breeze blew off the cove. Rachel grabbed her sweater, then slipped into the front seat of Nate's convertible, a relatively new acquisition. He'd chosen a candy-apple red and she'd fallen in love with it the minute he'd brought it over the first time.

The wind blew her hair into total chaos, not that Rachel cared. She was with Nate, and they had the whole day together. The weather was a bonus, but it wouldn't have mattered if the skies had opened and drenched them with rain. In that case, they would've had their picnic on her living room floor.

They wandered through the park, finally choosing a secluded spot where Nate spread out a blanket. The picnic basket boasted fried chicken, potato salad, rolls and coleslaw, which Nate had picked up at a chicken franchise before coming to collect her.

He'd also brought some white wine that was way more expensive than anything she ever chose.

When they'd eaten, Nate sprawled out with his head nestled in her lap. Rachel lazily stroked his hair and savored this peaceful afternoon together. Nate's eyes drifted shut and Rachel discovered that she felt sleepy, too. The sun's warmth, the wine and the food and, most of all, being with Nate produced a sense of well-being and uncomplicated joy.

The tranquility of the moment was shattered by the shrill ring of Nate's cell phone.

Jerking upright, Nate frowned and reached for the phone, clipped to his waist. "Hello," he answered tersely. But then his demeanor changed and he relaxed.

After a minute or two of conversation, Rachel realized it was Nate's mother on the phone.

"A political rally for Dad," he repeated. He looked at Rachel and smiled reassuringly. "In October. I can request leave, but Mom, there's no guarantee. Yes, yes, of course, I understand this is important. I'll do what I can." He touched his index finger to his mouth and kissed it, then pressed it against Rachel's lips.

She smiled and brought his finger into her mouth and gently sucked on it.

Nate darted her a warning glance before he withdrew his finger.

"I'm with Rachel," he said unexpectedly. "This would be a good time to introduce yourself."

A feeling of dread washed over her. Nate's

powerful, wealthy family made her feel insecure. Her sole disagreement with him while he was away at sea for six months had been about the difference between their stations in life. In defiance of his father, Nate had enlisted in the navy and, through his own skills, had risen to the grade of warrant officer, the highest of any noncommissioned rank.

Apparently Nate had something else to prove to his father, and she was afraid that *something* was his relationship with her. Rachel's biggest fear was that dating her was another act of defiance on his part, although Nate fervently assured her otherwise.

Nevertheless, Rachel kept a close guard on her heart. She was apprehensive, justifiably so, in her opinion. Still she found herself drawn to him despite everything. She treasured the hours they could spend together and looked forward to their conversations. Even when he wasn't at sea, they e-mailed each other often. Rachel sometimes used the computer at the salon during her breaks, although privacy wasn't exactly in great supply.

"Here, why don't you talk to Rachel," Nate said next and without warning handed her the cell phone.

She glared at him and shook her head, refusing to accept it. Nate insisted, however, and given no choice, she took the cell.

"Hello, Mrs. Olsen, this is Rachel Pendergast," she said, making a face at him.

Nate smiled and brought her right hand to his

mouth, sucking on her finger. She yanked it away and turned around so she could concentrate on his mother.

"Hello, Rachel," his mother greeted her warmly. "It's nice to finally get a chance to meet you, even if it is over my son's cell. And please, call me Patrice."

"All right, Patrice," she said, nearly stumbling over the name. "It's lovely to meet you, too." Rachel's heart felt lodged in her throat as she struggled to think of some appropriate comment.

"You certainly seem to have captured our son's interest."

Rachel glanced over her shoulder and exchanged a smile with Nate. "He's wonderful."

"I'm sure you know he broke off a long-standing relationship with the daughter of one of our dearest friends because of you."

Nate had made it clear on their first date that he had a girlfriend back home.

"Yes, he did mention that. I hope it hasn't caused any problems with your friends." Nate had also mentioned that he was glad to be out of the relationship and that the girl—she didn't remember her name— was already engaged to someone else.

Patrice's returning laughter sounded a bit strained. "No problem at all. Please don't concern yourself. Everything's fine. I, uh, hear you're a bit older than Nate."

This, too, had led to arguments between Nate and Rachel. "Five years," she murmured. "I'm five years older." On their first meeting, Nate had seemed so young, and at thirty, Rachel had felt worlds older. But Nate had eventually convinced her that those few years meant nothing. Every now and then, she reminded herself that when she'd graduated from high school, Nate had been in seventh grade.

"Five years isn't that much of a difference," Patrice said reassuringly. "I didn't know what to think when Nate said you were older. It would be just like him to arrive with a forty-year-old divorcée on his arm. He does things like that, you know? I swear, it's just another way of defying his father and me. He did that as a youngster, too." She laughed lightly, as if a little embarrassed.

"Did Nate tell you I'm a nail tech?" Rachel felt she needed to bring up her occupation. Might as well put it all out there.

"You're in the navy, too?" Patrice asked, sounding surprised.

"No, I work in a salon and do hair and nails. That kind of tech."

Silence. Then, "Oh."

Her reaction told Rachel that Nate hadn't said anything about it.

Patrice recovered quickly. "No, but that's our Nate. He likes to deliver his little surprises. I'm sure you're very talented with hair and, ah, fingernails."

"Thank you," Rachel managed. "Perhaps I should pass the phone back to Nate."

"Yes, please."

Rachel gladly returned the cell phone, and while Nate ended the conversation, she started walking. She needed to think about the emotions this brief conversation with his mother had brought to the surface. She was afraid she'd made a terrible impression. His mother's attitude was clear and unmistakable: Without even meeting her, Patrice Olsen had decided Rachel was an inappropriate choice for her only son.

Nate caught up with her a few minutes later and she was grateful to see he was no longer talking on his cell.

"Rachel, wait," he said, grabbing her shoulders. "What did my mother say?"

She shook her head. "Nothing. She was very nice." Even as she spoke, Rachel's stomach knotted. "I can't believe I let this happen," she whispered, covering her face with both hands. Despite the inner voice that had warned her about the dangers of this relationship, she'd resisted. Almost from the first, she'd known that dating this young officer wouldn't work for either of them. His father was a congressman, for heaven's sake!

"Rachel, tell me," he pleaded.

"She had no idea that I'm employed as a nail tech. She thought it had something to do with the navy." She hiccupped a laugh at the absurdity of such a comment. His mother had to know about nail techs, but Rachel didn't want to assume the comment had been deliberate. Any more than she wanted to think the remarks about her age and his previous girlfriend hid some malicious intent.

"I'm phoning Mom back and asking her to apologize," Nate said, reaching for the cell clipped to his belt.

"No, please, don't." Her hand stopped him. "It's nothing."

"Then why are you upset?"

"I…I don't belong in your world."

"Wrong," he declared. "We belong together. I knew it from the beginning." He walked away, pacing restlessly, as though he couldn't bear to stand still. "This isn't the first time my parents have done this kind of thing. They feel this need to control my life, and I'm not letting it happen. I love you, Rachel. Do you hear me?"

She stared at him, afraid to believe what he was saying.

"I love you," he repeated, "and furthermore, I don't give a damn what my parents think about it. The minute they meet you, they'll love you, too, and if they don't, then it's their loss. I won't allow them to come between us."

She wanted to trust in the depth of their feelings, but while he might be sure of how he felt right now, at some point that could all change. "Nate, please don't. It'd be best all the way round if we just ended this."

"No way! You aren't doing this to me again. You've *got* to *believe* in us, Rach."

She did, and yet she was afraid.

He drew her into his arms, and his hold on her tightened as she struggled with her resolve. "You can't let every little roadblock dissuade you," he whispered.

That was true but…

"Are you so willing to give up on us? Do I mean so little to you?" Already Rachel felt herself weakening. Nate was right; she needed to be determined, especially where his family was concerned. She had to accept the strength of their love. She had to believe.

Twenty-Four

On the last Saturday of May, Charlotte and Ben decided to visit the Farmers' Market at the Cedar Cove waterfront. She loved the displays of flowers and baked goods, plus the various crafts. And she always made a point of visiting the animal shelter's booth, where Grace often volunteered. It was still too early for much fresh produce but the market did a thriving business, nonetheless.

Although the day was overcast, Charlotte chose to be optimistic and suggested they walk. Being a good sport, Ben agreed.

"Look," Charlotte said as soon as they entered the market. "There's fresh rhubarb this week." Her own garden had once yielded an abundant supply. She hurried forward to buy half a dozen stalks.

"I don't suppose I've mentioned that rhubarb pie's

my absolute favorite," Ben said as he took the sack from the vendor.

"I thought peach pie was your favorite," Charlotte teased.

Her husband recovered quickly. "Peach pie is indeed my favorite—in August. My favorite pie changes seasonally, sort of like those flags you hang out on the porch and have me switch around according to the months." The current flag celebrated spring.

"Ah, that explains it," Charlotte said, holding back a smile as she hooked her arm through Ben's. What she appreciated most about him was his gratitude for the little things she did—and, of course, everything he did for her. He seemed to genuinely enjoy her company and, while they didn't live in each other's hip pockets, he often accompanied her on outings. Grocery shopping was a good example. Ben seemed to actually like driving her around town, and she was grateful not to have to do it herself. He loved her children and grandchildren, too.

Recently he'd been in contact with his ex-daughter-in law, David's first wife and the mother of a little girl. Ben didn't want to lose touch with his granddaughter and had taken to calling her every week.

"I thought we'd pick up some fresh clams for dinner," Charlotte said. "What do you think?"

"Anything you do with clams is bound to be delicious," Ben commented.

As they waited their turn at the popular fishmonger's, Cliff Harding came up beside them.

"Why, Cliff," Charlotte said delightedly. She'd met Cliff five years earlier through his grandfather, Tom Harding, better known as the Yodeling Cowboy of 1930s and 40s movie fame. These days Cliff was considered almost family. Now that he was married to Grace, Olivia's lifelong friend, Charlotte felt a special closeness to him.

"You're looking well," Charlotte said, accepting his hug. "Married life seems to agree with you."

Cliff grinned a bit sheepishly. "A man could easily get accustomed to having a wife."

"Couldn't have said it better myself," Ben murmured.

"Is Grace still at the shelter booth?" Charlotte asked, glancing around.

Cliff nodded toward the far corner of the market. "Yup. She's trying to get a couple more of those kittens adopted out."

"Have you heard from Cal?" Ben asked.

Charlotte was curious, too. Cliff and Grace had had a send-off party for him before he went to Wyoming. It had been a lovely evening complete with a barbecue and buffet. Charlotte was furious about the slaughter of those horses, and she felt grateful that Cliff and Cal cared enough to take action. She'd made a healthy contribution to one of the adoption facilities. Because of Grace, the local animal shelter had heard about the plight of the mustangs, too, and collected several hundred dollars' worth of donations.

"Cal keeps in touch as often as he can. He's linked up with a rancher in the area, and there's lots of interest from folks here in Cedar Cove. Vicki Newman, the vet, has decided to volunteer, too. Some of these mustangs are in dire need of medical attention. She has a new partner, who agreed Vicki should go, so she's meeting Cal there."

"That's great. When do you expect him back?" Charlotte knew Linnette McAfee missed Cal terribly. Corrie, her mom, had mentioned it when Charlotte had seen her and Peggy Belden at lunch recently.

"I can't say for sure," Cliff told her. "He checks in whenever he can, but apparently he's in an area that doesn't get good cell phone reception. Sometimes I don't hear from him for three or four days."

"Well, I for one think what you're doing is a great thing," Ben said heartily.

Charlotte nodded. "I know Cal's the one who's actually out there in the wild west, but you're just as involved, Cliff, since you're paying him and he's using your horse trailer *and* you're going to adopt some of those mustangs. I'm proud of you, Cliff."

By the time they'd finished chatting, and purchased the fresh clams, rain had started to fall. "We'd better head home before we get soaked," Ben told her when Cliff had hurried off.

The walk up the hill from the waterfront left

Charlotte a bit breathless. "I think I'll heat up some tomato soup for lunch," she said as they neared the house.

"With toasted cheese sandwiches?" Ben asked.

"If you like."

The gentle pressure from his arm around her waist said it was exactly what he'd like. This man loved a good meal and so, for that matter, did she.

Harry, her guard cat, was waiting impatiently when they returned to the house. He peered out from the safety of the doorway and promptly went back to his spot on top of the sofa, where he curled up and resumed his sleep.

After unpacking their purchases and drying off, Charlotte put the leftover soup on the stove and got out bread for sandwiches. When the doorbell rang, she let Ben answer it. Curious, she stuck her head around the kitchen door a moment later to see who'd decided to visit at lunchtime.

Ben's son, David, stood on the porch.

"David!" she burst out before she could stop herself.

Her husband hesitated, then invited him in.

"This is unexpected," Ben said, and if David didn't notice Ben's lack of welcome, Charlotte did.

"You're just in time for lunch." Charlotte felt obliged to include him. "I have homemade tomato basil soup and toasted cheddar cheese sandwiches."

"I'm sure my son has other plans," Ben said, his voice unemotional.

David, impeccably dressed as always, looked uncertain. "I can stay," he said, "but I don't want to intrude."

"Of course you're not intruding! Now what brings you to Cedar Cove?" Charlotte asked, joining her husband.

David seemed surprised by the question. "I came to visit you. I was in Seattle on business, and it's been several months since we saw each other. I felt I should at least make an effort to visit my own father."

"What a good idea," Charlotte said, leading him to the sofa. "Lunch will be ready in a few minutes."

"Thank you, Charlotte." He sent her a smile. David Rhodes was an attractive man, but unfortunately she'd discovered that he wasn't to be trusted. It was a sad reality they had to come to terms with. Still, he was Ben's son and as such, was welcome in her home.

Remaining stoic and unemotional, Ben sat down opposite his son. "I appreciate the check, David," he said after an awkward silence. He leaned back in his chair, crossing his arms. "However, it bounced."

David's eyes flew open as though in shock. "Oh, my goodness, Dad, I'm really sorry. I had no idea. Why didn't you say anything?"

Charlotte wanted to stay and listen, but she dared not or their lunch would be ruined. As quickly as she could, she ladled out three bowls of soup and cut up the sandwiches, then arranged peanut butter cookies on a plate.

"Lunch is ready," she announced, carrying two soup bowls into the dining room.

Ben came to help her, but not David, who eagerly took his seat at the table. Charlotte returned for the platter of sandwiches, and Ben followed with the third soup bowl and the cookies.

David immediately started his meal until his father stopped him. "We say grace before we eat."

Somewhat embarrassed, David set his spoon aside and bowed his head while his father said a few simple words of thanksgiving. David then had the good sense to wait until Charlotte reached for her spoon before he took up his own. She did so want to think well of Ben's son and could see that he was trying.

"I'll write you another check," David insisted after he'd finished his soup, on which he'd complimented Charlotte any number of times.

Ben didn't encourage him, nor did he refuse his son's offer.

"You're staying in Seattle, David?" she asked, making conversation.

He nodded. "I'm at a hotel downtown."

"How long will you be there?" Charlotte asked next, wanting to cover the uncomfortable silence.

"I leave tomorrow. Say," David said, "on my way into town, I drove past the waterfront. What happened to The Lighthouse restaurant? It's gone."

"It was destroyed by a fire," Ben responded, "that seems to have been set by an arsonist."

David's brows shot up and he leaned forward. "Here in Cedar Cove? That's hard to believe."

"It was terribly shocking," Charlotte agreed. "Poor Justine and Seth have been beside themselves. Until everything's settled, Justine is working part-time at the bank and Seth has taken a sales job."

"What about the fire? Is there a suspect?"

Ben exhaled slowly, as though loath to discuss the subject. "A high-school boy appears to be responsible. The sheriff has called Anson Butler a 'person of interest.' The boy hasn't been seen since the fire and apparently Seth let him go shortly beforehand."

"Everyone in town is heartbroken for Seth and Justine," Charlotte said. "But I'm sure they'll rebuild soon."

"I feel bad for them," David said, sounding sincere. "I hope everything works out for your granddaughter, Charlotte."

She was touched by his words and thanked David. "A cookie?" she asked, passing him the plate.

David took two.

Before he left, he wrote his father another check. "I couldn't be more embarrassed, Dad," he said. "You shouldn't have any problem with this one." He shifted his eyes from Ben to Charlotte, then stared at the floor. "You might want to wait until the first of the month, though, if that's not inconvenient."

Again Ben didn't comment. He accepted the check, nodded his head at David's request and walked his son to the door.

"Next time, let us know when you plan to stop by," Charlotte chastised him gently. "That way I can make you a real dinner."

"Thank you, Charlotte," David said, kissing her cheek. "Next visit, I'll give you plenty of notice."

Charlotte and Ben stood out on the porch with him. It was cool, and the drizzle continued. Ben put his arm around her shoulders.

"Come and see us again soon," she said as David ran to his car. She waited until he'd started the engine and driven off before she went back inside, Ben at her heels.

"It was good of David to stop by," she commented, watching her husband closely.

"Like you said, David should've let us know he was coming," Ben murmured. He helped her clear the table. "Frankly, it would've suited me just fine if he hadn't bothered."

"Ben! That's a terrible thing to say about your own son."

Her husband shook his head. "I know David." With that, he reached for the check his son had given him and tore it in several pieces. "This is as worthless as the first one he wrote." Ben's eyes filled with pain as he crumpled the scraps and dropped them in the garbage.

Charlotte walked over to him and slipped her arms around his neck. "I'm sorry about this," she whispered, wishing she knew how to ease the ache in his heart.

"So am I," Ben said, holding her close. "So am I."

Twenty-Five

The morning before the senior prom, Allison drove into Silverdale to pick up her dress. She'd dreamed that Anson would be her date on prom night. That wasn't possible, but rather than stay home feeling depressed, she was attending with her friend Kaci. Her parents didn't understand why she'd refused to go with any of the three boys who'd invited her, and Allison knew her mother was disappointed on her behalf.

Her cell phone rang as she walked through the mall to the parking lot, the dress draped over her arm. She'd purchased the cell with her own funds, hoping against hope to get the number to Anson so they could talk privately. So far, there hadn't been any opportunity. He hadn't phoned her again and his mother had no way of getting in touch with him, either.

"Hello," she said as she walked toward her mother's car, expecting to hear Kaci's voice.

"Allison?"

She stopped cold. It was Anson.

"Can you talk?"

"Yes," she said, hardly able to believe it. Despite her fears, her heart did a little jig of happiness. She had so much to tell him, so much she wanted to ask.

"Are you alone?"

"Yes," she said. "I'm in the parking lot outside the Silverdale Mall."

"Good."

Before he told her anything else, she had to warn him. "Don't tell me where you are. All right? I'd have to tell the sheriff, so it's better that I not know. You aren't on a phone that can be traced, are you?"

"No."

"Thank goodness." She breathed easier. "How did you get my number?" she asked. His call seemed like the answer to a prayer, the granting of a wish, but she didn't think it was the result of either divine intervention or fairy-tale magic.

"I'll explain in a minute. There's something I have to say first."

"What?"

"You're probably going to the prom tomorrow night," he said, "and I *want* you to go. It's important to me that you do. I don't want you sitting home alone because of me. If you think you're being loyal to me by staying away, then don't."

Her throat hurt as she held back tears, and she found it hard to swallow, hard to speak. She was moved beyond words that he cared about her…that he'd even remembered the dance. "I'm going with Kaci," she finally said. Because of all the traffic noise outside the mall, she unlocked the car and sat in the driver's seat. She tossed her dress on the empty space beside her.

"But Allison…"

"You're my date, Anson. I can't imagine dancing at the prom with anyone but you." Closing her eyes, she could almost feel his arms around her.

"I'd give anything to be there with you," he whispered.

Her heart felt like it was about to break. "How did you get my number?" she asked again, trying to maintain some semblance of control.

"Eddie. I had a friend phone the house pretending to be a guy from school and Eddie answered and gave him the number of your cell."

"Now that I have my own phone, can you talk more often?" She had so many questions. Although she was desperate to ask about the pewter cross found in the fire, she was also afraid of what he might tell her. All she needed now, she decided, was the sound of his voice. The questions could wait.

"I'm not sure it's a good idea for me to call you," he said.

"Please! I have to know you're all right."

"I'm okay. There's nothing to worry about."

"I do worry, Anson." She wanted him to come back to Cedar Cove, and yet she was terrified of what might happen when—if—he did. A part of her yearned to tell him to stay hidden, otherwise he might end up in jail. At the same time, she longed for his name to be cleared. Only she wasn't convinced anymore that was possible....

"What can you tell me about The Lighthouse?" he asked. "Is there any news? Has anyone been arrested?"

Allison closed her eyes again, fearing this very subject. She hesitated.

"Allison?"

"Your cross was found in the ashes. It'd partially melted and there was a picture of it in the *Chronicle*."

He muttered something best not repeated.

"You were there that night, weren't you?" Asking him this required all the courage she could muster. Her hand was trembling and damp with perspiration as she clutched the phone.

"Yes," he said, "but I swear to you, Allison, I didn't set the fire. I did everything I could to put it out. I realized I'd lost my cross, but I didn't know where.

Tell the sheriff to check the fire extinguisher. My fingerprints should be all over it."

"I'll tell him," she said, eager to do anything that would help prove his innocence.

"Have you lost faith in me, Allison?" Before she could answer, he continued. "I swear to you I had nothing to do with the fire."

"Who else could have done it?" she asked rather than admit her faith had been shaken.

"I saw him." Anson's voice was so low she could hardly hear it.

"What?" she said breathlessly. "Who?"

"I can't tell you."

"Why not?" she nearly shouted. She wasn't stupid and she wasn't going to let him lie to her, either.

"I don't know his name," Anson groaned, his frustration evident. "I've seen him before, but I don't know who he is. He ate at the restaurant. But I only saw him one time and then again the night of the fire. I swear that's the truth. I shouldn't have told you this much… I don't want to involve you any more than I already have."

"But Anson, I—"

"All I'm asking," he said, cutting her off, "all I want from you is to believe me. If you can't do that, there's nothing more for me to say…."

"Don't hang up," she cried.

She heard the drone of silence and tears welled up in her eyes.

"Anson?"

"I'm here. I should go," he said.

"No, please." She felt like she was grasping at wind.

"I can't talk anymore."

"I went to see your mother," she rushed to tell him. "I understand now what you meant when you came to me that night. You said it was better if I didn't know what you'd done. You meant the money you stole, didn't you?" She could only hope that was all he'd meant.

"I took that money from my mother," Anson admitted. "I'm not proud of it and I'll pay back every penny. I promised I would and I will."

"She let me read your letter," Allison told him, "and I told her about your phone call."

"Did Cherry tell you about the fires I started as a kid, too?" he asked.

Allison heard gruff voices in the background. She couldn't decipher what was being said, but it was clear that Anson needed to get off the phone.

"Yes, she told me."

"No wonder you don't believe me," he said. "Listen. I *didn't* nearly burn the house down when I was a kid. My mother was drinking and she left a cigarette burning. She blamed me, but it was her fault. The other incident wasn't me, either. It was another kid from the neighborhood. I know this looks bad, Allison, but I swear I wasn't responsible for the fire at The Lighthouse."

"I *want* to believe you. With all my heart, Anson."

"Thank you," he whispered and then, before she was ready, he disconnected.

Allison's hand tightened around her phone and she held on for a long moment, trying to maintain the sense of closeness they'd shared.

Anson had told her far more than he had in his previous call or the night of the fire, and it gave her hope that he was telling the truth.

As she drove back to Cedar Cove, Allison's thoughts whirled in a hundred different directions. On impulse, she stopped at the First National Bank. The last time she'd made a deposit, Allison had seen Justine Gunderson there.

Ms. Gunderson was talking with a client at her desk when she entered the bank. Allison sat in the waiting area until Justine was free. During that time, Allison changed her mind twice before she found the courage to approach the owner of the burned-out restaurant.

"Can I help you?" Ms. Gunderson asked pleasantly as Allison walked toward her.

Her knees felt weak, and Allison sat down in the chair opposite Justine. "I'm Allison Cox," she said. Because she felt it was important to maintain a businesslike facade, she extended her hand across the desk.

Justine shook it and seemed to take her seriously, which reassured Allison. "I don't know if you remember me," she said. They'd met at The Lighthouse and at a party held by her parents a couple of Christmases ago.

She waited, but Ms. Gunderson gave no indication that she did.

"I'm Zach Cox's daughter—and Anson Butler's girlfriend," she said in as straightforward a manner as she could.

Justine's eyes flickered with recognition.

"I talked to Anson today. A little more than thirty minutes ago."

Justine leaned forward, her elbows on the desk. When she spoke, her voice was low and tense. "Does Anson know the sheriff wants to talk to him regarding the fire?" she asked in a conspiratorial whisper.

"Anson knows."

"Is there a reason he won't talk to the authorities?"

Allison wasn't sure how to answer that. "I want him to come back to Cedar Cove more than anything."

"My husband and I realize he was upset after we laid him off."

Allison had never seen Anson more distressed than the day last autumn when he'd found her in the mall. He'd been so negative, convinced the world was against him. Convinced that nothing he said or did would ever be good enough.

"He was so hurt and angry when he lost his job. He didn't take that money, Ms. Gunderson. I *know* that. He'd tried really hard to do everything right—and then to be falsely accused… You can't imagine what it did to him."

Justine sighed. "My husband felt bad about the way he handled the situation. We'd never had anything like that come up before. Seth liked Anson. In fact, he'd recently made him a prep cook."

— Allison nodded vigorously. "Anson thought he was making progress and that he'd be able to pay off the shed and—"

"The shed?" she asked.

Allison lowered her eyes. "He was making restitution for the fire in the city park."

Ms. Gunderson went very quiet. "I'd forgotten about that," she said after a moment. She pressed her fingertips to her forehead. "I've tried to put as much of this behind me as I can. As you might've guessed, this whole episode has been devastating for Seth and me."

"Your husband knew about Anson's past. My father talked to him about it and Mr. Gunderson agreed to give him this job."

"You believe in your friend, don't you?" Justine said gently.

"Yes!" She wanted to defend Anson, explain that he was a good and honest person and how intelligent he was. None of that made any difference, though, unless there was evidence exonerating him.

"If he's truly innocent, then your friend'll return of his own free will and answer the sheriff's questions."

"I'll talk to him about it," Allison said. The next time Anson phoned, she'd make sure he understood how important it was to contact the authorities if he hoped to clear his name. Otherwise, this fire would hang over his head for the rest of his life. Otherwise, the entire town would lay the blame at his feet. His reputation had cast a shadow of doubt over him, and his disappearance only reinforced people's suspicions. Refusing to step forward hindered his chances.

It hindered *their* chances.

Twenty-Six

Linnette was waiting for her sister at the high-school track. Gloria had finally convinced her to try running, which she claimed kept her in good shape and allowed her to pass the police department's regular fitness tests.

Gloria was supposed to join her when her shift ended. Together they'd do a lazy mile, she'd said. Then, in a few weeks, after Linnette had built up her endurance, they'd run farther. Gloria had made it sound like fun and as a physician assistant, Linnette often advised patients on the health benefits of exercise. The least she could do was practice what she preached. Besides, seeing her fit and firm would be a nice surprise for Cal when he returned.

Gloria was only a few minutes behind her; she pulled into the lot and parked next to Linnette.

"Hey, you look great," Gloria said as she stepped out of her car.

Linnette did a full turn so her sister could get a complete view of her jogging suit. "I should. This running outfit cost me over a hundred bucks."

Gloria rolled her eyes. "You don't need designer clothes to run—an old pair of jeans and a T-shirt would've worked fine."

"Not for me. I figure that if I'm going to sweat, I want to look as good as I can while I'm doing it."

Shaking her head, Gloria led the way. It was late enough that the school had finished with the track, which was now open to the public. Several other runners circled it; a few more walked.

"Chad asked me to send his greetings," Linnette said, watching for her sister's reaction. Gloria didn't give any indication that she cared. "Hey, that's quite the poker face," she teased.

"What?"

"I mentioned Chad's name and you didn't even raise an eyebrow. When are you going to admit you're as interested in him as he is in you?"

"Do you want to run or not?" Gloria asked, ignoring the question.

"Run, of course." She was looking forward to some brisk exercise and, in the process, spending time with her sister. All they seemed to do when they got together was go out for meals, which defeated her goal of getting into shape. Gloria was the one who'd suggested they start running and Linnette had happily agreed.

Gloria demonstrated a few warm-up exercises.

Linnette carefully followed her instructions. "Hey, this is great. I feel better already."

"We aren't running yet."

Linnette jumped up and down a few times, showing her sister that she had plenty of energy in reserve. "Lead on and don't hold back on my account," she said, gesturing dramatically at the track.

"We'll start off nice and easy," Gloria told her. "I wouldn't want to kill my sister, the health care professional."

"It's nice to have a sister, isn't it?" Linnette murmured, basking in the glow of first finding a friend and then learning that friend was also her sister.

"I agree—a sister is a good thing," Gloria said with a smile.

They took off down the track, and to Linnette's surprise it wasn't bad. She could breathe almost normally. But by the end of the first lap, her breathing had grown heavier and her speed had decreased. "How many laps in a mile again?"

"Four."

Gloria had to be kidding. Each time around felt that far. "That was a joke, right?"

"You're already a quarter there." Gloria cast her a knowing look.

This wasn't welcome news. Her lungs ached, and her legs didn't want to cooperate. She felt suddenly depressed to realize she still had three laps to go before she was finished. Besides, in addition to her aches and pains, she noticed that perspiration was running freely down her face. "Maybe you were right about starting off slow and easy," Linnette managed, although it stung her pride to suggest she wasn't up to the challenge.

"We're practically walking now," Gloria said. "Why don't we talk—that'll distract you."

"What do you want to talk about? Chad?" Linnette asked.

Once again, Gloria ignored the mention of his name. "What do you hear from Cal?"

"Not much. I talked to him this weekend. He was in a honky-tonk bar, if the background music was any indication." Linnette frowned at the memory. She might not know much about mustangs, but even as a greenhorn she was bright enough to recognize that there weren't a lot of wild horses hanging around in bars. Rethinking the conversation, she recalled a number of other things that had bothered her. "While we were talking, Cal began to stutter again. That tells me he's tense or nervous about something."

"Maybe he just needs to get back to the speech therapist."

"Maybe." Still, Linnette didn't think that was the problem. There was something on his mind he wasn't telling her. They hardly talked anymore. When he phoned, it felt more like the fulfilling of an obligation than any desire to talk to her. A recent article in the *Cedar Cove Chronicle* stated that local veterinarian Vicki Newman had joined Cal. She remembered their meeting at the ranch earlier and the odd sensation that had come over her when she saw Cal talking to Vicki. She'd felt threatened, and she couldn't figure out exactly why. Vicki was so…ordinary. Linnette hated to say it, but the veterinarian, with her sharp facial features, lank hair and mannish build, was downright unattractive. She seemed nice enough, Linnette supposed. But Cal hadn't told her Vicki was going to Wyoming, too, and that worried her.

During their last call, Linnette had told him how much it dismayed her, but Cal hadn't responded. Instead, he'd changed the subject.

They never argued. Cal would walk away from a disagreement rather than talk about it rationally. It didn't help, she told herself, that he had a difficult time controlling his speech when he was upset, which only made him more disinclined to discuss problems.

"What about you and Chad?" Linnette asked again, rather than focus on her own relationship. "You talk about Chad and I'll discuss Cal."

"There's nothing to talk about."

"Why aren't you going out with him?" Linnette didn't understand it.

Gloria shrugged. "Should I be?"

"No, I guess not," Linnette said reluctantly. And yet the two of them looked at no one else whenever they were together.

"If anyone *isn't* interested in Chad, it's me," Linnette said on the off-chance Gloria was denying her feelings out of misplaced loyalty to her.

"Then why are we discussing him?"

"Because I know how he feels about you."

Gloria increased her pace, and Linnette had to struggle to keep up. "Hey, slow down, would you?"

"Not if you want to talk about Chad."

Linnette frowned, blinking as the sweat slid down her face. "Am I missing something here?"

"No." Gloria's response was much too quick.

Linnette was nearly panting in her effort to keep pace with her sister, who seemed to be trying to break a world speed record. "Maybe it'd be best if we didn't talk," she suggested, breathing heavily.

"Maybe," Gloria agreed and immediately slowed to a kinder pace.

"This was supposed to be a *lazy* mile," Linnette reminded her.

Round two was completed, and two more remained. It would be a miracle if she managed four full laps.

"A lazy mile doesn't mean we're going to crawl," Gloria snapped.

"You've had more practice at this than I have." Linnette tried not to sound apologetic.

"I thought we weren't going to talk."

"I *have* to talk." Linnette couldn't stop, much as she'd prefer to. If she did, then all she'd think about was how much her body didn't want to do this. Her calf muscles were about to spasm. Her face burned, her stomach had begun to churn with nausea. "How often do you come out here?" she asked.

"Every day. I run between three and five miles."

Linnette groaned. "You just said that to make me feel bad, didn't you?"

Gloria laughed, raced ahead, then spun around and ran backward, facing Linnette. "Hey, are we having our first sisterly disagreement?"

If she'd had the energy, Linnette would've laughed, too. "Yeah, I think we are." Seeing that she was holding Gloria up, she gestured for her to run on. "Leave me," she panted. "I'll walk these last two laps."

"You sure?"

"Go, before I require resuscitation."

Gloria grinned and took off at a speed that would've caused Linnette to have a cardiac arrest. As she'd promised, she continued walking, astonished at Gloria who literally ran circles around her. Actually, now that she was moving at a relaxed speed, Linnette found she didn't object to exercising.

Without Gloria there to distract her, though, her mind was free to roam. But the subject in the forefront of her thoughts was an uncomfortable one.

Cal.

While his mission was undeniably noble, he'd seemed too eager to get away from Cedar Cove—away from her. Her brother, Mack, had warned her that she was suffocating him. At the time, Linnette hadn't been willing to listen, but now she felt she had to give his words some heed.

When she rounded the last curve, Linnette was surprised to see Chad standing outside the fence, watching them. When he looked in her direction, she waved. He returned her greeting, but his gaze immediately went to Gloria. In that brief moment, Linnette saw such longing in his eyes that it took her aback.

She didn't know what to think. Was it possible they were already involved? Yet that didn't make sense. Chad would've mentioned it, she was sure, since they worked together every day.

Gloria was certainly closemouthed, but Linnette resolved to mind her own business from now on. She couldn't figure out what was happening in her own relationship, so she hardly felt qualified to diagnose the problems between Gloria and Chad.

After the evening meal at Lonny Ellison's Wyoming ranch, where they were staying as guests, Cal found Vicki outside, standing at the corral. He hesitated before joining her. They'd been working together twelve and fifteen hours a day for two weeks now. His new feelings had crept up on him unawares.

She'd been around Cliff's ranch from the time he'd hired on, and they'd always been friendly but nothing more. He wasn't sure when it'd happened, but Vicki had become someone who mattered to him. Maybe it had started the week he left, when they'd met to make plans for this trip....

Vicki ignored him and rested her arms on the top rung. She stared straight ahead as several of the mustangs dashed around inside the pen, snorting at their unaccustomed boundaries, kicking up dust and generally letting their displeasure be known.

"It was a mistake for me to come to Wyoming," she said without looking at him.

Cal couldn't let her think that. "No. You've been a real asset." He began to remind her of everything she'd done for the mustangs, but she stopped him.

"It was a mistake for other reasons," she said. "I'm sorry, Cal."

She still hadn't looked at him.

He swallowed hard. He refused to believe that she shouldn't be there—or that she was sorry. Although he'd been careful to avoid touching her, he couldn't keep from doing so now. He placed his hand on her shoulder and watched as her eyes drifted shut, as if she, too, was fighting their strong physical attraction. "I didn't mean for this to happen," he whispered.

"I'm going to turn in for the night," she said.

"Don't," he pleaded. "Not yet." He moved closer, stroking her hair with his other hand.

"You don't understand!" she said, breaking free.

"Understand what?" Despite the desire to pull her back into his arms, he let her step out of his embrace. "What?" he pressed.

She held his gaze until her own eyes filled with tears. "You really don't know, do you?"

He frowned. "Know what?"

"Oh, Cal, how could you be so blind? I've been in love with you for two years!"

She couldn't have shocked him more if she'd poked him with a cattle prod. His mouth fell open, but he couldn't speak for at least a minute. He just gawked at her.

"You never let on," he said numbly.

"How could I?" she asked, jerking her hand across her face, smearing the tears. "I...I didn't know how, and then you started seeing Linnette and she's so lovely and I'm—well, I'm not. Why do you think I didn't want to go on this trip at first?"

Cal hated to appear dense, but apparently he was exactly that. "I—thought it had s-something to do with your office."

"I only said that because I was afraid I wouldn't be able to hide my feelings, and now look what's happened."

"What's happened," Cal said, exhaling sharply, "is that I've fallen in love with you, too."

He had no idea how Vicki would accept this news; however, he didn't expect her to lash out with her fist and clobber him in the chest. "Don't you *dare* say that to me, Cal Washburn! Don't you dare!" She punctuated each word with another solid punch.

"Ouch." Cal backed away and rubbed his chest, confounded by the vehemence of her attack. "Ow, dammit. What did you do that for?"

"Don't you touch me again, either."

"I thought—I hoped you shared my f-feelings."

"I do," she muttered, "but that doesn't change the fact that Linnette's in Cedar Cove patiently waiting for your return. What about *her*? She loves you, too."

Cal felt the color drain from his face. Vicki was right. He had no business declaring his feelings or kissing her until he'd resolved the situation with Linnette. The problem was, he had no idea how to do that.

Twenty-Seven

Memorial Day, Cecilia got up early, even before Aaron woke her for his feeding. Not wanting to disturb Ian, she got quietly out of bed and pulled on her robe. Then she tiptoed into the kitchen to make a pot of coffee. The clock on the microwave told her it was barely five. Nevertheless she was wide awake.

A quick check on the baby assured her that Aaron was sound asleep. Taking these few moments to herself, savoring the silence, Cecilia poured a mug of coffee and sat in her favorite chair in the living room. She was happy, she realized, truly content with her life. Memorial Day was a little less sad this year, mostly because she had Aaron. For the past few years, she'd visited the cemetery on this holiday, so it had come to remind her of the most profound loss she'd ever experienced—the death of her daughter, Allison.

All this time, her arms and her heart had ached for the baby she'd held so briefly. Her son would never *replace* Allison, but she loved him just as much. Her grief no longer seemed as raw, as overwhelming.

A year ago on Memorial Day, when Cecilia was still pregnant with Aaron, and Ian had been at sea, she'd driven out to the cemetery and placed flowers on Allison's gravesite. The loss of her little girl still affected her, and Ian, too, although he wasn't as willing to discuss the subject as she was. Every now and then in the middle of the night, he'd reach for her and they'd talk about Allison. She could never doubt Ian's love for the daughter he'd never seen or held.

"Cecilia?" Ian said groggily. He stood in the hall doorway wearing his pajama bottoms. "What are you doing up so early?"

"I was awake and it's such a lovely morning, I decided to get up." She was hoping to do a bit of yard work later, after they'd been out to the cemetery. She'd started tending the garden and hoped to coax Grace's rosebushes and perennials back to vibrant life. She longed to show the Hardings how well she and Ian were caring for the house and yard.

"It's only about five," Ian said.

"I know. Why don't you go back to bed?" She had plans for him later and didn't want him telling her he was too tired.

"Are you all right?" he asked, sounding worried.

"Yes," she told him.

He didn't look as if he believed her.

"Ian," she said, smiling softly. "I couldn't be happier. I love you and our babies so much, and Aaron is healthy and thriving. We live in a lovely home. My life's never been better."

"Babies," Ian repeated carefully.

"Yes, babies." Allison would always live in Cecilia's heart, would always be her daughter.

"So we're going to the cemetery today," he said.

Cecilia had already purchased a small bouquet of flowers. She nodded. "I have every year. I couldn't imagine not going."

"Me, neither," Ian concurred sadly. He yawned and turned away, then walked into the room with slow, measured steps. To her surprise, he sat down on the nearby ottoman, his shoulders slumped.

Cecilia leaned forward and placed her hand on his bare back, pressing a kiss to his shoulder. He didn't say anything for a long time. Long enough for her to recognize that he had something on his mind. Something that weighed on him.

"Ian?" she said. "What's wrong?"

He didn't answer; instead, he stared down at the floor.

"Ian?"

"I've been transferred."

The words hung in the air. Ian *transferred?*

Cecilia swallowed hard, trying to make sense of what he was telling her. Ian had been stationed at the same base for nearly six years, two more years than the usual four-year assignment. Those two extra years could be attributed to the fact that he'd moved from a submarine to an aircraft carrier.

After Allison's death, the navy had given him a new duty assignment. Because Ian had been under the polar ice cap at the time of Allison's birth, he hadn't even known until his return that his daughter had been born, had died and already been buried. He'd suffered severe emotional trauma as a result.

"We have to move?" Cecilia asked, choking off an automatic protest. The day they'd come to view the house, Ian had said they couldn't sign a full year's lease. He'd said there was a rumor they might be transferred. Cecilia had known it was a possibility, only she'd convinced herself it wouldn't really happen.

Ian had told her when they were first married that the navy might require frequent moves. But Cedar Cove was their *home*. It was where they'd met, where they'd fallen in love and married, and where they—

No. Bile rose in the back of her throat. Their daughter was buried here. A transfer meant they'd be leaving Allison behind.

"I put off telling you as long as I could," he mumbled. "I was afraid one of the other wives would say something, and I didn't want you hearing this from anyone else. The *George Washington's* new home base is San Diego."

"Just like that, we have to pack up and leave?" she said in a small voice.

He nodded. "I'm sorry, Cecilia." He shrugged helplessly. "There's nothing I can do."

"What about Allison? Who'll visit her grave? Who'll make sure it's properly taken care of if we're not here?" Fears and denials crowded her mind but she quickly swallowed a cry of alarm. This had to be hard on Ian, too, and her dissolving into tears wouldn't change anything.

"I don't know what to tell you. All I can say is that the navy's sending us to another duty station. When I signed my name on the enlistment agreement, I knew this was bound to happen sooner or later. You knew it, too."

Cecilia did. Two weeks ago, her closest friend, Cathy Lackey, had revealed that her husband had received transfer papers that would send the small family to Scotland. Cecilia and Cathy had shed a lot of tears, but they'd vowed to keep in touch through e-mail and letters. Cecilia was determined to hold on to that precious friendship.

"What about the house?" she asked next. They'd only just settled in; the packing boxes were still in the garage. Cecilia loved this house, and so did Ian. "I thought we might own it one day."

"I know." Her husband sounded as miserable as

she felt. "We are on a month-to-month agreement, though. I've already spoken to Mrs. Harding. She was disappointed, too, but she understood."

Cecilia hardly knew what to say. She'd be walking away from the friends she'd made, the daughter she'd buried, the job she enjoyed and the teenage girl she'd befriended. Everything—her whole life—was here in Cedar Cove.

"You'll like San Diego," Ian said gamely.

"I'm sure I will," she murmured with no particular enthusiasm.

When Ian spoke again, his voice was void of emotion. "I've been doing a lot of thinking, and I know how much you love it here." He paused. "If you wanted, you could stay," he suggested with obvious reluctance. "I could make the commute for a while. I'm at sea for six months—and, well, there are ways around this if you don't feel you can uproot your life and leave Allison."

"Oh, Ian." That would be disastrous for their marriage. She needed to be with her husband, regardless of where he was assigned. They were a family.

"Is that what you'd like to do?" he asked, his eyes intense and sad as he studied her.

"I hate leaving Cedar Cove," she said softly, rubbing her hand down his bare back. "But Ian, don't you see? I could never live apart from you." She managed a shaky laugh. "At least, not any more than the navy already requires."

He brought his arms around her then, and they clung to each other. Words weren't necessary. He wanted her and Aaron with him, and yet he'd been willing to compromise, to give her what he felt would make her happy.

"I love you so much," he whispered. "You have no idea how much I dreaded telling you this."

She hadn't made it easy, Cecilia realized. Every day she'd been full of joy about the house and working hard to make it comfortable and welcoming.

"We can start packing this afternoon," she said, tears spilling from her eyes.

"We'll go visit Allison first."

Yes, and while she was there, Cecilia would tell her baby girl goodbye.

Twenty-Eight

Justine glanced at her watch, surprised it was almost noon. With a staff meeting and back-to-back appointments, the morning had gotten away from her. She grabbed her purse and hurried out from behind her desk. She should've left ten minutes ago. She was meeting Seth and their insurance agent at The Lighthouse, or rather where The Lighthouse used to be. The site had been cleared now, and decisions needed to be made.

As Justine headed out, she nearly collided with Warren Saget, who was just entering the bank.

"Justine," he said catching her by the shoulders. "I almost bowled you over."

"Warren," she said, nearly breathless. "Oh, my goodness, I'm sorry. I'm in a rush—I'm supposed to meet Seth and our insurance agent."

"Oh." His face fell, his disappointment obvious. "I was hoping to convince you to have lunch with me."

"I can't," she told him. "I have to run. I'm already late."

"Will the meeting take long? I could wait."

She didn't want to hurt his feelings, but Seth had asked her not to see Warren again. Her mother had been critical of her, too, for that one lunch meeting. Olivia didn't know the nature of her relationship with Warren, although Seth, of course, did. Warren was impotent, and they'd been friends who'd provided each other with certain mutual benefits, including company in social or business situations.

"I'm going to be at D.D.'s on the Cove," Warren told her as she started backing away from him. "They do marvelous crab cakes. That was your favorite entrée, wasn't it?"

"You go on ahead," she told him, eager to get away. She realized she hadn't explicitly turned him down.

"Meet me if you can," he said.

Justine nodded and, because she was late, decided to drive rather than walk. She rushed across the parking lot where she'd left her car. Seth had been so busy at the boatyard lately that they hadn't had a chance to discuss their plans for the restaurant. She still had mixed feelings about rebuilding. The restaurant was too demanding; it took too much time away from their family life.

Tragic and distressing as the arson had been, she loved the freedom the last few months had given her. Seth was doing so well in sales, and each commission he collected was more than they'd cleared in any single month at the restaurant. In her heart of hearts, she hoped Seth would see that rebuilding The Lighthouse would be too hard on them. At the same time, she understood what he was saying about not wasting all the effort of the last five years. Besides, she had an idea, one she'd come up with during a recent visit at her mother's and briefly discussed with Seth. He seemed to listen but she wasn't convinced that he'd truly grasped her vision.

Seth and Robert Beckman, their insurance agent, were already at the site. Justine parked and hurried across the street to join them. The view of the cove was dramatic and beautiful, part of the reason this was such a valuable piece of real estate.

When she approached Seth and Robert, they were deep in conversation, pausing only to smile at her. Still speaking, her husband put his arm around her waist and brought her close.

"Robert was just saying he's reviewed the architect's plans," he told Justine. "With a fresh start, we can make some necessary changes and update the old floor plan."

Justine unsuccessfully hid her surprise. Construction plans? No one had mentioned any of this to her. "I have a few ideas of my own," she inserted.

"Because of the fire," Seth said, ignoring her comment, "we have the opportunity of a lifetime." He grinned wryly. "Ironic, huh?"

She understood what he meant. They'd purchased the old Captain's Galley restaurant and done extensive renovations before opening and renaming it The Lighthouse. Even with all the money they'd sunk into the business, they were stuck with the original floor plan and kitchen. Rebuilding from the ground up gave them the opportunity to change everything. "What about my idea?" she asked. "What about the tearoom I told you about?"

Seth frowned and went right on speaking. "Robert's saying that in the rebuild, we can add a banquet room, which I'd already discussed with the architect. We can do the things we dreamed of doing. You could make the banquet room a tearoom, too, if that's what you want," he said, in an obvious concession to her. The longer he spoke the more animated he became.

"Not a restaurant like we had before," she said, refusing to let go of the idea. "But a tearoom for women in the area. This has nothing to do with adding a banquet room," she said slowly.

"For women?" Seth repeated. "That wouldn't work. When we rebuild, it'll be a whole new Lighthouse. Can't you just see it?" he asked, smiling down at her. "We'll have the banquet room we've always wanted."

Again and again Seth had bemoaned the fact that

The Lighthouse didn't have an area large enough to hold private banquets. He'd made the most of the space they had. But the restaurant lacked the facilities for wedding receptions and when they'd hosted any big occasions—like the charity auction and her grandmother Charlotte's wedding—they'd been required to close the restaurant.

"You know how badly we need a banquet room," her husband said again, puzzled at her decided lack of enthusiasm.

Justine didn't answer. In talking to Robert about rebuilding—and this was obviously not the first such conversation—Seth made it clear that he hadn't heard a single thing she'd said in the last two and a half months.

"Justine?" Seth studied her, frowning slightly.

Pointedly she looked away from him. "Actually I can see I'm not needed here. You two appear to have everything under control. I was invited to lunch, so if you'll both excuse me I'll join my friend." Before Seth could question her or object, she left. If she hadn't been so angry, Justine would've burst into tears; as it was, she was fighting for her composure.

When she reached her car, she heard hard footsteps coming up behind her. She turned to find Seth.

"What's the matter?" he asked.

"You aren't even listening to me," she said, unable to hide the hurt she felt. "I really think my idea would work, Seth."

"I'm not letting the last five years go down the drain so you can build a *tearoom* for a bunch of bored women. If we're going to rebuild, it needs to be something that involves me, too. I want to make The Lighthouse what it was always meant to be."

"Then you go ahead and do that." Her voice remained calm, belying her anger.

"You think a tearoom's actually going to be some kind of improvement?"

"Yes, I do. Don't you understand, Seth? I've seen more of you these last few months than I have in years. Leif is thriving. He loves having both his parents around for more than an hour a day."

"You're exaggerating."

"Am I, Seth?"

He shook his head, as if he couldn't make sense of what she was telling him. "This is a golden opportunity for us. It's not the time to consider doing something else. We have a chance to start over—"

"Then do it," she broke in, glaring at him. "Just do it. If you want The Lighthouse back so badly, then rebuild." She nearly choked on the words as she whirled around and opened her door.

Seth looked utterly perplexed as she slipped inside her car, thrust the key into the ignition and drove off. In her rearview mirror, she saw him standing at the side of the street, staring after her.

Her hands trembled and she bit her lip hard. She was hurt and angry and wanted to lash out at him.

He objected to her seeing Warren? Well, too bad. Warren was her friend and at the moment he seemed to be a better one than her own husband.

She walked into the foyer at D.D's on the Cove, then scanned the room. Warren sat at a table next to the window, facing the front of the restaurant. When he saw her, he brightened visibly. He stood, and came eagerly toward her.

"Justine," he said meeting her at the entrance. "I hoped you'd come." He kissed her on the cheek and steered her toward his table. Every eye in the room was on them.

This wasn't a small, out-of-the-way café like the place they'd met before. Soon everyone in town would be talking about her and Warren. So be it.

The instant they reached the table, he pulled out her chair with a flourish. Next he got the waitress's attention and asked for a menu. Justine felt a small shock as she recognized Diana, who'd worked as a waitress at The Lighthouse. They exchanged a few stilted words, and Justine hoped Diana wouldn't mention her presence here—with Warren—to anyone who might know her mother. Crazy as it sounded, she worried more about Olivia finding out than Seth. Her husband could not have made it plainer that he didn't care about *her* feelings, so she couldn't see any reason to be too concerned about his.

"Would you like a glass of wine?" Warren asked as she glanced over the menu.

"The way I feel right now, you can order an entire bottle."

Warren's laughter pleased her. "Then I will."

He did, and he didn't spare any expense, either, choosing a sixty-dollar bottle of chardonnay.

Despite her lack of appetite, Justine ordered the crab cakes and a small salad.

"All right," Warren said, leaning toward her. "Tell me what happened."

She waited until her wineglass had been filled. "Oh, Warren. I'm so upset."

"I can tell," he said, immediately solicitous.

"It's Seth. He wants to rebuild the restaurant. I'd talked to him about another idea and he completely ignored me."

He seemed a little surprised himself. "You don't want to rebuild?"

"Not The Lighthouse. Not the way it was." If what her mother had said was true and Warren was trying to get on her good side, hoping to be awarded the construction contract, he'd take her husband's part in this. "For the first time since we opened The Lighthouse," she explained, "Seth and I have time together like a normal couple. Leif is doing so well. The Lighthouse was strangling us, and now that we've been without it, I don't want to return to that kind of life."

"But the restaurant was your livelihood," Warren

said, immediately siding with her husband. "It's only natural that Seth wouldn't want to give up his only source of income."

So, maybe Olivia was right, and Warren did have an agenda. "It *used* to be our livelihood, but Seth went to work for Larry Boone and he's making more money as a salesman than we ever did with the restaurant."

"I see," Warren murmured thoughtfully. "Have you told Seth how you feel?"

"I made my feelings very clear." Had Seth already forgotten the endlessly long hours and the constant struggle to meet their expenses and still make a living?

What hurt most was how matter-of-factly her husband had dismissed her. All he saw was the opportunity to add a banquet room to the redesigned restaurant. He was even willing to put them in a position of taking on more debt.

"I wish things were different," Warren said, his eyes warm and sympathetic.

Well, maybe Olivia wasn't right about Warren's intent, after all. His sympathy seemed real, and it felt good to be with someone who understood her frustration.

Since Seth had started work at the boatyard, he seemed content for the first time since the fire. Not only that, he excelled at sales. Justine had real hope that their lives would finally settle into something resembling normalcy. Then, almost without warning, Seth was back to letting the restaurant obsess him.

"What am I going to do?" she asked, sipping her wine.

"Talk to him," Warren advised.

"I already have, and he isn't listening." Her eyes brimmed with tears and she quickly blinked them away.

"Then do something that'll make him sit up and take notice." Warren gave a low, soft laugh. "You could always move in with me. That would get Seth's attention fast enough."

She choked on her wine. Coughing and sputtering, she said, "You're kidding!"

Warren smiled and reached for her hand. "I wish I was. I can't tell you how much I've missed you, Justine. Nothing's been the same without you. We were good together, you and me. I realize what a fool I was to ever let you go."

He'd grown so serious it made her uneasy. Not knowing how to answer him, Justine looked away.

"I can see that I've embarrassed us both," Warren said, releasing her hand. "Forget I said that."

She smiled, silently reassuring him that all was forgiven. Fortunately she didn't need to say anything, because Diana arrived with their salads. She frowned at Justine in obvious disapproval.

Justine pretended not to see. Despite Warren's

urging, she drank just the one glass of wine. For the rest of the leisurely meal, Warren was attentive and entertaining, working hard to distract her from her woes. After he'd paid the bill, she thanked him and left to pick up Leif from his friend's house earlier than planned. She'd made the babysitting arrangement that morning, hoping to talk to Seth about her ideas over lunch—but that, of course, hadn't happened.

Leif was tired and cranky and fell asleep in the car on the short ride home. When she arrived at 6 Rainier Drive, Seth's car was parked out front. Actually, she was glad he was home; she'd take the opportunity to talk to him.

Lifting her still-sleeping son out of his car seat, she carried him into the house.

Justine hadn't even stepped through the door when Seth loomed in front of her. "Exactly where did you disappear?" he demanded.

She ignored him, the same way he had her, and carried her son into his room, with Penny following her. She placed Leif in his bed and covered him with a blanket. Then she quietly closed the door behind her.

Seth stood in the hallway waiting. "I told you I met a friend for lunch," she explained patiently.

Seth's eyes were narrowed and accusatory. "I don't suppose that friend was Warren Saget?"

"What if it was?" she said and walked into the kitchen, where she sorted the mail on the counter.

"You promised me you wouldn't see him again."

She tossed the bills into one pile and the advertisements into another. "Warren's a friend, nothing more."

Seth angrily paced the kitchen floor. He stopped abruptly and seemed about to say something, then changed his mind. As quickly as it had flared, the anger was gone, replaced with what appeared to be disappointment and sadness. "In other words, you feel Warren Saget is a better friend to you than I am."

That was exactly what she'd told herself earlier. She shrugged. "Warren listens to me." She glanced up and met his eyes. "You obviously don't."

Twenty-Nine

Relaxing on a lounge chair, soaking up the June sunshine—it was the perfect way to spend a Saturday afternoon. The deck had become Maryellen's favorite spot, and she savored every moment outside the house, brief as those times were.

Jon was taking photographs in the Olympic rain forest, one of his preferred locations. Those pictures had also been among his most popular. Her biggest fear was that his job with the portrait studio would kill his love of photography. This was the first Saturday he'd gone out on a shoot in weeks. His parents had made it possible, although he'd never admit it.

With her knitting in her lap—the baby blanket was progressing more slowly than she would've liked—Maryellen watched Katie chase a butterfly with her grandfather, who kept a close eye on her. Ellen was in the kitchen, making a fresh pitcher of lemonade.

"Here you go," she said, bringing Maryellen a tall glass of lemonade, with ice and a wedge of lemon and even a fresh sprig of mint. Maryellen appreciated these appealing details, the lovely little touches her mother-in-law brought to everything she did.

"Oh, thanks," she said, immediately setting her knitting aside. Ellen took the chair beside hers.

"I don't mind telling you what joy Katie has brought Joe and me," she said, smiling at the little girl and her husband. "She's given us a new lease on life. We'd always heard how precious grandchildren were, but we had no idea it would be anything like this."

The feeling was mutual. "Katie adores the two of you."

"We love her," Ellen said simply. "From the moment we received the pictures you mailed us… It's hard to explain. Our world changed overnight. We had a grandchild, and now we're about to have a second one. I can't even *begin* to tell you what a difference Katie has made in our lives."

Maryellen hardly knew what to say. They never discussed their granddaughter's father. Really, what could they say? So far, both Joseph and Ellen had abided by Jon's wishes and had no contact with their son. As far as she knew, he hadn't said a word to either of them. Not a single word.

"Oh, look, Joe, look!" Ellen cried out, pointing at Katie. "She wants to play hide-and-seek."

Katie had hidden behind a flowering rhododendron bush and was peeking around, just waiting to be discovered.

Everything her daughter said and did seemed to thrill Katie's grandparents. They were completely smitten with her and she flourished under their love and care and attention.

Surely Jon had noticed. Maryellen didn't think he could help seeing the transformation in their daughter. Katie had gone from being whiny and difficult to a contented three-year-old once again. It was as if their daughter had absorbed the stress and uncertainty of Maryellen's pregnancy and reflected it in her behavior. Her disposition had returned to normal soon after Jon's parents arrived.

And yet Jon had never once commented.

"Joe, Joe," Ellen shouted, playing along. "Where's Katie?"

Joseph pretended he couldn't see her anywhere, which delighted Katie to the point of giggles.

The baby kicked and stretched inside her, and Maryellen rubbed her stomach. *Soon.* She felt she couldn't stand another minute, and yet Dr. DeGroot had told her she needed to be patient and do everything she could to forestall labor. Each single day improved the baby's chances.

When bed rest was first ordered, it had seemed an

impossible situation to Maryellen. She'd already miscarried one baby. Although no one had told her outright, she felt this was her last chance for a second child. Didn't Jon realize what his parents were doing for them? They'd given Maryellen peace, they'd taken Katie into their hearts—and they'd allowed Jon to do the work he needed to do. She didn't know how he could continue to ignore what should be so obvious.

She wanted to berate him for the way he behaved toward his parents. She couldn't, however. Jon had to find it in his own heart to forgive them. He persisted in holding on to his hatred, yet she didn't understand how he could.

"Where's my Katie-girl?" Joseph asked, again pretending that he couldn't find the little girl. He did a good job of seeming to search high and low.

Katie loved thinking she'd outsmarted her grandfather. She giggled and giggled, and Joseph acted beautifully.

Ellen laughed, and Maryellen, too, was amused by their antics.

When she couldn't bear to remain hidden any longer, Katie raced around the bush and presented herself in true theatrical fashion. Seeking her reward, she rushed toward Joseph with her arms held wide.

Joseph caught her and, scooping her into his embrace, whirled her around and around.

Maryellen was so intent on watching them that

she didn't realize Jon's vehicle had pulled into the driveway. He'd parked, climbed out and was standing in front of his car before she noticed. Maryellen's breath seemed to be trapped in her lungs as Jon stared at Katie and his father.

Joseph continued to whirl her around until he saw Jon. He stopped abruptly. Katie threw her arms around Joseph's neck and gave him a kiss on the cheek. Then she saw her father and immediately wanted to be put down.

"Daddy! Daddy!" she cried.

Joseph lowered her to the lawn, and Katie started eagerly toward Jon.

Crouching, Jon held his arms open to his little girl. Laughing and chattering, Katie fell into his embrace. Jon glanced at Maryellen, but when he saw his stepmother sitting at her side, he turned away.

"I can see it's time for us to go," Ellen said, unable to disguise her pain. She stood, reached for her empty glass and carried it into the kitchen.

Maryellen watched as Jon slowly straightened, Katie in his arms. Joseph faced his son and they looked at each other in silence.

"She's a delightful little girl," Joseph said after a long, tense moment.

Jon didn't respond.

"I know you don't want us here." Joseph rubbed his hands in nervous agitation. "Ellen and I have done our best to respect your wishes, because we know that's the only way you're comfortable with having us near your family."

Katie squirmed, and Jon set her down. Not understanding, she turned to her grandfather and raised her arms, demanding to be picked up.

As though asking his son's permission, Joseph glanced at Jon.

Maryellen bit her lip when Jon gave a slight nod, a gesture of permission.

Joseph reached for Katie. "I know you named her after your mother. She would've been so proud. And I—I'm proud of you, Jon, prouder than I can say." He had to stop because tears started to run down his weathered cheeks.

Jon seemed about to say something, but didn't.

"I understand why you can't forgive me," Joseph went on. "I do…and I have to say I can't blame you. What I did was despicable. I won't offer you an excuse. I…I deserve your hatred."

Ellen stepped onto the deck and stood completely still when she saw Joseph talking to his son. She brought her hand to her mouth, as if she feared she might make some sound that would destroy the fragile mood.

"I want to thank you, though," Joseph said. His words, choked out with emotion, were difficult to understand. "This time with Maryellen and Katie has been a blessing I never thought I'd receive." His father put Katie back down on the grass. Confused, the little girl looked from one man to the other.

Jon slid his gaze toward Maryellen. She gave him a shaky smile and picked up her knitting, although her fingers were suddenly uncooperative. The scene unfolding before her was of far more interest than the yarn and knitting needles she held.

"Thank you, son," Joseph said. "For letting Ellen and me come here. We'll leave you to your family now."

"Joe."

He didn't call him Dad, which was more than Maryellen would have expected.

Joseph paused and waited.

"Maryellen and I appreciate what you've done." His voice was gruff and didn't sound like him. He gathered Katie into his arms and headed for the house.

Nearly overwhelmed by emotion, Ellen hurried to Joseph and they hugged each other before driving away.

Jon didn't join Maryellen on the deck the way he normally did. Instead, he went immediately into his darkroom, taking Katie with him. He wanted a few minutes alone. Maryellen understood.

Those were the first words Jon had spoken to his father in fifteen years. In her heart, she knew this was a new beginning for all of them.

Thirty

It was graduation day.

When Anson had first disappeared, Allison was sure he'd return before now. She realized she'd set herself up for disappointment, but she couldn't stop believing that he'd find a way for them to be together.

She'd talked to him twice, and he hadn't even mentioned the possibility of coming back. If anything, especially now the pewter cross had been discovered, returning to clear his name seemed increasingly unlikely. Despite his claim that he'd seen the arsonist, and his insistence that he hadn't set those fires during his childhood, all the evidence pointed to him.

Now, as she stood with her classmates, wearing her cap and gown, she was forced to accept that Anson wouldn't show up at the last minute the way she'd dreamed.

Graduation day should be an important event, a day of triumph, yet all she felt was a sense of loss and betrayal. She wanted Anson with her so they could graduate together. Had he stayed in school, everything would've been different. She was positive he would've been awarded an academic scholarship. They'd talked about attending the same college. They'd talked about a lot of things. Every dream he'd ever shared with her had gone up in flames with The Lighthouse.

Allison's closest friends had gathered in the waiting area, talking animatedly, laughing nervously, discussing plans and exchanging bits of gossip. The stadium was filled with family and friends. The chatter and all the noise made her want to clamp her hands over her ears. Soon "Pomp and Circumstance" would begin, and Allison, along with the rest of her classmates, would file into the Tacoma Dome, where their families had assembled.

"Allison."

At the sound of her name, she turned to find Shaw Wilson slipping between two other graduates. He insisted on being called Shaw—she had no idea why—although his real name was Phillip. He'd once been a Goth friend of Anson's. Apparently he hadn't earned enough credits to graduate or he would've been required to wear a cap and gown. As usual, he'd dressed entirely in black. The June evening was mild, but he wore a full-length black coat that was long enough to drag on the floor. His face was heavily made up with black eye shadow.

Allison remembered that Shaw and Anson had hung around together at the beginning of the school year. She hadn't seen Shaw with him much after Anson began working at The Lighthouse. Shaw was the first person she'd gone to after Anson's disappearance, certain the other boy would know where he was and what had happened to him. Shaw swore he didn't and she believed him.

"Hi, Shaw," she said, doing her best to hide her misery.

Her classmate moved uncomfortably close and stared at her.

In that instant Allison knew. "You heard from him?" She kept her voice low and didn't dare say Anson's name aloud.

Shaw gave the slightest nod of his head.

"Is he all right?" she breathed.

He shrugged one shoulder. "Not if you ask me. He says otherwise."

Allison bit her lip for fear she'd cry out. "He phoned you?"

Again he nodded, glaring at her as if she were a traitor. "He wanted to tell you more but he couldn't because he knows you'll tell the sheriff. I told him you can't trust a girl. At least he listened to me about that much."

"Does he need anything?" After her graduation

announcements had gone out, Allison had received
gifts of money from family friends and relatives she'd
barely even met. If he needed it, Allison would send
Anson every penny.

"He says not."

"He hasn't phoned me." Allison knew why, too.
She'd lost her faith in him. Still, she waited every
single day, worrying endlessly about where he was
and how he was living. He didn't have any relatives
who could help him, and even his mother didn't
know where he'd gone.

Shaw held up his hand, stopping her. "Don't ask
me anything, because I can't tell you."

"How can I help?" That was all she really wanted
to do. Innocent or guilty, she still loved him.

"You don't really care what happens to him."
Shaw's eyes burned into hers.

"I do!" She wanted to shout the words. She cared
so much that she was near tears.

Glancing around, obviously afraid people might
be watching them, Shaw whispered something un-
intelligible in her ear.

Frowning, she looked up at him. "Pardon?"

"S U L," he said. "Those are the first three letters of
the license plate belonging to the person he saw that
night." Shaw kept his head down and spoke in a voice
so low she could hardly hear. "He didn't get a good look
at the car, but from the back it seemed to be dark.
Midsize. A sedan. Pretty common, in other words."

Hope, faith, love, all three came to her in a blinding flash. Perhaps there *had* been someone else there that night—and that someone was responsible for the fire. Almost immediately this flicker of hope was extinguished by doubt.

"Why didn't he tell me this earlier?" she asked. If Anson could trust anyone, it should be her. Not Shaw. *She* was the one who'd stood up for him, defending him to her classmates and anyone who'd listen. *She* was the one who'd believed.

He sighed loudly. "Anson wanted to keep you out of this. I checked around, but I couldn't come up with anything. He said I should tell you now."

"Thank you," she said gratefully. She hugged Shaw, who backed away in surprise.

Desperate for hope, she asked, "Is he coming?" Her voice rose excitedly. "He's here, isn't he?"

Shaw's demeanor changed as he shook his head. "No way, man. He isn't stupid enough to do that, not even for you. Just remember—See You Later."

"See you later," she repeated, not understanding.

"It's how I remember the letters."

The music started and everyone scrambled to get into their assigned positions. Before Shaw could leave, she grabbed his arm. "Is there anything else you can tell me?"

"No." He shook his head more emphatically than before.

"Is there anything else you're *not* telling me?"

His eyes narrowed, then he slowly nodded. "He swore me to secrecy. I can't tell you, so don't ask. Later, you're going to get something from him. When you do, make sure the sheriff knows I was the one who arranged it for Anson. Me. You understand?" With that he left her, disappearing into the throng of students.

Allison didn't know what he meant and didn't have time to question him further. Already the line of graduates had begun to move and Allison, shaking from the inside out, searched frantically for her cap before joining her friends as they filed into the pavilion.

The graduation went smoothly. When her name was announced, Allison Rose Cox crossed the stage to accept her diploma. Clutching it in her hand, she descended the steps and reclaimed her chair. She sat through all the speeches and awards, but her mind wasn't on any of them. She was thinking about Anson. He'd sent Shaw to her in an attempt to prove his innocence. He needed her to have faith in him and she'd faltered, but she wouldn't let him down again.

After the ceremony Allison wandered through the crowd until she found her family. Her mother held a damp, crumpled tissue. "It's so hard to believe you're eighteen. An adult," Rosie Cox said, dabbing her eyes. She hugged Allison and her father did, too. Eddie shifted from foot to foot, looking bored. Her brother's turn was coming; next year he'd be in high school, too.

Allison was ushered home, where her grandparents and aunts and uncles had gathered for a big family party. Everyone seemed so pleased for her and so excited. There was lots of talk about the future and the fact that she'd be leaving for college in September. None of it seemed real.

As soon as she could, Allison broke away from her relatives and sought out her father. "I need to talk to Sheriff Davis," she told him. She trusted her dad beyond anyone else. Her mother, too, of course, but her father was the more approachable, at least about something like this.

Zach quietly pulled her into his den. "You heard from Anson again?"

"Not directly. This has to do with the fire, though. It's important, Dad. I have some information that might help identify the arsonist."

"Okay." He nodded solemnly. "I'll contact Sheriff Davis first thing in the morning. We'll go in and see him together."

"Thank you." She was glad he'd simply taken her word, without insisting on details. Placing her hands on his shoulders, she kissed his cheek. It'd been a long time since she'd done that and she wasn't sure why she did it now. Perhaps it was to show her gratitude. Not just for this but for everything.

"What about Grad Party?" her father asked. She suspected he'd purposely steered the conversation away from anything too emotional.

"I'll go in a little while. Wake me in the morning,

okay?" Grad Party, with nearly her entire graduation class, was scheduled for later that evening. It was the last time this senior class would be together. From this point forward, they would go their separate ways.

"Okay, good." Her father left the den to attend to their guests.

Allison returned to her bedroom for a moment's solitude—and hoped she'd made the right decision.

"Allison," her mother called from out in the hallway.

"I'm in here, Mom," she said, forcing herself to smile. "I needed to change my shoes," she said, offering a convenient excuse.

"Here." Rosie handed her a single red rose in a crystal vase. "This came for you. It was delivered just now, and there's a card with it, too. Who would do something so sweet?"

Allison didn't need to guess; she knew. Anson. He hadn't come himself, but he'd done the next best thing.

Taking the rose and the card, she looked up at her mother, and the expression in her eyes must have conveyed the truth.

"Anson?" her mother whispered.

"I think so."

"Rosie, we're out of punch," Zach announced from the hall.

Allison could have kissed him. Her mother turned around and spoke briefly to her father as she walked past.

"That's from Anson?" her father asked.

Allison shrugged. "I think so," she said again.

He hesitated for only an instant before he left her to open the card in privacy. Inside was a simple message. *I will always love you. Anson.*

Allison closed her eyes and, leaning against the wall, whispered back, "I will always love you, too. Always, always, always."

Thirty-One

The only person Teri could talk to about this was Rachel Pendergast and rather than spill her heart out over the phone, she drove to her friend's rental. By the time she arrived at Rachel's, her eyes had flooded with tears and she was an emotional wreck, shaking from head to foot. She'd almost expected to get a speeding ticket on her way here.

Rachel answered her door, and immediately grabbed Teri's arm and pulled her inside. "Good grief, what's wrong?"

Collapsing onto her friend's sofa, Teri covered her face and burst into tears. She doubled over, leaning her forehead against her knees. Rachel sat down next to her, placing one arm around Teri's shoulders, and made soft, comforting sounds.

"I've done something really stupid," Teri bellowed

out between sobs. All at once she was so furious she couldn't contain her anger.

"You'd better tell me," Rachel said in a soothing voice as she continued to rub her back.

Teri pounded her foot against the carpet. "I am so *stupid*, I can't believe this. I just can't believe it!"

"Teri." Rachel was beginning to sound frustrated with her.

"It's his fault," she cried. "It's all Bobby's fault."

"What is?" Rachel asked.

Teri held out her hand. As she'd expected, Rachel gasped when she saw the huge diamond engagement ring.

"I'm in love," Teri shouted. "I said I'd marry him." She wept noisily. "It's never going to work. Bobby is…Bobby." She stamped her foot some more. "He loves me! At first I didn't think it was possible. He doesn't even know me, the real me, but he says it doesn't matter."

"He phones you every day, doesn't he?"

"Three times a day." No matter where he was in the world, he managed to reach her, and the sad part was, Teri lived for his calls. They never lasted long, but he made her laugh without even trying. And his innocent expressions of love brought her to tears.

He claimed he didn't "do" emotion and that he didn't "get" romance, but he was about the most romantic man she'd ever met. He loved her. She didn't understand why, and yet he loved her. No man had ever cared about her the way Bobby Polgar did. He was constantly proving it. If she made even the most casual comment, some silly remark like she enjoyed pickles, then he had a case delivered to her doorstep. He showered her with gifts, half of which she refused. The only thing he'd ever asked of her was to marry him. He'd asked over and over, and in a moment of weakness she'd said yes. But a chess genius shouldn't be married to someone like her. Bobby needed a wife who was his intellectual equal. She wasn't even close. She had to back out of this ridiculous engagement.

"He phones three times a day?" Rachel repeated.

Teri sniffled. "Before I go to work in the morning, at noon and then before I go to bed." Bobby's chess-playing had never been better, and he was convinced it was all due to her. He wasn't talking about the haircuts she'd given him, either.

"Why are you crying?" Rachel asked. "You should be over the moon that Bobby loves you."

"Because..." Teri was hardly able to speak. "He wants to marry me. And it's just not possible... and...and I have to tell him that."

"Why is it so impossible?" Rachel demanded. "He says you're good for him, and I know he's good for you. I've never seen you happier. He thinks you're fabulous, and you are."

"He doesn't really know me," Teri snapped. "Someone needs to tell him about all the loser men I've had in my life."

"He wants *you*," Rachel argued. "He doesn't care about the past."

Teri was annoyed that her best friend would be so obtuse. "Bobby only *thinks* he loves me. Why am I the only levelheaded one in the bunch? I don't care what you say, Rachel, I'm telling Bobby no." To prove her point, she yanked off the diamond ring and set it on the coffee table. Then fearing she might lose it, she grabbed it and slid it onto her finger again. That diamond probably cost more money than she'd make in her whole life as a hairstylist.

"I'm giving it back to him," Teri announced. "I *have* to."

"Teri," Rachel said, "don't do that."

"No, I mean it. He's flying in tonight and that'll be the end of it. I'm giving him the ring and then I'm telling him I don't want to hear from him or see him again." She'd tried to convince him once before, and it hadn't worked. This time she'd make sure he understood.

"Don't be ridiculous! You love this guy."

Teri shook her head adamantly. "I'm all wrong for Bobby."

Rachel gave an impatient sigh. "*He* doesn't seem to think so, and for what it's worth, I don't, either. You're perfect for each other."

"How can you *say* that?" Teri wailed. "Can't you just see what would happen if some television reporter interviewed me? I'd say something stupid that'd make Bobby the laughingstock of the chess world. No, I'm not going to do it."

"If you walk away from him, you'll regret it for the rest of your life."

This wasn't what Teri had come to hear. She needed her conviction shored up, needed the strength to send Bobby away, once and for all. "You're no help," she cried and she stormed out the door.

Sniffling and carrying on wasn't going to help, either, Teri told herself on the drive home. The ring kept glinting in the evening sunlight and it was all she could do not to stare at it. If she didn't watch what she was doing, she'd drive off the road.

Just as she feared, the stretch limo stood in front of her apartment complex.

As soon as she'd parked in her allotted space, James was there to open her car door.

Teri glared at the tall, skinny man and sniffed loudly.

"Are you unwell, Miss Teri?" he asked.

Bobby had sent him to collect her. This was her opportunity to make a stand. She'd let him deliver the news to Bobby. "I'm not going."

James shook his head, his expression confused. "Bobby is expecting you." It was understood that no one kept Bobby Polgar waiting. Not that refusing to go would do any good, anyway. James would simply come back for her and the next time Bobby would be with him.

Still holding the steering wheel with both hands, Teri laid her forehead against it and started to cry.

Poor James was beside himself. "Shall I phone for a doctor?" he asked anxiously.

"No," she sobbed, giving up. If she didn't go to Bobby, it would only make matters worse. He'd come himself. There'd be a scene. Before long, the entire apartment complex would get involved, with everyone offering opinions and taking sides. Teri could see it already. Much as she wanted to avoid a confrontation with Bobby, she didn't have a choice. "I'll go," she said dully.

"Your suitcase?" James asked.

"I don't have one." If that shocked him, James didn't let on. She didn't need a suitcase because she wasn't going anywhere with Bobby. She wasn't marrying Bobby Polgar, and that was final.

Reluctantly climbing out of the car, she picked up her purse and let James escort her to the gleaming black limo with its tinted windows. He opened the door and she crawled inside and began to cry all over again.

Because this ludicrous vehicle was as long as a bowling alley, she couldn't tell what James was doing, but she suspected he was on the phone the instant he peeled out of the parking lot. She could imagine what he was saying to Bobby.

"Get a grip," Teri said aloud as she fought to compose herself. Wiping her face, she realized they were headed for the Bremerton airport; Bobby must have hired a private jet. This man wasn't only a chess champion, he had more money than the United States treasury. He flew all over the world. A hop between London, England, and Bremerton, Washington, was nothing to him.

As soon as James turned the car into the small airport, Teri saw the Learjet parked on the runway. Her heart began to pound and all her efforts to dry her tears were pointless. A new deluge was coming and she couldn't hold it back. By the time James had driven up to the jet and the door was opened for her, Teri was a blubbering mess all over again.

Bobby was waiting for her inside the jet, and once she appeared, he dismissed everyone from the plane. He stood in the doorway with his hands locked behind his back.

Sobbing so hard her shoulders shook, Teri climbed the steps and the second she reached the top, she jerked the huge diamond ring from her finger and gave it to Bobby.

Bobby dropped it carefully inside his pocket, then hit a button just inside the aircraft. The staircase refolded and the door slid shut.

"I'm not staying and I'm not marrying you." There, she'd said it. She'd made her stand.

Bobby ignored that. "Sit." He gestured to a swivel

chair covered in soft white leather. He handed Teri a tissue, which she gladly accepted. She blew her nose and thought it sounded like a trumpet call. She wasn't one of those women who could weep elegantly.

"Why won't you marry me?" he asked. He looked puzzled again, as if he'd done something wrong.

"Don't you see?" she cried. "I don't want to love you, but I do."

"I know."

"It's *your* fault," she cried.

"Maybe," he said. "I worked hard so you'd love me. You're funny and wise and beautiful."

"You don't think I'm fat?" she asked him.

"Well…a little. It doesn't matter, though. I like you the way you are. Can we get married now?"

"Bobby," she said, recovering quickly. "*No*. I'm sorry, no."

He frowned, then got down on one knee in front of her. "I told you I'm not good with emotion. I think too much, but when I'm with you I don't want to think, I want to *feel* and I like that. That's never happened before. When I'm with you, I want to do…things that don't involve chess."

"What sort of things?" she asked, growing suspicious.

His eyes were so honest and full of love that she couldn't have looked away for anything. He kissed her. She enjoyed Bobby's kisses because they were different from those she generally received. With other men, there was a hot urgency. But Bobby's kisses were gentle and lingering, as if he savored her. She craved his touch. His kisses were unselfish and they made her feel as if she'd never been kissed before. Ironically, she was the one with the sexual experience, not Bobby.

She needed every ounce of strength she possessed to break off his kiss.

"Will you marry me *now?*" he asked. With child-like innocence, his eyes implored her.

Teri swallowed back tears and shook her head. The things he hadn't heard about her yet—and there were a lot—would change his mind fast enough, and sooner or later he'd find it all out. "You don't know me."

Instead of arguing, he kissed the side of her neck. Teri thought she'd dissolve into a puddle at his feet. The only sure way to end this was to enlighten him with the truth. "I've…there've been lots of other men."

"Yes, I know. From now on there will be only me."

She gripped his shoulders and pushed him away. "You *know?*"

He nodded.

She swallowed and in a small voice asked, "Everything?"

He nodded again.

The thought of Bobby learning about the litany

of stupid, lethal relationships she'd stumbled into and out of mortified her.

"How?" Her eyes narrowed.

"Can I kiss you again?"

"No. Answer the question."

"If I answer the question, can I kiss you?"

She sighed and nodded. She didn't have the strength of will to refuse him.

She'd meant he could kiss her *after* he'd answered, but he didn't wait. He gave her a long, loving kiss that made her go weak inside.

"All right," she said, her eyes still closed as he ended the kiss. "What do you know about me?"

"Dwight Connell." The jerk who'd emptied her bank account. "Ray Hawkins." The guy she'd had to throw out of her apartment with the sheriff's help. "Carl Jackson." Her first boyfriend, now in jail. "Randy—"

"All right, all right. How did you learn all that?"

"It wasn't hard." He paused. "My job is to play chess and yours is to cut hair. There are people whose job it is to find things out, and I asked one of them."

"Oh." She didn't have the energy to feel offended. She would've told him all of that, anyway.

He pulled the ring out of his pocket and took her hand. The diamond glided onto her finger as if that was where it belonged.

She couldn't stop staring as Bobby pushed the same button he had earlier. The door opened and the stairs descended. Two uniformed men boarded the plane, followed by James, and walked past Teri into the cockpit, each murmuring a polite "Hello."

Within minutes, the plane was at the end of the runway. "Where are we going?" she asked Bobby.

He seemed surprised by the question. "Las Vegas."

Teri was speechless. How had this happened? Thirty minutes ago, she'd categorically refused to see this man again. Ten minutes ago, she'd still felt that way—and now all of a sudden she was flying to Vegas to marry Bobby Polgar, a man she'd seen a grand total of three times in her life. She hadn't even slept with him, and she was about to marry him.

"Did I agree to this?" she asked tentatively.

"You want to marry me and I want to marry you." Apparently that seemed an unquestionable fact to him, so he'd taken the next logical step—they were on their way to Vegas.

"I...I didn't bring any clothes with me."

Bobby smiled. "You won't need clothes."

Teri giggled, suddenly so happy she wanted to sing—and she had a terrible voice. Whenever she broke into song, the dogs in the neighborhood joined in. Using a special phone Bobby handed her, she called Rachel and asked if she'd cover for her the next few days and promised to keep in touch.

As she hung up the receiver, she thought of something else. "I don't have any form of birth control, either."

His smile faded and an adoring look stole over his face. "I'd like to get you pregnant," he said softly. "With your wide hips, you should have an easy birth."

The man said the most outrageous things! "Fine. Then, *you* can go through labor."

"I would if it was possible. I don't think I could stand to see you suffer."

Was it any wonder she loved him? "Okay, but there's one little fact you should know. No child of mine's going to have the smarts to be a chess champion."

He accepted that without argument. "Good. I want my child to live a more normal life than I have."

When they landed in Vegas nearly three hours later, they were ushered into another limo and driven down the Strip. Teri opened the sunroof and stood with her head and arms out, yelling to the crowds at the top of her lungs. *"I'm getting married!"* she screeched, waving madly and flashing her diamond.

A minister was waiting for them in the penthouse suite of a posh casino hotel. The room was filled with flowers, all white. Everything was ready. All Teri had to do was sign the paperwork and show her identification.

Then she and Bobby exchanged vows. James was the witness. Two minutes after the ceremony, they were alone. Bobby kissed her again. "Can I make love to you now?" he asked.

He was so sincere, so sweet. She nodded. "Please."

Bobby led her into the bedroom, looking a bit self-conscious. He turned off the light.

All at once, Teri was nervous. She was no novice to bedroom antics. As one of her loser boyfriends had said, she'd been around the block more often than the mailman. While she wasn't happy about her past, she wasn't ashamed, either. But just then, she would've given everything she had in this world to have come to her husband a virgin.

Whatever fears and regrets she had faded the instant Bobby took her in his arms.

He was gentle, as she knew he would be, and generous and tender. For her, it might as well have been the first time because that was how he made her feel. Lying in his arms, she wept silently. He kissed her tears away and explored her body with his hands and lips, between the sweetest and most exquisite of kisses.

"I love you," she whispered.

"Do you think I gave you a baby?" he asked.

"Hmm." Teri considered his question. "I'm not sure. Maybe we should try again."

Bobby laughed and she thought she'd never heard him sound this happy. That thrilled her, knowing she was capable of pleasing him.

In the wee hours, she woke to find Bobby leaning

on one elbow staring down at her. With his index finger, he outlined the shape of her eyebrow. Teri smiled up at him.

"Can we…again?" he asked shyly.

Her smile widened, and she threw her arms around his neck, and let him know she had absolutely no objections.

They slept late, only to be awakened by James pounding on the door, announcing that Bobby was needed downstairs.

At the noise, Bobby leaped out of bed, glanced at the clock and searched frantically for his pants. "I'm late."

"You have a match this morning?" For modesty's sake, Teri pulled up the sheet to cover her naked breasts. She dropped it. There was no reason to be shy with Bobby. Her husband had spent plenty of time holding, touching and kissing her breasts the night before.

"I have a tournament here." He jerked up his pants and scrabbled around for his socks and shoes.

"This morning?"

"Yes. At nine." He found his shirt and buttoned it crookedly. She crawled across the bed and refastened it for him. "I don't want to go. I'm sorry," he told her.

"Me, too. My favorite time to make love is in the morning."

His eyes widened. "Stay here," he said, his voice

husky. He cleared his throat and spoke again. "I'll be back. Soon."

"But…"

He pointed at her and at the bed, and stammered, "Please. Order breakfast, have a…have a shower, but…don't leave this room."

"I won't," she promised. "Is the match televised?"

"Yes." He dragged in a deep breath.

"Come here," she said, kneeling at the foot of the bed.

James knocked again but Bobby moved toward Teri. Wrapping her arms around her husband's neck, she kissed him in a way that guaranteed his return. "That was for luck."

Bobby's breathing went shallow, and he backed out of the room.

Teri ordered coffee, which arrived when she'd finished her shower. She uncovered the television remote, and after flipping through various channels, found the station broadcasting the live chess match. The commentator was talking about Bobby, and Teri sat up in bed, sipping coffee, listening as the highlights of her husband's illustrious career were described. *Husband*—oh, that word had a wonderful sound.

She watched as Bobby faced his opponent, a well-known Russian player, according to the commentator. Teri had never heard of him but that wasn't saying much.

Twenty moves later, the game was over. The

audience was stunned. When Bobby stood up to leave, the man who'd been commenting on the game tried to interview him. Shaking his head, Bobby walked directly past him. He simply marched out of the room. Five minutes later, Teri heard the door to their suite open.

Bobby already had his shirt off by the time he made it into the bedroom. He stood at the end of the bed, and his eyes glowed with warmth as he smiled at her.

She repeated what the television commentator had announced. "Bobby Polgar just made chess history."

"I hurried."

Teri held her arms open. "How long before the next game?"

"An hour," he said, frowning.

"That's enough time," she assured him.

His smile was back.

Bobby Polgar, husband of Teri Miller Polgar, continued to make chess history for the rest of that week. Without explanation, he disappeared after each match and arrived late for several of them. Refusing all interviews, he was less social and more reclusive than he'd been since entering the international chess arena. Speculation ran rampant.

Teri didn't leave the suite for five days. She had everything she could want or need at her fingertips. In fact, she had more than she'd ever dreamed possible.

Thirty-Two

"**I**'d like to talk to you a moment," Seth said after a silent dinner on Wednesday evening. They hadn't mentioned the subject of the restaurant since last Friday, although it loomed between them. He hadn't said any more about her idea for a tearoom, and Justine hadn't brought it up. She was so bitterly disappointed in her husband that she could barely look at him. He'd acted as though her ideas and suggestions meant nothing. What hurt even more was that Seth hadn't told her about his ideas, either. He'd just moved forward without her.

"All right," she murmured, turning away from the sink. They'd spoken very little for the past five days, exchanging only mundane remarks about Leif's needs. They still slept in the same bed, but as far from each other as possible, and they never went upstairs at the same time.

Seth had been avoiding her. He put in long hours at work. At least she assumed that was where he spent his time. For all she knew, he could've been in meetings with a builder and broken ground. Sad to say, she wasn't privy to her husband's plans.

Drying her hands on a dish towel, she glanced into the living room and saw that Leif was putting together a puzzle, Penny curled up beside him. He'd be content for a few more minutes. Pulling out a kitchen chair, she sat down while Seth poured himself a cup of coffee.

Instead of joining her at the table, he remained standing, leaning against the counter. Justine felt at a disadvantage, sitting while he stood, but didn't have the energy to get up.

"I owe you an apology," Seth admitted, surprising her. "I didn't take this tearoom idea of yours seriously. I should've given it more consideration and I didn't. Instead, I went ahead with my plans to rebuild— without discussing them with you first."

Justine kept her eyes lowered. "I didn't even know you'd made any plans, Seth. It was a shock."

"No more of a shock than you seeing Warren behind my back," he retaliated.

She opened her mouth to defend herself and swallowed a retort. Arguing wouldn't help, and she didn't want to say anything in front of their son. Leif had heard far too many of their disagreements already.

"Forget I said that," Seth murmured, brushing his blond hair away from his face. Despite his words, his mouth was pinched, his expression disapproving.

"All right, I will."

Her husband exhaled, as though he had difficulty controlling his frustration. "I want you to know I've done some serious thinking about what we should do."

She dared to raise her eyes, almost afraid to hope Seth would be willing to hear her ideas.

"I love you, Justine," he said, his eyes meeting hers. "You and Leif mean more to me than anything. I can't risk losing you."

Justine felt a lump form in her throat.

"I won't destroy our marriage because I'm too stubborn to let go of an idea."

Justine blinked rapidly to hold back tears. "I love you, too," she said.

"More than Warren Saget?"

"Yes," she cried. "A thousand times more!"

Seth pulled out another chair and sat across from her. He reached for her hand. Justine struggled not to cry; she hadn't slept well in days, and she doubted Seth had, either. Lack of sleep had made her emotions more volatile than they already were.

"I think the best thing to do, since we can't agree, is to sell the property. I've contacted a real estate agent and I've decided—" he hesitated "—if you concur, that is, we'll put the property on the market."

Justine was sure she hadn't heard him correctly.

"You're willing to sell the land?" That wasn't what she wanted, although at one time she'd thought perhaps she did.

He shrugged. "With the way property values have gone up in the last five years," he continued, "plus what we'll collect from the insurance company, we should be able to walk away debt-free."

They could pay off everything they owed, but… "In other words, we won't have anything to show for all the work we put into The Lighthouse?" She realized she was stating the very argument he'd made earlier. She saw the discouragement in his eyes and in the tight set of his mouth. She and Seth had taken a risk when they'd opened the restaurant. From the first day they'd opened for business, Seth had been determined to succeed.

He'd worked hard. So had Justine. And yet, after five long years, they had nothing. The fire had wiped them out.

"What do you think?" he asked.

"But…" *Sell the property?* Even now, he didn't want to listen to her ideas. She wouldn't force them on him. "Can I sleep on it?"

He bowed his head. "Of course." He leaned forward, not looking at her. "It's just… I've put so much into this."

What about me? she thought resentfully. The restaurant had been *their* dream, the project they'd worked on together. Justine felt cast aside, unimportant. Once again, Seth had made her feel as though her contribution and her concerns were of little value.

Her reaction last Friday had been childish, and she regretted seeing Warren. Her willingness to have lunch with him that day had only encouraged him. Every day since, he'd made an excuse to visit the bank. She'd declined his invitations for meals and drinks, but nothing she said seemed to convince him. As he told her repeatedly, he'd achieved the success he had by persisting, and her polite rejections had only made him redouble his efforts. In fact, he'd sent flowers to the bank twice. His attention had become conspicuous—and embarrassing.

Maybe it would be best all the way around if they did sell the property. Justine tucked a strand of hair behind her ear as she considered. "You're still enjoying sales?" she asked.

Seth grinned. "I appear to have a knack for it."

That was true enough; after only a few weeks, Seth was the company's top salesperson.

"Before you make your decision, there's something you should know," Seth said. "If we list the property, there's a strong likelihood it'll sell right away."

"You can't be sure of that."

"Actually, I am. From what I understand, a fast-food franchise is looking for prime property here in Cedar Cove."

"But…"

"We'd get full price and the deal can close within the month."

"The real estate agent told you this?" Justine asked. Seth nodded.

"Would you have any regrets?" she asked, studying him.

"No," he said, and he seemed sincere. "Not anymore. I hate the thought of someone selling hamburgers and fries at the waterfront, where our restaurant once stood, but I'd get used to it."

Seth might, but Justine wondered if she would as easily.

"Let's sleep on it," she said again. "Both of us."

Seth put Leif to bed while Justine walked the dog. When she got back, he was still reading stories to their son. Eventually Leif fell asleep in the middle of *Good Night, Moon,* which both she and Seth could practically recite from memory. Justine took a long soak in the tub, perfuming the water with gardenia-scented bubble bath. Seth's favorite. Her body was glistening when she finally climbed out of the water.

Seth paused in the bathroom doorway, watching her dress for bed. He gave her a slow, lazy smile. "Are you thinking what I'm thinking?" he said, his voice husky with suggestion.

Justine smiled. "I certainly hope so."

It was still light out when they went to bed. Seth reached for her, and Justine turned willingly into his arms. Their lovemaking was full of deep sighs and hoarse whispers.

Afterward Seth held her close. Nestled in her husband's embrace, Justine felt content for the first time in weeks.

"I could get pregnant, you know." She hadn't bothered to resume her birth control pills—with Seth's agreement. Not that it'd mattered much recently.

"Good."

She grinned sleepily. "You'd like that, wouldn't you?"

"As a matter of fact, I would. It's time." He kissed the top of her head. "Do you think twins might run in the family?"

Her eyes flew open as she considered the idea. She was a twin. "It's a possibility, I suppose. What makes you ask?"

Seth twined his fingers through her hair. "If you had two babies, you'd be too busy to give Warren Saget a second's thought."

"Seth," she whispered, raising her head to meet his gaze, "don't tell me you're actually jealous."

He slid his hand down her spine, and she arched her back. "In case you hadn't noticed," he said. "I'm green with it."

"There's absolutely no need to feel the slightest bit of jealousy. I promise you that."

"I'm glad to hear it."

She kissed his jaw. "If you don't object, I'll give the bank my notice."

She felt his smile against her temple. "No objection here."

She loved the feel of his skin against her own. Justine smoothed her hand along his bare shoulders and over his chest. "I didn't think you'd mind." Suddenly tired, she yawned. "I like falling asleep in your arms," she murmured. With the long hours Seth had spent at The Lighthouse, there'd been few opportunities for them to go to bed at the same time. And lately—ever since last week—they'd been so angry with each other, they hadn't wanted to.

"I love you," she whispered, yawning again.

"Sleep," Seth urged and she did, falling into the soundest, deepest rest since before the fire had laid claim to her security.

Justine woke about five in the morning, feeling energetic and alert. She tossed aside the covers, got out of bed and quickly donned her robe. Then she hurried to the kitchen and, even before starting a pot of coffee, grabbed a pen and paper. She'd never been good at drawing, but her vision of a tearoom wouldn't leave her alone. She had tried to push it out of her mind, afraid that discussing it would only upset Seth. Now she was determined to make him listen, to demand that he give her idea a fair hearing.

Seth found her standing over the table, sipping coffee. He slipped his arms around her middle and hugged her from behind, pressing his cheek against her back.

"You're awake early." Working his hands inside her robe, he cupped her breasts.

It was difficult not to get caught up in the sheer sensual nature of his caress. "Seth," she breathed, even as her nipples hardened in the palms of his hands. "I don't want to list the property until after you listen to me."

He seemed to stop breathing. "You're still thinking about a tearoom for women?" He removed his hands and stepped away from her. "Justine, we can't keep doing this. We have to make a clear decision and go on with our lives. Isn't that what you've been saying?"

"Yes, but do you honestly want to see a fast-food joint on the waterfront overlooking the cove?" In her view that would be a terrible misuse of the land.

"All right. Convince me a tearoom would be a success."

"Here," she said, shoving the tablet toward him. Her artistic talents were limited, but she'd done a fairly good job of drawing a Victorian structure with one turret and two gables.

Seth glanced down at her sketch and then at her. "It looks like a Victorian house. You want to build a house that serves tea where we once had the restaurant? I don't mean to discourage you, Justine, but I don't think the city would grant a permit for us to put a residence in a commercial zone."

"It only *looks* like a house, Seth. It's a Victorian Tea Room."

"A Victorian Tea Room," he repeated. "That's different from a regular tearoom?"

"Well, maybe not, but that isn't the point. First, we'd only be open for breakfast and lunch, and I'd be home in the evenings. I thought we could add a gift store, too. We'd serve high tea once a month, more often if there's a demand."

"In Cedar Cove?"

"It would be a special place for women to meet. We could have small receptions there and an outside patio for special occasions and—" She stopped because she was getting ahead of herself. "It occurred to me that we were wasting all the valuable lessons we learned from The Lighthouse."

"How so?" he asked, studying her drawing. "For the record, I agree. But I'd like to hear what you think."

Those words made her smile. "When we were open for lunch and dinner, our working hours were much too long. I wouldn't want a liquor license, either." Because they'd served evening meals, it was a necessity and where they'd garnered their highest profits.

"I can understand that," Seth murmured. "I have to admit you've come up with an interesting compromise...."

"With just the two meals, I'd be home in time for dinner with you and Leif."

"All right," he said, and seemed to be slowly absorbing her thoughts. "Here's my next question—would I be part of this?"

"Only if you wanted to be. And only to the extent that you wanted to be. The thing is, Seth, you're good at sales. You're happy, and the money so far is great. We wouldn't need to rely solely on the earnings from the tearoom."

He frowned. "In other words, you want to do this…alone?"

"Absolutely not! I'd need you. Not to work in the restaurant necessarily—unless you felt like it—but I'll need your counsel and suggestions and input and encouragement. And your love."

"I can give you all that," he said. "Gladly."

"We can do this, Seth, I know we can."

He set aside his coffee and drew her into his arms. Justine accepted his kiss. This was the perfect solution—for both of them.

Thirty-Three

Linnette didn't know where else to turn. It'd been a week since she'd heard from Cal. In the beginning, Cal had contacted her every few days, and then less often. Now, not at all.

Linnette understood his reasons for leaving Cedar Cove. Or, at least, she tried to. Everyone said saving wild mustangs was a worthy cause, and she knew it was. She also understood that cell phone reception in rural Wyoming was poor to nonexistent. But whenever they did manage to speak, it seemed that he ended the call as quickly as possible.

Linnette didn't need anyone to tell her something was wrong. Because she didn't know what else to do or whom to trust, she went to see Grace Harding, Cliff's wife. Grace might be as completely in the dark as Linnette, but she hoped the librarian might be able to give her *some* information. Linnette couldn't go on like this, not when she loved Cal so much.

She visited the library on Thursday during her lunch break. This was the first time she'd actually set foot inside. The truth was, she hadn't read very much since moving to Cedar Cove—mostly medical journals in order to keep current. What novels she did enjoy had been passed along by her mother. Sad as it was to admit, she'd lived in Cedar Cove for more than a year and hadn't even bothered to get a library card.

The library was an inviting place to be. The floor was carpeted to absorb sound and the reading area with its overstuffed chairs and displays of books welcomed anyone stepping inside.

Linnette saw Grace right away. She stood behind the counter, chatting with a woman who was checking out a stack of books. Glancing up, she waved at Linnette.

Linnette moved toward the counter and waited until Grace had finished checking out the other woman's books.

"Hello, Linnette," Grace said with a friendly smile. "Good to see you."

"You, too." Her throat started to close up and for half a second she was afraid she might cry, which would have mortified her. This just proved how despondent she was over Cal.

"What can I do for you?" Grace asked.

Linnette had always liked Cliff's wife. Her mother spoke highly of Grace, too. From a brief remark her father had once dropped, Linnette was fairly sure Grace had been a client at one time.

"I don't have a library card yet," she murmured, feeling more than a little ill at ease.

"Then it's past time you did," Grace said cheerfully. She handed Linnette a clipboard. "If you'll fill out the application, I'll take care of this personally."

"Thank you." Her hand trembled as she took it, but if Grace noticed, she didn't comment.

"Actually," Linnette said, clearing her throat. She held the clipboard against her, as if it offered some form of protection. "Coming in for a library card is an excuse so I could talk to you."

"To me?" Grace asked, obviously surprised. "You're welcome to talk to me anytime you want, Linnette, library card or not."

"About Cal?" she asked in uneven tones.

"Oh." Grace's face betrayed her. Apparently Cal was a subject she'd rather avoid.

Linnette was afraid of exactly this.

"Perhaps we should talk somewhere a little more private," Grace suggested. She excused herself and conferred briefly with one of the other employees. Then she retrieved her purse. "I'll take an early lunch this afternoon," she told Linnette, leading the way out of the library.

"Thank you," Linnette whispered as she followed obediently. She left the clipboard on the counter.

The waterfront area was decorated by flowering baskets that hung from the light posts. Linnette had always loved strolling by the marina. She'd done this with Cal many times, walking side by side, holding hands and talking. Okay, she did most of the talking, but that was what Cal preferred. Even when his speech therapy was completed, she suspected he'd never be much of a conversationalist.

As if deep in thought, Grace didn't say anything as they walked. Her pace was slow.

"Have you heard from Cal recently?" Linnette asked when she couldn't bear the silence anymore. She matched her steps to Grace's, although she normally walked much faster.

"He phoned Cliff the other day."

He hadn't called Linnette, though. "Everything's all right, isn't it?"

Grace nodded. She began to say something else, then apparently thought better of it.

Linnette could tell there was much more to Cal's conversation with Cliff, but whatever it was, Grace seemed reluctant to tell her.

"Cal hasn't been hurt, has he?" she asked anxiously.

"No, no, it's nothing like that." She walked over to the espresso stand and ordered a latte with sugar-free vanilla flavoring. After she'd ordered, she turned to Linnette. "Would you like anything?"

"No, thanks. Is that all you're having for lunch?" Linnette asked. She hadn't eaten herself and doubted she would. Getting anything past the lump in her throat would've been impossible.

"I generally have a sandwich with a latte or soup for lunch," Grace explained as she paid for her drink. "I should probably be watching my weight more than I do," she grumbled. "I seem to have a small problem with it, unlike others I could name, including your mother and Olivia," she said with a laugh. "I'll eat something later."

As soon as the latte was ready, Grace and Linnette walked to the gazebo near the waterfront park. Grace took a seat on a bench that faced the water and Linnette sat down beside her.

"I'd appreciate it if you just told me what's wrong," Linnette said.

Grace sipped her latte, then sighed. "You know that Cal's in Wyoming with Vicki Newman, right?"

"She joined him there later, didn't she?"

Grace nodded. "Vicki's a very good vet."

"I'm sure she is."

"The problem is that a lot of these mustangs have medical problems."

"I'm sure that's true," Linnette whispered. She already knew what Grace was trying to tell her. Cal had fallen for Vicki. It didn't seem possible, but she felt intuitively that must be it.

Again Grace grew quiet, as if considering her words.

"Cal's involved with Vicki, isn't he?" Linnette said bluntly.

"I...didn't speak to him personally, you understand," Grace murmured. "But from what Cliff said, Cal does seem to...have feelings for her."

"I see." A cold sensation came over Linnette. Cal supposedly had feelings for her, too. Apparently she was an out-of-sight, out-of-mind kind of girl.

Grace shook her head. "I know Vicki, and I don't want you to think she'd go after someone else's man. Because she just wouldn't."

This wasn't exactly reassuring, in light of the fact that Cal was obviously interested in her.

Grace shrugged. "She doesn't even seem to pay much attention to male-female stuff." She sipped her latte. "I'm not putting this well and I'm not even sure how to explain Vicki."

"Go on," Linnette said from between clenched teeth. "Try."

"Well, first, you and I both know that Vicki's rather...unfeminine in appearance. I don't mean to be unkind, but that's just a fact. She wears her hair skinned back and doesn't style it. I've never seen her wear makeup or attractive clothes. We've never heard of her having any boyfriends or even a social life. To tell you the truth, all of this comes as a shock to Cliff and me."

All of this. "Go on," Linnette urged, needing to

know, regardless of how much it hurt. Not knowing was worse.

"The two of them have been working closely together, day in and day out...."

But Cal had said he loved *her*. If he felt anything for this other woman, it was a brief attraction and nothing more. As soon as he returned to Cedar Cove, everything would be all right again. Cal would come to his senses and his feelings for Linnette would reassert themselves.

"That's about all I can tell you, Linnette."

Linnette could think of a thousand things she'd rather hear. "This is just a temporary infatuation," she said, making an effort to sound confident. Trying to rationalize what she'd been told.

The librarian didn't answer.

"I need to talk to him," Linnette insisted, urgency building inside her. "It won't be long before Cal's back, so we should get this resolved." Linnette could understand how such an infatuation, presumably mutual, might come about. Working closely together in an isolated location. Sharing a cause. Yes, she saw how *all of this* could happen. But once Cal was home again, he'd forget his feelings for this other woman.

Cal wasn't himself. He wasn't thinking clearly.

"I'm certain you'll have the opportunity to talk this out with him soon," Grace murmured.

"Of course I will," Linnette said.

The opportunity came much sooner than she'd

expected. When Linnette got back to her car, she found a voice message from Cal on her cell phone. Sitting in the library parking lot, she returned his call.

Cal didn't answer, so she left a message for him. Since she was afraid they'd keep missing each other, she phoned again and told him she'd be home that evening and would wait for his call there.

She didn't hear from him until nearly eight.

The waiting was agony, and she could feel one of her headaches coming on. Pressing her fingertips to her temples, she paced the carpet, oblivious to the view of the cove or the Bremerton shipyard with its massive aircraft carriers and retired submarines. Late-evening sunlight dappled her deck but she hardly noticed.

By the time Cal finally did phone, Linnette was almost convinced he hadn't received her message.

"Linnette," he began.

"You'd better tell me what's going on between you and Vicki Newman," she snapped, without giving him a chance to greet her. At this stage, Linnette was long past exchanging pleasantries.

"Y-you know?"

"About Vicki, you mean?" She didn't let him respond. "I thought you'd… I hoped we could speak honestly with each other. I think we owe each other that, don't you?"

"I'm-m-m s-sorry."

"You should be!"

"Linnette, stop." His voice took on a strength and conviction that startled her.

"Stop?"

"I apologize."

She sighed. "All right then, you're forgiven." Perhaps she'd blown everything out of proportion. Grace hadn't talked to him personally and it seemed that Cal had already regained his sanity. Relief settled over her, easing the tension between her shoulder blades. The throbbing headache that had started to pound began to subside.

"I love Vicki."

Linnette gasped. She refused to believe it. Cal wasn't making any sense. "You just said you were sorry. You—"

"I volunteered to travel to Wyoming to rescue the mustangs because it's important to me, yes, b-but also because I needed to get away and think. I needed to get away from you."

He was telling her he'd purposely left to escape her. *"What?"*

"I appreciate everything, I truly d-do." He paused as if to control his tendency to rush the words. "I wanted to talk to you. I tried, but I c-couldn't."

"Why not?"

"I don't do well with words. I thought once I was here, I'd write to you. But when I arrived, a letter seemed so...callous."

"And this isn't?"

"I'd give anything not to hurt you," he said in a low voice.

It was too late for that. Pain swirled through her, cutting off her breath, undermining even her ability to stand upright. Sinking into a chair, she clutched the phone with one hand and held the other against her forehead.

"There's nothing physical between Vicki and me," he said. "I haven't even kissed her."

"And you believe you're in love with her?"

"I know I am."

"Okay, okay," she said, thinking fast. "You need to examine everything, Cal. Your feelings and reactions. The two of you are out there alone, and it makes sense that you might be attracted to her, but that'll all change when you're back home."

"No," he stated flatly. "It won't change."

She noticed how controlled his voice was, as if he knew exactly what he planned to say and had rehearsed it any number of times.

"I'm coming back to Cedar Cove. I'm leaving in the morning."

"Thank God," she breathed. Once he got back, he'd realize what a mistake he was making.

"My feelings for Vicki aren't going to change, Linnette," he insisted. "I intend to ask her to be my wife."

Thirty-Four

Grace arrived at the Pancake Palace three minutes ahead of Olivia for their weekly splurge of pie and coffee. They'd both earned it after an hour's worth of aerobic exercise. If it was just up to Grace, she'd skip the workout and go straight for the pie. Olivia wouldn't hear of that, however, and was determined that Grace join her for class. Although she complained, Grace actually looked forward to exercising with her best friend. The bonus was that Wednesday evenings were also their time to catch up on each other's news.

Grace slid into the booth by the window and Goldie, the crusty, retirement-age waitress, immediately brought over a pot of decaffeinated coffee. Grace turned over the ceramic mug—a ritual at the Pancake Palace.

"Olivia's right behind me," she said. Reaching for Olivia's cup, she righted it.

"You girls want the usual?" Goldie asked as she filled both mugs.

Grace nodded. She'd been friends with Olivia so long that she felt she could speak for her. They'd met in first grade and been best friends all through school. Although they were both in their fifties, and into their second marriages, they remained as close now as when they were girls. They'd come here, to this very same restaurant, for sodas after class. The Pancake Palace was a venerable Cedar Cove institution, and Goldie had been there since Grace and Olivia really *were* girls.

"Why don't you live a little?" Goldie suggested. "Go for the big-time. I've got apple pan dowdy in the kitchen."

Grace nearly choked on her coffee. "Apple pan dowdy over coconut cream pie? I don't think so."

"What about chocolate cream pie?" Goldie said next, her hand on her hip.

Grace considered that, but only briefly. "Not interested, sorry."

"Blueberry?"

"Coconut cream."

Goldie shook her head, as if bitterly disappointed. "The judge, too?"

Grace nodded. Olivia and Grace remained steadfastly loyal to coconut cream—and to each other.

Still shaking her head, Goldie disappeared into the kitchen.

Sipping her coffee, Grace recalled the afternoon shortly before their high-school graduation, when she'd told Olivia she was pregnant. They'd been sitting in a booth at the Pancake Palace then, too. This was weeks before she'd had the courage to tell her teenage boyfriend. She'd married Dan and shortly afterward he'd joined the army and was shipped off to Vietnam. Grace sighed; she didn't know why her mind was traveling down that road.

She looked up to see Olivia walking into the restaurant, and although they'd just finished a strenuous physical workout, her friend had hardly a hair out of place. She'd always been like that; she was such a contrast to Jack Griffin, which made their marriage very interesting indeed. Olivia craved order and Jack...well, Jack didn't. Despite that, or maybe because of it, they succeeded as a couple.

"I ordered the pie," Grace said when Olivia sat down across from her.

"Great." She picked up her coffee and after the first sip, exhaled with satisfaction. "How was your week?"

Grace shrugged. "All right, I guess."

"You *guess*?"

She'd never managed to keep anything from her friend, she thought with a slight smile. "Cliff talked to Cal, and he's on his way back to Cedar Cove with two mustangs."

Olivia studied her carefully and after a short pause, said, "That should be good news, right?"

Grace lowered her gaze. "Normally it would be." With Cal away in Wyoming, Cliff had been doing Cal's work as well as his own. Grace didn't feel she was much help, but she did her best to assist her husband in Cal's absence.

"What's going on?" Olivia asked.

Until now, Grace had kept the romance developing between Cal and Vicki Newman to herself. She didn't believe she had the right to say anything, especially when he'd been so close to Linnette McAfee. Then last Thursday, Linnette had come to her because she'd sensed that something was wrong. Grace wanted to kick Cal for not being more straightforward with the girl.

"Grace?" Olivia said, breaking into her thoughts. "You look a million miles away."

"Oh, sorry. It's Cal."

"You said he's on his way back."

"He is, but he dropped a bombshell when he spoke to Cliff last night." She cupped her hands around the warm mug, letting the heat warm her palms. "He said he wants to marry Vicki Newman."

"The vet?" Olivia's eyes grew wide. "Isn't he seeing Linnette McAfee?"

"He is…was."

Olivia opened her mouth, and then abruptly closed it. All she said was a soft, "Oh, my."

"I know." Grace shared her friend's feelings.

"Does Linnette have any idea?"

"Cliff didn't mention that part, but I assume Cal must've at least given her a few hints. She was in the library last week and asked me point-blank if Cliff and I had heard from Cal."

"You told her?"

Grace felt dreadful about it now. She nodded. "Cliff told me what he suspected was happening between Cal and Vicki. I felt I had to tell her. I tried to be gentle."

"None of this is your fault."

It wasn't her business, either, but she couldn't leave the poor girl wondering. Now she felt responsible for breaking Linnette's heart.

Olivia's hands tightened around her own coffee mug. "Don't you just want to wring his neck?"

"I certainly think Cal could've handled the situation better. Linnette is devastated. From what Corrie said, this is her first really serious relationship."

"The poor girl," Olivia murmured sympathetically.

Grace had suspected, at his farewell dinner, that things weren't going as smoothly between Cal and Linnette as she'd assumed. When she'd discussed it with Cliff later, her husband had said that Cal was awfully eager to leave for Wyoming, eager to get away. Yes, he was genuinely concerned about the mustangs but it was more than that. Cliff hadn't really understood it at the time; now, however, everything seemed to add up.

"What do you know about Vicki Newman?" Olivia asked.

Grace had taken Buttercup, her golden retriever, to see the vet when the dog had a cancer scare, and she'd been impressed with Vicki's affection for animals. Sherlock, her cat, had only been in for routine checkups and shots. Vicki was often out at the ranch because of the horses, and had occasionally joined her and Cliff for a coffee. Their conversations tended to be rather stilted.

"She seems nice, but…"

"But what?"

Grace hated to say it out loud. "I find her rather…different. Don't misunderstand me. I like her, and she's certainly a skillful vet. She's always been cordial enough. It's just that she…communicates better with animals than with people."

"That could be said for Cal, too, couldn't it?"

Grace had to agree. "Especially before he started working with the speech therapist," she recalled. "It was the oddest thing…."

"What was?"

"Whenever he was around the horses, he didn't stutter at all." She frowned. "Even though his speech has improved, it's going to take a lot of effort on his part to learn communication skills. If the way he's dealt with Linnette is any indication…" Grace couldn't imagine Cal ever being talkative. She suspected he'd always have trouble sharing his thoughts and feelings with others.

Goldie delivered the pie and refilled their coffee mugs, then stepped away from the table.

"I feel so bad for Linnette."

"Me, too." Grace sliced into the pie, feeling a strange sense of sadness. "I just hope Cal's made the right decision."

"I do, too."

"Any news at your end?" Grace asked, eager to hear what Olivia had been up to all week.

"Actually, two pieces of information," Olivia said.

"I'm all ears."

"First," Olivia said, "Mom told me that Ben heard from his older son, Steven."

"The one who lives in California?"

"No, that's David. Steven lives on Saint Simons Island in Georgia."

"Right." Grace remembered that now. Will Jefferson, Olivia's brother, lived in the same state; he was definitely not someone she wanted to think about.

"Apparently, David's in some kind of financial mess and went to his brother for a loan. Steven called to tell his father about it."

Grace leaned back. "David's money problem surprises you?"

"Not really. I remember how he tried to swindle

my mother out of five thousand dollars." Olivia's eyes narrowed. "It makes me mad every time I think about him giving my mother this ludicrous story about needing surgery."

"Oh, brother."

"Apparently he already declared bankruptcy a couple of years ago and now there's no easy solution."

"He's being hounded by creditors?" Grace asked. She'd had some experience of that soon after Dan disappeared. It'd been a nightmarish time in her life. She didn't wish those kinds of pressures on anyone, David Rhodes included. "What I recall is that he asked you to fix his traffic ticket."

"Like I'd even *consider* such a thing."

Grace swallowed another bite of pie. "You said you had two pieces of information."

Olivia set her fork aside and seemed to be carefully choosing her words. "I don't think there's anything to be concerned about," she began.

"What?" Grace demanded. "Concerned about what?"

"It has to do with my brother, Will," Olivia informed her.

Grace did her best to appear completely indifferent. "What about him?" He was nothing to her any longer, other than a source of profound embarrassment.

"I know I probably mentioned that he and Georgia

are getting divorced. They've sold the house and the proceeds have been equally divided between them."

"Oh." Grace responded to the news with sadness—not for Will but for his long-suffering wife. Poor Georgia. Grace could all too easily imagine what she must've endured through the years. Closing her eyes, Grace acknowledged a sense of guilt for her part in this, and regret that she might have caused the other woman pain. She'd been foolish to get involved with Will. So foolish... Grace had known he was married, which only intensified her guilt. She suspected their emotional affair wasn't his first, nor was it likely his last. Granted, she hadn't slept with him but probably would have if the relationship had continued. And according to Olivia, he'd had other actual affairs.

Olivia seemed to be watching her closely.

Grace gave a beleaguered sigh. "There's more, isn't there." She could feel it coming.

Olivia nodded. "Will told Mom he was moving back to Cedar Cove."

Grace stared at her in horrified silence. "You've got to be kidding! What about his job?"

"He's retired now and seems to be at loose ends."

Grace closed her eyes. The last time Will came to town had been a disaster. This was shortly after she'd broken off the relationship. He'd insisted she didn't know what she was doing and that he loved her. At one point, Cliff had stepped in and, in a fit of anger and jealousy, Will had taken a swing at him. It'd been a dreadful scene, a public spectacle, with Will threatening to press charges. Thankfully Olivia had witnessed the episode and made it clear that Will didn't stand a chance of having any charges stick.

"I'm worried," Olivia said.

"About me and Cliff?" Grace asked and made a weak dismissive gesture with her hand. "Don't be."

"No," Olivia told her. "I'm concerned about Will. Mom is, too. She suggested he rethink this move. It's too drastic, especially so soon after the divorce. He needs to stay where he is. And…"

Olivia hesitated and took a deep breath. "What bothers me more than anything is that my brother, who can be as clueless as a Keystone Cop, might assume you're still available."

"Will *knows* I'm married." She remembered that Olivia had expressly told him.

"He knows, all right," Olivia said. "But a little thing like a wedding band, including the one on *his* finger, hasn't stopped him before. He might have the mistaken impression that it won't stop you, either."

Grace swallowed. "Then I'll just have to tell him." Cliff would be happy to oblige in that regard, too; however, she had every intention of keeping the two men away from each other.

Thirty-Five

The first time Anson Butler kissed Allison Cox was last October, after a Friday-night football game. Instead of attending the Homecoming dance, they'd sat in the bleachers and talked long after everyone else had left. Allison remembered that kiss as clearly as if it'd just happened. She'd had boyfriends before and had dated a jock while she was a junior. Clay was a really nice guy, popular and funny, but his interests were limited and they didn't have much in common. They broke up shortly after the prom.

Anson was different. They'd had a couple of classes together the year before, but she hadn't really noticed him until this year, when they sat across from each other in French. His language skills were impressive, and he seemed to catch on faster than anyone else. Allison hated the way he'd downplayed his abilities and made light of his intelligence. Thinking back, she decided it was his sense of humor, unexpectedly wry, that had initially attracted her.

Sitting in the bleachers now, in the same row as she had during that first kiss, Allison closed her eyes and tried to recapture the exciting sensations she'd experienced that night.

It'd been really cold, she recalled, and the lights on the field were off. Clouds scudding across the sky had frequently obscured the full moon; the intermittent darkness had given them a feeling of seclusion, of privacy. Anson wore his long black coat with a knit stocking cap pulled down over his ears. He didn't wear gloves and his hands had been cold to the touch. Unlike him, Allison was bundled up head to foot in a red coat and scarf, hat, mittens and boots with wool socks.

They sat huddled together against the wind. The music spilled faintly from the gym, where everyone was dancing. He'd ditched his friends and she had hers.

Anson had amused her that night, speaking in French, making up words. She'd laughed at something he'd said and then, for no reason, they weren't laughing anymore. Anson had leaned forward to kiss her, hesitant, as if waiting for Allison to stop him. All she could do was hope that he *wouldn't* stop. When their lips met, his were cold and chapped. Hers were warm and moist, and she parted them slightly, wanting him to know how glad she was to receive his kiss.

The moment was perfect. Afterward, they'd stared at each other for a long time, and then Anson had said that kissing her was even better than he'd expected. For her, too.

Her phone rang, jolting Allison out of those comforting memories. She snapped open her cell and saw that he was right on time. "Anson?" she whispered.

"I'm here. You got the message from Shaw?"

She nodded. His friend had called the night before and told her Anson would phone at nine. That was all he said, then he'd simply cut off the connection. "He seems to enjoy playing courier."

"Shaw's a good friend," he said.

"I know," she said. "Oh, Anson, I miss you so much." She tried to keep the emotion out of her voice, but she'd had some bad news and was struggling to hold it in. The last thing Anson needed was her dissolving into tears over a matter that didn't involve him. There was nothing he could do.

"How was graduation?" he asked.

"All right. I wish you were there. The rose was beautiful. Thank you so much for that, and the message, too." Her faith in him might have wavered, but Anson continued to love her.

"You talked to the sheriff?" he asked, getting directly to the point. "About the information Shaw gave you?"

"Yes. I told my father and we went in to see the

sheriff on Monday." This next part shouldn't come as any surprise, so she drew in a deep breath. "Sheriff Davis wants to talk to you."

Anson snickered. "Sure he does."

"Anson, you can't stay in hiding for the rest of your life!"

The returning silence rang like an alarm between them.

"I tried," he finally said.

"You tried?" she repeated. "What do you mean?"

"I phoned the sheriff."

"You talked to Sheriff Davis?" This was wonderful news, but no one had said a word to her. "I didn't know, I thought—"

"No, I didn't talk to him," Anson said. "I *tried* to talk to him. He wasn't there. I asked when he'd be available and I got this runaround. No one seemed to be able to tell me."

Allison found that difficult to believe, until she remembered overhearing a conversation between her parents. "Oh, I can explain. His wife died recently. You must've phoned at that time."

"What happened to his wife?"

"I'm not sure exactly, but Mom said she'd been sick for years." It all made sense now. "He took some time off after the funeral." She was encouraged by Anson's effort. "Try again, okay?"

Anson seemed to consider her suggestion. "Maybe I will."

"You didn't tell the people at the sheriff's office who you were—did you?" She felt positive he would've received more cooperation if he'd identified himself.

"No… The only person I want to talk to is the sheriff himself."

"Well. I know he's back in the office. My dad mentioned it last night."

"Okay."

All at once there didn't seem to be anything more to say. "Thank you for the rose," she said again. Allison had pressed it between the pages of a thick book, wanting to save it forever. The card, too.

"I'd've given anything to be with you."

"I know."

Some unidentifiable noise drifted into the background, and she wondered where Anson was. "I should go," he murmured.

"Are you taking care of yourself?" she asked.

"I'm doing all right. What about you?"

"I'm okay."

"Just okay?" he asked.

She was silent for a moment. "Do you know where I am, Anson?" Of course he didn't. "The football field," she told him.

"In the bleachers?"

She smiled, holding the small phone close to her ear. "And do you know why this spot is so special to me?"

"It's where I kissed you the first time."

He did remember.

"All I could think about that night was kissing you. You looked so pretty. Your cheeks were rosy with the cold and you wore this bright red coat…. I figured you could go with any guy you wanted and yet you were with me."

"Don't," she said, her throat tightening.

"Don't?"

"If you keep on talking like that, I might start to cry." She tried for a humorous approach. "I look terrible when I cry."

"I wish I could kiss you right now."

"Me, too." It was at this point that she lost her composure. "Oh, Anson. I can't go on like this."

He didn't speak right away; when he did, his voice was low and harsh. "You're all I think about. That's what gets me through each day. I don't know where I'd be now if it wasn't for you. Just remember that, okay? No matter what happens about this fire or anything else, just remember you're the best thing in my life."

"Okay," she whispered.

"I realize you don't know if you can trust me," he said. "But for my sake try. Please, Allison, try."

"I will."

"There's something else bothering you."

She was surprised he'd noticed. "Don't worry about me."

"What is it?" Anson asked.

"It has nothing to do with you or the fire or any-thing."

"Tell me," he insisted.

She couldn't hold back a sob. "Remember my friend Cecilia?"

"The woman who works for your dad?"

"Worked," she corrected, and swiped at the tears that ran down her cheeks. "She's moving. Her hus-band's in the navy, and he was transferred and she's moving to San Diego."

"I'm sorry."

"Why do the people I love best all go away?"

"Allison…"

"No, I'm the one who's sorry. You have enough worries—you don't need to hear that."

"I love you."

The tears were coming in full force now. "I know."

"Tell me about Cecilia," he said. He seemed to un-derstand how badly she wanted to talk to someone about this loss.

"She's been such a good friend to me. She's like the older sister I never had. You probably don't remember what I was like when my parents divorced, but I went through a really dark period." She sobbed again. No one else knew this next part. No one, not even Cecilia.

"Go on," he said softly.

"She told me what it was like when her parents split up. I didn't want to hear it and tried to block out everything she said. As much as possible I made her life miserable.

"Then one afternoon I came into the break room and found her by herself and she was crying. She didn't want me to see, but I could tell she was looking at a picture. When I had the chance, I got into her purse and took out the picture." If anyone had caught her, she would've been in serious trouble. "The photo was of her little girl who died. Later I learned she'd named her baby Allison, and that was one of the reasons she felt so close to me."

The tears fell unrestrained, ruining her makeup. "I talk to Cecilia all the time and, oh, Anson, I don't know if I can bear losing you both."

"You'll be able to keep in touch with her."

"That's what Cecilia said, too, and we've promised we always will."

"I'm coming back to you, Allison," he promised. "Somehow, I'll make it happen."

This was the hope that got her through each day. Just as Anson's memories of her were the thing that sustained him.

Thirty-Six

Saturday, at the end of a long shift, Rachel checked her phone messages and found a slip with Nate's name on it. Instead of returning his call, she dropped it inside her apron pocket, along with the two already there. She knew what he wanted. His parents were in town. The very thought of meeting Nate's father and mother was enough to shoot chills of dread down her spine.

Thankfully Teri had given her a wonderful reason to avoid it. The fact that she'd eloped with Bobby Polgar meant everyone at the shop was doing double duty. As much as her own schedule would allow, Rachel had taken over Teri's clients. Now she and Jane were the only staff left at the end of a long, frustrating Saturday.

Then, as if she'd just gone out for a few minutes, Teri Miller Polgar casually sauntered in.

The instant she saw her friend, Rachel squealed with delight. "Look at you," she cried as she jogged across the salon and threw both arms around her. Teri radiated happiness. She positively glowed with it.

"It's about time you got back," Jane shouted from the reception desk where she'd laid out the cash. She came around and hugged Teri, too, and then grabbed her hand to examine her engagement and wedding rings. "Wow! Look at the size of that rock."

"That's not the only thing that's big." Teri loved saying the outlandish.

"Teri," Rachel chastised, slapping her friend's hand.

"Speaking of big, where is the mighty Mr. Polgar?" Jane asked.

Teri shrugged. "I was distracting him too much," she said, and her eyes twinkled. "He's off to Russia on some big chess tour."

"You're not going?"

"Do I look like I have a passport?" Teri chided, hand on her hip. "James brought me home, but I'm already miserable without my Bobby. I'll bet he feels *exactly* the same way."

"James the chauffeur?" Jane asked in a mock-dignified voice with a stagy British accent.

"The very one. He's waiting for me outside." Smiling, she surveyed the salon. "Believe it or not, I missed the place. I had James bring me here even before I went home."

"Tell me," Rachel said, dying of curiosity. "What's it like being married to someone famous?"

Teri cocked her head to one side. "I don't really see Bobby as famous, you know? He's just Bobby. He thinks about chess almost all the time, and talks about it, too." She grinned smugly. "Except when we're in bed." She giggled, then grew serious again. "I'm crazy about him. Me and Bobby Polgar—who would've guessed it?"

"Are you coming back to work?" Jane wanted to know.

"Of course," Teri said, as if that should be understood. "I told Bobby I need to work. He can do his thing, but I have mine."

"You *need* to work?" Rachel asked. Anyone who spent as much money as Bobby obviously had it.

"For my sanity, I do," Teri said. "I could follow Bobby around from city to city and match to match, but I'd hate it. I'd hardly ever see him and I'd be by myself most of the time. This way, he'll fly in to stay with me as much as possible, and I can meet him in New York once in a while. I've got to keep an eye on my kid brother, too, you know. And my sister, Christie, needs me—she's finally dumping her loser husband."

"New York?" Jane repeated enviously, back at the receptionist's desk. That seemed to be all she'd heard.

"Bobby's got a place somewhere in Manhattan. A penthouse, I think. I haven't seen it yet, but I will soon."

"He's got a penthouse in Manhattan and you've got a tiny apartment in Cedar Cove," Jane muttered. "Hmm. Sounds perfect." She shook her head. "You guys are about as mismatched as any two people on earth."

"Jane," Rachel said, "they're in love, and that's what matters."

"Look who's talking." Jane glanced up from the desk where she was bundling the bills. "You keep ignoring Nate's calls. Why is that, might I ask?"

"That's completely different! Nate has nothing to do with this."

"It's exactly the same. Love conquers all, remember? You're afraid to meet his parents, so you don't answer his calls. It wouldn't surprise me if he just showed up one evening and took the decision out of your hands."

"I have Jolene this weekend. Nate knows that."

"And you made sure of it, too, didn't you?" Jane challenged. "You arranged it on purpose."

She had, but Rachel wasn't admitting it. "Don't be ridiculous." Turning her back on Jane, she faced Teri. "I want to hear all about Vegas."

Teri's eyes brightened. "We barely left the bedroom. So there I was in Vegas and I didn't play a single slot machine. Do you want to hear how Bobby kept me occupied?"

"I think we already know." Some details were best not shared.

To her astonishment, Teri hugged her hard. "Thank you so much," she whispered. "I've never been happier in my life. You were the one who convinced me to go with him. I'm so glad I did. Bobby is wonderful." Her eyes welled with tears. "I know it's hard to believe, but he needs me. And he loves me."

Rachel didn't find that hard to believe at all.

The phone rang again. Jane started for it, then paused, looking over at Rachel. "You want me to get that or should I let the answering machine pick up?"

"The machine," she said.

Jane frowned. "Coward."

It was true; Rachel was terrified of Nate's parents, especially his mother. She couldn't help it. That one brief phone conversation with Patrice Olsen had confirmed every fear Rachel had. They hadn't even met, and already his mother didn't like her. Not only that, Mrs. Olsen had driven home the fact that Rachel didn't belong in their world—and Rachel wasn't so sure she wanted to be there.

"Rachel?" Teri eyed her skeptically.

"Forget all that," she said, unwilling to discuss her relationship with Nate. "I want to hear about you and Bobby."

Teri was eager to tell her. "He wants me to buy a house while he's away. I haven't told him yet, but I've decided to learn about chess, too. I've been reading up on it. Did you know chess started out as a four-handed dice game in India about fourteen hundred years ago?"

Both women shook their heads.

"Me, neither. Some really interesting people played chess, too. Charles Dickens played and Tolstoy and Sir Walter Scott. Humphrey Bogart was a chess player, and John Wayne. It's all really fascinating. Although," she said with a wink, "I didn't do a *lot* of reading."

Deciding she should change the subject, Rachel asked, "What about the lease on your apartment?"

"Oh, he's already taken care of all that. Bobby had one of his people do it. You know what is so…so wonderful?" Teri whispered. "He makes me feel like I'm the only woman in the universe."

"Teri, I'm so happy for you."

"I'm happy, too," Teri said dreamily. "So happy I can't believe it. I don't know what I ever did to deserve this…."

"You cut his hair," Jane said, snapping a rubber band around a pile of bills. "One free haircut, and you're set for life. Go figure."

Not one to take offense, Teri giggled. "You guys want to come to my place for dinner?"

"Sorry, I can't tonight," Jane said. "We're going to my in-laws."

"I can't, either," Rachel said.

"You coming back to work on Tuesday?" Jane asked Teri.

"I'll be here."

"Good. Everyone'll be thrilled to see you."

"Where are you off to?" Teri asked as Rachel finished cleaning up her station for the night.

"Home. Bruce is bringing Jolene over and—"

"She's avoiding you-know-who," Jane supplied unnecessarily.

Rachel reached for her purse and after a brief farewell, she and Teri left the salon. "You want to stop by my place?" she invited. "The neighbors'll get a kick out of seeing the limo and James."

Teri shook her head. "I can't. Bobby's phoning as soon as he lands."

"You can take his call at my house," Rachel told her.

With a silly grin, Teri said, "No, I can't. I wouldn't want Jolene listening in on that conversation."

Rachel laughed. "You're right."

Teri walked out to the parking lot with her. James stood outside the stretch limo, awaiting her instructions.

Her friend paused and studied her. "You still care about Nate?"

Rachel sighed. She was crazy about this guy, but not crazy enough to have a face to face with his mother. She supposed she'd have to meet the dragon lady sometime, but she wasn't ready for that yet.

They hugged once more and each went their separate ways. Rachel had only been home a few minutes when Bruce arrived with Jolene.

"We brought dinner," he said as his daughter skipped into the house, carefully holding a pizza box.

Bruce followed, carrying the little girl's overnight bag, which he set down in the living room.

"You can go now," Jolene said, dismissing him.

Rachel laughed at the shocked look on Bruce's face. "I guess you got your marching orders."

He seemed downright perplexed. "Don't I get any dinner? I paid for that pizza, I'll have you know."

Jolene sent Rachel an enquiring glance. "Let him stay," Rachel said with a smile.

"All right," his daughter agreed reluctantly. "But you have to leave after you eat. You can't watch the movie with us."

"What movie?"

"*The Princess Bride*," Rachel whispered. "It's her favorite."

"I heard that," Jolene said. "It's your favorite, too."

"Okay, it's my favorite, too."

Bruce rolled his eyes. "Personally I'd rather paint the living room—which is exactly what I'm going to be doing."

Rachel went into her small kitchen and got three plates, setting them on the table.

"Do you have any red pepper flakes?" Bruce asked.

"Top shelf, right-hand side," she instructed, her head in the refrigerator as she dug out three cans of soda.

The doorbell chimed, and Jolene immediately shouted, "I'll get it!"

A sick feeling grabbed Rachel's stomach even before she turned to see who it was. Sure enough, Nate Olsen stood in the doorway. With both his parents.

Thirty-Seven

Justine had just spent two hours with a Bremerton architect, and everything had gone as well as she'd hoped. Excited and happy, she phoned her mother, who suggested she visit on her way home. The courts were closed for Flag Day, and while the rest of the business world went about its normal tasks, all state and federal employees enjoyed a one-day vacation.

Justine had always loved 16 Lighthouse Drive; seeing this house never failed to bring her a feeling of peace. The sweeping front porch was like an invitation to come in, to linger, to relax with family and friends.

When she walked up the steps, Justine could hear the vacuum cleaner running. So this was how her mother had chosen to spend her day off. Olivia was cleaning house. That was typical; her mother was a stickler for order. According to Olivia and to Charlotte, as well, that old bromide about cleanliness being next to godliness was one hundred percent true. While Justine agreed in theory, she had other priorities and struggled to keep up with her young son and her husband, her friends, the house, plus her job. Justine had handed in her notice the previous Friday; the manager hated to see her leave and had offered her an employment package that sounded tempting. Justine, however, had other plans.

After knocking, she let herself in the front door. Only it wasn't her mother doing the vacuuming, as she'd assumed. Jack Griffin stood in the middle of the living room wearing headphones, one of her mother's frilly white aprons tied around his waist. His eyes grew wide with shock when he saw her.

"Well, well, well," Justine said, unable to hold back an amused grin.

Jack glared at her and removed the headphones.

"Now, this is news," she murmured. "Should I call for a reporter from the *Chronicle?*"

"You tell a soul about this and you're dead meat," Jack threatened, scowling into the kitchen at Olivia.

"Children, children," her mother called, as she entered the room, drying her hands on a dish towel.

Jack held Justine's gaze. "Your mother said vacuuming ranked right up there with jogging," he muttered. "She made a convincing case. It seemed an easy way to get my daily exercise."

"And the apron?" Justine asked.

Jack's gaze connected with Olivia's. "That was your mother's idea, too. Something about dusting the bookshelves…" He quickly pulled off the offending apparel and tossed it on the sofa. "You aren't going to say anything, are you? This is our little secret, right?"

Justine raised her hand as if swearing an oath. "My lips are sealed."

Shaking her head, Olivia walked over and hugged Justine. "It's wonderful to see you, sweetheart. So your appointment with the architect went well?"

Justine smiled brightly. "Mom, I really think this idea of yours is going to work."

"Of course it's going to work," Olivia said as if she'd never doubted that for a moment. "And it wasn't really *my* idea. If you recall, we came up with it together. I just happened to comment how nice it would be to have a special place to go for an elegant tea. Next thing I know, you've got everything in motion."

"I don't have to eat at this tearoom, do I?" Jack asked as he unplugged the vacuum and rolled it toward the hallway closet. He thrust his little finger in the air and sipped from an imaginary cup.

"Not unless you wear your apron," Justine teased, saluting him with her own hooked pinkie.

Her comment earned her a dirty look from Jack. "Very funny."

"Next time I'll lock the front door," Olivia promised him.

"There won't be a next time."

"Yes, dear."

Jack checked his watch. "I'd better get to the office. Some of us have to work, you know." He kissed Olivia long enough to cause her mother to blush profusely. With a flourish Jack bowed, then started for the door. Just before he left, he caught Justine's gaze and winked. She winked back.

Justine loved the changes she'd seen in her mother since Olivia's marriage to Jack. For the first time since Jordan's death, she felt her mother was truly happy. Come to think of it, *she* was happy, too. The fire had changed everything for a while and she'd faltered; so had Seth. They were finally coming out of this stupor and finding themselves again.

Justine and her mother talked over cups of tea, exchanging ideas. Olivia suggested a brand of tea she particularly enjoyed. They talked about dishes for the tearoom and Justine decided to purchase an assortment of teapots of different colors and styles. Justine wondered if her grandmother would share her recipe for coconut cake, a longtime family favorite. Olivia was sure she would. Lunches would be soups, salads and sandwiches, with a special each day. They wrote out lists of recipe ideas and discussed decor.

Justine picked Leif up from preschool at noon. While he napped, she spread out the architect's rough drawings on the kitchen table, and made notes in pencil, incorporating some of the ideas she and her mother had come up with.

By the time Leif was awake, everything had been put away. Dinner was in the oven, the salad was made, and a bottle of wine was cooling on ice while she waited for Seth's return from the boatyard. She had so much to tell him, so much to share.

The doorbell rang, surprising her. Penny, who was in their fenced yard, was barking wildly. Before Justine could stop him, Leif raced ahead of her and happily threw open the front door. He stared blankly at the man who stood there.

"Warren," Justine said, trying not to frown.

"Hello, Justine," he said. When she didn't immediately invite him inside, he asked, "Would it be all right if I came in?"

Seth was due home any minute and wouldn't be pleased to find her entertaining Warren Saget. "I suppose so." She hoped the hesitation in her voice let him know she was reluctant.

She unlocked the screen door and held it open. Regarding their guest suspiciously, Leif wrapped his arm around her leg, and Justine reached down to pick up her son.

"What can I do for you?" she asked. She didn't mean to be inhospitable, but she wasn't interested in his company. She wanted him to state the purpose of his visit and then leave. That was it.

Warren wore a pained look at her reaction. "I

stopped at the bank last Friday. You weren't there but I learned that you've given notice. You never mentioned that you'd decided to quit."

Justine felt it was none of his concern, but didn't say so. "The job was only for the interim while Seth and I figured out what we were going to do about the restaurant."

"So you've made a decision?" he asked curiously.

"We have," she said, her enthusiasm bubbling to the surface. "We're going to rebuild."

"When we spoke earlier, you told me you were disappointed that Seth hadn't listened to your ideas. Has he had a change of heart?"

Rather than explain the complexities of her business—and her marriage—she just nodded. "Something like that."

"Well, great. We've been friends for many years, and I hope we can work together on this."

Justine was sorry she'd confided in him at all, friend or no friend. She now felt disloyal to Seth for saying anything. She didn't answer.

"Tell me what you've decided," he pressed.

"I don't have time to go into it now. But I will say I'm quite excited about it."

Warren smiled. "That's wonderful, Justine."

Bored now, Leif squirmed and she set her son back on the floor. He tugged at her shirt. "Read me a story, Mommy," he clamored. "Now, okay? Read me *Goodnight, Moon.*"

Justine shushed him. "I need to get back to my family," she said, hoping Warren would get the message and leave.

"I understand," he muttered, edging toward the front door. "You will give me an opportunity to bid on the construction project, won't you?"

"I'm sure we can do that," Justine said, although she already knew Seth wouldn't want Warren on the job. For one thing, his methods and materials were sloppy; for another, he'd use every opportunity to spend time with Justine.

At the door, Warren hesitated and turned back. "I've never made my feelings for you a secret," he said. "I'd like to be more than your builder."

"Warren, please!"

"We have a long-standing friendship, Justine. I've missed you. I hoped you'd realize how much I care for you. You mean the world to me, and you always have."

"Warren," she said firmly, "I'm married. I love my husband and my son."

"You haven't been happy," he insisted. "I know you, Justine. I can see it in your eyes. You didn't want me to find out, but you couldn't hide it from me."

"That's changed."

"Has it?" he asked softly. "Or is this just a temporary fix?"

The door off the kitchen opened and Seth entered the house. Penny bounded in with him, then charged toward Warren, but skidded to a stop at one curt word from Seth.

Her husband looked slowly from Justine to the other man.

"Hello, sweetheart," she said, grateful to see her husband. She walked over and kissed his cheek, circling his waist with her arm. She was silently letting Warren know that her loyalty and her love belonged to her husband. Seth scooped up Leif and kissed him, then petted the dog, who sat obediently beside him.

"Warren." Seth nodded stiffly.

Warren did the same. "Seth."

"Warren was just leaving," Justine said pointedly. She'd explain Warren's presence as soon as he'd gone.

"I came to talk to Justine about the rebuilding project," Warren said affably enough. He seemed more inclined to stay and chat than to leave.

"I see," Seth said. Without even a hint of welcome, he strode to the door and held it open.

For his part, Warren didn't budge, and the two of them exchanged lethal glares.

"Would you kindly stop," Justine snapped, hands on her hips. "Both of you." She stepped between them, saying, "Warren, please go."

He cast her a hurt-little-boy look, his voice petulant. "I think you should tell Seth."

"Tell me what?" Seth demanded.

The dog barked but stayed in her sitting position, and Leif ran into the other room.

"There is *nothing* to tell." Justine felt like shouting. Warren was clearly trying to cause trouble between her and Seth, and she wasn't going to allow it.

"Warren, stay away from me. I mean it. Is that plain enough for you?" He'd overstepped the bounds, and from this moment forward, she wanted nothing more to do with him.

Thirty-Eight

Maryellen was feeling very pregnant. The baby could be born at any time, and she'd never looked forward to anything more. She was ready. Her bag was packed, the house was clean, thanks to Ellen and Joe, and her baby blanket was finished. She'd bring the baby home from the hospital wrapped in the pale yellow blanket she'd knit herself.

It was another sunny day, and Maryellen sat on the sofa, gazing out at the yard and folding a batch of towels still warm from the dryer. Jon was at home, working in his downstairs office. That was where he had his darkroom, along with his computer and printer for digital photographs. He'd willingly stayed in the same vicinity as his parents, which was a sign that his attitude had changed, at least a little.

Joe and Ellen had taken Katie outside to enjoy the sunshine. Like any toddler, Katie loved exploring her world. Through the sliding glass door, Maryellen could see the three of them walking around the yard, exclaiming at the flowers and studying each blade of grass.

Katie had not only grown close to her grandparents, she talked about them tirelessly. If Jon was there, he found an excuse to change the subject. He never spoke against his parents to Katie, but he didn't discuss them with her, either.

Recently Maryellen had noticed the slightest softening toward his family. It'd started the afternoon he found his father playing with Katie as she chased butterflies. That was the day they'd first spoken. They'd exchanged a few brief remarks since then, friendly but noncommittal.

The phone rang and Maryellen automatically reached for it. Now that her due date was almost upon them, her mother called twice a day and visited often. Her sister, Kelly, was due in a few weeks, and they kept in frequent touch. This was probably Kelly; she usually phoned in the early afternoon.

"Hello," she said, expecting to hear her sister's voice. She did.

"How are you feeling?" Kelly asked.

"How are *you* feeling?"

"Pregnant," Kelly said, giggling.

"Me, too." Only Maryellen wasn't laughing.

"My goodness, who knew nine months could take

so long," Kelly complained. Unlike Maryellen, her sister had difficulty getting pregnant, but—again unlike Maryellen—she had no difficulty staying pregnant. "Nothing fits anymore and I've got new stretch marks every day. Not that I'm complaining, mind you. It's just that I'd forgotten how uncomfortable pregnancy can be."

Maryellen was hard pressed not to remind her younger sister that she'd spent most of her own pregnancy trapped on the sofa in their living room. The comforts she longed for were the simple, ordinary aspects of what used to be her life. She yearned for the time she could crawl into bed and cuddle with her husband. The pleasure of a real bath was a forbidden luxury. Climbing stairs was out, too, and since the baby's bedroom was on the second level, she'd had to leave the decorating to her mother and Ellen. It didn't feel right not to be personally involved. She hadn't even seen it yet.

If that wasn't enough to unnerve Maryellen, she endured constant worries about the baby. She tried to be positive; nevertheless, she worried. Because of the problems associated with the pregnancy, she was deathly afraid that something might be wrong with her baby.

Early on, there'd been numerous blood tests and ultrasounds, and then, as the fetus developed, fewer and fewer. The physicians assured both Maryellen and Jon that everything appeared to be normal, but their words were always followed by a statement indicating that the ultrasounds offered no guarantee.

Maryellen had already accepted that because of her age and the problems she'd encountered, this pregnancy would be her last.

As was their habit, Kelly and Maryellen talked for about ten minutes. When she turned off the phone and set it aside, she was surprised to see Ellen in the kitchen, preparing a salad for dinner.

"Where's Katie?" Maryellen asked as she folded a thick yellow towel.

Ellen glanced up, lettuce in her hands. "She's still outside with Joe."

Thinking she might have missed seeing her daughter, Maryellen looked again. The yard was empty, and she saw no evidence of either her father-in-law or her daughter.

"I don't see them," she said, struggling awkwardly to her feet.

"I'm sure they're there." Ellen washed her hands, and taking the dish towel with her, walked outside.

Maryellen stood at the open glass door, watching Ellen as she strolled casually about the yard. When Ellen didn't see her husband or granddaughter, either, she moved out of Maryellen's sight.

After a few minutes, she heard Ellen shout, calling their names. Her voice became increasingly shrill when she couldn't locate them.

Maryellen's heart started to pound. *Something was*

wrong. She could feel it. Every maternal instinct she possessed went on full alert. Feeling light-headed, she made her way to the stairs that led to Jon's office.

"Jon," she called, trying to sound calm and collected. "Could you come here right away?"

Her fears must have been evident in her voice, because he was up the stairs in a flash.

His eyes immediately locked with hers. "What is it?"

She swallowed hard, fearing his reaction. "Joseph and Katie are missing."

"Missing," he repeated, gripping her shoulders. "What do you mean *missing?*"

"Katie was outside with Joe and Ellen. I was on the phone with Kelly. When we finished, Ellen was in the kitchen and I couldn't see Katie or your father. You know how much Katie loves the water and—"

She didn't get a chance to finish.

Jon was out the door, and she saw him dash across the yard toward the creek at the back of their property. The rushing water flowed down the embankment that led to Colvis Passage. If Katie had fallen in the swollen creek, it could carry her all the way to Puget Sound.

Standing on the deck, Maryellen pressed her hand against her forehead. Breathless, Ellen emerged from the bushes that lined the far end of the property. She looked at Maryellen and shook her head.

"Where's Jon?" Maryellen shouted.

"He went down to the creek. I couldn't make it."

"Joe?" she asked.

"I—I don't know. He couldn't have made it to the creek, either. The banks are much too steep."

Nausea built in the back of her throat, and for a moment Maryellen was afraid she'd throw up. This *couldn't* be happening. None of this could possibly be real, and yet the terror that overwhelmed her *was* real. She had a blinding headache, and feeling nausea and dizziness, she clutched the back of a patio chair.

"I don't know how this could've happened," Ellen cried, and tears filled her eyes. "Joe was with her…."

But it only took an instant to lose sight of Katie. The little girl loved to play hide-and-seek; all Joe had to do was turn his back for a few seconds, and Katie would see it as an opportunity to slip away.

Maryellen couldn't tell how much time passed. It felt like an eternity. Just as she was about to give way to panic, she saw movement in the bushes. Then she heard Katie's frightened wail. The relief that shot through her made her knees buckle.

Jon broke out of the thick underbrush and onto the grass, carrying Katie. The three-year-old was covered in mud from head to foot. He held her tightly in his arms.

"Where's Joseph?" Ellen cried as she rushed toward him.

Maryellen couldn't hear what was being said. Ellen ran forward, and Jon handed Katie to his stepmother. As soon as he had, he quickly went back to the same path he'd just left. Within seconds, he was completely invisible in the dense trees and shrubs that edged three sides of their property.

Katie continued to wail, but her deep, gulping sobs didn't signal pain so much as fear. Ellen brought Katie to Maryellen. As soon as Katie was in her arms and Maryellen had a fresh towel around her, the little girl stopped sobbing. She thrust her thumb into her mouth, then released a shuddering sigh as Maryellen sat and gently rocked her daughter and allowed her own heart to return to normal.

"Joe, dear God in heaven," Ellen wept, pressing her hand over her mouth.

Maryellen raised her head to see Jon leading his father through the brush and toward the house. Joe was drenched and shivering with cold.

"What happened?" Ellen asked, coming toward them.

Joseph hardly seemed able to speak. Between deep breaths, he explained. "Katie was playing hide-and-seek, and she went into the woods." Joe gasped for oxygen. His skin was ashen and his lips blue. "She got too close to the edge. I saw her slip and fall in, so I went after her."

Maryellen could picture the older man, racing down to the creek, stumbling over rocks and fallen trees in an effort to catch his granddaughter before she was swept away.

"I slipped, too," he choked out as he leaned forward, his hands on his knees, fighting for breath.

Jon ran into the house and got a blanket to wrap around his father. Maryellen could see the barely restrained anger in his movements as he spread it over his father's back.

"Ellen," he said sternly, "get Dad to emergency now."

His stepmother hurried into the house for her purse.

"Do you need me to drive you?" he asked when she returned.

Ellen seemed to be in a daze. She hesitated, and then declined, shaking her head. "No. Just take care of Katie."

"Have them check his heart."

"I'm fine," Joseph insisted. "As long as Katie's all right, then I am, too."

"Do what I say," Jon barked, and Ellen nodded obediently.

Refusing to listen to any protest, Jon took his father to the car and helped him inside. Ellen was already behind the wheel and had started the engine.

Jon stepped away from the vehicle as Ellen pulled out, the wheels spitting dirt and gravel. He stood there watching until she turned onto the road.

When he joined Maryellen on the deck, Jon looked about to collapse. "Katie?" he asked.

"She's shaken up but she's fine."

"Thank God." He closed his eyes and lowered his head.

Maryellen did thank God. They'd almost lost their daughter. If Joseph hadn't gone after her when he did, Katie could have drowned—probably *would* have drowned.

After a few deep breaths, Jon reached for the child and hugged her tight. Then he carried her upstairs for a warm bath and fresh clothes.

Maryellen changed her muddy top and when she sat down realized she was still trembling. She was shaking from the inside out, her knees literally knocking against each other.

They'd come so close to losing Katie, she thought again. So close.

When Jon reappeared, she was afraid he was going to chastise her or declare that his parents were no longer welcome in his home. From the moment Joseph and Ellen had arrived, he'd looked for any small infraction as an excuse to send them packing. He'd never said so, but Maryellen knew.

This afternoon, Joseph had given him the perfect reason. And yet…Jon had called him "Dad."

Warm and dry now, Katie acted as if the events of the afternoon hadn't distressed her in the least. Maryellen felt ready for a mental ward while their daughter chattered happily away.

"Are you all right?" Maryellen asked Jon.

He grimaced and took her hand. "I don't ever want to live through another afternoon like this one."

"Me, neither."

"When I saw Joseph holding her, I didn't know what to say. I wanted to rant at him and berate him for letting Katie out of his sight."

"You didn't?"

"No. I think he was on the verge of having a heart attack himself."

"Oh, no…" She wanted to ask Jon how that made him feel but she couldn't. His father had saved Katie's life, yet Jon couldn't acknowledge that, not explicitly, not in so many words.

An hour later, Ellen phoned to report that Joe had been seen by Dr. Timmons at the medical clinic and his heart was fine. His blood pressure was elevated but that was understandable. They were both back at the hotel and resting comfortably.

Grace phoned, and after she'd learned of the frightening episode, she and Cliff came over with dinner. Maryellen barely touched the chicken-and-rice casserole. She assumed it was because of the terror she'd felt earlier, but her appetite was nonexistent.

After straightening the kitchen, her mother was getting ready to leave, and Maryellen clambered up from the sofa to hug her mother and Cliff goodbye. She suddenly noticed how much her back ached. Then and only then did she recognize what was happening.

She was in labor.

"Can you stay for a while?" she asked her mother.

Grace glanced at Cliff, then nodded. "Of course."

"Jon." Smiling, she stretched out her arms to her husband. "I think it would be a good idea if you took me to the hospital now."

Thirty-Nine

Charlotte spent the morning with her friends at the Senior Center. The knitting group get-together had included a lunch of sandwiches and coffee— and a thoroughly enjoyable gossip fest. Although it was a lovely afternoon—the official first day of summer—and the house was only a few blocks from the center, she drove. She usually enjoyed the short walk, but today she needed to run errands.

Ben had decided to remain at the house, which meant he wouldn't be playing bridge with his friends while she visited with hers. It meant he wouldn't be running errands with her, either. From the moment they'd started seeing each other, Ben had willingly accompanied her on such routine tasks, and Charlotte had come to rely on his companionship.

Something was bothering him. Had they been

married longer, she might have known instinctively what it was. She was becoming familiar with his moods, but this latest one was new—and it worried her.

As she pulled into the grocery store lot, she found a convenient parking spot, turned off the engine and sat in her car for a few minutes while she thought about this. She'd hoped Ben would feel comfortable enough to share his troubles with her. Apparently he didn't. But rather than take offense, she tried to think of ways to ease his worries. Perhaps she should ask him outright why he seemed so distressed. That was what she'd do, she decided.

Olivia was walking out of the grocery just as Charlotte was going in.

"Mom!" her daughter said excitedly. "Maryellen's having the baby."

"Now?"

"She might even have delivered already. Grace phoned yesterday evening to tell me. She and Cliff spent the night out at Jon and Maryellen's. They're watching Katie."

"That's wonderful news." Charlotte was so pleased for Maryellen—and her mother. Grace was having a good year, and she deserved it. Two grandbabies due within a few weeks of each other, a new husband and—Charlotte frowned. Although Grace's happiness was unmistakable, a cloud darkened the horizon. Will was returning to Cedar Cove. Her son's sudden desire to move here concerned Charlotte. Her fear was that Will intended to meddle in Grace's relationship with Cliff.

"Mom?" Olivia asked.

"Oh, sorry, I was just thinking."

"I have to get back to the courthouse—I came to pick up something I need for dinner. It's tofu, but don't tell Jack. He eats it all the time, only I don't let him know."

"Good for you." Grabbing a cart, Charlotte entered the store. "Be sure and call me when you hear about the baby."

"I will," Olivia promised. "Talk to you later."

Charlotte exhaled heavily. Life did have its share of worries. Her first concern was Ben; she'd tackle Will later. Ben had been so preoccupied lately, so distracted, and try as she might, she couldn't put her finger on what was wrong. That thought weighed on her as she hurriedly finished her tasks. She bought milk and bread, went to the cleaners, then headed home.

Yes, she'd ask him. Further deliberation had confirmed her decision. Asking him was the only *sensible* way to handle the situation. Charlotte was a *sensible* woman, or she had been, until she'd fallen in love with Ben Rhodes.

On the drive back to the house, Charlotte stopped at a roadside stand selling strawberries freshly picked on Vashon Island. She purchased two large flats to put up strawberry preserves. Perhaps she could tempt Ben by serving scones topped with sweetened strawberries and whipped cream for dessert this evening. He enjoyed scones, especially when they were hot from the oven. As she'd always known, a clever woman had ways of getting information from a man. Her granddaughter might tell her this was an old-fashioned approach, but whatever worked…

The moment she got home, Ben came out to carry in the strawberries and the few groceries she'd bought.

Charlotte followed with the dry cleaning. The prices they charged for pressing a shirt were highway robbery, but Ben insisted. He didn't want her expending time or energy at the ironing board when the cleaner was happy to do it.

Ben brought everything into the kitchen, and she saw that he hadn't eaten the lunch she'd left for him. Rather than comment, she mentioned Olivia's news. "Maryellen's having the baby."

Her words fell on deaf ears.

"Did you hear me, Ben? Maryellen's in labor."

"Oh, sorry," he said, recovering quickly. "That's great."

"It is," Charlotte agreed. "Olivia said she'd let us know as soon as Grace calls her."

"Good."

Shaking her head, Charlotte set the kettle on the stove to heat water for tea. Whatever was wrong had grown markedly worse in the time she'd been away.

"These are a lot of strawberries," Ben commented as he picked up a large red one.

"Let me wash a few of those for you to nibble on," Charlotte suggested. "They were just picked this morning and couldn't be sweeter." The vendor had told her as much.

Ben set the strawberry down and shook his head. "Thanks, but no."

Charlotte couldn't stand it a minute longer; she had to know. "Is everything all right, Ben?" she asked.

He walked over to where Harry had curled himself up on a kitchen chair and began to pet her cat. "Of course."

"I don't mean to pry," she continued, "but you just haven't been yourself lately."

Ben pulled her close and hugged her, sighing deeply. "Are you *sure* you want to know?"

"Of course."

"It's my son," he confessed.

"David?"

He sighed again. "Yes."

"Here," she said, the practical side of her nature immediately taking over. "I'll pour water in the teapot and while it steeps we can start to talk."

"I don't want to burden you with this," Ben said, dismissing the offer.

"Nonsense! I'm your wife."

"But—"

"Ben, please. Unless you confide in me, I won't

feel comfortable sharing my worries about my own children."

"Your children are nothing like mine—especially David," he murmured.

"That's not true, but we can discuss Will later."

"Will?" Ben looked up, his face a picture of astonishment.

"I'll say more about him when we're finished. Please, tell me what's got you in such a state."

He seemed relieved to finally tell her, and Charlotte silently scolded herself for delaying this conversation. Instead of fretting, she should've asked him sooner.

He waited until she'd poured hot water in the teapot and assembled cups. When she sat down with him at the table, she noticed that he'd placed Harry on his lap. Not so long ago, the cat had taken exception to sharing Charlotte's affections, but Ben had won him over—as well as everyone else in her life. Harry purred contentedly as Ben stroked his sleek body.

"You know Steven phoned a little while ago."

"Yes." Charlotte had talked briefly with Ben's older son. It'd been a bit awkward at first, but Steven sounded like a fine young man. Unlike his brother, he wasn't a charmer and seemed to have difficulty carrying on a conversation. Fortunately Charlotte had no such problem and she'd done her best to let him know how pleased she was to be part of his family.

"Do you remember Steven said that David had gotten himself into a financial mess—again?"

"Yes. He declared bankruptcy a few years ago, didn't he?"

"Right," Ben confirmed. He looked past Charlotte, not meeting her eyes. "What I didn't tell you has to do with yet another mess my son's gotten himself into. I'm not sure of all the details. According to Steven, David was recently arrested for fraud. It was because of an insurance claim he made."

Arrested? "Oh, dear," she gasped.

Ben continued to pet Harry, his fingers smoothing the cat's soft fur. "Then all of a sudden, he had the money to hire a high-priced attorney to represent him."

"All of a sudden?" Charlotte repeated. "You mean he came into some unexpected funds?"

Ben grew very still. "Apparently this was shortly after the break-in and arson at The Lighthouse."

Charlotte felt a chill. "Are you saying David might somehow have been involved in that?"

"Yes," he said hoarsely.

"Ben, surely David would never do anything so…so vile."

"You think I *want* to believe my own son could do something like this?" he asked. "I have lived with this information for nearly a week now, and I can't ignore the possibility any longer. I checked the dates and they coincide."

"Oh, Ben."

All the color had drained from Ben's face. "I didn't

say anything earlier because…because I didn't know if I could. It's one thing to suspect my son of such an ugly, underhanded crime and another to give his name to Sheriff Davis as a suspect."

Charlotte's heart ached for her husband. What an impossible decision he had to make. Regardless of anything else, the young man was Ben's son. No father wanted to be responsible for turning his own child over to the authorities.

"While you were at the Senior Center this morning, I paid Sheriff Davis a visit."

"Oh, Ben." Charlotte stretched her arm across the table, wanting to clasp his hand, to offer what comfort she could. He didn't seem to notice.

"Sheriff Davis took down all the information and said he'd look into it," Ben said stoically, gazing down at the cat. "If it does turn out that David had something to do with the fire, promise me, Charlotte, that you and your family—" He seemed incapable of continuing.

"I love you, Ben. If David *is* involved, you can rest assured that no one in this family will blame you in any way for your son's actions."

Her husband glanced up, and his eyes shone with appreciation. "Thank you," he whispered, taking her hand at last. "If David did this, I'll personally reimburse Justine and Seth for their losses."

"Ben! You can't possibly do that." Restitution for The Lighthouse wasn't *his* obligation—and it would wipe him out financially. "They have insurance."

"It doesn't matter," he said. "I won't allow my son to hurt you, directly or indirectly."

Charlotte thought she might weep for his pain, for his disappointment in David and his nobility in assuming an obligation he didn't need to.

But that was Ben, wasn't it? And those were the reasons she loved him.

Forty

"Can't you do something to help my wife?" Jon pleaded with the labor room nurse. The middle-aged woman with gray-streaked hair wore a name tag that identified her as Stacy Eagleton.

"Honey, I'm fine," Maryellen whispered, her brow damp with perspiration. Her death grip on Jon's hand said differently.

Jon was worried. Maryellen had been in labor for nearly twenty hours, and with each passing minute, his fears mounted. Everything about this pregnancy had been difficult. He didn't know why he'd assumed the labor would go smoothly when nothing else had.

The hospital staff had all assured him that his wife's labor was progressing normally. "These things take time," Stacy had repeatedly told him. If one more person uttered that trite remark, Jon thought he might not be able to control his temper. Twenty hours *wasn't* normal. It couldn't be. Katie had arrived with far less effort on Maryellen's part.

"Give her something for the pain," he instructed the nurse.

His wife opened her eyes and lifted her head from the pillow. She'd grown so pale, so weak. "No," she said in a surprisingly strong voice. "It's not good for the baby."

At this point, Jon was far more concerned about his wife.

Before he could try to convince her to accept medication, Maryellen groaned. Then, as if she couldn't bear the agony another second, she tossed her head from side to side. Jon did everything he could think of to help her, but she no longer wanted him to touch her or massage her back. The most she'd let him do was count off the seconds, and that seemed so damn little.

"Excellent, excellent," Stacy encouraged Maryellen, after checking to see if dilation was complete. "Everything's looking good. I'll get Dr. DeGroot for the delivery."

Kissing Maryellen's hand, Jon whispered, "It won't be long now."

His wife offered him a feeble smile. "I don't think our baby is all that willing to be born."

Jon remembered the elated feeling he'd experienced at Katie's birth. The miracle of bringing a new life into the world had left him awed and humbled, although much of the labor remained a blur in his memory. How oblivious he'd been to the reality he faced now as he watched his wife struggle to give birth to his child.

He loved Maryellen deeply, but never more than he did just then. He laid a cool cloth across her brow and kissed her temple and whispered his love.

"Are Joseph and Ellen still in the waiting room?" she asked, looking up at him.

Jon nodded. Grace had called them, and as soon as his father and stepmother learned that Maryellen had gone into labor, they'd rushed to the hospital. The truth was, he didn't want them there. All that prevented Jon from asking them to leave was his love for Maryellen.

"Have you talked to them?" she asked.

Although he knew he was a disappointment to her, Jon shook his head. "I've had the nurse give them regular updates."

Her smile faded.

Jon leaned his forehead against the edge of the mattress. He couldn't remember the last time he'd slept. But he knew the tiredness he felt didn't compare to what Maryellen had endured during these twenty hours.

She moaned slightly, and her grip on his hand was punishing. Trying to help her, he softly counted off the seconds. The pain lasted a full minute and a half, and her contractions came so quickly now, there was barely a moment between them. When this latest one had passed, a tear rolled from the corner of her eye.

Dr. DeGroot arrived and nodded at Jon. "This seems like a good day to be born, don't you think?" he said, as he took his position at the end of the birthing bed.

Everyone suddenly seemed to get busy. Several nurses surrounded Maryellen and there was a noticeable surge of energy now that the birth was imminent.

"Let's see what we have here," the physician murmured. "Okay, Maryellen, get ready to push."

Jon felt a little extraneous, as though he had no real role anymore. There was some problem, but he didn't completely understand it. Apparently the baby was facing up instead of down, which had contributed to the lengthy labor.

The pain that followed seemed to be the worst so far. Maryellen gritted her teeth and bore down with what appeared to be an excruciating effort. She half rose from the bed and groaned loudly.

"Good, good," Dr. DeGroot said encouragingly.

Jon was mesmerized. He watched as the baby slipped free of Maryellen's body and into the physician's waiting hands with a lusty cry. The doctor smiled and turned to Jon. "Congratulations! You have a son."

Jon smiled at Maryellen. "It's a boy," he told her unnecessarily.

"Is he all right?" she asked anxiously.

"He's perfect," Jon announced, although he couldn't really see anything through the tears that clouded his vision.

"Welcome, little Drake," Jon whispered. This was the name Maryellen had liked best. They'd discussed names a hundred different times, poring through baby-name books Grace had brought them from the library. Unreasonable as it seemed now, he'd assumed the baby would be another girl; if it was, they'd settled on Emily.

"We don't have a middle name," Maryellen said, reminding Jon that he'd promised to choose a second name. "Drake Jonathon has a nice ring to it." She smiled up at him and he leaned forward and kissed her, putting all his love, all his pride in her into that kiss.

"There's plenty of time to choose one," he said, entwining his fingers with hers.

When he straightened, the nurse handed Jon his son. Maryellen was right; little Drake found the world the most irritating of environments. The baby cried until Jon rocked him gently, then placed him in Maryellen's arms.

As if she needed to see for herself, she pulled back the receiving blanket and examined his fingers and toes. Drake gazed up at her and instantly settled down to sleep. Like Jon, his son had found his contentment in Maryellen's arms.

"I believe your family's waiting for the news," Stacy Eagleton told him after finishing with Maryellen.

"Will you tell them?" Maryellen asked, her eyes imploring.

It was decision time for Jon. A part of him wanted to ignore the fact that his father and stepmother were even at the hospital. He'd vowed not to let them back in his life. He'd fought to maintain this promise to himself. He didn't *want* to care about his father. The man had turned his back on Jon when he'd counted on his family to come forward with the truth. He'd lied. Even knowing his oldest son was innocent, Joseph had sent him to prison.

"Jon?" Maryellen whispered.

Her soft voice drew him from his reverie. As he stared down at his sleeping son, Jon's heart filled with such overwhelming love that he thought it might burst wide open. For the first time, he understood his father's dilemma.

Jon had two children now, too. Katie and Drake, and he loved them equally. If he had to choose to send one to prison over the other, which would it be? He didn't ever want to find himself in such a horrible position—sacrificing one child to protect the other. Granted, Joseph had no legal or moral right to make such a choice, to play God in this way, but Jon could understand it now, at least a little. Yes, Jim had been guilty, but he was a weak and vulnerable man, easily broken. He'd lied about Jon's culpability, and Joseph had backed him up. Joseph had chosen to sacrifice Jon because he was stronger than his brother. Prison would have destroyed Jim. In the end, of course, Jim had destroyed himself, despite Joseph's attempts to save him with rehab and counseling and unstinting support.

"I'll tell them," he said.

Maryellen clasped his hand. "Thank you."

"They've been here nearly twenty hours, too," he reminded her.

As he walked into the waiting area, Ellen and Joseph immediately stood. Two other people who sat at the far end glanced over, then returned to their conversation. His parents looked at him, their eyes wide with expectation. They were both tired and disheveled, especially his father. Only the day before, Joseph had frantically stumbled through knee-deep running water in a desperate attempt to save Katie. His father, with a weak heart, had nearly suffered a heart attack while rescuing his granddaughter.

If he lived another hundred years, Jon would never forget the panic in his father's eyes when Jon found him sitting on a fallen log, holding a sobbing Katie in his arms. He'd been panting with relief and physical exertion and was deathly pale. Seeing the embankment his father had clambered down in his struggle to reach Katie, Jon thought it was a miracle the old man hadn't been swept away himself.

"We have a son," Jon told them.

Ellen brought her hands to her mouth and tears streamed from her eyes.

"A boy," his father repeated, grinning proudly.

"He's perfect."

"Maryellen's okay?" Joe asked.

"She's exhausted. I'm married to an incredible woman, you know that?"

Joseph grinned again and nodded in obvious agreement.

"How much does he weigh?" his stepmother asked.

"Six pounds, thirteen ounces," Jon said. "He measured twenty-one inches."

"He's going to be lanky like his father," Joseph commented.

"And grandfather," Ellen added, looping her arm around her husband's waist. She leaned her head against his arm. "Have you and Maryellen chosen a name?"

Jon looked at the two of them. "We decided on Drake," he said.

"Drake. Drake Bowman." His father seemed to test the name, then nodded approvingly. "I like it."

"Drake Joseph Bowman," Jon said, his gaze connecting with his father's.

Joseph stared at him, and then his eyes filled with tears that ran down his cheeks.

"Oh, Jon." Ellen was sobbing now. She held out her arms to him and after the briefest hesitation, Jon hugged his stepmother and then his father.

He hadn't known he was capable of forgiveness until that moment. What he'd discovered was that when a man found love, the kind of love and contentment he'd discovered with Maryellen, there wasn't room in his life for hatred.

Forty-One

Teri stirred the boiling macaroni and tasted it to see if it was done. She sometimes overcooked it, and that would ruin everything. This dinner was special—she was cooking for Bobby.

Although she'd been married for more than two weeks, it was the first meal she'd put together for her husband. Bobby was flying in from someplace in Russia following an important match. She'd had no idea the demands on his time would be this constant.

Although he was faithful about phoning each and every day, and often more than that, Bobby hadn't contacted her when he'd finished this match. As far as Teri could figure, Bobby was on a plane. He'd caught a flight immediately after the competition and was landing in Seattle at five. James was with him and would drive him from Sea-Tac to Cedar

Cove—to their home. Yes, they had a real home now, at 74 Seaside Avenue.

Within days of her return from Las Vegas, Teri had purchased the house. Bobby insisted she move out of her apartment and into a place big enough for both of them. He'd written the check, and she'd moved in so quickly that her head was still spinning. She'd learned that when Bobby Polgar wanted something done, it got done.

He'd given her a credit card, which she'd used to buy new furniture from a high-class Seattle shop, including a leather sofa, the price of which shocked her, and a solid-wood dining suite. And then there was the bed....

Eager to show her husband the house and cook for him, Teri had decided to make one of her favorite meals. The macaroni-and-cheese dish was a hit whenever she brought it to the Christmas potluck at work. She had a couple of variations on it, too. Sometimes she added cooked taco meat, which was just hamburger and taco seasonings. Occasionally she threw in some chopped tomatoes.

Teri wanted Bobby to like her cooking. When he'd taken her out for dinner, or—more frequently—ordered room service, they'd always had fancy food, lobster and such. She thought he'd enjoy some more basic fare. Her kind of food.

It seemed strange but they'd been apart longer than they'd been married. She needed her husband, missed being with him and, yes, sleeping with him. Although the truth was, neither of them seemed too interested in sleep. She smiled, recalling how much Bobby seemed to enjoy the marriage bed. Well, it'd mostly been hotel beds, but that wasn't the point.

Peering out the window, she saw the stretch limo pull up in front of the house. Too excited to wait a second longer, Teri dashed out the door. Bobby hadn't even taken two steps toward her when she hurled herself into his arms. The impact nearly knocked him off his feet. If not for the fact that the vehicle was directly behind him, Bobby would've keeled straight over.

Teri spread eager kisses across his face, setting his glasses askew. She quickly realized he wasn't nearly as enthusiastic as he normally was.

"Bobby?" she asked, leaning back to get a good look at him. "What's wrong?"

He didn't answer right away. In fact, it was James who explained in hushed tones. "You didn't hear?" he asked. "Bobby lost."

Well, those things happened. He couldn't possibly win every time. You win some and you lose some; that was her philosophy of life. In Bobby's case, he won more often than he lost because he was so darned good at what he did.

"He doesn't like to lose, Miss Teri," James explained further.

"No one enjoys losing," she said calmly. "Does this mean our entire visit is ruined?"

"He doesn't lose often," James continued.

Bobby didn't even seem to be listening. James dragged his suitcase into the house and placed it just inside the living room.

"I'm afraid he's taken the defeat hard," James said in a low voice as he walked past her on his return to the limo. "He needs a bit of TLC, and he'll be fine. I'll be back to pick him up in two days."

Pulling her husband gently by the hand, Teri led him into the house. "Let me give you a tour," she said.

He seemed to be in some kind of trance. "Bobby, are you listening?" She waved her fingers in front of his face with no result. Instead he walked over to the chessboard she'd set up on a small oak table and sat down. She'd studied a diagram to position the pieces correctly. Without a word, he started moving them around.

Teri could see it would do no good to interrupt him with a little thing like…life. His concentration was so complete that he didn't seem to be aware of where he was or that she was with him. Rather than pouting or making a fuss, Teri dished up a bowl of her specialty macaroni and cheese, squirted on some ketchup and sat cross-legged on the carpet beside him to wait.

An hour later, Bobby glanced up, apparently shocked to find her there. "Teri?"

"Hello, Bobby. Welcome home."

"I lost."

She sat down on the sofa next to him and brushed his hair aside. "I heard," she said tenderly. "I'm sorry."

"I don't like to lose."

No kidding. "Did you figure out what went wrong?" she asked, looking over the chessboard and the pieces he had scattered about.

He nodded.

"Are you hungry?"

Her question resulted in a furrowed brow, as if he wasn't sure how to answer.

"Never mind, I'll get you a dish."

"I could wait," he said, and his eyes held hers for the longest moment.

Teri might not have been married long but she knew that look. "Perhaps you'd like to see the rest of the house," she suggested. "Shall we begin with the master bedroom?"

For the first time since he'd arrived, Bobby smiled. He trotted down the hallway behind her and into the bedroom. Then he shut the door.

An hour later, Teri lay next to him in bed, sighing with contentment. Bobby held her close. "Losing doesn't seem so bad when I hold you," he murmured.

"Good. I'm glad."

"I'm hungry now," he said and, as if to prove his point, his stomach growled.

"You should be," she said, kissing his jaw. "That was quite a workout I gave you."

Bobby smiled again, and Teri wondered how many people in this world had actually seen her husband do that. Not many, she suspected. She climbed out of bed and got her robe, slipping her arms into the sleeves.

"Do you like the house?" she asked, tying her sash. She'd felt a bit anxious about that, since she'd made the decision without Bobby.

He sat up and grinned. "Very much. Especially the bedroom."

Teri swatted his shoulder playfully. "Come on, husband of mine, and I'll serve you my specialty."

He tilted his head to one side, and gazed up at her, his expression intense.

"Bobby?" She wasn't sure what he was thinking when he stared at her like that.

A deep frown wrinkled his brow and the perplexed look gradually turned into one of pleasure—and wonderment. "I love you," he said simply. "I really love you."

She leaned over and kissed him softly on the lips. "I love you, too."

Their time together was brief, too brief to suit Teri. They had three nights and two full days. Every evening she cooked for him. He enjoyed her macaroni and cheese, and her chili pie, another dish she'd invented, and her broccoli quiche, which she'd made using a recipe she'd cut out from the *Chronicle*. They listened to music and she taught him how to play Yahtzee and strip poker. He preferred the poker.

He liked the fact that he didn't yet know anyone in Cedar Cove. She'd taken Saturday off, so they had the whole weekend, during which they saw only each other—no friends or neighbors. Teri didn't even answer her phone.

Except for the five days they'd spent on their honeymoon, they'd had almost no time together. Those days in Vegas weren't a true indication of what life with Bobby would be like. Now that he was home, she'd been surprised by how little he actually slept. He'd told her once that he spent a lot of time thinking, and that had been no exaggeration. He required four hours or less of sleep a night. Often she found him sitting in the living room in front of the chessboard, studying it intently, working out moves in his mind.

Sometimes he seemed to forget she was with him. Teri didn't take offense at his lack of attention. Because when he did remember, he made her feel more cherished and loved than she'd ever felt in her life.

When he said he loved her, he meant it. Loving someone seemed to be a new experience for Bobby, and it was important to him that she know how strong his feelings were. Every day they were together he bought her gifts, ordering them by phone or Internet, and no doubt paying a premium for quick delivery. These weren't minor gifts, either. The first day it was a diamond tennis bracelet and a tennis racket to go with it. Teri had never played tennis in her life. Bobby, however, believed the two were supposed to go together and she wasn't about to disillusion him. The following day it was a wall-mounted plasma-screen television with satellite hookup.

When James arrived, Teri had to swallow the words to ask her husband to stay a few extra days.

Bobby held her and then kissed her. She kissed him back. "When will I see you again?" she asked, thinking any more than a few hours would be too long.

He explained his travel schedule, the upcoming matches. His answer was lengthy, technical and confusing. She looked to James for a translation.

"A week."

"I can last a week," she whispered.

Bobby smiled and hugged her a final time.

"Take care of him," she told James, her hand lingering on her husband's arm.

"I will." He opened the car door for Bobby, who reluctantly climbed in the backseat.

Folding her arms, Teri stepped away from the curb.

"You did a great job," the chauffeur said under his breath as he walked around the limo. "I've only known Bobby to lose one other match in all the years I've worked for him. Afterward, he sank into a depression that lasted for months."

"He'll be all right now," she assured the driver.

James touched the rim of his cap. "You're good for him, Miss Teri."

What she didn't tell James was that Bobby was good for her, too.

Forty-Two

Linnette had waited for this moment ever since she'd heard Cal was back from Wyoming. After a week, he'd phoned and asked if they could meet.

She had restrained herself from calling him, and the fact that he'd taken so long to get in touch only compounded the pain. Hoping to put them both at ease, she'd suggested the waterfront park. It was neutral territory, and in the early afternoon, there were few occupants besides the seagulls. On Thursday evenings during the summer, the park held Concerts on the Cove, with free entertainment ranging from rock-and-roll groups to folk singers and swing bands. Linnette hadn't yet attended a single one, although she knew her parents enjoyed the outings. It didn't strike her as something that would appeal to her father, but he went, primarily to please her mother. It was their once-a-week summer date. If it wasn't so ironic, it would be laughable. Her married parents dated more often than she did.

As Linnette sat in the bleachers waiting for Cal, she wondered how she'd react when he told her face-to-face that he no longer wanted to be part of her life. For reasons she couldn't really explain, she needed him to tell her in person. Ending their relationship with a phone call was just wrong.

She saw Cal drive into the lot next to the park and climb out of his pickup. Her heart went on alert, and her pulse accelerated at the sight of him. The memory of all the good times they'd had together brought hot, stinging tears to her eyes. That embarrassed her, and she quickly blinked them away. As Cal approached, she stood up.

He looked tanned and handsome, even more attractive than he'd looked before. He wore jeans and a Western-style shirt, and his Stetson was pulled forward to shade his face.

"Hi," she said evenly. "Welcome back."

"Thanks," was his reply. He stood awkwardly in front of her, his thumbs hooked in his jeans pockets. "It's good to be home." No hint of a stutter, she noticed.

She sat down again and he joined her on the bottom bleacher. For a few seconds, neither said a word. To Linnette's way of thinking, Cal should be the first to speak.

"I don't want to hurt you, Linnette."

Well, it was too late for that. She *was* deeply hurt, and fighting not to show it. She tried to tell him to save his breath, but the words didn't make it past the constriction in her throat.

"I never meant to fall in love with Vicki."

"You're sure you love her?" That was the important question.

"I'm sure," Cal said. "We have a lot in common."

If this was supposed to make her feel better, it hadn't worked.

She could see that he was waiting for her to say something, and despite the emotions that simmered inside her, she couldn't. She'd wanted this meeting and agreed to see him when he'd phoned. She didn't know what she'd expected—certainly not this crush of pain and loss. Perhaps it would've been best to simply walk away and not look back.

Cal glanced at her. "Aren't you going to yell at me or anything?"

She managed a smile and stared down at her feet in their neat, polished pumps. "I thought I would, especially when you first told me. I guess I'm past the angry stage." She wasn't really, but couldn't see any point in discussing it or telling him it often took years to get over rejection. At least that was how she felt about it.

"I…I don't have much experience in relationships," she said. This grief was new to her, a life-lesson she didn't *want* to learn—or repeat.

"I know and—"

"You don't know any more about relationships than I do," she told him.

"No, I don't," Cal murmured amenably. "I think we both liked the idea of being in love."

She didn't agree with him, but there was no reason to argue. "Perhaps," was all she said.

Cal sighed and looked out over the cove. "I guess your entire family's upset with me, and I'm sorry about that. I like your family."

She shrugged. "Mom and Dad both think you're the greatest thing since flu shots."

Cal cracked a smile. Then, apparently feeling it was necessary to predict a positive future for her, he said, "One day you're going to meet someone who'll love you more than I did."

Linnette supposed Cal meant that as a compliment, but it didn't sound like one. "I should hope so. I'd hate to think getting dumped is going to be a regular occurrence for me."

"That's not what I meant."

"I know." Then, to her dismay, a tear escaped. Hoping he hadn't noticed, she quickly wiped it away. She hadn't anticipated this heart-wrenching sense of regret and wasn't sure how to react to it. She'd truly loved Cal and tried to help him. Perhaps that was where she'd gone wrong. Perhaps no man wanted to be helped by the woman he loved—or thought he loved.

"Vicki asked me if she should come and talk to you herself. I—I didn't think that was a good idea."

"Probably not." Linnette figured it wouldn't look too impressive if one of the community health-care professionals scratched out another's woman's eyes. The thought produced a near smile.

"I have an announcement of my own," she said with false enthusiasm.

Cal looked directly at her then, for the first time since their conversation began.

"I've decided to leave Cedar Cove." She made it sound as if she'd received the opportunity of a lifetime, when no such prospect existed. In fact, she'd be breaking her contract and her lease, packing her bags and walking away with no destination and no plans.

"You're moving?" He seemed shocked by that.

She was astonished that he actually thought she'd stay in Cedar Cove.

"I've always wanted to see other states."

"You have a job?" he asked.

Not yet she didn't. But it shouldn't be a problem finding employment in one of the small towns that dotted middle America. "Do you think I'd move without a job?" she asked, implying what she knew he wanted to hear.

"What did your parents say?"

Of course she hadn't told them yet. This had been a recent decision—made all of two minutes ago. And yet…it felt right.

She had to leave Cedar Cove. It was difficult enough to recover from a broken heart, but it would become impossible if she had to see Cal and Vicki around town. No, the only reasonable solution was to pack her bags.

"I'm sorry," Cal said wretchedly. Linnette knew he was sincere. In two words he'd told her he would have spared her this pain if he could.

"Don't worry about it," she said with a flippant air. "I'm learning lessons most girls learn in high school. I…I always was a late bloomer."

She stood abruptly, needing to get away. "Goodbye, Cal."

He stood, too, looking at the ground, shuffling his feet, obviously ill at ease. "I'll always be grateful to you."

He'd be grateful. Well, that was nice, but it didn't make up for the fact that he didn't love her anymore. Linnette walked home to her waterfront apartment, which wouldn't be home for much longer, and climbed the stairs. Not once did she glance back, which was an accomplishment of its own.

Coward that she was, Linnette phoned the medical facility so she could talk to the personnel director and give notice verbally. A formal letter would be coming, she said. When she got off the phone, she wrote and printed out the letter, as promised. And then, because she needed to do something physical, she pulled out her suitcases and started to pack.

Forty minutes later, her doorbell chimed, and for a fleeting moment, hope emerged and had her rushing to answer the door. But it wasn't Cal, and she'd been deluded to even think it might've been. Instead Dr. Chad Timmons stood there.

"You've given your notice?" he demanded, pushing his way past her, irritation written on his face. He was still dressed in his whites and had obviously come straight from the clinic.

She nodded.

"I won't let you."

"Sorry, too late. I've already had that discussion with Alma McDonald," Linnette said without emotion. "I've written my letter of resignation. Besides, what makes you think you can force me to stay?"

"You can't leave," Chad insisted, his hard gaze holding hers. "Okay, so you had an important relationship go sour. Happens to all of us sooner or later."

It had never happened to her until now, and she wasn't sticking around to see Cal and his new girlfriend together at every community function. Perhaps a stronger, better woman would be capable of that, but Linnette couldn't do it.

"Do you intend to run away every time you hit a difficult patch emotionally?" he asked. "Is this the kind of pattern you want to set in your life? Come on, Linnette, get a grip. You're an adult. Act like one."

The harshness of his words felt like an attack. She

stood up to it, though. In little more than a year, she'd experienced two disappointments in romance. She wanted out. Okay, her reactions were childish; she didn't care. Besides, she didn't know why Chad felt so concerned about this, since he was interested in Gloria, not her. Fine, she'd dealt with that, and really it hadn't been so painful because Cal had entered her life. She'd sure made a mess of that relationship.

"Sorry," she said, meeting his eyes. "I'll let you know where I land."

Chad frowned. "You're really going?"

She nodded. No one else knew yet. She still had to tell her parents and Gloria, but she was leaving Cedar Cove.

That much was certain, even if nothing else was.

Forty-Three

"Allison." Her father's voice rang over her cell phone. "Could you stop by the sheriff's office?"

"Now?" she asked, glancing regretfully at her two friends. She was on her way to the Silverdale Mall for a much-needed shopping break. Her mom had let her use the car, and Allison had volunteered to drive. Since graduation, all she'd done was work at her dad's office. She had less and less of a social life these days. It seemed pointless to date anyone else, because no matter how this whole arson mess ended, she loved Anson.

"Yes, now," her father insisted. "It's important."

"Does...does this have anything to do with Anson?" Her friends looked at her, and their conversation instantly died.

"It does."

Her heart leaped into her throat. "I'll be there in ten minutes." After apologizing to her friends as she dropped them at a bus stop, Allison reversed her direction and headed back into Cedar Cove. Her stomach was in knots. Something had happened.

The sheriff's door was closed, and Seth and Justine Gunderson sat outside his office. So did Roy McAfee, the private investigator she'd once gone to on Anson's behalf. They all smiled warmly when they saw her.

"Hello," she said nervously.

"Hello," Justine said. "I think you're supposed to wait here, too."

Allison took the fourth chair and twisted her purse strap around her palm. "Is my father talking to the sheriff?" she asked.

Mr. Gunderson nodded. He began to speak, but the door opened then, and her father stepped into the hallway. He brightened when he saw her.

"Can you tell me what this is about, Dad?" she asked, coming to her feet.

"I sure can." Her father smiled. "Actually, it wasn't Sheriff Davis or I who asked to see you." He held open the door and gestured her inside.

Wondering at his words, Allison entered the small office and noticed Sheriff Davis right away. A soldier stood next to him, a handsome young man, wearing fatigues and a cap. The name tag on his jacket said Butler.

Butler.

No, it couldn't be. Allison looked again. It was.

"Anson?" she whispered, hardly able to believe what she saw.

He smiled and held out his arms. Even with her father and the sheriff watching, she didn't hesitate. Allison rushed forward for the biggest, most precious hug of her life. Her throat was crowded with tears of joy. "You enlisted in the army? All this time you were in the *army?*"

Anson grinned. "There aren't a whole lot of options for someone hoping to escape a few unpleasant complications."

"When?" she asked, astounded at the changes in him. He looked better, healthier than at any other time she'd seen him.

"I'd made the decision before the fire that burned down The Lighthouse. I talked to a recruiter and saw there were more opportunities for me with the military than anyplace else. I enlisted in Silverdale. Even though I was a 'person of interest' with regard to the fire, I wasn't charged with anything, so it didn't stand in my way. I had all the credits I needed to graduate."

Relieved though she was, Allison felt angry, too. He could have trusted her! "Why didn't you tell me?"

"I wanted to graduate from basic training first— prove I could do it. I needed to consider my choices."

"Which are?"

"To return to Cedar Cove and answer a few questions, for one," Sheriff Davis put in.

"I couldn't drag you into this," Anson said, turning to Allison.

"Anson wasn't responsible for the fire," she argued, ready to do battle even now.

"We already know that," her father assured her.

"We have another person of interest we're planning to question," Sheriff Davis explained. He nodded at Anson. "We appreciate your help, son. You're free to go." They exchanged handshakes. "Thanks to you," he added, "we're pretty sure who set that fire."

"Thank you, sir," Anson said respectfully. He turned to Zach. "Do I have your permission to speak to Allison privately, Mr. Cox?" he asked.

Allison's father smiled at his daughter. "If I said no, I fear I'd have a family mutiny on my hands."

It was all Allison could do not to hug her father. Before anything could prevent their departure, she linked her hand with Anson's, and they walked out together. As they were leaving, Sheriff Davis asked the Gundersons to step into his office.

Allison had so many questions, she wasn't sure which one to ask first. "You know who set the fire?" she blurted out. "Was it because of the license plate?"

"Partly. I didn't know his name, but I'd seen him

around town. He saw me, and I knew it wasn't safe for me to stick around, so I ran. The way I figured it, with my record, I'd get blamed for the fire anyway." They left the building and before they could walk toward the parking lot, Anson stopped abruptly. He pulled her under an outside stairwell. "Listen, Allison, I know this is crazy, but I swear if I don't kiss you right here and now, I'll lose my mind."

"Funny," she whispered. "I was thinking that, too."

Anson took her into his arms and brought his mouth to hers. She'd waited months and months for this kiss, and she wasn't going to let the fact that anyone could see them detract from the joy she felt.

"I have missed you so much," she murmured, her arms around his neck.

"Thinking about you was all that got me through basic training," Anson murmured as he ran his hands down her back.

They clung to each other for the longest time. Finally Allison couldn't stand not knowing, couldn't stand it for another second. "Who did it?" she asked breathlessly. "Who started the fire?"

"Like I said, I didn't know his name but I'd seen him in the restaurant and around town. He's a builder, I guess. It wasn't until very recently that I found out who he is. Warren Saget."

"Warren Saget," Allison repeated. "My dad does his taxes."

"Yeah, I know. Your father mentioned that."

"How did you identify him?"

"His picture was in the paper. Shaw's been mailing me the *Cedar Cove Chronicle*, which is how I managed to keep up with what's been happening around town. Saget was photographed in an ad for his construction company. Once I had a name to go with the face, I phoned the sheriff." He smiled grimly. "The license plate—first three letters *SUL*—checked out."

It was one thing to identify Warren Saget as the arsonist and another to prove it. All the information she'd seen and read—on TV shows and in mystery novels—indicated that there had to be more than circumstantial evidence or even eyewitness reports. The only physical evidence was the pewter cross discovered in the ashes—the cross that belonged to Anson.

"How will Sheriff Davis ever prove he's the arsonist?" she asked.

"Well, I'm a witness and I've agreed to testify in court. The sheriff and Mr. McAfee had another idea, though. He didn't tell me what it was, but it involves Mrs. Gunderson. That's why she was there with her husband. My guess," he said thoughtfully, "is that Sheriff Davis is going to arrange a showdown, a face to face with Saget." Anson shook his head. "The sheriff didn't confide in me. All I know is that if it's necessary, I'll testify against him in court."

She had another question, an important one. "How did my dad get involved?"

Anson rested his forehead against hers. "I called him. It was on his advice that I spoke to the sheriff."

"*What?*" He couldn't have shocked her more had he confessed to setting the fire himself. "When?"

"Last Friday. Like I said, I saw Saget's photograph and recognized him as the arsonist. I figured if I was ever going to step forward, the time was now. Otherwise I was afraid this would hang over me for the rest of my life. Your dad arranged today's meeting." He paused. "There are only a handful of people I trust in this world, and your father is one of them."

"Not me?" She realized she sounded hurt; she couldn't help it, even though she wanted to be more mature.

"I wouldn't put you in that situation." He kissed her again, letting his lips linger on hers. "I knew you wanted to believe in me. All I could do was pray that your father did, too."

Her father hadn't breathed a word of this.

"How long can you stay?" Allison already dreaded the day he'd have to leave her again.

"Just a week, and then I'm headed for specialized training. I'm going into Army Intelligence, working with computers. Whether I continue with the military or not, this is training I can always use."

"You're one of the smartest people I know." She couldn't keep the admiration from her voice.

He'd never been able to accept compliments well. He did now, though, because he believed it himself. "You're the only person who ever said that to me, and the funny part is, the tests I took proved it's true."

"I *know* it is."

"After I enlisted, the army put me through a lot of testing. I ranked high in languages and computer skills and a bunch of other stuff. Basically, I could have my pick, and I went with Army Intelligence."

"I'm so proud of you, Anson, so *proud*."

"You're the one who gave me the power to believe in myself," he said.

They left their haven under the stairwell and walked into the parking lot. Allison unlocked her mom's car, and Anson slid into the passenger seat beside her. "Where would you like to go?" she asked him.

"If you don't mind, I'd like to see my mother first. I have her money. Then Shaw." He grinned. "I don't think either of them will recognize me."

"I didn't at first."

"I know," he said with a delighted laugh. "I wish you could've seen the look on your face when it dawned on you that this short-haired soldier was me. It was priceless."

"You think you're funny, don't you?" she said, laughing, too.

"No, I think I'm the most fortunate man in Cedar

Cove. I don't need to run or hide. I have you back, and my life's on course. For the first time ever, I can smile at the future."

So could Allison.

Forty-Four

In Rachel's opinion, dinner with Nate's parents on Tuesday evening couldn't have gone worse. She'd felt miserable and out of her element the entire evening. They were in an outrageously expensive Seattle restaurant, where each place setting featured more cutlery than Rachel owned. That was bad enough. Even worse was the fact that Nate didn't even seem to notice how uncomfortable she was. Nate's mother had used every opportunity to belittle Rachel, and she'd done it in the most subtle way. Again and again, she brought up subjects that excluded Rachel and made no effort to explain who or what she meant.

Once when Rachel had the temerity to ask a question about someone she'd mentioned, Patrice Olsen raised her eyebrows—as if it should be understood that she was referring to the English ambassador's daughter. Following that, Rachel hadn't dared ask a single thing. They'd all started off on the wrong foot the night Nate had showed up at her house, his parents in tow. The fact that Bruce and Jolene were there seemed to give his mother even more of a reason to dislike her. Patrice obviously assumed that Rachel was cheating on her son.

After dinner, which seemed to last forever, Nate wished his parents a safe trip home. He appeared to be pleased with what he considered a successful evening. Now as he drove Rachel home, she tried to figure out how Nate had missed his mother's unmistakable attempts to thwart their relationship.

"I told you there was nothing to worry about," Nate said, briefly glancing away from the road. His right hand reached for hers and gave it a gentle squeeze. He looked happy and content, while Rachel felt just the opposite. "I knew the minute Mom met you, she'd love you, too," he continued, "and I was right. Mom thinks you're fabulous."

"How can you say that?" she asked, her voice barely above a whisper. "I was a nervous wreck all night." She didn't mention their initial introduction, but surely he could guess that was part of the reason!

"You were?"

"Yes," she said, close to tears. "Nate, I was so far out of my comfort zone I could hardly breathe."

He glanced away from the road again. "It didn't

show. You're a classy woman, Rach, and my parents thought you were great, but I knew they would."

Apparently he hadn't noticed that she hadn't swallowed a single bite of that expensive dinner. "Your parents really care about you," she said.

Nate shrugged. "Dad and I have had our differences over the years. As you already know, he didn't approve when I enlisted in the navy. We had a big blowup about that, but underneath it all, I know he's proud of me and my decision. He's come to trust my judgment. Mom, too." He cast a meaningful look in her direction as they drove across the Tacoma Narrows Bridge on their way back into Cedar Cove.

"Your parents have plenty of reasons to be proud of you, Nate." All Rachel wanted was to get home. Her head hurt and her cheeks ached from constantly smiling. She had less of a problem with Nate's father; unlike his wife, Nathaniel Olsen was a straight shooter. Mrs. Olsen had made it evident from the moment they were introduced that she found Rachel lacking. No, even before tonight, Rachel thought, recalling the phone conversation in the park. It wasn't anything personal; his mother just didn't consider Rachel Pendergast good enough for her only son.

They got to her house before Rachel was ready. She didn't want Nate to leave and yet at the same time she wanted to be alone. How could she explain the way his mother made her feel? If she tried, Nate would assume she was being paranoid and childish.

Nate parked his car at the curb and turned to smile at her. The look in his eyes told her he wasn't ready for the evening to end, either.

"Would you like to come in and talk for a bit?" Rachel asked. There was nothing to do at the moment but put tonight's dinner behind her. Later, when she'd had time to assimilate the evening's events, she'd be able to make some decisions.

"I would love a cup of coffee," Nate said and gently kissed her. His kisses had always been her downfall. The first time they'd kissed, Rachel had felt her world crumble at her feet. That hadn't changed in the months they'd been seeing each other; if anything the physical attraction between them had grown stronger.

Nate helped her out of the car and when they'd walked up to her front door, he took the keys from her hand and unlocked it for her. He observed these small courtesies, old-fashioned courtesies, which he'd obviously grown up with. The contrast between Nate and Bruce when it came to these details of courtship was striking. Not that she was dating Bruce. The fact that he'd even enter her mind at a time like this was an irritation she could do without.

"Thanks," she said when Nate gave her back the key ring. The living room was dark and she switched on a lamp on her way into the kitchen. Although she wasn't really interested in coffee, preparing a pot gave her something to do while she collected her thoughts.

"It looks like you've got a message on your answering machine," Nate commented as he pulled out a kitchen chair.

Without thinking, Rachel pushed the button. Almost immediately she heard Jolene's sweet voice. "Hi, Rachel." She sounded disappointed not to find Rachel at home. "I wish you were there. I was hoping we could go to a movie together. Dad says the one I want to see is a chick flick and I should ask you." She gave an exasperated sigh that made Rachel laugh. "You know men. Call me back soon, okay?"

Suddenly she saw that Nate was frowning. "They take a lot for granted, don't they?" he murmured.

"Not really." Now Rachel frowned, finding herself oddly defensive of Bruce and Jolene.

"I have news," Nate said. He'd waited until after she'd poured him a mug of coffee.

"Good news, I hope," she said as she joined him at the table. She stirred a teaspoon of sugar into her coffee.

"Rachel." He reached across the table, stilling her hand. "The *George Washington* has been transferred to San Diego."

It took longer than it should have to understand what that meant. "You're leaving Cedar Cove?" she asked.

He nodded. "I wanted to say something sooner, but with my parents in town and you so busy most of the time…"

"I haven't been *that* busy at work," she countered. "Not since Teri got back." But she knew what he'd say. Twice in the last month, he'd wanted to go out and she'd had to turn him down because of previous commitments to Jolene.

"You're always doing something with that girl."

"She has a name, Nate. It's Jolene, and she's my friend."

He shrugged. "I'm not sure it's healthy for you to spend so much time with her."

The anger Rachel experienced was hot and immediate, but she forced it back. This wasn't the time to discuss her relationship with Jolene. There were other pressing matters at hand. It had only begun to sink in that Nate would be leaving Cedar Cove. "You…you should've said you were being transferred," she said. "You should've told me earlier."

"I know." He covered her hands and gazed into her eyes. "I hate to tell you like this," he said quietly, "especially since we're heading out so soon."

"When?" she asked in a strained voice.

"Next week."

She gasped. "No…"

He nodded. "I'm sorry."

"I…" She didn't know how to react to this shocking news. The evening and the uncomfortable dinner were the least of her worries now. Nate had been transferred. Within a week, this man she loved would be gone.

Her mouth went dry. "What will that mean for us?" she managed to ask.

"It means," Nate said, exhaling deeply, "that you and I need to make a decision. A very important decision."

Her stomach tensed, and she could hear her heart pounding in her ears.

He paused as if to gauge her response to his announcement. "You know how I feel about you."

"Yes..." She felt the same way about him. Although he was a few years younger and the son of a wealthy and powerful politician, he'd managed to steal her heart. During the six months he'd been at sea, they'd written each other long letters, then later e-mailed on a daily basis, and in the process had grown close. When she'd first learned about his family, she'd wanted to end their relationship, but he'd persuaded her not to. Now the navy was taking him away from her.

"What about the others?" She'd become good friends with several of the navy wives, especially Cecilia Randall. Since Aaron's birth, she hadn't seen as much of Cecilia, and now Rachel understood why. Cecilia was adjusting to more than her newborn son, more than her move to Grace Harding's house on Rosewood Lane. She was packing up for San Diego.

"They're all moving, too," he said, "Almost everyone associated with the *George Washington* has been transferred."

"Oh." She hoped there'd be an opportunity to say goodbye to her friends and to exchange addresses and promises to keep in touch.

"I want you to think about something," Nate continued. "I want you to go there, too."

He couldn't be serious! Did he expect her to pack up her own life and become a camp follower?

"With your job you could work anywhere, right?"

He left her reeling from one shock and then another. "You want me to move, too? Just like that?"

"I know it's a lot to ask. I know it's unfair, but I have a reason for asking."

It didn't matter. "I can't, Nate. My life is here in Cedar Cove. My closest friends are here—Teri and Jane and—"

"Jolene," Nate finished.

"Yes, Jolene," she confirmed. If Rachel moved, the child would be devastated. She'd lost her mother a few years ago, and Rachel's leaving would make her feel like she'd been abandoned a second time. Rachel couldn't do that to her.

Nate brought her hand to his lips and gently kissed her knuckles. "Why don't we give it three months?"

"All right." Already she missed him. She knew instinctively that this would be different from when he was at sea. "Three months," she repeated, wondering, *Three months until what?*

"At the end of three months, we should both know," Nate said casually.

"Know *what?*"

"If this is something we can do, live apart like this," Nate explained, again sounding very casual, as if everything was clear. As if she understood.

She frowned slightly. "And if we decide we can't, what will that mean?"

"I'm hoping it means you'll be willing to join me."

"Join you?"

Nate's sensual mouth turned upward in a warm, inviting smile. "In other words, Rachel, I'm hoping you'll consider becoming my wife."

Forty-Five

Teri took a bite of her taco salad and realized that her appetite just wasn't what it used to be. Love did that to her. When Ray had first moved in with her, she'd lost ten pounds. Of course, that weight had reappeared, plus five additional pounds once she'd kicked him out, but that was beside the point. This time she was living with the right man and she'd never been happier in her life. In fact, she hadn't expected to be this happy, ever. Falling in love with a decent man who loved her back didn't happen to women like her. Only it had, and she thanked God every day for bringing Bobby into her life.

"Are you taking your lunch break now?" Teri said to Rachel, who'd wandered into the lunchroom. Her friend had been depressed all morning. Yesterday, she'd gotten the news that Nate was shipping out, and she was taking it hard.

"I'll be with you in a minute," Rachel said as she slipped a Lean Cuisine meal into the microwave and punched in four minutes. "The truth is, I don't have much of an appetite."

"Me, neither," Teri moaned. "What's wrong with us?"

"Men," Jane said, coming into the room. "That's usually what it is, anyway."

Teri laughed. "I miss Bobby," she admitted. She probably said this a dozen times a day. In order to maintain his ranking, he had to play tournaments all over the world. Teri hoped that in a year or two, he'd be able to slow down this relentless pace.

"Where is he now?" Jane asked, waiting for her turn at the microwave.

"New York City." She'd talked to him before she left for work. "He wants me to meet him there this weekend."

"Are you going?"

Teri shrugged indifferently, although she was dying to be with Bobby and to see his Manhattan apartment. She might even talk him into taking her to a real Broadway show. Aw, who was she kidding? When Bobby was in a tournament, chess was his sole focus. With one exception—their honeymoon. They'd had another subject on their minds in Las Vegas, and it didn't have anything to do with gambling. Just thinking about the hours they'd spent in bed made her miss her husband even more.

"You really love that chess geek, don't you?" Jane said, watching her closely.

"Bobby isn't a geek." He was, but Teri had no intention of admitting it, especially to Jane. "He's a *genius*, and he needs me, and yes, I love him."

"He likes her macaroni and cheese, too," Rachel teased, smiling at Teri.

"You just wait," Teri told her friends as the microwave buzzed. "One day you're going to fall this much in love and then you'll understand."

"Rachel *is* in love, aren't you?" Jane said, stepping around her to insert her frozen entrée into the microwave.

"Yeah," Rachel said, "but I didn't expect love to be this complicated."

"How so?" Jane asked, crossing her arms and leaning against the wall.

Rachel seemed about to explain, then changed her mind. Sighing, she lifted one shoulder. "It just is."

"Are you going to follow Nate to San Diego?" Teri asked. She'd hate it if Rachel moved away. Get Nailed wouldn't be the same without her, although she also wondered how long she'd be able to maintain her own splintered life, with Bobby's home on the east coast and hers on the west. More and more, she felt that her place was with her husband. They needed each other, although it was an odd feeling to need anyone. *Being* needed, yes; she was used to that. But needing someone? Having lived her life as independently as possible, Teri found this difficult to grasp.

Still, she didn't want to leave Cedar Cove. And she didn't know how these new contradictions in her life could be resolved.

"I don't know what I'm going to do," Rachel said.

"Just remember," Jane told her, "if you marry Nate, you're married to the United States Navy, too. You go where they tell you and when they tell you, and you do it without complaint."

"Aye, aye, Captain," Rachel teased, saluting Jane. She sat down and dipped her fork in the steaming chicken and rice entrée. "Actually, it isn't the navy that scares me. I can deal with navy life, but I'm not sure I can cope with Nate's mother."

Just then, Denise, the receptionist, came into the break room. "There's someone here to see you," she said, directing the comment to Teri.

"I don't have an appointment until one," she muttered, eyeing her half-eaten lunch.

"It's not a customer," she said. "It's that tall, skinny driver."

"James?" The only reason James would be in Cedar Cove was if he'd driven Bobby.

"There's someone else with him, too," Denise added, curling her lip as if to say she didn't like his companion. "A big, beefy guy."

"Is everything all right with Bobby?" Teri asked, instantly concerned. She immediately set aside her salad and got to her feet.

"He didn't say," Denise told her.

Pushing back the drape, Teri hurried into the salon foyer. Sure enough, James was there. She didn't recognize the man with him. Like Denise said, he resembled a wrestler with huge biceps beneath a black suit.

"Teri," James said. "Come with us."

"Is Bobby with you?" she asked

"He's in the car," the other man answered for him, speaking with a heavy accent. One Teri couldn't identify.

"He is? Why didn't you say so?" She started out of the shop, with James and his friend following behind. But when she entered the mall parking lot, she couldn't see the limo.

"Over there," James said, pointing.

The other man led the way to a white van, where a third man waited. "James?" she asked, suddenly suspicious. Something wasn't right.

James avoided her gaze.

"What's going on?" she asked urgently.

"Just do what he tells you," Bobby's driver instructed her in a quiet voice.

"Now, just a minute," Teri said, standing her ground. She wasn't about to walk off with this…this gangster, not without a very good reason, anyway. "What's going on here?" she asked again.

James's cell phone rang, and he looked at the other man before answering. The wrestler type nodded, and James flipped it open. His gaze shot to Teri.

"She's with me," he answered, his voice unnaturally high. "No, no, we haven't been hurt."

"Is that Bobby?" Teri asked. She noticed that the big guy was walking away.

James nodded.

"Give me the phone," she said, and James complied. "Bobby?"

"Did they hurt you?"

"You've got to be kidding," Teri said. "What's all this about? Did they threaten you?" She was tempted to race after the big guy and give him a kick he wouldn't forget. How dare he frighten Bobby this way! "You don't have anything to worry about," she assured her husband. "I can take care of myself."

Bobby didn't respond.

"Give me James," he said a moment later.

Teri handed the cell phone back to his driver. The two spoke for a few minutes and then James closed the phone. He offered her a tentative smile. "Nothing's going to happen," he announced, his voice trembling.

"Did those gorillas threaten Bobby?" she demanded.

"No," James said, wiping the perspiration from his forehead. "They threatened you."

"*Me?*" she cried. "I'd like to see them try."

"No, you wouldn't," James said in the same shaky voice. "Trust me, you wouldn't."

The outrage was building in her. "Who *are* they?" she demanded. The first thing she intended to do was inform the sheriff and have them arrested for—she didn't know what but she'd find out. Uttering threats? Blackmail? They were clearly guilty of something.

"I don't know exactly who they are." James seemed on the verge of collapse.

Teri took him back inside the shop and into the break room, which had emptied. Jane and Rachel cast her quizzical looks, but she ignored them both.

"That was just to let Bobby know they could get to you anytime they wanted," James told her.

If this was supposed to frighten Teri, it didn't. Perhaps she was being foolish, but she really *could* take care of herself. Bobby had enough on his mind without worrying about her.

As soon as James was seated, Teri poured him a glass of cold water, which he drank in giant gulps.

"All right," she said angrily. "How much money did they want?"

James stared at her. "They weren't after money."

She frowned. What was the point of this charade if it wasn't money?

"They want Bobby to throw a chess match," James explained.

That was when Teri started to laugh. "They don't know, do they?" she said.

"Don't know what?" James asked.

Teri shook her head. "Don't they realize how much my husband hates to lose?"

Forty-Six

Justine had arranged to meet Warren Saget at D.D.'s On the Cove. Even now, several days after the shocking revelations, she had difficulty believing he'd set the fire. It tore her up to think he could hurt her like this, and yet in a strange way, it all made sense.

Warren already had a table and was waiting for her when she arrived. He stood as she entered the room and held out a chair for her. This meeting hadn't been her idea, but she'd agreed to it, although neither Sheriff Davis nor Seth fully understood what they were asking of her.

"I can't tell you how happy it made me to get your phone call this morning," Warren said the moment she was seated.

In an effort to hide her uneasiness, Justine reached for the linen napkin and smoothed it across her lap.

"I appreciate your willingness to have lunch at the last minute like this."

"Could I refuse you anything?" Warren asked gallantly. His gaze was warm and appreciative. "I want to be your knight in shining armor—you know that."

"I do," she said, and in a flash she understood what had led this man to do the things he'd done. Later, she'd discuss her insight with Seth, but right now she had a role to play.

"What can I do for you?" Warren asked.

Justine mentally reviewed the tips Sheriff Davis had given her to guide the conversation. "I talked with an architect about building the Victorian Tea Room," she began.

"Fabulous. You do want me to look over the plans, don't you, and give you a construction bid?"

"That would be wonderful." She pretended to glance at the menu. "By the way, Seth met with the insurance people this morning, and there's been an interesting development in the case."

"Really?"

As she suspected, Warren's interest was immediately awakened. "It's all rather complicated."

"Complicated? How?"

Justine shrugged. "I don't want to discuss the fire—it upsets me. I still can't believe anyone would do something like that deliberately."

Warren nodded. "It's a cold, dark world out there."

"There doesn't seem to be a logical reason anyone

would want to hurt us. It just seems...irrational. I mean, there's no financial gain to be had."

"So, you think it was personal?" Warren asked.

"What *else* can I think?" she responded. "Whoever did this must hate me. Whoever did this must've been looking for a means to hurt me and my family."

"Not you, Justine," Warren said quickly. He glanced down at his own menu.

"Hurt Seth, then?"

"He's the one who laid off that dishwasher, isn't he?" Warren muttered.

She leaned toward him and placed her elbows on the table. "That's the interesting thing about all of this, Warren. Apparently it *wasn't* the young man we assumed. We have positive proof that Anson Butler wasn't involved in the fire."

Warren frowned. "I thought I read that his cross was found in the ashes."

"No one ever said it was *his* cross." Justine met his gaze.

"Perhaps I'm wrong, but it seems to me I heard that somewhere."

"You might have," Justine agreed. "All the evidence certainly pointed to Anson." Outwardly she remained calm, in contrast with the wild pounding of her heart. Turning to the menu again, she added, "Some other evidence has recently come to light. That's why Sheriff Davis contacted Seth."

"What evidence?" Warren asked sharply.

Playing her role to the hilt, Justine looked away and then sighed. "Unfortunately, I'm not at liberty to discuss the details, but from what I understand, it's pretty damning." Step by step, she was leading him on, leading him to an admission of guilt.

Alert now, Warren leaned close and lowered his voice. "You can tell me, Justine. I can be trusted."

"Can you, Warren?" she asked softly. And then, because this was so much more painful than she'd realized it would be, she stopped and swallowed hard. Tears clogged her throat as she thought about the day of her panic attack and how Warren had seen her through it. His kindness had seemed genuine, and yet all along he'd been the one responsible for bringing this sadness and stress into her life.

As best she could, she remained calm and set her menu aside. "I'll have the crab cakes."

Warren nodded, but he didn't appear willing to drop the subject. "Tell me," he coaxed. "You've always been able to trust me. What information does the sheriff have?"

Justine met his gaze. "You honestly think I should tell *you?*"

"Ah…" He seemed taken aback by that blunt question. "Of course."

"Really?" She had a hundred other questions she wanted to ask him. More and more she doubted she'd ever have the opportunity. This conversation might be her only chance.

By now, Warren had started to squirm.

"Warren," she said, looking straight at him, "you should know that the new evidence points directly to you."

He issued a harsh laugh. "This is a joke, right?"

"I wish it was." She meant that. "The reason I asked to meet you is so I could find out why you'd do such a thing."

His eyes widened and he scooted back his chair as if about to flee.

"If I could only ask you one question," Justine whispered, "it would be this." She paused, determined not to lose her composure. "*Why*, Warren? Why would you want to destroy the restaurant?"

He'd gone completely pale. He lowered his gaze and seemed to struggle to find the words. "Seeing you with Seth was...hard, knowing you'd chosen him over me. You were the only woman who ever understood me, the only woman who didn't hold my sexual inadequacies over my head." The bitterness in his voice was frightening. "I knew I had to find a way to get you back."

"Oh, Warren."

"Then that day six or seven months ago when I came in for lunch, I managed to convince you to have a glass of wine with me..."

Justine searched her memory. It'd been the day David Rhodes had come by to have lunch with her grandmother. He'd tried to weasel money out of

Charlotte. Justine had been outraged and badly shaken by the events of that afternoon.

"You seemed so tired, so drained."

"I was," she agreed but didn't explain why.

"Seth showed up and when he saw you with me he was—" Warren just shook his head.

Justine remembered that, too. There'd been tension between her and Seth, and they'd had an argument.

"He wore that smug look that told me no matter how much I loved and needed you, you were his and always would be his. Nothing," he said, "absolutely nothing I did would bring you back to me. At that moment, I knew I had to do something."

"But burn down the restaurant?"

"I wanted to hurt Seth, not you," he said, pleading with her like a repentant child. "I could never hurt you."

"But you did, Warren, you hurt us both."

He hung his head. "I see that now. But I thought of a way to make it up to you. I'd build you another restaurant, bigger and better than the first one. I'd give you the restaurant of your dreams and then you'd see how much I loved you."

"Warren, you don't prove your love by hurting other people."

He kept his eyes lowered and nodded sadly. "I'm sorry."

"I know."

Seth and Sheriff Davis walked across the room

and stood next to the table. Warren looked up and sighed deeply. "You talked to the dishwasher, didn't you?" he asked without showing any signs of distress. "He was there that night. He tried to put out the fire."

"So I understand." Sheriff Davis removed his handcuffs from his belt. "Warren Saget, you have the right to remain silent...."

"Yes, yes, I know," he snapped irritably. He stood then and held out his hands. Glaring at Seth, he said, "You could never love her the way I do."

Justine stood, too, and Seth slipped his arm around her waist. "No one could possibly love my wife more than I do, Warren. I'm sorry it's come to this."

"I'll deny everything," he sneered. "I have a good attorney."

"Ah, but we've got a confession right here on tape," Justine said, raising her shirt to reveal the wire taped to her midriff. "We have your confession, Warren, and you made these statements in a public place, in which you couldn't anticipate privacy. All the bases are covered."

Sheriff Davis clipped on the handcuffs and with everyone in the restaurant looking on, took Warren away.

"It's over," Seth said as he led Justine from the room. The relief in his voice was unmistakable.

"In the end, I nearly couldn't do it," she said. "Even knowing what he'd done, I had trouble deceiving him."

Seth turned to face her. "You still got what we needed, and that was a confession. It didn't matter how you went about it—all that matters is the end result."

It wasn't that she loved Warren, but she pitied him and perhaps she always had.

"I can't help feeling sorry for him," she said as Seth opened the car door for her.

They were both silent during the drive home. "It's sad, you know," she said once they arrived.

"Don't tell me you actually pity that slimeball."

"In a way I do," she admitted.

Seth didn't say anything for a long moment. "In a way I do, too." He smiled at her and together they walked into the house. "We have the whole afternoon to ourselves, don't we?"

No one had expected Warren's arrest to go this smoothly. "Yes," she said.

"We've got another two hours before we have to collect Leif."

Justine threw her arms around her husband's neck. "Any ideas for what we could do with that time?"

Seth chuckled. "Give me a minute and I might have a suggestion." Then, without warning, he swept her into his arms and carried her into the bedroom.

"Why, Seth Gunderson," she said in an exaggerated Southern accent. "Just *what* do you have in mind?" She fluttered her eyelashes at him.

"I was thinking," her husband said, a moment

before his lips claimed hers, "that this would be the perfect opportunity to work on expanding the family."

Justine agreed that was a fine suggestion, indeed.

Bobby Polgar studied the note in his hand. He wasn't a man who understood fear, but he felt it now. Teri's life was being threatened. His wife and James had been confronted by ruthless men. The message was clear. These men could kidnap Teri at any time and he could do nothing to protect her. The note told him he was to return to 74 Seaside Avenue and wait for further instructions.

* * * * *

Come back to Cedar Cove soon!

Join Teri and Bobby at 74 SEASIDE AVENUE to see how things develop. Keep in touch with Maryellen, Jon and their family and find out whether Rachel decides to stay with Nate.

Welcome to Cedar Cove –
a small town with a big heart!

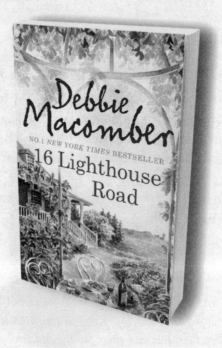

When family court judge Olivia Lockheart causes a scandal by denying a couple's divorce, the whole town starts talking about it.

Meanwhile, her daughter Justine must decide if she should stop waiting for love and accept a marriage of convenience.

And Olivia's best friend, Grace, wonders if her own husband is having an affair.

In Cedar Cove, nothing stays secret for long.

www.mirabooks.co.uk

Welcome to Cedar Cove –
a small town with a big heart!

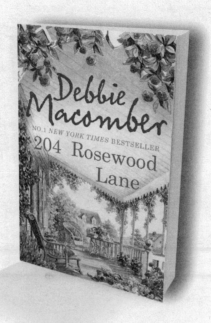

Grace Sherman's life was happy and untroubled –
until her husband just disappeared.

But life can – and does – go on. Cedar Cove is
abuzz with talk of weddings and babies. Romance
is blossoming between friends, and there
are troubled relationships to solve.

And will Grace ever find out what happened
to her husband?

www.mirabooks.co.uk

Welcome to Cedar Cove – a small town with a big heart!

Recently divorced Rosie and Zach's unusual custody arrangement means that they will be moving between each other's places, not the kids!

Will Judge Olivia stay with Jack, the local newspaper owner, or get back together with her ex-husband?

And who is the mysterious man who died at the local bed-and-breakfast?

In Cedar Cove, it won't be a mystery for long!

www.mirabooks.co.uk

Welcome to Cedar Cove –
a small town with a big heart!

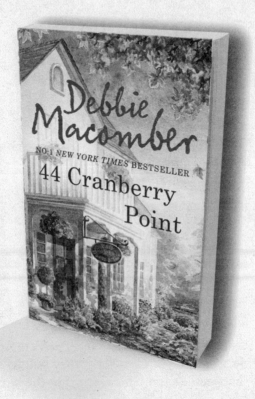

It turns out that the man who died at the Thyme & Tide
bed-and-breakfast was called Max. But why did he
come to Cedar Cove – and who killed him?

In other news, Jon and Maryellen are getting married.
And Maryellen's mother, Grace, has more than her share
of interested men. But who will she choose?

www.mirabooks.co.uk

Welcome to Cedar Cove – a small town with a big heart!

Local private detective Roy McAfee and his wife Corrie have been receiving anonymous postcards with messages asking if they "regret the past." What does it mean?

And it looks like the romance between Cliff at the horse farm and Grace Sherman is back on. Could a wedding be on the cards?

www.mirabooks.co.uk

Can you tell from first impressions whether someone could become your closest friend?

Lydia, Jacqueline, Carol and Alix are four very different women, each facing their own problems in life. When they are thrown together by the hands of fate, none of them could ever guess how close they would become or where their friendship would lead them.

Make time for friends.
Make time for Debbie Macomber.

www.mirabooks.co.uk

The No. 1
New York Times bestseller

Meet Phoebe, Alix, Margaret and – for the first time –
a man, Bryan Hutchinson, in Lydia's newest
knitting class "Knit to Quit".

Catch up with other Blossom Street regulars, including
Anne Marie and her adopted daughter Ellen.

With romance and friendship on the horizon,
it's going to be a busy summer on Blossom Street!

www.mirabooks.co.uk